SELECT ACCOLADES AND PRAISE FOR

IRON WIDOW

An Instant #1 *New York Times* and UK Bestseller

Winner of the Astounding Award for Best New Writer at the Hugo Awards, 2024

Winner of the British Science Fiction Association Award, 2021

Winner of the Barnes and Noble YA Book Award, 2022

Finalist for the Andre Norton Nebula Award, 2021

Finalist for the Locus Awards for Young Adult Novel and First Novel, 2022

'Raging against the patriarchy in spectacular style.'
Observer, best books of the year

'A ferociously original fusion of Chinese history and mecha sci-fi.'
Guardian

'Zetian is unstoppable, and I dare you not to cheer her on.'
Elizabeth Lim, author of *Spin the Dawn*

'Absolutely epic. This is the historical-inspired, futuristic sci-fi mash-up of my wildest dreams.'
Chloe Gong, author of *These Violent Delights*

'Zetian is the take-no-prisoners heroine you'll love to cheer on.'
Rebecca Schaeffer, author of *Not Even Bones*

'Thrilling, heart-wrenching and epic!'
Kat Cho, author of *Vicious Spirits*

'A searing, cinematic, gut-punch of a tale.'
Joan He, author of *The Ones We're Meant to Find*

'Think *The Handmaid's Tale* meets *Pacific Rim* and buckle up.'
Shelley Parker-Chan, author of *She Who Became the Sun*

'Brutal, bloodthirsty and full of rage.'
Julie C. Dao, author of *Forest of a Thousand Lanterns*

'A primal scream of a book.'
E.K. Johnston, author of *Aetherbound*

'Zetian is here to set the world on fire.'
Nicki Pau Preto, author of the Crown of Feathers trilogy

'A rip-roaring, blade-sharp rampage.'
Kat Dunn, author of *Dangerous Remedy*

XIRAN JAY ZHAO

HEAVENLY TYRANT

ROCK THE BOAT

A Rock the Boat Book

First published in the United Kingdom, Republic of Ireland and Australia
by Rock the Boat, an imprint of Oneworld Publications Ltd, 2024

Published by arrangement with Tundra Books, an imprint of Tundra Book Group,
a division of Penguin Random House of Canada Limited.

Text copyright © Xi Ran Zhao, 2024
Jacket art copyright © Ashley Mackenzie, 2024
Mecha illustrations copyright © Setodra, 2023

The moral right of Xi Ran Zhao to be identified as the
Author of this work has been asserted by them in accordance with the
Copyright, Designs and Patents Act 1988

All rights reserved
Copyright under Berne Convention
A CIP record for this title is available from the British Library

ISBN 978-0-86154-423-3 (hardback)
ISBN 978-0-86154-426-4 (paperback)
ISBN 978-0-86154-425-7 (ebook)

Printed and bound in India by Replika Press Pvt Ltd

This book is a work of fiction. Names, characters, businesses,
organisations, places and events are either the product of the author's
imagination or are used fictitiously. Any resemblance to actual persons,
living or dead, events, or locales is entirely coincidental.

Oneworld Publications Ltd
10 Bloomsbury Street
London WC1B 3SR
England

Stay up to date with the latest books,
special offers, and exclusive content from
Rock the Boat with our newsletter

Sign up on our website
rocktheboatbooks.com

To Qiu Jin, Rosa Luxemburg, Thomas Sankara,
Salvador Allende, and others who came before.
Along with those who will come after.

AUTHOR'S NOTE

Please beware that this book contains violence and abuse, body horror, mass murder, toxic relationship dynamics, discussions of reproductive coercion, allusions to childhood sexual abuse, and references to miscarriage, domestic violence, sexual assault, and suicide.

Although inspired by figures and events from across Chinese history, this book is not historical fiction, historical fantasy, or alternate history, but a futuristic story set in a science-fiction world entirely different from our own in the way that many sci-fi stories riff off of the Roman Empire. Historical figures are reimagined for the purpose of exploring the spirit they represented rather than accurately depicting their original life circumstances and upbringings. This book should not be taken as an educational guide in any way. To get an authentic view of history, please consult nonfiction sources.

The fictionalized characters in this novel make many morally questionable choices in the conditions unique to their world. Depictions do not equate to endorsement in real life, and parallels to reality should not be drawn without considering the impacts of the existence of fantasy plot devices such as Chrysalises.

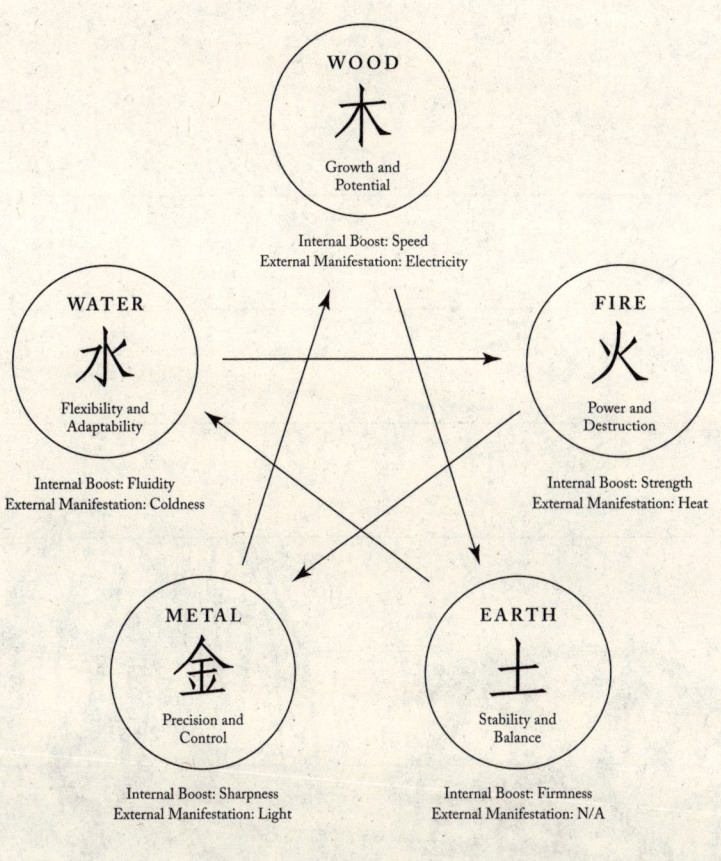

ATTRIBUTE: WOOD TYPE
WEIGHT: PRINCE CLASS
YÁNG PILOT: LIU CHE
YĪN PILOT: WEI ZIFU

STANDARD FORM   ASCENDED FORM

AZURE DRAGON

HEROIC FORM

ATTRIBUTE: WATER TYPE
WEIGHT: DUKE CLASS
YÁNG PILOT: ZHUANG ZHOU
YĪN PILOT: VARIABLE

STANDARD FORM

WHALE BIRD

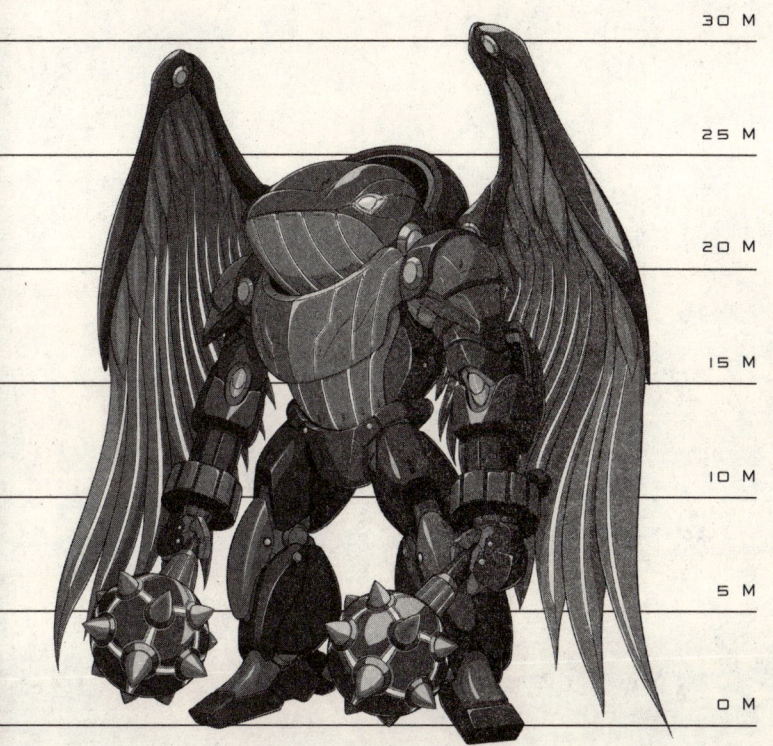

ASCENDED FORM

ATTRIBUTE: METAL TYPE
WEIGHT: COUNTESS CLASS
YĪN PILOT: LIANG YUHUAN
YÁNG PILOT: VARIABLE

STANDARD FORM

PLUM BLOSSOM DEER

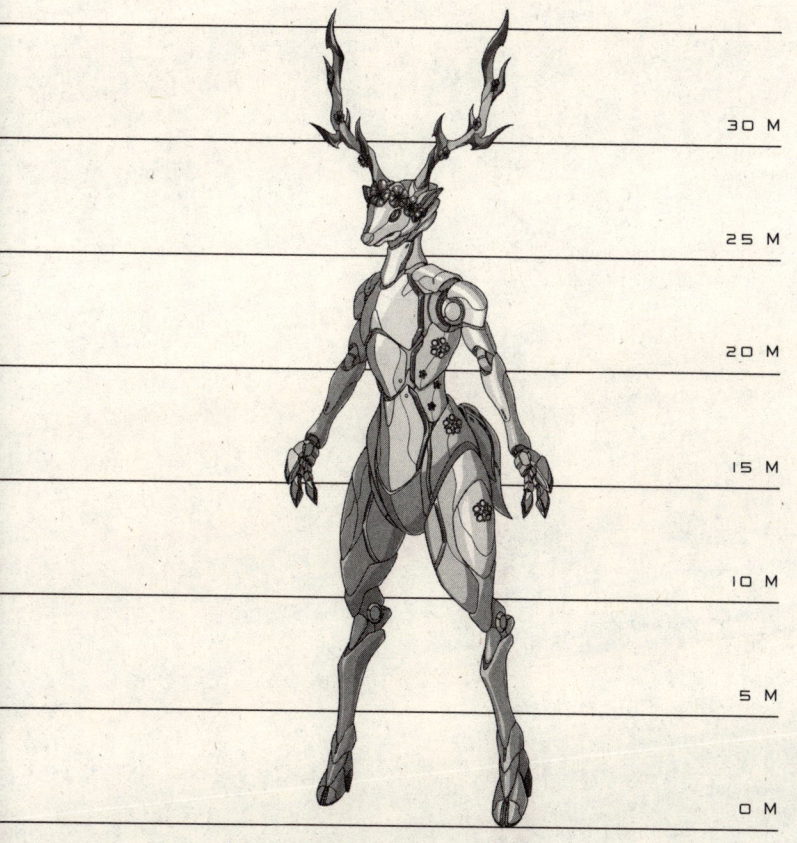

ASCENDED FORM

PROLOGUE

In a world teeming with those who wanted him dead, Qin Zheng never thought it'd be a plague that would take him down.

He had crushed Hunduns that dwarfed the greatest of manmade monuments. He had bested legions of Chrysalises commanded by fools who'd refused to surrender to him. He had roused the workers of seven bickering nations into rising against the industrialists, bankers, and landlords who subjugated them. And he was still young. He should have had so many more years to further his revolution. It was absurd that he was now at the mercy of something more minuscule than the eye could see. A virus, ravaging through his every organ, rending him from the inside, making pustules bloom like cursed flowers over his skin. He felt more powerless than when he'd been a gutter child spat on and laughed at for being the son of a whore. It was one thing to gaze up and dream of infinity; it was another to reach the peak, only to plummet with so little warning.

After burrowing the Yellow Dragon under Mount Zhurong, deep enough to access the living energy of the planet itself, he disconnected from the pilot link.

"*Shīfu* . . . This is not how I . . ." he began to say to the woman coming to consciousness in the yīn seat in front of him, someone he'd never thought he'd pilot a Chrysalis with, for she had always fought at his side in her own unit. Queen-General Mi Xuan, pilot of the Three-Legged Crow, leader of the Iron Widows. His mentor.

"Quit wasting your energy on talking," she grunted over her shoulder, her words muffled by her protective leather mask, its glass lenses fogging up. She was the only one left in his nascent empire of Huaxia who dared speak to him this way. She shed her temporary Yellow Dragon armor on the yīn seat like a golden husk and stood up in her black conduction suit. She'd brought her usual Three-Legged Crow armor into the cockpit, but she wouldn't need it for what would come next.

Qin Zheng sprouted thin needles out of his gauntlet palms to let her manipulate the qì flow between him and the Dragon. His Council of Sages had vehemently opposed this experiment, but they had not come up with any alternative solutions. He was showing symptoms of the most aggressive form of flowerpox. He had mere days before his organs began liquefying right in his body. A cure would not be produced within days.

Silently, he cursed the gods. Even after he had resumed tribute to them, they would not respond to his requests for dialogue. His sole remaining option was this audacious attempt to freeze himself in time.

"*Shīfu*," Qin Zheng said in a smaller voice than he had used in years. It pained him to leave Huaxia in the hands of others, but he could scarcely hold on to his existence, much less his empire. "Do not let them wake me until a cure is made. No matter how long it takes."

General Mi's steely eyes glistened behind the glass lenses of her mask. "That, I can promise you."

She pressed her bare palms into the needles on his gauntlets. Her jaw clenched. Blood trickled out between their hands. The meridians carrying her qì through her body darkened across the few swaths of visible skin on her neck and the backs of her hands. Water was the qì type she had the least affinity for, yet she wielded it like a roaring tide. Its coldness pervaded like slush into Qin Zheng's blood. His instinct was to control it, the way he controlled everything, but for once he let it happen to him. If a passive stream of qì could be established through the Dragon like a river flowing downhill, while its primal particles were fine-tuned to filter only Water type into Qin Zheng, this coldness could theoretically persist indefinitely.

"Xuan-*jiějiě* . . ." he breathed out as his consciousness frosted over. An improper way for a student to refer to their mentor. As improper as the way she, in turn, never used his imperial title.

A slight tremor went through her. Qin Zheng wanted to say more, but could no longer conjure the words to encapsulate everything he was feeling.

"Get some rest, Zheng'*er*," she murmured. "I will come back to you."

Please, he pleaded in the safety of his mind, because he would never do so out loud.

The cold closed over him like ice over a lake.

He swore it was less than a minute later when heat coursed through his body again. His eyes stuttered open to a winged blur in the dim cockpit. Had General Mi put on her Three-Legged Crow armor? The pressure of her hand on his gauntlet now pumped Fire qì into him. He momentarily feared the experiment hadn't worked, but there was someone else with her now, hand on his other gauntlet. Some time must have passed. She had indeed returned to him.

"Where's the cure?" Qin Zheng croaked out.

She and the other person stood in silence.

"Where's the cure?" he repeated, stale air wedging in and out of his thawing lungs.

Shouts rose in the shadows further ahead in the cockpit. Had they brought more people into the cockpit?

General Mi snapped into motion, fumbling with something in her free hand. "Open up!"

Her voice was wrong, higher-pitched and less raspy. Her qì felt off as well. And her armor was red and coarse, not black and form-fitting.

Before he could tell if this impression was the fault of his reviving senses, he felt a numbness in the right side of his body and a sagging in half his face. He and General Mi both cried out in surprise. He shook one gauntlet free to morph a mask of spirit metal over that half of his face, because, though he knew she would not care past the initial shock, he did not want her to see him like this.

As expected, she was dazed for but an instant before she stabbed a syringe into his neck. A cold liquid he assumed was the cure to flowerpox seeped into him. Slowly, his vision came to focus.

The sight was not what he wanted to see.

She was not General Mi. They looked remarkably similar, with the same eyes that promised vengeance and bloodshed, but it was impossible that General Mi had gotten younger and shorter.

What was going on? How long had it been? Where was the general?

"Can you pilot?" The girl's question pierced his spiraling thoughts. She spoke with a strange dialect, one he could not pinpoint. She detached the syringe from his neck and pressed down on the bleeding puncture. "I need your power, your Chrysalis. Now."

Qin Zheng kept his expression neutral. He could not show vulnerability in an unknown situation.

After feeling for her spirit pressure, he let out a dry laugh. Who did this little girl think she was? Had no one told her who *he* was? Piloting with him would be her death sentence. He channeled all five types of qì with the full force he could muster, showing her exactly what she'd be getting herself into.

Yet, after a few stunned seconds, she did not relent. She demanded he shift to the yīn seat—the *woman's* seat—and threatened to withhold further medicine if he did not. It was preposterous. He told her so.

"Do you want to live or die?" the girl shouted at him. "It's a simple question!"

"You wouldn't let me—"

"Qin Zheng, I know two hundred and twenty-one more years of what's going on than you do, and I have no time to explain!"

Her tirade continued, but his mind snagged on the number she'd spouted. *Two hundred and twenty-one years.*

Over two centuries.

The world seemed to turn on its axis, tipping Qin Zheng around and around and around. Two hundred and twenty-one times around the sun. Constellations cycling, trees rising and falling, lives beginning and ending.

His General Mi was dead, along with everyone and everything else he knew.

PART I

HEAVENLY EMPEROR

天皇 *Tiānhuáng*

How could you say you have no clothes to wear?
I will share my robe with you.
His Majesty has called his army;
I will prepare my ax and spear,
and share an enemy with you.
How could you say you have no clothes to wear?
I will share my shirt with you.
His Majesty has called his army;
I will prepare my lance and halberd,
and march together with you.
How could you say you have no clothes to wear?
I will share my skirts with you.
His Majesty has called his army;
I will prepare my armor and weapons,
and advance together with you.

—Qin folk song, from *The Classic of Songs* 诗经

CHAPTER ONE

THE LEGEND, THE TRUTH

I am ready to slaughter the gods.

If I can find them.

I soar in the Yellow Dragon, straining against the pull of gravity in search of the Heavenly Court's sailing twinkle in the ocean of stars above. The gods' unexpected message burns in my mind, fueling me onward even as exhaustion eats at my consciousness.

"If you do our bidding as the Sages did, we have ways to bring back what you've lost. But if you defy us or reveal the truth, you will lose everything."

Soon, the stars look less like stars and more like the static that pops behind my eyes whenever someone hits me hard on the head. Truthfully, I have no idea where I'm going. I flew the Yellow Dragon beyond the Kunlun Mountains right after the gods' message, but there's really nothing indicating I might find them in this direction. I guess I just instinctively headed for the unknown. The sands of what must be the Xihuang Desert drift far below, known to me as only a label on the very west of maps until now.

"You still possess no concrete understanding of what the gods are," Qin Zheng remarks with an air of incredulity, his spirit form sitting opposite mine in the yīn-yáng realm, that incorporeal space our minds share via the Yellow Dragon's pilot link.

"No, what are they?" I demand.

"You of the future should be enlightening *me*." He shakes his head, gaze distant and haunted. "Two hundred and twenty-one years, yet nothing has changed. They continue to lord over you, making you think of them as divine. Their power has not been broken."

The Yellow Dragon slows in its flight as more of my focus strays to Qin Zheng. "Why do you say that like things are supposed to be different?"

His spirit form looks at mine as if I'm telling him an absurd story. "You know not of the ultimatum I attempted, do you?"

"No, I don't! What are you talking about?"

"Three months ago . . . three months ago from *my* perspective, I halted all tribute to the gods, refusing to obey them blindly any longer. I had always doubted they were as mighty as they claimed, so I demanded to see their true faces. I told them that if Huaxia were to continue offering tribute, we must receive more in return. The gods responded only with warnings. Then, two weeks ago, I came down with this blasted pox." He touches his face. Flower-shaped pustules bloom over his skin, the way his body looks in real life.

I waver on the farthest stretches of my capacity to process what's happening. Two weeks ago from his perspective. Two hundred and twenty-one years from mine.

"They infected you?"

"Perhaps. At the very least, they left me to perish, even after I resumed the tributes." Hatred erupts from him, hitting me like ice water through our mind link. "*Me*, the strongest pilot to ever live, who crafted a plan to end the war. This confirms my suspicion that they have no interest in letting that occur. I would guess the Hundun husks we offer are much too valuable to them. If we annihilated the Hunduns, they would receive no more."

My mind spins at the reminder of the Hunduns.

"*This isn't our planet!*" Yizhi's words scour through my memories like a phantom wail.

"Did you know the truth about the Hunduns?" I choke out. "What they really are to this world? Of what we are to it?"

"Yes," Qin Zheng says, chillingly nonchalant. "The story of them as aggressive invaders and us as embattled defenders is useful fiction that maintains the resolve of the masses against the Hunduns. Those of us who reach the upper echelons of power know better. We need to, in order to know which studies and discoveries to nip in the bud. It is not difficult for an observant scholar to stumble upon findings that contradict our recorded history."

I wrench the Yellow Dragon around in midair. "We need to tell everyone."

"Absolutely not!" Qin Zheng seizes control of the Dragon, forcing it down from our considerable altitude. "This is the one matter I begrudgingly agree with the gods on. The fiction is effective. Exposing it would do more harm than good."

"What do you mean? How could telling the truth be—"

"You wish to rule? This is the cost!" He slaps the yīn-yáng realm's invisible ground. "Do you sincerely believe we can control and defend the entirety of Huaxia without maintaining certain illusions? Good pilots have always been in short supply, and I doubt that has changed, given how the war has gone nowhere. Revealing the truth would do nothing but dampen fighting spirits."

"So we lie to our entire world about why we're fighting? That's ridiculous!"

"Is it? Look how distraught you are, yet what can you do about our circumstances? The Hunduns will not cease their attacks, and we cannot cease to defend ourselves against them. Aside from creating turmoil in your heart, what practical difference has learning the truth made to you?"

I press my knuckles to my forehead, putting my everything into keeping myself from unraveling. "The truth means the Hunduns aren't mindless invaders. It means there's hope for peace."

"Peace?" Qin Zheng lets out a bitter laugh. "How shall we make peace with metallic bugs who cannot understand us?"

"Who says they can't? Didn't you hear the Water Emperor speaking in our heads?"

"*Spare us... Please...*" I remember it pleading as we drained it of qì with the Yellow Dragon near the end of our counterattack on the Zhou province.

"I heard no such thing," Qin Zheng says, though a trace of uncertainty slows his words. I think he genuinely never experienced anything like it in his era. But two hundred years is a long time, and we humans might not be the only ones who've grown and evolved.

"Your brain was still thawing!" I point out. "Before I woke you up, my army fought a Metal-type Emperor, too. Fly back and ask any pilot who was there. They'll tell you they heard it speak in their head."

There's no way any of them could forget that eerie voice stabbing into our minds, accompanied by a shrill melody, sending us all into unnatural panic. "*Get out!*" it said. "*Leave us alone!*"

I couldn't comprehend what was happening then, but now it makes sense. So much of my world is making more sense.

Qin Zheng's eyes flit side to side like he's reading something. "Even if these extraordinarily rare Emperor-class Hunduns somehow developed this ability, did you manage any proper dialogue with it? Have any other Hunduns demonstrated the same capacity?"

"We didn't know it was possible to try! But now we do, and surely we can figure out a way to communicate with—"

"The Hunduns will not indulge your delusions of peace! From their perspective, *we* are the invaders. The only way we can battle them with equal vigor is if we believe the same of them. This war has raged for centuries. How it started no longer matters. Many Rongdi tribes have folktales that tell of being 'cast from the heavens as divine punishment.' This suggests our ancestors were criminals exiled to this planet. We would not be accepted back to wherever they originated."

A sickness crawls over me. *Ancestors. Criminals.* How deep and ugly does the truth go?

I can barely think. I am so tired of these lies upon lies upon lies from those in power. The last thing I want to do is become the one maintaining them.

"Besides," Qin Zheng adds, "so long as the gods rule over us, they will not allow any prospect of peace. However," he leans close and drops his voice, "if you attempt to publicize the truth, I will not wait for the gods to end you. I will do it myself. Then I shall ensure your words are remembered as hysterical nonsense."

I flinch from his piercing gaze, though the threat isn't shocking when I remember who I'm dealing with. These eyes have set sight on countless enemies before watching them surrender or perish. It's honestly laughable that I brought up the word "peace" around him. This is Qin Zheng. Qin Fucking Zheng. I still can't quite believe he's alive before me, resurrected out of stories and legends, transcending time and death.

But this is no longer the world he ruled.

"I'd like to see how you'd pull that off when you have no idea how the modern world works," I say, refusing to cower.

"I have perused enough of your memories to be certain the masses would believe my word over yours, Iron Widow."

The Yellow Dragon hits the ground in a hefty, shuddering landing, having been descending by his will this whole time. Horror trembles at my core at the reminder that memories can spill across a mind link. How much has he learned of my life?

"You're really willing to bet on that?" I hold his stare in the yīn-yáng realm despite the icy nausea creeping through me.

After a lengthy silence, he cocks his head, gaze softening. "Do you not wish for your partner back?"

I wince as an image flashes in a deeper layer of my consciousness, that of a partial body suspended in a fluid-filled glass tank. I can't admit it's . . . it's . . .

"The gods are bluffing." Words tumble out of me. "There's no way, just no way, that someone can come back from that."

"The gods are capable of more than we can comprehend. The technological information they throw to us in exchange for our tribute is no doubt a mere fraction of their knowledge."

"Then how did you think you could bargain with them?"

"Because I would rather die fighting than languish in servitude. Is that not why *your* first impulse upon receiving their message was to hunt for them?"

Through the Dragon's eyes, I glance around the desolate landscape we've landed in, utterly different from the forests on the other side of the Kunlun Mountains. Wind sweeps up curls of sand like glimmering stardust under the full moon. An unknown territory I entered out of a sheer, seething desire to confront the gods, despite knowing logically I cannot win.

"I won't find the gods by wandering like this, though, will I?" I remark, more to myself than to Qin Zheng. I feel like I aged a decade in this one day. How was it just this morning that I was charging out from the Sui-Tang frontier with the cautious hope of retaking the Zhou province and leveraging it against the government? Now neither the Sui-Tang command center nor the central government exist anymore. I crushed them both to rubble.

Skies, did I really do that? How am I supposed to clean up this mess?

"This is folly indeed." Qin Zheng's eyes fall shut. "The wiser move would be to return to Chang'an and abide by the gods' commands for now. If we are to challenge them, we ought to formulate a more concrete plan."

We. The word catches at my mind like a thorn.

There is no "we," I want to insist.

Yet . . . isn't there?

I study Qin Zheng's spirit form, sitting like he's deep in meditation, shockingly composed for someone who woke up to find he overslept for two centuries. He is undeniably the most powerful co-pilot I could have. While we disagree on revealing the truth of the Hunduns, we have the same goal of challenging the gods. I'm not sure I can physically activate the Yellow Dragon again without him. He's also not wrong about going back to Chang'an. We won't find the Heavenly Court by blindly flying. We have to track its movements, plan a proper trajectory, something more.

When Qin Zheng's eyes stay shut and the Yellow Dragon remains on the ground, I realize he's leaving the decision to take off to me. Why? He cannot be someone used to yielding power.

Or is he? Maybe he's still too dazed from his thawing to pilot properly. What do I really know about him? His name. His power. His accomplishments. But who is he beyond the legend of a prostitute's son who united seven warring nations into Huaxia? I have no clue besides what I experienced in his mind realm: countless *èguǐ*, hungry ghosts, clawing through a frozen sea. Why is it like that? What did he go through that the stories don't speak of? How did he get those streaking scars over one side of his face? Who did he leave behind in his century?

I don't know.

I don't know.

I don't know.

No matter how hard I reach, I can't access any of his memories. Whatever.

I propel the Dragon into flight again. It's better than sitting around doing nothing.

He makes no effort to influence the Dragon's movements. As I fly over endless stretches of sand, I almost wish he would help. Now that I've lost my momentum and adrenaline, just pushing the Dragon forward is a strenuous endeavor. I doubt I can keep moving for much longer. I can't wait to settle down and rest.

When we finally approach the Kunlun Mountains again, a string of pings inside the Dragon's cockpit startles me.

Crap. We must've flown out of range of the radio wave transmitters in the trucks I placed around the mountains. I'd destroyed a whole line of them to cut off communication between the army and the strategists, and once I'd crushed the Kaihuang watchtower and the Palace of Sages, I replaced only a few on my return journey to maintain connectivity with Yizhi. What messages did I miss? I can't be slow to react at a time like this.

I land the Yellow Dragon around a mountain and disconnect from it. After a disorienting return to my human body, I check my wristlet.

"Zetian, you have to come back right now!" Yizhi's shout bursts from the speakers when I open his first voice message. "There are reports that Liu Che and Wei Zifu are flying here in the Azure Dragon!"

Blood drains from my face. Those two are the third and final Prince-class Balanced Match in Huaxia, the only pair I haven't met. I double-check the time Yizhi sent the message.

It's already been half an hour.

CHAPTER TWO

REMEMBER THIS

"*Going into the estate bunkers. Connection might be spotty.*"

That's the last message from Yizhi. No reply comes when I ask him for an update.

I connect to the Yellow Dragon once more and launch it airborne, praying I'll make it back to Chang'an in time.

To my agony, I can sense the Yellow Dragon doesn't have enough qì for the trip *and* a potential battle, so I'll have to recharge at Mount Zhurong first. I navigate by feeling for the spirit signatures of the other pilots that came to take back the Zhou province. Before I took off in search of the gods, I told them to stay put near the volcano.

Worst-case scenarios whirl through my mind as I race the Dragon over a blur of mountains and valleys sketched out by moonlight. Yizhi is using the Gao Estate as a base. I falter in my flight when I imagine the Azure Dragon destroying it like I destroyed the Palace of Sages. Yizhi said he went to hide in the estate's bunkers, but who knows if someone might jump at the chance to betray him? He just killed his father to take over Gao Enterprises. They only swore loyalty to him out of fear—fear of *me*. But I'm not there. How easily might they be swayed to Liu Che's side?

Even if I make it in time, how can I continue protecting Yizhi every second, every hour, every day?

Me and Yizhi against the world. It seemed so thrilling when I destroyed the Kaihuang watchtower and the Palace of Sages so the powerful men in them couldn't kill me first, but a cold new reality presses down on me, heavier by the second. How can two people hold down an entire nation that doesn't want them as rulers?

In the yīn-yáng realm, Qin Zheng's spirit form remains passively seated, eyes closed. I have no idea how dependable he'll be. Dread pounds in me like a frantic heartbeat, louder and louder. Despite the Yellow Dragon's unbeatable might, I am a human with limits, ones I'm stretching too thin. I was already close to collapsing, and now I have to deal with *this*.

But I can't give in. I can no longer drop my guard for a single second.

Soon, Mount Zhurong's jagged volcano opening cuts into view. Its ashen incline glimmers with shattered Hundun remains. Among them are the Chrysalises that survived the counterattack, deactivated in their Dormant Forms. Most pilots have their cockpits open and are sitting partly outside, barely visible on my scale. As we get closer, the tiny figures jerk to attention and vanish back inside their Chrysalises. In spurts of light, the army reactivates.

When I dip the Yellow Dragon's tail into the volcano to draw qì from within the planet, I have no choice but to land on the Hundun remains. Every gleaming shard fills me with nausea, reminding me of the Hunduns' bursts of anger and grief as we killed them.

"Hey!" The White Tiger leaps toward us in Standard Form, paws thudding against the mountain. Its mouth glows a dark green as it speaks, a mix of Qieluo's Wood-green qì and Yang Jian's Water-black qì. "What happened? Why'd you suddenly fly off?"

Right. I didn't tell them what I'd heard from Yizhi and the gods before leaving in a frenzy. The truth surges in me like bile, burning to spill free, but the unshakable presence of Qin Zheng's meditating form in the yīn-yáng realm makes me swallow it down. I don't doubt he'd kill me for letting it slip. I have to wait for a better time.

"I was looking for the gods," I tell part of the truth through the Yellow Dragon's mouth, "to see if they really took the Vermilion Bird's head as you saw."

The Tiger's eyes search the stars. "Did you ... find them?"

"No."

Loud metallic echoes cluster over the mountainside as other Chrysalises gather behind the White Tiger in the manner of awaiting command. When I'd first landed back here, before Qieluo and Yang Jian told me about the vanishing aircraft that took the Vermilion Bird's shattered head, I'd announced my destruction of the Palace of Sages to these pilots. They were dumbfounded, of course, but none of them raised any protest. Having Qin Zheng on my side is an effective deterrent, at least. However, it's one thing to not defy me; it's another to actively join me in changing everything about the world we know.

"Qieluo, Yang Jian." My voice shakes slightly as I address the White Tiger, the only unit to disobey the strategists and come to my aid before I dug up Qin Zheng. "When the Black Tortoise attacked the Vermilion Bird, why did you try to help us?"

They're quiet for a beat before saying, "Because it was proof that, sooner or later, we would've been next."

Their words reverberate deep inside me. In an instant, I understand what they mean. They're getting close to twenty-five years old, that mythical age when pilots are allowed to retire. Except it's an open secret in the army that aging pilots face the prospect of getting "tributed"—deliberately left to die in battle so the Hunduns can physically feel their spirit pressures extinguish, which tends to calm the Hunduns down for a while. Qieluo and Yang Jian may have believed their war accolades could save them from this fate, but the order to purge me and Shimin demonstrated that the government will dispose of any of us the moment we stop being useful, even if we win back a whole province for Huaxia.

Now that can change, and Qieluo and Yang Jian could be my strongest allies.

I raise the Dragon's head to speak to the wider army of Chrysalises. "Did you all hear what I revealed near the end of the counterattack, about the pilot system being deliberately skewed against female pilots?"

Hesitant murmurs go through the crowd.

"Yes," the White Tiger says with particular force, its green left eye shining brighter. "It explained a lot."

"Well, now is the time to create a new system! We can remedy not only this injustice, but others in the old order! May piloting no longer be a sentence to die young!"

Silence stretches uncomfortably long before one Chrysalis lets out a cheer. The rest quickly join in, their voices building to a wall of noise that soars toward the heavens. Many voices sound forced by fear, though. It'll take some time for them to accept that the world has turned upside down.

That's okay. I don't need all of them.

"Liu Che and Wei Zifu are heading for Chang'an," I say as quietly as I can to the White Tiger. "Will you come with us?"

"*Those* brats? We can come, but we won't be much help against the Azure Dragon. We can't fly."

"Just watching our backs is enough." I bow the Yellow Dragon's snout toward them. "Climb on, and call some other pilots you trust."

The White Tiger pounces onto the Yellow Dragon's head while shouting half a dozen unit names, including the Ocean-Filling Bird, the Quilled Ox, and the Long-Toothed Hog. I vaguely remember some of them from battle broadcasts.

They settle along the Dragon's long body. Once I feel it's filled to nearly full with qì from Mount Zhurong, I propel us all into flight.

"The rest of you, make camp!" I call to the army we're leaving behind.

The original post-counterattack plan was indeed for most of us to stay at the Zhou frontier, spread out across the Kunlun Mountains. Cockpits and radio trucks had packed plenty of rations and supplies for campsites. Additional personnel were supposed to come and restore the Great Wall around the Zhou frontier. I don't know how much of that will still happen. There's too much to think about.

I push the Yellow Dragon as fast as it will fly, guiding myself using a trail of crushed trees across the Zhou province. Although it's impossible to tell in the night, I like to think it's the exact path stomped out by me and Shimin in the Vermilion Bird this morning, leading me home.

Spots bloom and wane at the edges of my consciousness. The urge to ask Qin Zheng to do this mundane traveling for me bubbles in my mind, but I smack it down. After everything I went through to seize this power, there's no way I can willingly give up control of it.

Through a small eternity of flying, I pass the Great Wall, then rolling mountains with occasional patches of electric-lit villages and cities. I follow the brightest highways in the dark, which will inevitably lead to Chang'an. What are the ordinary people thinking after hearing their government was toppled? I imagine my old neighbors rushing out their doors, buzzing with the instinct to run for their lives yet drawing a blank on where they're supposed to go. They'll find no salvation closer to the heart of Huaxia, where I've taken hold. They can't retreat into the Hundun wilds, cleared for now but still a vast landscape of uncertainty.

Did I really cause this? Did I really break the world beyond repair? My mind drifts as though it can no longer connect with reality.

By the time I reach Chang'an, it feels like I've been awake for days. If the Yellow Dragon had eyelids, I'd be struggling to keep them open.

The capital is eerily silent, though every apartment window is bright with lights, making the cluttered buildings look like gleaming pillars. Millions of gawking eyes must be watching anxiously for how the world will change next. Before I took off for Zhou, I issued a curfew, ordering everyone back to their homes and forbidding them from leaving without permission. The streets are empty but for a few patrolling vehicles. Through his family's connections, Yizhi mobilized the capital soldiers to enforce the curfew. The fact that they're still complying is a relief. That means Yizhi is safe.

Maybe.

Hopefully.

The Yellow Dragon's shadow glides over Chang'an's Main Street, wide enough for six lanes of traffic. We pass Unification Plaza, which has a giant statue of Qin Zheng wielding spirit metal like mercury, placed amid a maelstrom of neon billboards. I try not to dwell on how surreal it is that I'm in a mind link with the exact historical figure that statue is based on.

Using my spirit sense, I feel for a powerful spirit pressure beyond the Chrysalises we're carrying. Indeed, one such signature speeds closer from the distance. That must be the Azure Dragon. We got here just before it.

"Wu Zetian." A flat voice suddenly speaks inside the Dragon's cockpit. It startles me so much that I lose some altitude.

"Wu Zetian." The voice speaks more loudly, echoing in the cockpit. It sounds artificial, like a text-to-speech program. But where precisely is it coming from? My wristlet? "You are forbidden from destroying the Azure Dragon or killing the pilots inside. They must be returned to the Han frontier to ensure the integrity of your Great Wall. Your Han province sent a significant number of Chrysalises to reinforce the Sui-Tang counterattack. It cannot lose another Prince-class unit."

What?

"Do not think of disobeying this command. There will be consequences."

I almost scoff, but then Yizhi's smiling face crosses my mind. I don't know where he is right now. I truly can't risk it.

I stumble into a thunderous landing over the ruins of the Palace of Sages, the one place in Chang'an where I can reasonably park the

Yellow Dragon. Rubble rolls down Mount Ziwei as I coil the length of the Dragon's body around it. The White Tiger and the other Chrysalises leap off, attention whipping toward the Azure Dragon's incoming spirit signature.

Defeat it without destroying it. That's not impossible. Back in the Kunlun Mountains, Qin Zheng defeated the Water Emperor by sapping its qì dry, not making a single scratch. The Azure Dragon should be even easier. It's made of Wood-type spirit metal, the leakiest type.

The sheer *sound* of it reaches us first, a parting of the night air like a monstrous roar. Then its long body streaks in across the cosmos like a skeletal dragon chiseled out of jade, one eye socket glowing Fire red and the other Earth yellow. Massive bat-like wings flap from its back, and its bare spine trails into a lashing, bony tail. Its chest looks like a bulk of spirit metal clasped by an exposed rib cage, which reminds me disturbingly of—

No. Don't think of that. Don't think of him.

With a blinding burst of light, the Azure Dragon transforms into Heroic Form. Its front claws split and shudder into four bony arms. Its wings grow wider. Its antlers lengthen. Its skeletal body wrenches itself into bipedal orientation, adorned with red and yellow highlights. The clashing colors blur against the night as it dives toward us, wings spreading against the stars.

I crouch down on the Yellow Dragon's many claws before springing into battle. According to the battle broadcasts that constantly played in my house, the Azure Dragon should be about fifty meters tall in its Heroic Form. Yet from my current perspective it doesn't look much bigger than a human. Its four arms cross over its chest to snap off four of its ribs, which then sharpen into swords.

Maneuvering the Yellow Dragon is much harder after my brief reprieve, like trying to pick up a heavy weight again after dropping it due to muscle-ripping pain.

"We don't need to fight!" I shout through the Yellow Dragon's mouth while dodging sword strikes. "The old government doesn't deserve your loyalty! If you join us, we can change the war system so you won't get tributed once you're in your twenties!"

"We will never join you, harlot!" the Azure Dragon yells back, mouth glowing orange from a blend of Earth yellow and Fire red.

Harlot? What is going on with their vocabulary?

"We could give your families massive plots of land in the Zhou province!" I throw out a promise. I'll think about the logistics later. "We did just free the whole thing, you know!"

"We will not be tempted by the darkness!"

My confusion about the overdramatic way they're talking scatters when I remember Liu Che is fourteen and Wei Zifu is thirteen.

There'll be no reasoning with them.

I pounce toward the Azure Dragon, aiming to sap it dry and get this over with. Yet it swerves behind me with shocking speed, wings sailing on the air. I turn, grabbing at it, only to miss by an embarrassing distance.

Oh, no. Wood-type Chrysalises are the fastest, so fast the Yellow Dragon can't keep up. It's like trying to swat a fly with a brick column I can barely lift. I twist the Yellow Dragon around with much difficulty and retreat toward the palace ruins. Maybe I can bait a battle closer to the ground, which will—

The Azure Dragon catches up before I reach the mountain and lands a pair of crisscrossed strikes on the Yellow Dragon's head. Pain singes into me. I reflexively grasp my spirit form's head in the yīn-yáng realm.

In a wild rush of color, the Azure Dragon vaults off the Yellow Dragon's snout—too fast for me to sap any qì—and flips in the air. Its four swords blaze red with Liu Che's Fire qì, extra destructive as it channels through Wood-type spirit metal. Too late, I remember Wood has a type advantage against Earth.

Briefly upside down, the Azure Dragon delivers another two slashes near its previous cuts. I double over in the yīn-yáng realm from the scalp-tearing sting. The Yellow Dragon crash-lands in a messy heap over Mount Ziwei, narrowly avoiding the White Tiger and the other Chrysalises we brought. The ones who can do ranged attacks blast their qì at the Azure Dragon, but it dodges with swift jerks of its skeletal body and comes for me again.

The absurd possibility that I might lose by having a Chrysalis that's *too big* quivers at my core.

No. No way.

I can't. *We* can't.

"Qin Zheng, tell them to stand down! They'll listen if it's your voice!" I cry in the yīn-yáng realm. No matter how much I don't want to surrender my hold on the Yellow Dragon, it's slipping from me. I'm too worn out.

Qin Zheng's spirit form remains still, eyes closed. In my increasingly hazy view through the Yellow Dragon's eyes, the White Tiger leaps while swinging its dagger-ax but misses the Azure Dragon.

"Qin Zheng!" I shake his spirit form. "Do something! They'll kill you, too!"

He makes no move. But he has to be conscious, or he wouldn't be in the yīn-yáng realm with me.

Don't make me beg, I scream in a deeper level of my mind.

Though . . . is that exactly what he wants?

I contemplate forcing his hand by just letting go of the Yellow Dragon, but I have a feeling I won't be able to stop from dropping all the way to unconsciousness if I relaxed like that. I can't risk it. I have to stay awake.

There's no more room for pride.

My hands slacken on his shoulders and slide down to his chest. "Qin Zheng, help me. Please."

His eyes flash open. He pinches my chin and lifts it.

"Remember this lesson, little girl."

The Yellow Dragon's gargantuan weight lifts from my mind. Before I can collapse in relief, my perception of the real world shifts entirely. I panic at first, thinking Qin Zheng threw me out of the cockpit—except I'm still with him in the yīn-yáng realm. Yet nothing else is the same. Everything, from the trees to the rubble to the battling Chrysalises, got larger in an instant. My passive awareness of the Yellow Dragon perceives an utterly different shape, no longer long and serpentine but *humanoid*.

With no more control over it, I can only piece together what happened by what passes through its point of view. Golden arms glimmering under the full moon, patterned with small squares like Qin Zheng's spirit armor. Flapping flashes of massive wings that rival the Azure Dragon's.

The Azure Dragon now looks equal in size, yet it's screaming incoherently and diving away from us. When we twist in the air in pursuit of it, I glimpse the scene back on the mountain.

Finally, what Qin Zheng did sinks in. In less than a second, he separated a smaller, humanoid subunit out of the Yellow Dragon. The rest of it slumps on Mount Ziwei like a husk, its head hollowed out. Bewildered looks from the other Chrysalises swing between it and us.

My view of the others reels away when Qin Zheng takes the Azure Dragon spiraling through the night, locking the subunit's arms around it. Stars and city lights blend into a dizzying vortex. Distantly, many screams rise from the masses.

With a harsh wrench to the side, Qin Zheng avoids the residential blocks and lands in Unification Plaza, destroying the statue of himself. Every billboard and window shatters on the skyscrapers nearby, drawing another wave of screams. The Plaza plunges into a darkness it likely hasn't seen in years.

"You dare raise your blade against your emperor?" he roars through the subunit's mouth, pinning down the Azure Dragon. "Open your cockpit!"

Its forehead pops open, revealing Liu Che and Wei Zifu, faces blanched under pure moonlight. I don't think they're aware we've been commanded not to kill them or damage their Chrysalis beyond salvaging.

"How did you do this?" I ask Qin Zheng in the yīn-yáng realm. I don't even know what to call this subunit. My mind stutters at the idea that a higher transformation of a Chrysalis could be *smaller*. Not to mention the instantaneous way he produced it.

Qin Zheng's eyes narrow. "It seems there is much they no longer teach pilots."

"No, they—We—You can reconnect this with the rest of the Dragon, right?"

"Obviously. It operates by the same principle as spirit armor."

But spirit armor is pre-made. This subunit didn't exist within the Yellow Dragon before he conjured it into existence. Whether a detached part can reconnect to a Chrysalis depends a lot on how clean the break is. This subunit doesn't match the hole in the Yellow Dragon's head at all.

I'm about to ask more jumbled questions when a cold realization hits me: if launching this subunit was an option all along, I didn't need to crush my family along with the Palace of Sages. I could've scooped them out of the way before destroying everything else with more strategic and controlled damage.

"Why didn't you tell me this was possible?" I grab Qin Zheng in the yīn-yáng realm. "Before I crushed the Palace, you must've felt how conflicted I was—why didn't you *stop me*?"

His gaze roves over me. "Because I wished to see if you would do it." The corners of his mouth curl ever so slightly upward. "I wished to see what lengths you would go to for power."

I know I'm too exhausted to think clearly. I know I'm not in my right mind. I know it's unfair to pin any responsibility on him when *I* made the choice. Yet, with a broken scream, I punch his spirit form in the face. He falls backwards. I clamber over him and go for another blow, then another, then another.

In the middle of my fifth swing, he yanks my arm away and clamps my spirit form against his.

"That's enough." His fingers dig like claws into my back.

Before I can make a noise, he tears my spine out.

CHAPTER THREE

TO QUENCH THIRST WITH POISON

I'm falling, falling, falling.

When I land, the impact shatters me to pieces. I am a wreckage of garbled limbs and protruding bones. My heart and lungs struggle behind fractured, exposed ribs.

With excruciating effort, I flip myself over and drag my ravaged body forward. There's someone standing ahead. I open my mouth to plead for help, yet the voice that rasps out of my throat isn't mine.

"Zetian . . ."

My perspective jumps. I am now the one standing, looking down. The crawling one lifts his head. Bloody hollows gape where his eyes should be.

"Zetian . . . How could you leave me like this, Zetian?"

I'm sorry, I try to cry, yet it's as if someone has sewn my lips shut. I stagger backward. *I'm sorry I'm sorry I'm sorry . . .*

He crawls quicker after me, leaving a wide trail of blood behind his partial body. "Help me, Zetian . . ."

I trip and land painfully on the ground.

He snatches my leg with a mangled hand. "Make . . . me . . . whole . . ."

The apologies trapped in my head sharpen into a silent scream. I jerk my leg free and roll away, only to feel another bloody hand on the ground. Its contorted fingers lock with mine like a trap. Ma Xiuying's eyes, once so soft and kind as she gave me advice, stare emptily at me, upside down. Her body lies pulverized to muddled gore in a pile of metallic shards.

"You did this . . ." Her voice surrounds me, though there's no movement of her jaw, dislocated and smashed to one side. "You claim you're fighting for the sake of women, yet you did this to me . . . Me, only trying to protect my children . . ."

What was I supposed to do, let you kill me? I want to shout but can't. I rip my hand from her grasp and scramble in another direction.

This time, my mother's and grandmother's crushed bodies block my path.

"You should've saved us." Their words echo around me, on and on and on. "You could've saved us."

I didn't know how!

My justifications can't reach any of them. More ruined bodies crawl to me, clawing and tugging at my limbs. No matter where I turn, there is no way out. They overwhelm me, tearing the flesh from my bones. I feel every rip of skin, every laceration of muscle, while not being able to make a single sound.

When I shudder awake, nothing makes sense. I don't recognize my surroundings. It takes a while to remember myself, to separate reality from nightmare.

"No—" I lurch up in an unfamiliar bed. Dizziness comes over me. My head sways.

A chain rattles, accompanied by a pressure at my wrist.

I break into a cold sweat. I'm shackled to a post on a canopied bed. An infusion line tugs at my other arm, connected to a fluid bag dripping high on a metal stand. Squinting, I make out part of the text on the bag. Some kind of nutrient solution that aids in qì recovery.

"My lady!" A girl springs up from a fancy cushioned chair near the door. She turns and calls out, "The lady is awake!"

"Where am I?" I croak. My heart thrashes as I take in more of the room. It's expensive-looking, with intricate rosewood furniture and dark walls painted with golden scrollwork. Amber light seeps from a wooden lattice on the ceiling. No windows. I have no idea if it's night or day.

Shit, how long has it been and what have I missed? What happened to the Azure Dragon, to Qin Zheng, to Yizhi, to the other Chrysalises? And *why am I chained up*?

The girl shuffles to my bedside and bows. This might be the Gao Estate, because she's dressed like their maidservants, with a pink vest over a white blouse tucked into a blue pleated skirt. Her hair is done up in twin bundles on either side of her face and topped with a hairpiece shaped like cat ears.

"You're in the new palace, my lady," she says, keeping her head low. "You've been in a coma for about three days."

Fuck! That is way too much time to have missed. Like—what does she mean, "new palace"?

"This isn't the Gao Estate?" I demand.

"Not anymore, my lady."

Okay, so it *is*. They're just calling it by a different name.

Knowing where I am brings no relief when the weight of the manacle hangs on my wrist. Yizhi would never do this to me, so what's going on?

"Who brought me here?" I examine myself. I've been stripped of my armor and conduction suit and put in a short-sleeved sheer robe tinged with gold. There's no spirit metal left on me, not even the spinal brace pilots keep in our backs so we don't have to stab ourselves with needles every time we put on our armor. I think I've been washed, too. My skin gives off a faint floral fragrance. My hair has been brushed soft and smooth. Nausea churns in me as I imagine strangers handling my naked, unconscious body. Whoever wrapped my feet back up did it particularly wrong; they throb with a dull, burning pain. "Where's Yizhi? Gao Yizhi?"

The maidservant's gaze remains on the polished floorboards. "His Majesty will be here to answer your questions soon, my lady."

His Majesty?

Oh, no.

As I begin to fear my questions will have answers I don't like, the door bursts open. Qin Zheng marches in, armor clattering, a black, gold-embroidered cape sweeping behind him. His half-masked face carries noticeably fewer flowery marks than when I first awakened him. Most seem to have scabbed over and flaked off, leaving faint white traces on his skin.

"Take your leave." He waves a hand at the maidservant.

She bows and scuttles backwards out the door, never turning her back on him. I catch sight of two soldiers stationed outside.

My skin prickles the moment the door clicks shut, leaving Qin Zheng alone with me. It's chilling to think back on how calculating he was while acting too dazed to pilot. He was observing me, determining how best to turn my weaknesses—my pride—against me. He let me wear myself out on purpose.

"Remember this lesson, little girl."

I will. I must never underestimate him again.

"I'd like to know why I'm cuffed, Your Majesty." I raise my chained arm and speak in the flattest tone I can manage, the archaic title feeling so strange on my tongue.

"A precaution," he says, no longer using the dialect he woke up speaking, but something closer to radio-standard Hanyu. "I could not be sure how you would react upon awakening. I discovered you're quite fond of causing public disturbances."

He flexes his fingers. A curl of spirit metal swirls out of his gauntlet and morphs into a key in his grasp. I thought the stories exaggerated his abilities, but given the way he sculpted that Yellow Dragon subunit in the blink of an eye, they didn't laud him *enough*.

I can't help but shrink against the headboard when he strides toward me.

"Fret not," he says, with an edge of bitterness. "The physicians determined that my strain of the pox is practically harmless in this era. How lucky you all are in the future, with your herd immunity and sophisticated vaccines."

Every time I remember he's from two hundred years in the past, it throws me off kilter all over again. This is weird. This is *so* weird.

When he lifts my wrist to unlock the shackle, I fight the urge to pull my blankets over this flimsy robe that barely covers anything. I cannot betray how vulnerable I feel, how I can scarcely breathe with him so close. I thought of him as a boy when I first saw him in the Yellow Dragon's cockpit because the legends fixate on how young he was when he activated the Dragon, but this is definitely a full-grown man. Biologically in his twenties, if I'm doing the math right. His crown, like a tall, antlered headdress topped by a platform with bead veils in the front and back, casts strings of shadow over his forehead. The mask that curves over half his face and hooks behind his ear has gained a dragon-scale texture since his first, hasty creation. I'm not sure what made that side of his face look like it was melting as he came back to life, if it had anything to do with his scars, but otherwise he seems . . . fine?

"All technicians involved in decoding information from the old palace were assassinated," he whispers near my ear.

I snap out of my stupor. "What? How?"

"Sniper wounds to the head. Current theory points to hit men hired over the . . . dark networks." He trips over the term, surely unfamiliar to him. "I have investigators tracking the hit men down, but I do not expect the trail to end anywhere but in untraceable messages. This was a warning from the gods. Speak no more about them out loud."

He drops the opened shackle. It clanks against the headboard on its chain. I don't fail to notice how he's leaving it dangling there like a threat, but that pales in comparison to my most urgent concern—

"Yizhi," I gasp. "Did they get Gao Yizhi? The boy who rode in the Yellow Dragon with us?"

"No." Qin Zheng melts the key back into his gauntlet. "He is too well protected. He is my Imperial Secretary now, after all."

"Wh—" I feel like *I'm* the one who woke up in a different world. "So you—Your Majesty spoke to Yizhi after the battle?"

"Indeed. He offered this estate as Huaxia's new governing palace, so I rewarded him with the position. He has been of tremendous assistance in navigating the intricacies of this future."

"Where is he? I need to speak with him." I look for my wristlet on the nightstand beside the bed but can't find it anywhere.

"It would not be proper for him to come here."

"What do you mean? This is his home."

"No. Did you misunderstand me?" Qin Zheng enunciates. "He relinquished ownership of the estate. I am allowing him and his family to continue living in the side buildings out of courtesy, but this estate now belongs to the government of Huaxia. It's *mine*."

The way he says that word sends a chill down my spine. I knew he might pose a problem, but I hoped he'd be too disoriented by his displacement in time to do much. Then I could just kill him if he proved too difficult to deal with. Yet in a mere three days, he's reclaimed his power at the top of the world. I can't believe Yizhi helped him, though I can't deny it was the right choice. If he didn't immediately snag Qin Zheng's favor, a whole city of other rich and powerful people would've pushed and shoved to do it first.

But where does this leave *me*?

"Why am *I* here, then?" I say, twisting my sheets. "What does Your Majesty plan on doing with me?"

Qin Zheng puts his hands on his hips and looks me up and down. "Well, I was never one for marriage, but given that you announced yourself as the Empress of Huaxia, I suppose I must marry you to avoid the inelegance of having to refute that statement."

I know I should disguise my reactions, but my mouth falls open. Coming from him, "empress" means something completely different from what I intended. All of a sudden, I get why he said it wouldn't be proper for Yizhi to come see me.

Qin Zheng flips his cape aside and sits down on the bed. This time, I don't hold back from gathering my covers over myself.

"Oh, do not flatter yourself," he says. "I find you far too mentally childish and physically repulsive to have any carnal interest in you. This arrangement shall be strictly political."

My grip on my covers loosens. There's indeed no lust in his eyes, just cold calculation. Which is preferable in this moment, but much more unpredictable in the long run.

"Listen." He puts a hand near me. "I am aware you wished to take the throne for yourself. It was amusing to watch, and I understand the feeling of invulnerability the Yellow Dragon can confer. But it was a foolish, impulsive move that would have brought you to a very quick end. However, I am not one to dismantle the bridge that let me cross the river, so to speak, and it would be a shame to let you perish when you have almost as much raw piloting talent as my nine-year-old self, so I am saving your life from the considerable number of calls for your death."

"Considerable number?" I feign shock. "For what reason?"

It's not that I'm surprised, but I'd like to know what, exactly, they're saying to him.

"You are . . . not liked." He peers at me with a mix of pity and amusement. "They tell me you are vulgar, dangerous, bloodthirsty, self-absorbed, manipulative, and an all-around affront to sensibility. What do you have to say for yourself, Wu Zetian?"

I fold my arms over my chest. No point denying any of that when he's been inside my head.

"Yes, that's pretty much who I am. Still want to marry me, Your Majesty?" I say it like a challenge.

I don't believe he's saving me out of *gratitude*. He has other plans for me, probably to use me as a steady co-pilot to kill more Hunduns en masse. The thought makes my stomach turn, but I need to ensure my survival before worrying about issues beyond me. If this marriage proposal is in name only, I have more to gain from accepting it than being squeamish.

A small smile curls his lips. "Frankly, I am offended by the insinuation that I would not be able to control you. Though, I must admit, when you invited me on a coup, I did not realize you were launching it with no power base at all among the masses. Not even a local dissident network? No assessment of which critical roads, ports, infrastructure, and military storehouses to secure? What was your plan?"

My face goes hot. "To not get killed. The Sages were bent on doing that, so I killed them first."

"Oh, you ought to garner at least *some* support among the people before you start a revolution, little girl. You cannot simply skip the middle steps."

I don't argue. I can't in good faith accuse him of being wrong.

"No matter." He strokes his chin. "I can work with this. Not my first time turning a military coup into a proper revolution. Rest assured: I announced to the masses that you deserve the immense credit of freeing me from my slumber and alerting me to the extent of corruption among the Sages. I made it clear that I then decided it would be easier to create a new government than to work with that rotten mess, so I ordered you to crush them with me once we finished the battle at the Zhou province."

"That's *not* what happened," I blurt.

"Is it not? Do you prefer the version of the tale that would intensify the calls for your blood? Would you like to speculate on what would have been done to your unconscious body if I had left it in the street?"

I shake away the horrible images rushing behind my eyes. "Don't act so noble. You only saved me to use me for your war plans."

His demeanor darkens like a gathering storm. "Do not speak to me of using others!" He lunges over me, backing me against the headboard. "*You* are the one who awakened me into a world I no longer recognize. You are the one who sought my power and my Chrysalis to free yourself from your conundrum. Did you think you could use me as a game piece only to discard me?" He runs his fingers down the chain hanging near my head. "I blame you not. Plenty of others have endeavored to do the same. It's never worked out quite as they intended."

My throat goes dry under the pressure of his scrutiny, his face so close I notice the eye on the masked side of his face is slightly cloudy. He must not have great vision on that side. Noted.

"Your Majesty is a little close," I make myself say.

Slowly, he pulls away. His gaze drifts toward the wall.

"Do you know the sharpest sentiment I felt since awakening? It's *disappointment*. Nothing about this future is how I imagined, aside from the minor miracle of Huaxia holding together as a single entity. I've discovered that I made the mistake of leaving too many reactionary forces alive in my time. As soon as I vanished, they leaped to purge my government and reverse my most revolutionary policies. They retaliated without mercy against the workers and peasants who rose up at my call. Now, despite all the improvements in technology, the rich have gotten richer, and the poor have gotten poorer. The war has gone nowhere. Pilots have devolved into *entertainment*. The masses lose themselves in flashy yet meaningless amusements, or they take their misery out on those more vulnerable than themselves." He glances in disgust at the outline of my bound feet beneath the covers. "Look at you, made physically useless for the sake of vanity."

A sourness prickles like acid beneath my skin. "It wasn't my decision," I say, though I don't know why I'm defending myself. I shouldn't have to.

"It better not have been. I cannot stand women content to be nothing but a pretty face and a birthing vessel. Once you recover from the surgery, I expect you to do your fair share of labor."

I'm about to argue most women don't get a choice, but something else sticks out in what he said. "Surgery? What surgery?"

"I had your foot situation reversed." He twirls a finger above my covers. "The best that the top orthopedic surgeon of this era could do, anyhow. The bones realigned, the flesh reattached, implants used where necessary."

I hurl my covers off my legs. I thought my feet felt weird because whoever clothed me messed up the binding technique, but my feet are, in fact, noticeably longer and wrapped in medical bandages.

"You had surgery done on me?"

"Insolence!" Qin Zheng chides. "Do not raise your voice to me. Would you have *wanted* your feet to remain in their putrid state?"

"I—" Admittedly, I've fantasized plenty about getting this kind of surgery. If the recovery period wouldn't have left me dangerously vulnerable for too long, I would've demanded it before the counterattack. But that is not the point! "Your Majesty should've asked me first!"

"There is no need to get emotional." He flashes his hand at me. "You were comatose, and time was of the essence."

As I do my very, very best to not scream at him, I notice my legs are perfectly smooth. I touch my face and inspect my arms. There are barely any hairs left on my skin. "Did you have me shaved, too?"

"Something better. I was informed there now exists a treatment with"—he gestures vaguely—"concentrated beams of light that can remove body hairs permanently. And so I bestowed it upon you. You were in urgent need of it."

"You mean *lasers*?" I've seen ads about this all over Chang'an the few times I traveled its streets.

"If you are to become my empress, you must be at least halfway presentable. Which also includes no longer having this 'lotus feet' ignominy." He snarls. "In my time, only so-called high society families in certain regions did this to their daughters, a grotesque symbol of their lack of need to toil for a living. So proud were they to live off the labor of others that they delighted in having wives unable to function without servants. I banned this ludicrous practice, but after my disappearance the ban was repealed in the name of 'personal liberty.'" He utters the term as if he wants to bite whoever coined it. "To think it's spread to even the peasant class! Outrageous."

Every sentence he speaks gives me a different whiplash of emotion, my urge to call him a pig extinguished by the thought that foot-binding could've been eradicated two centuries ago if he'd lived a few more years. That would've changed the fate of so many girls, including me.

"This is the kind of revolutionary policies Your Majesty was talking about?" I say, caught between guarded hope and stinging grief.

He raises his chin. "Did you think I unified Huaxia for the thrill of conquest alone? I was born into a world that saw me as less than dirt due to the circumstances of my birth. I spent my life proving the injustice of this judgment, because a society that values birthright over merit is fundamentally broken and nonsensical. I was out to transform it, to rid it of those parasites who amassed their riches by exploiting the less fortunate. Only by destroying this system can we most effectively harness the talent among our population to win our freedom."

I tense up at that last line. It's natural to assume he means victory against the Hunduns, but according to him that can't happen as long as the gods exist. So then . . . ?

"Are you with me?" Qin Zheng asks in a low voice, staring into my eyes as if he can see the turmoil behind them.

"Yes, if Your Majesty is sincere about transforming the world," I mutter. "But how exactly can we defea—"

He puts a finger to his lips and shakes his head. His eyes flick upward.

I catch his meaning. We have no idea how closely the gods can watch us. We can't plot against them without taking more precautions.

"I have a plan for Huaxia," he says. "I shall let you know when you have a role to play. Until then, do not get any stray ideas."

I don't like the way he said that, but I have to pick my battles. Whatever gets me closer to the changes I want. "As long as that plan includes no more foot-binding and no more unequal inputs in the yīn and yáng seats."

"Done. I have no love for unproductive practices."

I blink. That's it? It's that easy? A few words, and lives will change by the thousands? Millions, even?

So this is what it's like to have power.

Of course, the power is his, not mine. Something I don't think he intends to let me forget. How do I change this situation?

I need information from someone who isn't him, at the very least.

"Also, can Your Majesty give my wristlet back?" I ask in my most unassuming voice. "I would like to talk to Yizhi."

"No." Qin Zheng gets to his feet and adjusts his gauntlets, looking ready to leave. "I do not trust you with any device capable of spreading information on a wide scale."

"*What?* Why?"

"*You know why.*" His eyes burn with a reminder of our argument over the truth.

My palms go clammy. "Fine, I promise not to say anything Your Majesty doesn't want me to say. Just let me talk to Yizhi."

"You expect me to take you at your word?" He scoffs. "Besides, I've been told those advanced devices carry significant security risks. If hijacked remotely, they could transmit audio and visual information to nefarious parties. Why would anyone keep such things on their person? I shall call for writing utensils. Whatever you wish to say to whomever, you can write on paper, and I shall check and deliver it."

There is no way I'm taking that option.

Seeing no cane to use, I clutch my drip stand and swing my legs over the side of the bed. I will find Yizhi, even if I have to crawl through every building in the estate.

Qin Zheng holds me down by the shoulder. "What do you think you're doing?"

I bite back a reflexive demand for him to get his hand off me. That is not the way to get through to a man like him when I have so little leverage. He'd refuse out of spite alone.

"I'd like to not be touched," I say calmly. A request, not a command.

To my mild surprise, he actually takes his hand away. "You are in no condition to walk. Not to mention it is far too dangerous for you to wander about."

"Then Your Majesty will give back my spirit armor so I can protect myself, right?"

"You are in no condition to wield that, either. You are lucky not to have suffered permanent brain damage from overexerting yourself. Forcibly taking in large amounts of qì in a short time is extremely grating on your meridians. You must rest for the next few weeks to recover. This is for your own good."

I make an indignant noise before I can help it.

He tilts his head. "If you insist on being difficult, you leave me no choice but to chain you up again."

Dealing with him is impossible. I rise to get past him, biting my lip as I put my bandaged feet on the floor. It sends up a hotter, more swollen kind of pain than what I'm used to.

Qin Zheng shoves my shoulder. I flop back down on the bed, breath leaving my lungs. Heat surges in my face as I get up on my elbows, though I hiss when the movement rips the infusion needle out of my arm.

"That hardly took any strength." He lowers his hand. "The soldiers at the door have orders to keep you safe. I would love to see you attempt to get past them. Really, it would *delight* me."

I briefly fantasize about tackling him to the ground and strangling him. I want to scream, I want to fight, but I would lose, and that would only prove his point.

"Then I want to see Dugu Qieluo." I pick up my infusion needle to stop it from dribbling onto my sheets. "The White Tiger's yīn pilot. What did Your Majesty do with her and the other pilots who came with us?"

"I have them aiding in the efforts to excavate the old palace ruins. Including that insolent pair of children who had the gall to challenge us." Qin Zheng shakes his head while opening a drawer in the nightstand. "Children these days. Nothing like community service to make them repent."

There's a certain relief in knowing it's unlikely we'll face more Chrysalis attacks after Qin Zheng has taken charge so aggressively, but the price is that . . . Qin Zheng has taken charge very aggressively. The last thing I wanted was to trade one prison for another.

He opens a small, flat package from the drawer and pulls my arm toward himself. I resist until I see he's holding an alcohol swab. With circular motions, he cleans the skin around my needle puncture. The tiny squares of metal that make up his gauntlets are so fine they fit his hands like snakeskin.

I look away from what he's doing. "Well, there shouldn't be a problem with Qieluo visiting me since she's a woman, right?"

"I suppose not. I shall summon her."

He opens another package from the drawer for a fresh needle. When he takes my arm again, a fluid loop of spirit metal from his gauntlet tightens around my elbow as a tourniquet. Squinting in concentration, he pushes the needle into my vein. I swallow my protests. If a doctor has me on this drip, I probably need it. Yizhi may have had no choice but to go along with confining me to this room, but he wouldn't have let them go as far as drugging me with something dangerous.

Qin Zheng tapes the needle down before hooking my dripping infusion line onto it.

"You're awfully familiar with doing this," I remark, shivering when the cold fluid enters my blood.

"My mother used to need many such treatments. The setup has changed little in the past two centuries."

His mother the prostitute, I automatically think before immediately feeling bad. For her, not him. Surely she deserves to be known for more than her profession.

"Now, behave yourself. I have much work to do." Qin Zheng leaves without another look at me, cape sweeping behind him.

I watch the door close, thumbing the needle in my skin. The room falls deathly quiet, aside from the pounding of my heart and the drags of my breathing.

Empress. Fancy title for a girl who can't even leave a room as she wishes. I stare at my feet, operated on without my knowledge, and see a long future where Qin Zheng makes every decision in my life according to his whims. I went through all I did, sacrificed my family, just to end up in *this* situation?

And I brought it on myself. I was so desperate when I unleashed him that I didn't consider the danger he might pose. I almost laugh out loud at myself when I remember a proverb: "to quench thirst with poison."

I drag my nails down my chest, leaving red streaks. What would it take for me to no longer be a woman? If I cut off my breasts? If I cut out my womb?

I glance around for something that could do the job, but whoever prepared the room swept it well. No sharp objects anywhere. Even if there were, and I mutilated myself with them, would it change anything?

I'm a prisoner in this world, in this era, in this room, in this body. It never ends. It will never end.

CHAPTER FOUR

SAME SHIT, DIFFERENT MAN

"You look like crap."

I rouse from beneath my covers as Qieluo stomps into my room.

"Same to you," I grumble, scooting up against the headboard. The dark circles under her eyes testify to her qì-exhaustion from the counterattack. She's not wearing her armor, just her white-hemmed black pilot uniform.

When she hoists the chair near the door toward me, a soldier follows her in and closes the door behind him.

"Hey, not you." I flash my palm.

He gets into a military stance as if he didn't hear me, hands clasped behind his back, though he bows his head.

"His Majesty's orders." Qieluo sets the chair beside my bed and sits down. "No one who's capable of killing you is allowed to be alone with you. I even had to ditch my armor."

A cold dread sinks through my innards. I can't say anything without Qin Zheng knowing. I can't tell the truth about our world to anyone without paying with my life and then getting slandered into a liar.

Qieluo crosses her legs. "So . . . empress, huh?"

"Supposedly," I grumble.

"Forgive me if I don't bother with etiquette until you're officially crowned. I need to get the insolence out of my system while I still can."

"Whatever. Just tell me what's happening out there. You're the only one I trust to not bullshit me." I eye the soldier warily as I speak, but I have too many questions to hesitate because he's here.

Placing her elbow on an elegantly carved armrest, Qieluo scratches her temple. "Well, at first it was chaos, obviously. No one could figure out what was going on. All kinds of rumors were flying around on the networks. People were calling all the footage of the Yellow Dragon fake. But once we explained what a livestream is to His Majesty, he made several announcements that settled things down. He's back, he's reclaiming his throne, and that's that." She recoils, as though she doesn't understand the language coming out of her own mouth. "I still can't really believe it. It's a gods-sent miracle."

Oh, how enraged Qin Zheng would be at the gods getting any credit for his return.

"What else has he done these last few days?"

"Mostly he's been getting filled in on over two hundred years of political drama by the new Sages. We've gone back to the old system where they're supposed to be advisors to a pilot ruler. They're using the banquet hall here as an assembly chamber now."

"There are new Sages?"

"His Majesty summoned what was left of the central government and had them vote in nine of their peers as a new council. The rest kind of just . . . promoted themselves to fill the positions of those who didn't respond to the summons. Since they're probably, you know, dead."

I tip my head against the headboard, studying the light seeping out of the wooden lattice in the ceiling. "Have you found any survivors in the ruins?"

Qieluo lets out a chortle. "You and His Majesty smashed that palace through to the bunkers. All we've been able to pull out is minced meat."

I squeeze my eyes shut against a barrage of mental images: corrupt officials, toiling governmental clerks, and innocent servants all crumpling with my family under steel, concrete, wood, glass, and the Yellow Dragon's claws. Bones snapping, skulls popping, blood soaking their clothes. Then Xiuying and Zhu Yuanzhang dying the same way in the Dragon's clutches, then Shimin—

A sharp breath slices into me before shuddering out.

Crushed alive. What a horrible way to die.

After a few seconds, I wrench my eyes open. I did what I did, made the decision I thought best with the information I had. I can't undo it. I can't hide from it.

"Their families should be compensated," I say. It's not penitence, but it's *something*. "And Xiuying and Zhu Yuanzhang's children—can you make sure they'll be well looked after?"

Now that I've had some distance, I can't bring myself to hate Xiuying for accepting the secret task of killing me and Shimin. The Sages held the real power, driving us both into impossible choices.

"I can submit a proposal to His Majesty," Qieluo says. "That's the way we have to do everything now. Paper trails everywhere, no more secret deals, no more bribery, no more sloppy accounting. Officials won't be able to expense even a restaurant bill without getting questioned. Not that it's a bad thing. Officials *shouldn't* be comfortable in their power." She crosses her arms, looking lost in thought. "Honestly, I may have followed you to Chang'an because I was already in too deep, but I was pretty worried about how things would turn out. Now that I've seen His Majesty take charge, though, I'm not worried anymore."

"Yes, he has quite the way of imposing his will on others." I shoot another look at the soldier.

Qieluo releases a long breath and leans back in her chair. "I can't tell you what you did wasn't extreme, but I think it may have been for the better. With so many of those corrupt old men at the top wiped out, the replacement newbies are scared out of their minds. His Majesty can change things for real, make decisions only a pilot has the guts to make. He can lead us into winning the war."

A silent scream rises in me. I clench my jaw, my throat, my bedsheets. "How can we keep the war going when the pilot system is so messed up, especially for girls?"

"That's another thing His Majesty has already ordered reforms to. He's a lot less closed-minded than those geezers you squashed. Turns out history doesn't always move in a better direction, huh?" Qieluo rubs her chin. "I bet you could convince him to enact better legislation for women. Some more protections during pregnancy and divorce would be great."

"What makes you think I can convince him to do anything? I can't even convince him to let me out of this room!"

"To be fair, it *is* pretty dangerous for you right now. All the officials are telling His Majesty you're a poor choice for empress and should be executed instead. They're saying you exaggerated how terrible Huaxia was after you woke him up and misled him into destroying the Palace of Sages. You 'stained his venerable hands with senseless blood,' they say."

"If he'd disagreed with anything I did, I wouldn't have been able to do it," I say with an acrid taste in my mouth. "Trust me."

"That's what His Majesty told the officials! But, you see, it's not about the truth. It's about his plans to drastically transform Huaxia. It's got them shitting their court robes. I think one of them fainted when His Majesty mentioned something about limiting property rights. They don't want him to change things so radically, so this is how they're pushing back. They can't question Emperor Qin, the legend, but they can question the information he got when he woke up in this utterly different era. The idea is if His Majesty wants to back off, he can save face by going with the story that you tricked him."

"Will . . . he?" I grow acutely aware of the soldier's presence and how he could report our every word to Qin Zheng, but I have to know.

"Oh, absolutely not," Qieluo says without hesitation. "It's only made His Majesty more determined to make you empress. It's like you've become a symbolic measure for how much his judgment can be questioned. If he accedes to the wishes of the officials and executes you, they'll hold it over him forever. Every time he makes a decision they don't like, they'll be able to say, 'Is Your Majesty sure about having reliable information regarding the situation? Remember the time that wicked woman almost tricked you into abolishing private property?'"

"I don't even know what that means!"

"I think it's when no one's allowed to own stuff anymore," Qieluo says with a frown, not sounding sure. "My point is, you do need to lie low for a while. Don't give the officials any more excuses to call you a conniving vixen."

I snort. "As if they'll ever stop."

"You still have to try! You've basically gotten onto the back of a wild, raging beast. There's no getting off without breaking every bone in your body, so you need to do whatever you can to stay on. Look." She pulls a handheld device out of her pilot coat. After assuring the soldier she won't let me touch the screen, she shows me a picture.

My stomach plunges. It's a shot of Qin Zheng coming out of the Yellow Dragon with my unconscious body in his arms, uncannily similar to when I carried Yang Guang's corpse out of the Nine-Tailed Fox. It's as if all the fight I put up, all the pain I endured, and all the power I thought I'd grasped since that moment has come undone in one image.

"This is the kind of thing that will save you." Qieluo's voice reaches through a hollow ringing in my ears. She shakes the device for emphasis. "You have to act like His Majesty, uh, mellowed you out."

"This is the same thing they tried with me and Shimin! Same shit, different man! And nobody bought it then!"

"Yes, but . . . this is no ordinary man. Not that I'm saying Pilot Li was ordinary, but . . . *you know*. This time, if you act like you've been 'fixed,' people will believe it. They could get used to it, and you could influence His Majesty into doing more for women."

"Ugh." I bury my face in my hands. For that short, precious while when I believed I'd overcome everything in my way, I thought I could be the one to make the changes. Now, whatever I want I'll have to grovel for from Qin Zheng.

"I'm sorry about Tengri, by the way," Qieluo mumbles.

"Tengri?"

"That was Pilot Li's Xianbei name. Daye Tengri. He told me during that time Gao Qiu crammed us onto the same hovercraft to Chang'an."

My heart squeezes painfully. I didn't know Shimin had a Xianbei name. Even after all those times we entered a mind link, there's so much I don't know about him. We had so little time together.

It's not fair.

Qieluo has no idea he's still alive ... maybe, in the most horrifying way possible. And I can't tell her.

Her eyes flick toward the floor. "And I'm ... sorry for how I acted when we first met. I think I just didn't know how to react to you. I knew the strategists didn't like me and my personality, but for years I thought they had no choice but to put up with me because I was the strongest female pilot. Then you showed up, and just like that, I wasn't the strongest anymore." She lets out a huff, shaking her head. "But clearly the power rankings mean nothing if they truly want a pilot gone."

"Well, they're dead and we're alive, so who's laughing now?"

We crack faint smiles at each other, yet we're not really laughing, either. I don't think I can laugh ever again.

Qieluo sneaks a glance at the soldier over her shoulder, then leans forward, speaking quietly. "I'm sure Tengri would want you to do whatever is best to protect yourself. And honestly, you could do worse than the most powerful man in Huaxia's history."

"Right." A throbbing intensifies in my post-surgical feet. I swallow the bitter bile in my throat. "How is Gao Yizhi doing? Is it true he's now the Imperial Secretary?"

Qieluo balks, blinking.

Ah, that probably sounded like a very abrupt tangent, to someone who doesn't know what we were to each other.

"He was just as close to Shimin as I was," I hastily explain. "That's why I'm worried about him."

Qieluo leans back. "The three of you had a weird relationship."

"You have no idea."

"Well, Imperial Secretary Pretty Boy's been very busy. He did a lot of work pulling lines of communications together so His Majesty can run the government again. I can't imagine the rest of the Gao family is happy with him declaring their company nationalized and handing their entire fortune to the state treasury, but they have His Majesty's favor for it, so they can't complain."

"He gave all their money to the government?"

"All of it. On paper, this family is destitute."

No wonder Qin Zheng is willing to trust him.

I relax a little. Yizhi is making the best out of this situation, seizing whatever power he can. Maybe I can do the same. Being a political symbol to Qin Zheng means I have more leverage than I thought. I can use it to make him give me what I want, like my spirit armor. I need to show him I'm not a doll to cut up and use as he pleases.

"Given that you announced yourself as the Empress of Huaxia, I suppose I must marry you to avoid the inelegance of having to refute that statement," he said. A remark that betrays more weakness than he intended, now that I think about it. In his version of the story, the coup was *his* idea, and everything that happened was by his will. If the officials or the masses find out my declaration was something I yelled in the heat of the moment with no prompting or approval from him whatsoever, his story falls apart. He'd be admitting he wasn't in control. I'm no longer sure how functional his mind really was during the coup, but if he doesn't want people to get suspicious, he *has* to defend the idea of me becoming empress

as if it was his own carefully considered decision, told to me before we reached the Palace of Sages.

"Can you bring Secretary Gao a message from me?" I say to Qieluo. "Tell him ... tell him to not worry about me. I'll be okay."

"Funny. He told me to tell you the same thing."

CHAPTER FIVE

THE STRIKE

After Qieluo leaves, the maidservant who took care of me while I was comatose brings in a lacquered wooden bed tray with porridge and steamed vegetables. I take better note of her this time. She looks very young, which is interesting. One would think Qin Zheng would've entrusted an older, more experienced servant with the responsibility of watching me. Or was it Yizhi who picked her? For any particular reason?

"What's your name?" I ask while she sets up the tray for me to eat in bed.

She bows her head so deeply her chin almost touches her throat. "It's Wan'er, my lady. Shangguan Wan'er."

"How old are you?"

"Twenty-four, my lady."

"Oh, wow, really?"

Never mind, I am terrible at guessing ages. But that's still young compared to some of the aunties I've seen around the estate.

Color blooms in Wan'er's round cheeks. "It's all right. I'm often told I look younger than I am, my lady."

"Who sent you to look after me and why? Secretary Gao or Qin Zheng?"

Her eyes go huge.

Right, it's technically a great disrespect to refer to him directly by name.

"I mean, or *the emperor*," I say, so she feels more comfortable continuing this conversation.

She lets out a breath of relief. "It was His Majesty, my lady. He summoned all of us newly hired last month to ask us some questions. I answered honestly. Then I was told to serve you."

So Qin Zheng deliberately picked a servant who hadn't had time to develop any loyalty to the Gao family. Yizhi and I can't trust her to relay messages between us, then, even though I can talk to her without any soldiers present. She's one more set of eyes and ears for Qin Zheng.

"What kind of questions did he ask?" I interrogate further.

She's oddly quiet before saying, "If any of us knew much about laborism."

"What is that?"

Surprise flickers across her face. "The belief that people deserve to reap the fruits of their own labor. That no one should exploit the labor of others for profit."

"Well, yeah. Doesn't everyone believe that?"

"Far from it, my lady. Much of the exploitation occurs in ways we don't think to question. For example, does your family own the land you farm?"

I wince at the mention of my family, but by the casual way she said it, I don't think she knows what I did to them. I'm not sure exactly what footage is floating around out there. I decide not to bring it up before answering, "No, there's this family who owns half the mountain my village is on. We pay a portion of our harvests to them each year to use their land."

"But do your landlords ever contribute to the tilling?"

I snort. "They live in the town down the mountain. I've never even seen them."

"So your family does all the labor on the land, yet your landlords receive a big portion of its yield without so much as setting foot on it?" The nervousness leaves Wan'er's voice as she speaks.

Her back straightens. Her eyes meet mine. "Does this not seem unfair, my lady?"

I blink at her before giving a slow shrug. "They own the land. My ancestors were refugees from Zhou. They had to settle wherever they could."

"But imagine if your village collectively stopped recognizing that family's abstract ownership of the land you work on. You wouldn't have to hand any more harvests to them again."

"We—we can't just do that!"

"Why not?"

Is she serious? I open my mouth to list the obvious consequences, yet my words don't come out so smoothly. "They'd . . . take us to court. It's their land, bought with their money."

"My lady," Wan'er says with particular emphasis, "you and His Majesty control the courts now. It's the state that enforces ownership, and you have seized the state. Also, however much your landlords purchased the land for, I'm certain your village has made it back for them many times over. Yet the land will never be yours as long as your landlords extract too much for you to amass the savings to buy it. Do you have no desire to dismantle this system?"

My mind goes blank.

Then I come to my senses. "No, no, *I* can't change anything. I don't control anything. Our dearest emperor does."

"I think you'll find His Majesty to be a staunch laborist, my lady. Our history books try their hardest to erase this, but he is. His analysis of the countryside, though, has always been flawed. You can be a voice of the peasantry to him. I believe it's worth thinking about what changes you could push for to truly transform Huaxia."

Did she just criticize Qin Zheng?

I look around in reflexive fear of him listening through the walls. Maybe he is. Maybe he got her to say this on purpose to test my reaction. What does he want to hear? Me chastising her? Me asserting I have no ambition to interfere in politics?

The idea of letting everyone defy their landlords is . . . bold. It would cause exponentially more chaos than what I've already unleashed. If this were a week ago, I'd be sure this woman was baiting me to say something subversive so there would be a legal excuse to execute me. But Qin Zheng did rant about rich people and how he wants to "rid society of parasites." Is he for real? If he is, does he want to hear me enthusiastically support his agenda?

No, enough about what he wants. I need to get what *I* want.

I shove away the tray of food. "If our dearest emperor is sincere about freeing the masses, he'd be a hypocrite for holding me prisoner. Tell him I won't eat a single bite until he gives back my spirit armor and lets me into his council meetings."

He's not going to let me into his meetings while fighting allegations of being manipulated by me, but the first rule of haggling is to aim high.

Wan'er goes pale. "My lady, you can't—!"

"You have no say in what I can or cannot do," I snap. I have to keep my distance from her, or she'll be used against me. "Tell him what I want. If he doesn't like it, he can come deal with it himself."

Time passed more easily when I was unconscious.

The bedchamber's pervasive silence reminds me too much of when I was locked in a dark cell after I killed Yang Guang, waiting in limbo for my fate while knowing the world outside had forever changed because of my actions. The only difference is my prison is fancier this time.

I stick by my refusal to eat anything, but I let Wan'er change my bandages and help me wash up. My new feet are a monstrous sight, no longer looking like pointed hooves, but wider and flatter, like swollen, discolored pouches of flesh stitched together with black thread and tipped with vague hints of toes. The surgeon broke my bones all over again and realigned them with splints. Fortunately, Wan'er says the swelling will go down. By tying waterproof bags over my feet, I can use the tub in the bathroom, albeit inelegantly, my legs hanging over the edge while my qì-exhausted body immerses in the silky, readily available hot water. My mind strays frequently to my first visit to Chang'an, when I got to spend a week and a half of my recuperation period with Yizhi. On those nights, he would invite me into the washing pool dug into his bathroom floor. I think of the way water slipped down his tattooed skin, the glide of his hands spreading soap over my body, the contours of his hips as I straddled him underwater, the heat of our mouths meeting in the steam. And more innocent moments, too. Shampooing each other's hair, laughing as we splashed each other with foamy water.

Alone with my memories, I turn them over and over in my head. If I'd taken Yizhi's offer to go with him to Chang'an instead of letting myself get lifted to the Great Wall with a heart full of vengeance, would Shimin still be alive? Would he have preferred to have never met me? If I'd known where this sequence of events would lead, would I have stopped? Where could I have made a different, better move?

The mess in my head gets so tangled I come close to ridding myself of it by force. Unfortunately, it's impossible to drown myself in a bathtub. No matter how hard I try to hold myself underwater, I can't override the instinct to burst out and cling to life.

Wan'er brings me food every few hours. I ignore her every plea for me to eat. She swaps out trays of uneaten food for trays of uneaten food. I bat away her attempts to stick more infusion lines into me. I drink only a little water so I'm not too parched to bargain with Qin Zheng.

A couple of days later, I hear the furious clanging of his armor before he throws the door open. I push myself up, a gnawing in my stomach, my body heavy as a Chrysalis.

"Why must you insist on being so difficult?" He stomps to my side. No more pox scabs mottle his face, just faint white imprints.

My gut twists at how he's stronger and steadier each time I see him, but I rasp out my chief demand. "I want my armor."

"So you'll have the means to take down your guards and go roaming outside? Absolutely not."

"Then Your Glorious Majesty won't have an empress." I drop my head back on my pillow, my voice grating like sand through my throat. "I bet the officials will be *so* satisfied. They'll be able to look you in the eye and laugh in their hearts about how they prevented you from doing something you insisted you would do."

"The central court has nothing to do with your foolishness."

"That's not how they'll see it. And imagine how it'll look to the masses, seeing you break your promise to make the girl who resurrected you empress the moment you were secure on your throne."

"I never promised—!"

"Well, that's what people think you did. Or do you want them to suspect you actually got dragged into crushing a government in sheer confusion and then lied about it to save face?"

Qin Zheng makes a gruff noise. "I am keeping you safe in a world filled with those who wish you dead! Must you be so hung up on pride that you cannot accept this?"

"I'll decide for myself what I'll do for my safety and what I won't. I don't need Your Resplendent Majesty to make choices for me."

"Is that so?" He eyes my latest tray of neglected food on the nightstand. He lands a finger on the edge of a porridge bowl. "It seems you are choosing to compel me to tie you up and force meals down your throat."

Shimin's memories of being doused with alcohol flash through me. My stomach clenches.

"Go ahead. I can't wait for people to hear that you have so little influence over me you can't even get me to eat by my own will. How's that for an auspicious start to your new reign? You think you can hide something like this when the court is looking for reasons to question you?"

Qin Zheng's gaze darkens. Right as I fear he's about to force-feed me anyway, he says, "Tell me something: what exactly is your relationship with Gao Yizhi?"

I go still as stone. He must have seen enough of my memories to know, or he wouldn't be bringing this up.

"Exactly what you think it is," I say with an air of nonchalance. Desperately denying it would only make him more keen to go after Yizhi.

"And you're aware that even if I need you alive, the same does not go for him?"

I let out a hoarse laugh, the shaking of my shoulders masking the tremor going through me. "You saw me crush my own family when they were being used against me. You felt me doing it even as it tore me apart inside, and you want to gamble on the softness of my heart?"

He frowns, mouth pinching shut.

I go on before I have to hear another threat on Yizhi's life. "Also, I wouldn't dismiss Gao Yizhi's usefulness to you. Who else would you trust to be Imperial Secretary? Everyone else in this era is an utter stranger to you. But if you've seen my memories, you know who Yizhi was before you woke up. You know what drives him."

He may be the only other person in Huaxia who wants to kill the gods as badly as you and me, I would add if it weren't too dangerous to say out loud. I hope Qin Zheng has realized this.

"Oh?" He tilts his head. "You imply that your memories of him, the side he has shown to you, are true reflections of who he is. Funny. I have already seen enough evidence to the contrary."

What is that supposed to mean? I bite my cheek to stop myself from asking. Qin Zheng is trying to mess with my head. I trust Yizhi. Whatever he did, it must've been necessary.

"No matter what," I say, "I will not let you dangle his life in front of me. The moment you do anything to him, I'll consider him lost. I'll accept that he's better off dead than being used to control me, and so will he. You'll . . ." A tremendous wave of grief rolls through me when I realize I must handle Shimin the same way. I have to think of him as gone. If I hold onto any hope of getting him back, I'll be like Kuafu from the folk stories, chasing the sun until my sweat runs dry and my body withers.

When I snap back to my senses, Qin Zheng is studying me in silence. I steel myself, continuing as if I didn't suffer the lapse. "You'll lose Yizhi as an asset, and I still won't do what you want. I'd weigh my options before making a move like that."

He releases a sigh that presses close to a growl. "You can roam as you wish once the frenzy dies down. Cease this childish fit and eat your meals." He picks up the bowl of porridge. "Have you any idea how much labor went into producing this? And you're letting it go to waste?"

I roll over in my bed. "Send it to a beggar or something."

He slams the bowl down on the tray. "I am far too busy for this nonsense." His cape flaps behind him as he heads for the door.

"Does it make you feel powerful, controlling me?" I croak after him. "Or does the idea of me having a little freedom scare you that much?"

He stops.

"I was asleep for two hundred and twenty-one years, yet all I had to do was wake up, and the world bowed to me once more." He cuts a glare at me over his shoulder. "I have no need to control you to feel powerful."

I don't know if Qin Zheng thinks I'm bluffing, or that I'll break eventually, but I persist in my refusal to eat. I stop drinking water as well.

Once I push past the most intense phase of hunger, it becomes easier to resist the scents of braised meats and fried tofu. No matter how Wan'er calls or nudges me, I don't respond. I can barely summon the strength to speak anyway. Sometimes she puts a finger under my nose to check if I'm breathing. Other times I wake to her sneaking spoonfuls of water past my cracked lips, and I have to whack her away. The clattering of all her meal deliveries blends together. I drift in and out of daydreams and nightmares, trying to think of anything except my sand-dry throat and hollow stomach.

My mind is swimming in darkness when a soft glow reaches through my eyelids. I peel them open to the sight of—

"Shimin?" I gasp.

He's kneeling at my bedside, faint and ethereal, like the mist that surrounded us when we first locked eyes on the Vermilion Bird's docking bridge.

"Mei-Niang..." He speaks like a wind, an echo. He brushes his knuckles over my cheek, the touch soft as silk. "Be strong. I believe in you."

My throat aches, and my eyes sting with hot tears. "You're not real. You can't be real."

He shakes his head with a sad smile. "I will always be with you."

He puts his hand over mine. I stop breathing, afraid that one stray flutter of air might scatter this illusion.

Then something else disturbs it—sudden sounds outside the bedchamber. Shouts, gunshots, metallic clanging. Flashes of red leak through the gap beneath the door.

Shimin and I exchange an alarmed look.

"Quick, hide!" he says.

I stumble out of bed, repressing a cry of pain as I put my weight on my feet. Their new shape throws me off balance. When I look up, Shimin is gone. I don't know what that was.

I stagger into the bathroom and fall against the sink counter, my limbs weak and my head woozy. Just after I lock the bathroom door, I hear the door of the bedchamber getting smashed open. Several beats of wood creaking and snapping, followed by a heavy thud.

The metallic clanking of armor rages closer.

"Harlot! Where are you?" a surprisingly boyish voice yells out.

That has to be Liu Che. He's still in Chang'an?

Right—Qin Zheng sapped the Azure Dragon dry of qì. The unit will need more time to recuperate before it can be flown back to the Han province.

Lights flick on in the bedchamber, spilling around the bathroom door. Heart pounding sluggishly, I feel around for something to defend myself with. The mirror has long since been removed, leaving me without the option to make a glass shiv. I twist open a bottle of hand soap instead and pour it in front of the door. Then I snatch a big towel hanging on the wall and take a few steps back, steadying myself against the sink.

The door handle rattles. The red radiance of Fire qì shines around the door's edges, then the lock glows like an ember. It melts.

"Meet *your* nightmare, harlot!" Liu Che kicks the door open, waving a sword.

Skies, that's not even the right line I said that one time!

I hurl the towel at him. It catches him over the head as I hoped. His sword stabs through the fabric and is inadvertently anchored. I duck around him as he stumbles against the door frame and then slips on the soaped tiles. He crashes onto his back with a massive metallic sound, yelping. With all the remaining strength I can squeeze out, I push through the pain in my feet and bolt for the lantern-lit hallway beyond the bedroom.

Liu Che roars out curses behind me, armor clattering as he gets up. Heat grazes my back. He must be firing qì blasts at me, but thankfully, Wood-type spirit metal doesn't concentrate qì as well as Fire-type, so it can't tear through me with explosive force.

However, I abandon any underestimation of Liu Che when I spot my guards on the hallway floor, slashed and burned with deep, charred gashes. The smell of roasted flesh lingers in the air, rousing my hunger in the worst possible way.

"Die, harlot!" Liu Che charges up behind me.

I trip in the hallway, landing hard on my elbows. I keep crawling over the polished wooden floor and trying to get up, but I've lost my momentum. I cry out when Liu Che stomps the back of my leg. He rolls me over with his foot. Blazing red eyes greet me. Fire qì heats like lava in his raised sword. I bare my teeth. I will not die with fear on my face.

"Enough!" Qin Zheng's voice booms through the hallway.

Liu Che lurches back, then drops to his knees. "Your Majesty!"

I glance behind me. Qin Zheng is marching down the hallway with an entourage of guards and servants. One of them darts out from behind his flowing black cape—

I clench every muscle in my body to not call out Yizhi's name. It feels like another hallucination, except I would never imagine Yizhi in the purple robes of a top-ranking official, his hair pulled up inside a black gauze hat with two flaps in the back. He clutches a large notepad to his chest.

Our eyes meet. There's a breathless moment in which a thousand things should have been said.

Horror blooms in his eyes at the sight of me. I must look as disheveled, starved, and worn down as I feel. My translucent robe exposes way too much, tracing angles of bones I've never been able to see through my skin until now. Heart twinging at Yizhi's expression, I draw my bandaged feet behind myself and try to at least sit straighter. I avoid looking at him directly so we're not staring conspicuously at each other.

In one smooth motion, Qin Zheng tugs his cape away from his shoulder guards and tosses it over me. I claw to get my head out from under the thick black fabric.

"Prince-Captain Liu." Qin Zheng plants himself before us. "Explain yourself."

Liu Che knocks his forehead against the floor and slaps his palms down flat. "Y-your Majesty, please believe I am acting out of the utmost concern for you and Huaxia. I was told this wicked harlot has deceived you and continues to trouble you!"

Qin Zheng steps past me. I shiver at the unnatural chill he exudes and draw the cape tighter around myself. He pivots and sinks to one knee beside Liu Che. "Who was it that informed you of this?"

Liu Che gapes like a fish while lifting his head. "E-everyone. Everyone is saying it."

"You trusted that rabble over my judgment?"

"Your Majesty, I only want what's best for Huaxia!"

"I appreciate your thoughtfulness, Captain Liu. I truly do. But I do not need anyone to question my capacity to make decisions," Qin Zheng hisses out.

"Please forgive me, Your Majesty!" Liu Che smashes his forehead thrice more on the ground. His green pilot crown, which sprouts vine-like antlers along his head, slips askew.

Qin Zheng gestures at the burned corpses near us. "These soldiers were good men who put their lives on the line for Huaxia. They were fathers to young children, sons to ailing elders. Yet you took them from their families forever, without a single thought."

"I was thinking of Huaxia, Your Majesty!" Liu Che says between sobs, disconcerting for a boy with fresh blood on his hands.

Then again, who am I to judge?

"You can't keep this wicked harlot around you!" Liu Che points at me. "She does nothing but lie and manipulate, and Your Majesty deserves better than a twice-used whore! She—"

Qin Zheng seizes Liu Che's hand with an expression that sends terror straight to my core.

"*Say that word in front of me again.*" He tightens his grip around Liu Che's little finger.

Oh. His mother.

Water qì runs black under the tiny squares that make up Qin Zheng's gauntlet. Liu Che screams, clutching at his hand. A burst of coldness reaches me, accompanied by the sound of crackling ice. With a heart-jolting noise, Qin Zheng snaps the finger off.

Liu Che's scream goes jagged. He gawks at the red stump on his hand, so frozen it doesn't bleed.

"Next time, it'll be your tongue." Qin Zheng stuffs the severed finger in Liu Che's skewed crown.

What little acid that's left in my shriveled stomach surges into my throat. The hallway tilts, and my vision goes black.

Cold arms catch me before I collide with the ground. When dark spots recede from my vision, Qin Zheng's half-masked face is right above mine. I fight to get away from him, but he lifts me up, wrapped in his cape.

"Let it be known!" He spins me toward his entourage, toward Yizhi. "By my decree, this woman by the name of Wu Zetian is to become the Empress of Huaxia, to be crowned in a ceremony on the first day of the fourth month! Her piloting power is vital to the war effort. I will not tolerate any further attempts on her life!"

I can't see Yizhi's face clearly anymore as he stands in the shadows between lanterns. I only catch the movement of his arm while he writes on his notepad. I shut my eyes and roll my head in the other direction. My cheek hits Qin Zheng's ice-cold shoulder guard.

As Liu Che wails and cries for forgiveness, Qin Zheng carries me back into the bedchamber.

"Get some food in you *now*," he mutters. "Aside from your spirit pressure, your moderately sumptuous figure was your sole redeeming quality."

Pointedly ignoring the remark, I wriggle an arm out from beneath his cape and pull myself higher by his neck. "This would not have happened if I'd had my armor," I snarl over the wretched sounds outside.

"Fine. However, I hope you have learned a lesson about the danger you're in."

I don't have the energy to respond to that. Cherishing his concession, I welcome the darkness that pulls me under.

CHAPTER SIX

STRESS-INDUCED METAMORPHOSIS

"Is this too tight?" Qin Zheng says with his fingers on my waist, his chin low but his eyes flicking up at mine. Meridians sprawl black across his face as he conducts Water qì to adjust the suit of Yellow Dragon armor he's put on me.

"A little," I wheeze. The icy metal pieces clutch me like a torture device. Shivering, I almost fall back on my heels. I'm kneeling upright on my bed in front of Qin Zheng—absolutely not a position I want to be in, but since I can't stand on my feet, this is the next most convenient pose for molding armor pieces around my body. I just have to lift my knees one at a time for him to encase my legs.

I push my own qì through the hair-thin needles freshly embedded in my spine, trying to shift the countless square pieces of my armor. The Earth-type spirit metal refuses to budge. I'm utterly baffled as to how Qin Zheng slid it over my body like molten gold. Though I guess I'm still weak from the hunger strike. I had to recover for a couple of days, slowly introducing food to my system, before I could even get up like this.

When my armor finally loosens to a more comfortable fit, I can tell it was by Qin Zheng's mental command instead of mine. It stops being flexible the moment his fingers leave my waist. Coldness recedes from the metal. A throttled breath escapes my lungs, and I rub the gaps between my gauntlets and shoulder guards, kept connected by thin strings. I swear he squeezed me on purpose. I'm starting to regret demanding this armor, but the protection and power it offers are too crucial to give up.

I don't know why I was imagining getting my Vermilion Bird armor back. Even disregarding the dubious condition it's in after Yizhi broke off a portion of it to smite his father, I can't wear anything associated with Shimin anymore. I'm supposed to be paired with Qin Zheng now.

Yang Guang, Shimin, Qin Zheng. I'd curse the world for binding me to man after man after man, yet I can't deny that with all three there was a moment in which I consciously chose them. Enlisting to be Yang Guang's concubine. Trusting Shimin. Awakening Qin Zheng. As I meet his eyes, I can't help but think: *There's a reason they call me the Iron Widow. You'd be number three.*

But there's a lot worth learning from him before I fulfill that title again. I won't survive outside this room if I can't wield my armor with ease. And if I can't even wield this armor, I can forget about ever piloting the Yellow Dragon without him. He must have some special tips and tricks.

Carefully, I sit down on the edge of the bed.

"How did you learn to do this?" I examine my golden gauntlets, as pliant as snakeskin gloves thanks to its complex texture.

Qin Zheng crosses his arms. "The manipulation of qì and spirit metal was considered an art in my time. We pilots honed our mastery of qì to ensure we did not burn our lives out in a few short years. I've been told that, these days, it's believed that pilots are doomed to perish before twenty-five years of age. That is nonsense. I know—*knew* many older pilots. Those of you in the future are mere shells of what you could be." He drops his voice. "Clearly, certain forces do not wish to see individual pilots grow too powerful again."

I glance toward the ceiling. Is he saying the gods interfered with the pilot training system to prevent another like him from challenging them?

"Well . . . how do we fix that?" I say in a near-whisper.

"Do not rely on so-called 'strategists' to do the thinking for you, for a start. What would a gaggle of flaccid scholars who never set foot on a battlefield know about wielding a Chrysalis? We pilots trained each other, the more senior ones mentoring the more junior."

"Really? Who trained *you*?"

His expression turns more sullen. "Have you heard of a pilot named Mi Xuan?"

"No?"

It's a while before he speaks again. "She was the commanding pilot of the Three-Legged Crow. Queen class, General rank."

My next breath catches in my throat. "You were trained by a female pilot?"

"Indeed. Are you certain you have no relation to anyone by the family name of Mi? It's written like the character for 'half,' except the top strokes are different."

I shrug. "I honestly can't tell you. My family lost our ancestral records when Zhou fell. They had to evacuate with nothing but the clothes on their backs. Why are you asking?"

He stares intensely at my face. "Wishful thinking, I suppose."

What is even happening in the recaptured Zhou province? I feel like I should ask, yet I can't summon the will to process what I might hear. Why burden myself with the knowledge? No way I could make the mighty conqueror Qin Fucking Zheng budge on matters of war.

His fingers tap against his elbow. He looks like he wants to say more, yet is hesitant for some reason. "The historical documents say those who competed for power after my disappearance blamed her for what happened to me," he finally says. "They executed her for it. Severed her at the waist and threw her into the streets to rot. Her absence, along with the fact that many pilots succumbed to the same flowerpox outbreak that caught me, played a large role in why Zhou fell. Yet, after the fall, the reactionaries persisted in their blaming. They executed many other Iron Widows and expunged their military achievements from the public record."

Nausea and shock churn at once in my chest. "Did you just say 'Iron Widows,' plural?"

"Yes. Such is what we called powerful female pilots in command of their own Chrysalis units. We had quite a few more of them, since the yīn-yáng seats weren't calibrated with unequal inputs."

"Wait, they weren't in your time? But the Yellow Dragon . . . when we switched seats . . ."

"It made no difference."

"Then why were you all offended about it?" I splutter.

"Since it made no difference, I had no clue why you were demanding that I switch! I was not in the mood to move around without a reason!"

"Unbelievable." I smack a hand over my face, though I'm breathing so heavily I feel like there's a volcano inside me. Just as I believed, Iron Widows existed before me, but they were erased. "How did this happen? Why did the Chrysalis engineers start making the inputs unequal? It makes no sense!"

"Since when did we as a species abide by good sense? Why do cowardly men strike their wives after a reprimand at work? Why do mothers scream at their children after a beating by their husbands? Those unable to conquer their misfortunes take their fury out on more convenient targets. It does not surprise me that women were forced into stricter subservience after Huaxia suffered a major defeat."

I search his eyes, wishing I could peer into his mind, or that I'd been able to catch a memory of the Iron Widows during my pilot link with him. What they were like, what they were capable of. I hate to think the sole remaining traces of their existence are in his head.

"Teach me everything Mi Xuan taught you," I plead, a tender warmth quavering at my lash line.

I don't realize I'm reaching for him, for the ghost of her within him, until my hand touches his armored chest. He startles, as if I've singed him, but steels his composure within a second.

"Eventually," he says, massaging his forehead. "When I have time. For now, I must keep my focus on matters of state. I am unhappy with nearly every single one of those spineless moderates in the central court, and finding suitable replacements will take much effort. If I allow myself any distractions, the court will certainly plot against me."

"Who would dare plot against *you*?"

He drops his hand from his face and glares at me with dead eyes. "Who, indeed? What kind of insolent cretin could possibly show no respect for me?"

My cheeks flush. "Just because I don't roll over to do whatever you say doesn't mean I'm plotting against you!" I say, hoping it sounds convincing. "We're on the same side. And surely you can spare, like, twenty minutes out of your day to help me ... become more useful against the political machinations you face. Come on, I'll start calling you 'Your Majesty' again."

"You should never have stopped!"

"I'll do it with extra enthusiasm as long as you train me, *Your Majesty*," I say in a sweet, high-pitched voice, because that allegedly works on men. "Or would you prefer Master Qin? *Qiiin-shīfu*?"

A whole-body shudder goes through him. "Not like that."

"Well, then," I continue in the same voice, "if you train me, I will stop."

He bends toward me with a scowl. "You should not take this so lightly, insolent girl. The ways of my time are much more intense than yours. We had to battle not only the Hunduns but other humans and their Chrysalises as well. We had no leisure to pose for photos, showboat in front of crowds, or *sell commercial products*," he says with utmost disgust. "Falling behind in pilot skill meant defeat and subjugation, and subjugation by fellow humans can be worse than being overrun by Hunduns. The Hunduns give a quick death. Humans may keep you alive in ways that make you wish you were never born."

"I'm well aware," I say, my tone colder and flatter. "So, tell me what you did to get so good with spirit metal. What made you . . . you?"

He straightens, appearing to weigh his next words very carefully. "I was nine years of age when I was first tested by drafters, and they estimated my spirit pressure to be around four hundred units."

"Four hundred?" I question, unsure if I heard right. "Was the scale different? Because nowadays you need at least five hundred to pilot a Chrysalis."

"The scale was the same. They took me precisely because my spirit pressure was close to the threshold but did not reach it. They used me in experiments studying stress-induced metamorphosis, the rare phenomenon of an extreme change in spirit pressure under extreme duress. They could not afford to risk Chrysalis-capable draftees on such experiments, but those like me had prime potential. They dropped me into a dungeon with nine other children, mostly orphans and street rats. A stream of water began pouring from a spout in the wall." Qin Zheng traces a circle in the air. "It was a small stream. Would have taken days to fill the dungeon. But they told us the hatch on the ceiling would not be opened until there remained only one of us alive." He tilts his head like he's trying to remember something. "To our credit, we made it to at least the second day before we began to kill each other."

My blood runs cold. The memory of his mind realm floods back to me—the frozen ocean, the hungry ghosts.

Qin Zheng goes on. "We tried plugging the water spout with our clothes. We tried bending it in on itself. We tried to open the hatch by forming a human pillar up to the ceiling. Nothing worked. In the end, it came down to strangling each other, bashing each other's heads against the wall, and holding each other beneath the water. I emerged as the final survivor with a spirit pressure in the thousands. The overall success rate of the experiments, however, was rather low, so I discontinued them after I seized control of the army."

I sit in silence, staring off to the side. *Stress-induced metamorphosis*. I think that might be how my own spirit pressure got so high.

"Still itching to be trained by me?" Qin Zheng says with a slight smirk, but there's something broken about it, like I'm seeing it in a cracked mirror.

I'd rather scramble far, far away from him. But then I imagine myself as one of those children in the dungeon, floating limp in the bloody water as he climbs to victory. There is no room in his world for weakness. There is no way out except by whatever means necessary.

I gather my wits and say, "That can't be the only way you got so powerful. You said they couldn't afford to risk Chrysalis-capable draftees, so your training after that must've been something other than death battles."

"Acute observation. My subsequent training was less deadly, true, but no less strenuous. The hottest fires forge the strongest weapons, they say."

"If you could handle that, so can I."

"We shall see." He turns to leave, but then stops and gives my face a long, troubled look.

He touches my armor's high collar. A thin layer of spirit metal liquefies and slithers up the back of my neck. As I squirm at the sudden coldness, it diverges over my ears to form a mask around my eyes. A veil of fine strands drops from the bottom of the mask, dangling over the lower half of my face.

"Hey, what the fuck?" I pry at the mask.

"*Language*," Qin Zheng chastises. "You are to become my empress. By tradition, no other man can touch you or see your face."

"Are you serious? Get this off!" I push at the mask from below, but it's so perfectly adhered to my face it won't budge. "Since when did you care about tradition?"

"*I* do not care, but the masses do. Having this as part of your new image will comfort them, and it will make it easier to pass body doubles off as you. We found a candidate with a figure similar to yours, but her facial features do not quite match up."

"You just want people to see that I'm under your control!" The veil of the mask dribbles like rain against my lips with my every word. This is going to get very annoying if I can't get rid of it.

"Which is an effective tactic to ensure your safety, is it not?"

"Wow, how noble of you!"

Qin Zheng flashes a smile. With deceptive nonchalance, he slides his hand around my neck and forces my head back. I inhale sharply at the iciness of his touch, my spine tensing onto an arc.

He leans until our faces almost touch. "My patience for your antics has limits. Understand this: I care not for whatever ... queer liaisons ... you were involved in before, but now that you belong to me, I will not tolerate any insult to my honor. We have an image to maintain. You will not be seen in the company of other men. You will not speak to me in your insolent way in public."

My pulse thrums against his hand. I should keep quiet and nod. That's what he wants. But I cannot let him think he can frighten me into submission, that he can make me *belong to him* by threatening me with violence.

"You call other men cowardly for laying a hand on their wives, yet here you are," I remark through the pressure of his grasp.

His hand slackens but doesn't leave my neck. "Do not reach for such a false equivalency. They do what they do to cope. I am doing this because you are an aggravating child who desperately requires discipline."

"I hope you know that, these days, it's very creepy to call your bride-to-be a child."

"I shall cease to treat you like a child when you cease to act like one!"

"And when will you stop treating me like property? A bit hypocritical, isn't it, when you claim to be for abolishing private property?"

"*What?* How is that relevant?" He recoils, releasing me, then squints. "Do you not know the difference between private property and personal property?"

I fold my arms, refusing to admit I'm confused by the question.

"Those are not the same!" he says, now sounding more annoyed than angry. "Private property is land, factories, utilities, infrastructure—resources needed by the whole of society but subject to the whims of private owners, giving them disproportionate and often unearned power. Things such as your clothes, furniture, jewelry, those are *personal* property, those are *possessions* that give you no economic power over others, and I have no intention of taking away . . ." He looks off in a vague direction. "Excuse me, I need to go reform the education system."

I shrink away from his weird outburst. "I didn't go to school."

"I can tell!" he yells over his shoulder while storming to the door. "Learn to manipulate the metal if you wish to adjust your armor!"

The moment the door slams, I double over, soothing the lingering chill around my neck. But my own touch is cold as well, startling me. I look down at the golden pieces enveloping nearly every part of my body. A sense of claustrophobia closes in. I thought this armor would be my strongest weapon, but if I can't learn to control it, it will be a cage only Qin Zheng can unlock.

CHAPTER SEVEN

A TESTAMENT TO WHY THEY SHOULD'VE USED LESS-CONFUSING TERMS IN METAPHYSICS

Wood boosts speed. Fire boosts strength. Earth boosts firmness. Metal boosts sharpness. Water boosts fluidity.

Sitting cross-legged on my bed as if I'm meditating, I mentally repeat the list of internal boosts the five types of qì can confer on spirit metal. I recall from Sima Yi's piloting lessons—with a bitter taste in my mouth about ever trusting him—that each type of spirit metal differs in whether it's better at channeling external manifestations or internal boosts. In the Fire-type Vermilion Bird, it was all about external manifestations. It was good at blasting Fire qì in powerful bursts, Wood qì like crackling lightning, or Metal qì like zapping lasers. Now I must adjust to the other end of the spectrum, where Earth-type spirit metal can't manifest qì externally at all. Even Qin Zheng's freezing power requires contact to work, despite the legends saying he could freeze whole herds of Hunduns at once. The coldness that exudes from him is just the surrounding air dropping in temperature, the way it would around a block of ice. However, if he were to put on the Vermilion Bird armor, he could indeed unleash his Water qì in a chilling black wave that freezes on a mass scale. Which would be pretty ironic when the armor is called a *Fire* type. Sometimes these metaphorical names get very confusing. Honestly, can Qin Zheng blame us for offloading the thinking onto drab old men who eagerly study metaphysics for years? The five types of qì can have *twenty-five* unique interactions with the five types of spirit metal, and exponentially more when multiple types of qì are involved. Give me a break.

. . . Except if I can't drill this into my head and match Qin Zheng in piloting skill, I'll always be at his mercy.

Ugh.

Eyes closed, I concentrate on trying to channel my dominant Metal qì out from my spine.

Metal boosts sharpness.

Theoretically, it'll let me etch fine details into my armor, such as clean splits down the arms, legs, and torso so I can take the pieces on and off. My inability to make the armor budge is causing serious problems. I had to get creative to use the bathroom, and the jutting shoulder guards are preventing me from sleeping on my side.

The mild coolness of Metal qì flows through the network of meridians in my body, yet it's like there's a clog where my spine meets my armor. I can passively feel the armor pieces as if through a sixth sense, but the sensation is dull, and I can't move them. My only progress has been figuring out I can attach the strings veiling my lower face to the sides of my mask near my ears so I can eat in peace.

Fire boosts strength. Fire boosts strength. Fire boosts strength.

A second circuit of my meridians floods with heat. The interlacing of Fire and Metal makes me hot and cold at once. I keep it up because Fire qì is more conductive than Metal qì, and therefore has a better chance at channeling into my armor. I sustain the surge until it feels like I'm in battle, my jaw gritting to the point of trembling, sweat beading on my forehead. I try conducting my qì at the highest spirit pressure I can manage. I try slowing it down, like rain soaking through earth. I try pulsing it like the blood in my arteries. I try summoning a third type of qì, Water or Wood.

Nothing.

Nothing.

Nothing.

I collapse against the headboard with an indignant howl.

If only the Iron Widows were never wiped out and suppressed. What I would do for a competent female mentor like General Mi...

Would it be possible to build a new generation of female pilots commanding their own Chryalises? The current most powerful female pilots like Qieluo and Wei Zifu are all locked in Balanced Matches. Splitting them from their partners would doom more concubine-pilots, something I'm not willing to suggest. Finding new candidates would require making the army do a sweep for girls with high spirit pressures, something they haven't taken seriously, since girls aren't conscripted like boys are. When a mobile testing team came to my village when I was fourteen, they only made vague estimates for us girls, while the boys got full rounds of tests.

But if they do a proper sweep, the girls will surely be urged to join the war—the last thing I want to think about right now.

I'm lost in a fantasy of how different my life would be if I lived in Qin Zheng's era when a knock raps on the door. It's familiar by now, after so many meal deliveries.

"Come in," I call out.

Wan'er elbows through the door, hauling a sack of books I asked her to get. I peek at the new guards outside. If the books prove useful, they just might help me overpower those guards if I need to.

"My lady, here's a good selection of texts on qì, spirit metal, and Chrysalises." Wan'er drops the sack on my bed, breathing hard, and wipes her forehead. "Please forgive me for taking so long. I got held up by Secretary Gao when coming back into the palace."

Every ligament in my body goes rigid. "Secretary Gao?"

"Yes, my lady. He wanted to inspect the books. He urges you to be cautious with what's brought in from the outside, though he suggests you start with this tome..." Wan'er digs through the sack and hands me a thick book with a worn cover.

I take it, heart pounding. Yizhi wouldn't have rifled through this book for no reason. A musty, smoky scent blooms in the air as I flip through its yellowed pages. I don't know what I'm looking for until I spot it—a tiny slip of paper with a line of handwritten text.

Tomorrow noon, estate temple.

Letting no reaction show on my face, I snatch the paper and hide it beneath my covers under the guise of adjusting them. Yizhi has to mean his family's ancestral shrine, though I'm not sure where it is in the estate. Asking Wan'er at this very moment would be too suspicious. I snap the book closed and pretend to consider its title, printed in a white box on its plain blue cover. I can't read half the characters in it.

"If I may, my lady, I agree with Secretary Gao's suggestion," Wan'er says. "Master Yan is a must-read."

"Is that so?" I say distractedly. "Who's Master Yan?"

"Oh, the philosopher Zou Yan of the pre-unification era. That's his *Theoretical Foundations of Metaphysics*. Some of the ideas in it are outdated, but as a starting point, it has no equal."

My thoughts snap away from Yizhi and temples. "You've read this yourself?"

Blushing, she lowers her head. "Yes, my lady. I checked out that same copy from the Chang'an Public Library ten years ago."

"You read this at *fourteen*?" I leaf through the book again. It's full of complex characters never reached in my rudimentary reading lessons from Yizhi. "How? Who taught you?"

"It was my mother, my lady."

My attention drops to her unbound feet, steady in embroidered slippers. I had the impression that only women from pompous families have the opportunities to be educated at a scholarly level, and those women almost always have bound feet, or they'd get shunned in marriage negotiations with other pompous families. So how did Wan'er end up as an unbound servant?

"How did your mother learn?" I keep questioning.

Wan'er nibbles her lip. "My grandfather was once a Sage, my lady. But then he . . . got caught up in political turmoil. It happened when I was a baby."

"A Sage?" I sit straighter.

Now things make sense. A disgraced family would see no point in binding their daughter's feet when they'll never have any good marital prospects again.

"Grandfather gave a lot of support to worker unions, so the big corporations lobbied for the other Sages to take him down on bogus charges," Wan'er says with a distant look in her eyes. Then she gives a start. "Not that I'm asking for a pardon!" She waves her hands. "I mean, I submitted an appeal to His Majesty, but I'm not trying to nudge you into supporting it or anything, my lady."

"I could, if you want. I can't promise he'll listen, but I could try. What's your grandfather's name?"

"Please, don't." She puts her hands together. "I don't want to jump the line because I happen to be your servant. I'm hoping this new government will move away from only doing things for people with connections. That's what my grandfather would truly want."

"All right, if you're sure. He sounds like one of the good ones, though."

"So I've heard." Wan'er's gaze drifts up.

Some believe the most enlightened among us ascend to the Heavenly Court once they die. On the slim chance that's true, I hope her grandfather's spirit can help Shimin in some way.

I tap the book thoughtfully, then hold it out to her. "Could I hear you read the first page of this out loud?"

"Oh, of course, my lady."

She takes the book and passes the test with astonishing grace, narrating the complicated passages as fluidly as a scholar-bureaucrat.

When she finishes, I gulp through a tender knot in my throat. "Your mother taught you well."

"She's read to me since I was very little." Wan'er returns the book and folds her hands in front of her blue pleated skirt. "Even though our family fell into its . . . situation, she raised me to love books as much as she does, everything from romances to epics to philosophy."

Lucky.

I weigh my options. Getting closer to her comes with risks, but my own shoddy reading skills won't get me anywhere with these books. I can't turn down the benefit of learning from someone with deep political knowledge, which I'll need to challenge Qin Zheng's power.

"Will you teach me, too?" I ask.

Her eyes spring wide. "Would that be allowed, my lady?"

"*Allowed?*" I snap, deliberately harsh. For her own safety, I can't get overly friendly with her. Qin Zheng will use her against me the moment he senses my heart softening. "I'm to be the Empress of Huaxia. What I do is at my own discretion. Bring that chair over and sit down."

Wan'er hurries to do so, apologizing when the chair briefly scrapes the floorboards.

"We'll read this entire book together," I say, opening it between us.

She takes a steadying breath and starts again from the beginning. Her finger glides across the text while she narrates it slowly. I follow every character she sounds out, mentally correcting my assumptions about their pronunciations. When I hum in confusion at a sentence, she explains it in her own words.

The introductory chapter explains the theory that the universe created itself out of primordial chaos—the *hùndùn*—by organizing into cycles of yīn and yáng, dialectical forces that give sense to the world. Without up, there is no down. Without summer, there is no winter. Without day, there is no night, and so on. Turns out this Zou Yan is the one to blame for popularizing the concept of the *wǔxíng*, from which the types of qì and spirit metal get their confusing names. Referencing five key substances in nature, he attempted to identify five distinct kinds of forces that arise from interactions between yīn and yáng. The flourishing force of Wood, the destructive force of Fire, the steadying force of Earth, the honing force of Metal, and the tempering force of Water.

As Wan'er's lesson goes on, a muted rage grows inside me. How much more would she know if her family hadn't been ousted from grace, if she'd had more teachers than her mother alone?

"I bet you could be a scholar-bureaucrat if they let you take the civil service exams," I mutter during a lull between sections. It's absurd that she's so smart, yet she's stuck being a servant.

Wan'er gives a frail smile. "I'm honored to simply serve you, my lady."

"Are you? If I changed the policies so women can take the exams, wouldn't you go for it?"

"You could really do that?"

Such bright hope lights up on her face that I flinch. "I . . . I mean, I could try."

When her expression wilts, I say, in a firmer tone, "I will do whatever I can to improve things for women. I didn't fight my way into this position just to let things stay the same."

"I hope so, my lady." Wan'er tames her reaction this time, but I don't miss the visible effort it takes for her to keep her mouth from curling at the corners.

The mood feels right for me to casually ask the question searing at the back of my mind. "By the way, there's a temple in this estate, right?"

"Yes, near the northern perimeter, I believe. Why do you ask, my lady?"

"Oh, I just think whatever's ahead for Huaxia, it'll be a rough road. I want to ask for a blessing from the gods."

Obviously, I don't use the same excuse with Qin Zheng.

"At least let me send off my old partner before we get married," I say when I get him to visit me the next morning. "He's haunting me. Let me go burn some incense for him. I can't stop thinking about what the gods have done to . . ."

I'm not even lying. Every night, I've gotten dragged through dreams of mangled flesh and broken bones.

To my surprise, Qin Zheng doesn't push back on letting me leave the bedchamber for this.

"Fine," he says, looking distracted. "But General Dugu must accompany you, and she must bring you back promptly. No detours."

Something's not right. His skin is almost translucently pale, and the under-eye circle visible on the unmasked side of his face is dark as a bruise. He doesn't make any snide comments when I grudgingly admit I'm having trouble taking off my armor. I wish I could've held out longer, but my feet are encased in its boots, and they might fester if I don't change the bandages soon. My pride is not worth blood poisoning.

I expected Qin Zheng to make me beg, but he touches his gauntlet to my armor without delay and mentally carves out seams that'll let me take the pieces on and off like magnets. He seems so unwell, I start wondering if freezing himself for over two centuries has had some side effects.

"So what actually happened to your face?" I ask, recalling something going wrong with it as he woke up, which led to him donning that mask.

"Ah. Turns out I had a minor stroke while I was thawing," he grumbles. "Explains why my mind felt so foggy for those initial hours."

"You had a *stroke?*" I exclaim, more alarmed than I want to be. I may be plotting his demise, but having it happen before I'm ready would create a whole lot of new problems. I don't know if I should be cheering *for* or *against* his health.

He shrugs. "The complications have largely passed. I've taken a liking to this mask, however. The cameras of this future are too powerful. They capture *everything*," he says, with a hint of horror.

I think of the grainy black-and-white photos and footage I've seen of him, in which I never noticed any scars. Going from being perceived as a fuzzy, blurred figure to being broadcast in full-color high-definition must've been quite the shock.

"Are you camera shy?" I mock him just a little. "You could get a makeup artist to put some foundation and concealer on you so you look less . . . pallid."

Shooting me a glare, he touches *my* mask. The veil strings I pinned near my ears drop back over my lower face. "Keep this down when you go outside."

I don't bother protesting. This is a minuscule price to pay to see Yizhi.

"Seriously, when was the last time you slept?" I question. "Shouldn't you be resting more after having a *stroke?*"

"I've done enough sleeping." He huffs, eyes closed and fingers on his brow. Then he leaves without further dallying.

It's the first time he came by this room without insulting or threatening me.

Huh. So there is such a thing as being too busy to be an asshole.

CHAPTER EIGHT

STRANGERS

Shortly before noon, Qieluo pushes me in a wheelchair through the roofed walkways between the many buildings and gardens of the Gao Estate. Or the Huaxia Palace now, I guess. The vibe is completely different from when I stayed here with Yizhi and Shimin a lifetime ago. Armed soldiers everywhere, for starters. No more silk-robed drunk people laughing and hollering at all hours. No members of Yizhi's absurdly large extended family coming to ask me invasive questions. I heard from Wan'er that many had to join the staff they used to boss around because the kitchens no longer cater to able-bodied adults who don't contribute labor.

There's a lot of work that needs doing as the government sets up offices in the residences here. I catch sight of a few scholar-bureaucrats shuffling through the walkways in their purple, red, or green robes, but always from a distance, and they immediately avert their eyes. Qin Zheng must've ordered the path from my residence to the temple cleared beforehand. I also spot, across a large lotus pond, what has to be one of Yizhi's younger sisters playing with a wooden yo-yo. The bound-foot woman she's with spins her away and hurries them both out of view, as if fleeing from a monstrosity.

A jitter builds in my stomach at the thought of seeing Yizhi himself soon. It may be a fatal mistake. No matter how discreetly Yizhi and I do this, there's always a chance Qin Zheng will find out the next time we pilot together, when my memories might spill over to him. But Yizhi would know the risks better than anyone. For him to call me out here regardless, there must be a very substantial reason.

The grinding of my wheelchair and the jangling of Qieluo's armor sound unnaturally loud when the only other noise is the trickling of water in garden ponds. The very air feels harder to breathe, as if the gray sky is pressing down on us.

"How's Liu Che?" I say to Qieluo to break the unnerving quiet.

"Staying put in the residence His Majesty threw him into." Qieluo turns my wheelchair onto a bumpy path across a rock garden. "He's scared shitless. Don't worry, though, he'll be scurrying away in the Azure Dragon after your coronation. That's right about when he'll be fully replenished with qì. I'll keep you safe from him until then."

"I'm not worried. I just can't believe that kid. Fourteen years old and already killing without blinking."

"Right? Thank heavens His Majesty is here to discipline him now."

I sigh as our path ends at a short set of stairs. Built on a mountain, the estate has an annoying number of these. Cautiously, I get to my bandaged feet and unlatch a metal cane from the back of my plain, foldable wheelchair. I don't know why Qin Zheng forbade me from using a motorized wheelchair when I couldn't have gotten far with it, no matter how fast it might go. Qieluo helps me traverse the stairs with one hand supporting my elbow and her other hand at the small of my back. It's like I have to learn to walk all over again. Not to mention how much the scuffle with Liu Che set back my healing. Every painful step plants me in that moment again: his hateful eyes, the roasted scent of the guards he killed to get to me.

Though it's not like I haven't committed my own share of horrors. It started with wanting to kill one boy in revenge. Then I was throwing soldiers out of the Vermilion Bird's cockpit. Torturing An Lushan to death. Squashing Xiuying and Zhu Yuanzhang in the Black Tortoise. Smashing the Kaihuang watchtower. Crushing the Palace of Sages, with my family in it.

In the fables, karma always catches up to the wicked, and kindness always gets rewarded in the end. Big Sister was the kindest person I knew, always putting others first, letting me or our little brother have more rice when there wasn't enough to go around, and taking responsibility when my fights with him wreaked havoc around the house. Although I could take a beating from our father and remain unrepentant, a weary admonishment from Big Sister would fill me with shame for days. For most of my life, I thought *I* was the broken one with the rotten heart, doomed to lose everything because I'm incapable of playing by the rules. Yet she's dead because of a depraved boy's whims, and I'm about to become the Empress of Huaxia.

It's almost paralyzing, gazing into the truth that the universe is indifferent at its core. There's no benevolent higher force that rights wrongs. No guarantee of justice. Our gods actively sabotage us. Those who create and enforce the rules are the ones who break them in the most heinous ways. Here at the highest levels of power, there is only *awful* battling *worse*.

"Qieluo, have you ever killed a person?" I ask when we reach a pavilion at the top of the stairs, my voice sounding far off to my own ears.

She snorts while going back to haul my wheelchair up. "As if the army would've let me get away with that."

"But if there were no consequences, would you do it?"

She sets the wheelchair next to me. "There are certainly people in this world I would rather not see alive anymore. Why?"

I lower myself into the wheelchair again. "Just wondering if there's something messed up in the head with all us pilots. If someone *has* to be messed up to be a strong pilot."

"Hey, don't drag me into this. I'm not messed up." She pushes me out of the pavilion and onto a stone bridge over a pond.

"You shoved me into a wall the first time we met! For something you saw in *Yang Jian's* mind!"

"No, no, I just didn't want to *talk to you* because of that. Then you got pissy and started insulting me, and that's what made me push you. Big difference."

"That's . . . never mind." I go slack in my wheelchair. The extent of Qieluo's violence is admittedly mild compared to Liu Che's. Or Qin Zheng's. Or Xiuying's. Or Zhu Yuanzhang's. Or Shimin's. Or mine.

"Do you think killing Hunduns makes it easier to kill humans?" I say in a near-whisper after a long silence.

"No? By that logic, all butchers are potential serial killers."

"You think killing Hunduns is the same as killing animals?" I look over my shoulder at her. "When you're in battle, don't you feel what the Hunduns feel, how complex their emotions are? Doesn't that ever make you hesitate?"

Qieluo scoffs. "That's just a defense mechanism, like a bee stinging you as it dies. This is war. If you fall for those tricks and hesitate, you perish. Though I can't deny that battles would feel a lot better if Chrysalis engineers could figure out how to keep the Hunduns from messing with our heads."

"Have you . . ." My next question lodges in my throat. This is a dangerous topic, too close to what Qin Zheng would kill me for. But I have to get Qieluo's opinion. "Have you ever wondered what it means for the Hunduns to be capable of feeling emotions so complex?" I ask in my lowest voice. "If they're self-aware, just like us?"

"No way. If they had our level of brains, they would've realized the moment we created Chrysalises that this invasion of theirs backfired spectacularly. I can't imagine any intelligent species staying here once we started piloting their corpses against them. They would've scrambled back to wherever they came from."

They can't! I want to scream, yet I bite my tongue. I imagine the way Qin Zheng's eyes would darken if he found out I'd said too much, the way he could crush me to a pulp with my own armor. I'm not afraid of death, but I'm afraid of the truth dying with me because I didn't wait for the right moment.

Still, my mind shrieks at every servant I see, hoping that somehow, someone can hear what's trapped in my head.

Of course, no one perceives anything but a stone-cold empress-to-be behind a mask and veil. The truth sinks through me like acid, eating me from the inside, bit by bit by bit.

The smell of incense stirs me out of my spiraling thoughts. We're approaching the temple. Dense, fluffy trees and manicured bushes huddle against the paved stone path that curves toward it. I grow tense when many voices carry on the wind, chanting a mantra over solemn music, though it's quickly apparent that it's a recording.

The temple is as Wan'er described it, a single-story building with red walls and pillars. Intoxicating smoke rises in wisps from a huge bronze incense vessel in front of it. The estate's northern wall juts out behind the temple, painted in white and topped with curls of barbed wire. A crow flutters out of the mountain forests beyond, its cry echoing across the swells and dips of other peaks.

The urge to climb the wall and escape into the woods pulses through me, the same old fantasy of vanishing into freedom.

If only.

Ganye Temple says a plaque above the temple's paper screen doors. The engraved calligraphy sends a jolt through my heart. The sturdy style reminds me too much of Shimin's.

Qieluo shoves the screen doors open before I'm ready. The chant recording pours louder over us. Dull daylight falls across a cushion for kneeling and a shrine loaded with rows of ancestral tablets. Fresh peaches sit on the shrine's offering altar. I scan the rest of the room, but I don't see Yizhi. Not yet.

Listening for any sound other than the chanting, I get up so Qieluo can carry my wheelchair over the threshold that's unfortunately at the entrance of every traditional building. Once I sit down again, she hands me a stick of lit incense from the bronze vessel, its tip glowing orange-red.

"I'll give you a moment alone," she says.

I nod in gratitude. She pulls the screen doors shut, though her silhouette remains in the wax paper in its frame.

With my free hand, I roll my wheelchair up to the shrine. Qin Zheng hasn't bothered to make this place his own yet. The Gao family's ancestral tablets persist in their rows like haughty spirits, right under the blaring brass speakers on the ceiling. Funny—if I had accepted Yizhi's marriage proposal, I would've had to pray to these tablets. In a nook at the top of the shrine stands a red-faced, green-robed statue of Lord Guan, the god of money, business, and brotherhood. Of course that's this family's patron deity. I snort before surveying the statues at the sides of the room. Chiyou, the monstrous god of war. Guanyin, the serenely smiling goddess of mercy. Nüwa, the snake-bodied goddess of creation. And more against the shadowed back wall, like a judgmental council staring down at me.

Are all of you real? I wonder, sweeping a challenging glare across them. *Do you really look like that? Do you really have those powers?*

Are you watching me?

My gaze follows the plume of smoke from my incense to the ceiling. I claimed to be coming here to pray for Shimin's spirit, but who am I supposed to pray to when the gods themselves are the ones dangling him between life and death?

Bowing my head, I raise the incense to no higher power in particular.

"Be free, Shimin," I whisper.

The words break something in me as they leave me. I double over, the metallic veil of my mask swinging onto an angle, and I clamp a hand over my mouth to stifle my sobs. The incense crumbles to ash in my hand. Tears patter over my armored legs.

It's not fair.

Come back. Please come back.

How could you have thrown me and Yizhi out of the Vermilion Bird without you?

I should've died with you.

I miss you.

I can't do this. I'm not ready.

I'm so scared.

I . . .

I will make them pay for this.

My eyes flash open to the concrete floor. The chant recording resounds in my ears. I clench the ashes in my hand. Twice before in my life, I've felt the sum of my pain and grief and anger condense into a hot core inside me, burning for a single purpose: *vengeance*. Destroy the ones who ripped away those I love—Big Sister, Shimin—or be destroyed by the force of my own anguish.

I don't lift my head. If the gods can really see my face through these statues in this moment, there'll be no more convincing them that I am capable of obeying them.

A backdoor creaks open behind the shrine. I lurch up in my wheelchair. Pink and blue emerge from the shadows. At first I think it's a maidservant coming to do maintenance, but then my mind readjusts its perception of her—*him*.

"Yizhi," I breathe out.

I check Qieluo's silhouette in the screen doors. Hopefully, the mantra recording is loud enough to keep her from hearing anything.

"Yizhi!" I whisper again, rolling my wheelchair toward him. My body aches with his absence, longing for the familiarity of his warmth.

Yizhi scuttles backward in his maidservant disguise and bows in the most formal way, his hands folded out in front of himself like a barrier against me.

"My lady," he says, almost inaudible over the chanting.

"No, no." I shake my head. "Don't call me that. Don't do this to me."

His throat bobs. He remains hunched over, not meeting my eyes. "It's good to see you well, my lady."

"I'm not well!" I cry under my breath. "I'm not okay! You know I'm not okay! Yizhi, look at me!"

"I'm afraid that would not be appropriate, my lady. This meeting is happening with His Majesty's permission. I will not betray his trust."

A chill slithers around my neck, as if I've been seized by the specter of Qin Zheng's grip. "He knows?"

"His Majesty is generously allowing us to find closure before settling into our new positions, so long as I dress like this so no one who might see us will get the wrong idea."

I almost spring up to shake Yizhi and scream at him. Only a dash of rationality roots me. Given that Qin Zheng knows what Yizhi and I are to each other, he was bound to suspect we'd try to meet up. Being upfront with him is indeed one way to put him at ease and elude his wrath.

No wonder he didn't hesitate to let me come. I can imagine what he told Yizhi: *Kill the part of her that longs for you. Crush her foolish yearning.*

"Did you call me here just to tell me goodbye?" My voice comes out small and cracked. It's maddening, being a mere pace apart yet unable to touch him.

Yizhi's bottom lip quivers. "This isn't goodbye. We'll still see each other around."

"If you can't even look me in the eye, we might as well be dead to each other."

Grimacing, he breathes slowly and deeply before speaking again. "His Majesty is the only one capable of protecting you, my lady."

"Haven't you heard about the way he treats me?" I slam my hands on my wheelchair's armrests. "I'm just a game piece to him. No, worse—a *doll*. I bet he doesn't put anyone in the central court under the knife because he doesn't like the way they look!"

A tremor starts in Yizhi's arms, still held out in a circle in front of him. "The rest of the world would do much worse to you if they could, my lady."

My mouth slips open.

Yizhi goes on. "His Majesty may have his . . . demands, but ultimately he will defend you against every threat to your life. He doesn't rule by mere whim. He wields power with a purpose beyond glory and fortune. He has some surprising beliefs the legends didn't pass down, don't you think?"

"If you're talking about how much he hates rich people, yeah. But in other ways, he's exactly what I expected."

Just another man who gets off on controlling women, I don't say out loud. Is this the choice I face? Let one man terrorize me or be terrorized by the world?

"More than anything, His Majesty is *right*," Yizhi says. "Huaxia has fallen too far into corruption and decadence. We've lost our way, and there is no one more capable of guiding us onto a better path than him. His Majesty defies impossibility. He remade the world once. He can do it again. For this, I'm willing to forsake my personal attachments, because what do they matter compared to the future of Huaxia?"

Each word of this spiel burrows a deeper cavern inside me, yet I can't demand that Yizhi tell me what he truly feels. To survive, he can't do anything but sing Qin Zheng's praises.

"My lady," he adds, "I've come to see that His Majesty is a reasonable man, more reasonable than we could've hoped for. He won't hurt you grievously if you don't give him reason to."

I can't listen to this anymore. This isn't Yizhi. This is an act, one he can never drop as long as Qin Zheng holds power over us. All the grief that aches to burst from my chest has to stay right where it is. I can't share it with a stranger.

I shouldn't have come here. The longer I stay, the more it hurts us both.

"I see your point. I should go." I turn my wheelchair toward the doors.

"Wait," Yizhi says. "There's something else I want you to know."

My attention swings back to him. He's finally dropped his arms, though he continues to speak without returning my look.

"I've done many things I couldn't risk admitting to you before my father . . . passed away. But I can tell you about them now."

"What kind of things?" I say, a numbness spreading out from my lips. Qin Zheng's taunting words ring in my head: *"You imply that your memories of him, the side he has shown to you, are true reflections of who he is. Funny. I have already seen enough evidence to the contrary."*

Yizhi straightens a bit but keeps his head low and his hands folded at his waist. "My tattoos . . . what they represent is my rank in the Brotherhood, a syndicate that controls the Chang'an underworld—its casinos, brothels, drug dens, all the places that don't operate in the light. Most of my family is involved. My father was its leader. That's how he amassed his fortune."

Goose bumps rise across my shoulders, intensified by the mantra recording resonating in my bones. But at the same time, I'm not surprised. It's no secret that Gao Qiu had dealings outside the law. I relied on that exact capacity of his to save myself and Shimin from the Sages. Until that stopped working, anyway.

What I didn't know was the extent of Yizhi's involvement.

"I swore my oath to the Brotherhood when I was a child, before I really knew what it would mean." Yizhi cracks a strange smile that doesn't reach his eyes. He scrunches up the pleated blue skirt of his maidservant disguise. "I'm rather lovely for a boy, aren't I? That's what they all say. My father thought so, too. He used to bring me to meetings with many powerful men. He would tell me beforehand to keep my eyes and ears alert for information to use against them, and then he would . . . leave me with them."

I forget how to breathe.

"For years, I dreamed of escaping to the frontier." He twists his skirt fabric tighter, his hands pale and trembling. "When I first met you in the mountains, that was after I'd finally made the attempt to run as far as I could."

I flash back to stumbling upon Yizhi in the woods, how I was so unsettled by the cleanliness of his robes that I attacked him with a branch to see if he was real. He should've warded me off before I backed him into a tree, yet instead he started asking why I was in the woods, if it was where I got my food, where my clothes came from, and more questions that unfurled into hours of conversation.

I suck in a sharp breath. "Is that why you asked me all those things about life on the frontier?"

"Yes. It made me realize the frontier had its own problems I'd been too naive to consider. And that as long as I had no power, nowhere in Huaxia could I truly be free. So I came back to Chang'an. But from then on, I was determined to climb higher through the Brotherhood's ranks. I took more initiative in getting information for my father. I found ways to leverage that information myself. I hoped one day I could rise high enough to be untouchable, and then I could take you here without anyone daring to question it. Whenever I felt like I couldn't go on, I thought about how much harder you had it in your village, and it would keep me—"

He gives a start, having come close to looking me in the eye. He bows deeper.

"I'm sorry I never told you any of this, my lady." His voice breaks. "Father had ways of knowing everything I did. Everything. He—he would've killed me for speaking of the Brotherhood to an outsider. He would've killed you."

"Don't apologize," I rush to say, reaching for him. At the last second before my hand touches his, I remember to stop myself. My armored fingers snap closed with a metallic noise. "Don't ever apologize for this. I'm glad you killed him first."

Gao Qiu died too quickly, even. I almost wish he were still alive so I could give him a death as long and painful as he deserved.

"So are you the Brotherhood's leader now?" I ask, trying to make sense of its existence.

Yizhi shakes his head. "Not exactly. No one could stop me from doing what I wished with my father's fortune because I had you and His Majesty behind me, but the Brotherhood's true heir is supposed to be my eldest brother, Changzong. Their loyalty to him runs a lot deeper. Many believe that killing my father was a breach of our oath never to harm a fellow Brother without provocation. They see me as a traitor."

"He provoked you plenty!" I hiss. "For your whole life!"

"That's not how those Brothers see it. But since I immediately got us more power under the new order, they're calm, for now. It remains to be seen if I can expand my own base of loyal underlings."

I break into a sweat under my armor, as if my wheelchair is hanging halfway off a skyscraper roof and Yizhi is beside me on the edge. He's been walking an even more precarious balance than I thought, one wrong step from being thrown off, not just by Qin Zheng, but by this Brotherhood that resents him for taking over.

I look to the back of the temple, thinking of the mountain forests outside.

"Run," I urge him. "Get away from here. Qin Zheng wouldn't care to chase you down, and the Brotherhood shouldn't be so thirsty for your blood that they'd go looking all over Huaxia for you. One day, when it's safer, I'll come find you again."

"I'm afraid I can't agree to that, my lady. I am not going anywhere."

"Yizhi!" I plead.

"I've given way too much to not get what I want!" His eyes snap to mine for the first time since Qin Zheng forced us apart.

The mantra recording drones on in the silence I'm too stunned to fill. Yizhi looks away again.

"What I want is for everything I did to get to this point to mean something." He speaks more quietly. "As His Majesty would say, power should belong to those who want to make real change, not those who indulge in empty pleasures. I've spent years collecting the secrets of everyone who had any significant power in the old order, and they are truly rotten through and through." He bares his teeth in a snarl. "I can name the exact people responsible for the worst corruption here in the heart of Huaxia, and I can help His Majesty clear them out."

I gulp through a drying throat. "I see. I understand."

I underestimated Yizhi. He isn't in this just to secure protection for us both. He has his own convictions, and they may be as strong as Qin Zheng's.

"Besides, I do have siblings I actually like," Yizhi adds. "I can't abandon them. Or you. Or . . ." His eyes flick upward, cautiously, briefly, but enough for me to know who he means.

There's a moment when we should take each other's hands and pull each other close, finding comfort in our shared grief. Yet the distance between us can no longer be crossed.

"There's no need to worry about me, my lady." Yizhi flashes a small smile. "I told you all of this so you'd see that. We're in *my* world now. I know how to play its games."

CHAPTER NINE

THE REUNION NOBODY WANTED

I decide to have faith in Yizhi and no longer twist myself into knots worrying about him. I immerse myself in lessons with Wan'er for the final few days before my coronation, kicking up no further fuss about leaving my room, spending only a couple of hours outside to attend a tech rehearsal for the coronation. I'll be in a much stronger position once I'm formally crowned the Empress of Huaxia and he can no longer depose me on a whim.

The night before the ceremony, though, he summons me to his throne room for a reason he won't specify to Qieluo, who once again escorts me through the estate.

Lanterns glow like fireflies under up-curled eaves, illuminating the stone paths and reflecting in sickles of light off dark ponds. The fragrances of grass and flowers drift on the air, released by dew. Freshly swaying from the rafters of many walkway roofs is the original flag of Huaxia, a golden dragon head against a red triangle on a black base. When I came across it a few days ago in a history lesson with Wan'er, she told me the red triangle represents the blood of rising laborers, while black was the national color of the ruthless Qin kingdom that Qin Zheng hails from. After the turmoil that followed his disappearance and the fall of Zhou, the flag got changed to the "less aggressive" one I'm more familiar with: a white lotus on a light-yellow base. But now the Dragon Head Flag has been revived with Qin Zheng.

He made a throne room out of a banquet hall in the estate's central building—the three-story structure that Gao Qiu emerged from during his welcome party for me and Shimin. Qieluo leaves me at the back entrance, saying Qin Zheng ordered her to stay outside. Having been to the throne room for the tech rehearsal, I have no problem navigating the revamped building. I ride the elevator to a hallway on the top floor. Here in one of the private rooms is where I had that horrible dinner to strike a deal with Gao Qiu. I roll my wheelchair along the same route I took to find Shimin afterwards. The entrance where the hallway used to open into the banquet hall is now veiled by a bead curtain, and the view beyond is cut off by a newly constructed dais.

I part the bead curtain and wheel around the lofty dais. The vast hall is somber as a tomb without the tech rehearsal crew around. The only light, low and warm, comes from atop the dais, where Qin Zheng is sitting in an ornate chair that is now the throne of Huaxia. Except he's . . . slumped across his desk?

Quietly as I can, I unlatch my cane from my wheelchair and make my way up the dais. I don't believe my eyes until I see it more clearly: Qin Zheng is passed out amid a storm of documents, graphs, handwritten notes, and open books on a long desk, one antler of his crown bent against the surface. Shit, did he actually drop dead?

No, no, he's breathing.

Wow, would I have panicked if he'd died? Ridiculous. I shouldn't need him. I don't *want* to need him.

An electric lantern casts shadows from his lashes over his ghost-pale cheek, the unmasked side of his face looking so delicate and fragile. The urge to do . . . *something* to him sharpens in me.

Then a map of Huaxia beside his head catches my eye. Little markings and dates adorn our borders. Hundun attacks in the past two weeks, clearly. My skin crawls at the concentrated number of them along the southern coast of the Han province, the supposed ancestral home of us Han people. Although I can't read most of the notes he's scribbled beneath them, I'd recognize the character for "dead" anywhere. *One dead. Three dead.* And so on.

Bile climbs into my throat. Of course. Just because I pushed the war out of my mind doesn't mean the Hunduns aren't persisting in trying to destroy our Chrysalises, smash down the Great Wall, and kill us all. They must've realized the Han frontier is short-handed. These casualty numbers probably aren't even counting concubine-pilots. They never do.

Hand-drawn arrows from Zhou to Han indicate that Qin Zheng is moving a few Chrysalises back, but it couldn't have been an easy decision, given that the Zhou frontier has no Great Wall. They're facing increasing attacks, too, from Hunduns coming across the Xihuang Desert. They need to keep as many units as possible during the reconstruction.

I assume Qin Zheng and I will be deploying soon after the coronation to alleviate this crisis. The thought makes me lightheaded, as though I'm on the verge of tumbling off the dais. I reach for him.

A sudden noise escapes his throat. In a blur of violent motion, the throne scrapes back and he's behind me, pinning me against himself while holding an ice-cold blade to my neck. Every cell in my body freezes around my thumping heart. His hot, shallow breaths gust near my ear. Through our connected armor, I'm aware of his entire contour, the rapid rise and fall of his chest against my back. The rhythm wanes several moments later, and he releases me with a gruff grunt. I brace against my cane and twist to face him, breathing hard as well.

"Don't startle me!" he chides, his spirit metal blade unraveling into tendrils and fusing back into his gauntlet. "Have you any idea how many assassinations I've had to fight off?"

"You're the one who called me here!" I rub my throat, though my anger goes muddled at the way he can barely keep his eyes open. "Have you seriously slept at all since . . . ?"

He scrubs his hand down his face. "I've gone longer during my unification campaigns. 'Specially against Chu. Now *that* was a fuckin' palaver." He's slipped into the coarse dialect he must've grown up speaking before he reinvented himself as a pompous ass.

"That doesn't mean you should keep doing it. You're as human as the rest of us."

"Yeah, yeah, I hear ya'. Come on." He beckons while turning away.

"Where?"

"You'll see soon enough." He heads down the dais.

"Uh, your antler—" I point. It's still crooked.

He looks back at me in bleary confusion, then breaks into an exasperated sigh when he notices the problem. He squints in concentration. The antler tilts outward, yet remains uneven with the other one.

"Ugh." I trudge down to him with my cane and grasp the antler myself. It'll bother me if I have to keep looking at it.

He jumps at the contact, but keeps the antler flexible to let me fix it. As I look at him up close, something feels increasingly off; his face is too flushed, and his eyes are unfocused, devoid of their usual domineering intensity. Before his guard can come up, I touch my knuckles to his forehead. A startling temperature comes through my gauntlet.

"You have a fever!"

"No, I'm channeling Fire qì," he says sarcastically, but his irises blaze red for real. With Fire-boosted strength, he picks me up by the waist with one arm.

"Hey—!" I cry, the sound cutting off in an embarrassing squeak.

He hauls me down the dais and dumps me like a sack of rice into my wheelchair.

"You're welcome." He pushes me forward.

"Can you *not*?" I scramble to keep my cane on my lap. He goes much faster and more fiercely than Qieluo. There's something about having my wheelchair in the control of someone I don't trust that's especially discomforting, as if he's seized one of my organs.

He turns me around the dais, through the bead curtain, and

into the hallway I came from. At the third door down, he comes to an abrupt stop. I nearly pitch out of my wheelchair. Another protest trips from my mouth, but I fall silent upon catching sight of the bronze plaque on the door. Specifically, the chrysanthemum engraved in front of the room's name.

It's the same private room where Shimin and I met with Gao Qiu.

Qin Zheng opens the door and pushes me in. My eyes squeeze shut ahead of an onslaught of bad memories.

"Lady Wu," says someone in the room.

The instant I place who the voice belongs to, my eyes fly open, and a killing rage bursts through my body.

"*Sima Yi!*" I spring up in my wheelchair.

Qin Zheng presses me down by my shoulder guard while kicking the door shut. My armor pieces lock around me. To my horror, I can't move anything. Even my lungs stop short of a full breath against my breastplate. I knew Qin Zheng might be able to do this, but to feel it for real injects me with a dread more potent than when he held that blade across my throat.

Sima Yi rises from the dining table, wearing a Sage's gold-embroidered purple robes and round black hat with two flaps in the back. "I figured we should have this meeting before you saw me at the coronation tomo—"

"You killed Shimin!" I scream with all the force my throttled lungs can muster, straining against the cage my armor has become. "Qin Zheng, let me go!"

"It was not my call!" Sima Yi raises his voice right back. "I argued against it, believe me! But orders were orders."

"Coward!"

Sima Yi breathes deeply. The room's amber lighting leaves much of his face in the gloom. "Can you blame the former Sages for making such a decision? Look what you did to them because you happened to survive!"

"Only because they tried to kill me first!"

"Only? What about Strategist An? Did you think we wouldn't find out what you and Pilot Li did to him?"

Memories rush to the forefront of my mind, of torturing and killing that bastard An Lushan after getting his confession that the pilot system is skewed against girls to ensure that boys have a better chance of surviving a battle link. My original plan was to upload the video as proof to the public, but with Qin Zheng himself decreeing the system be reset to equal inputs, the video became unnecessary. It would just corroborate the accusations of me being a bloodthirsty menace.

I don't regret it one bit, though. I'd do it again.

"You didn't even like An Lushan!" I yell. They must've found his body during our counterattack on Zhou.

"This is not a matter of personal feelings, but of basic humanity, of which you have none!"

"Chairman Sima," Qin Zheng warns, "I suggest you refrain from speaking to my empress-to-be in this way. I might not be able to hold her back much longer."

My armor loosens slightly. But, wait, did he just call Sima Yi—

"You made him the new *Chairman* of the Sages?"

Qin Zheng releases a low sigh. "As the envoy of the gods, he is entitled to the highest position in the central government."

"That's correct." Sima Yi straightens his deep purple robes. "After I narrowly escaped your wanton destruction of the Kaihuang watchtower and went into hiding, the venerated gods above called upon me. They tasked me with the duty of relaying their will to His Majesty. Since, as I understand it, there've been some *difficulties* in communication."

"What do you mean, they called upon you?" I demand. "How?"

"I received a message on my tablet unlike any other." He takes a handheld device out of his robes and holds it up like a sacred relic. "I didn't believe it at first, thinking it was a trick by you and the rich boy to lure me out. But then I was sent a video of Huaxia from high above, higher than any camera or aircraft could reach."

Wonder enraptures his face. "I saw the pattern of shining lights in every province, the shape of our coastline, and even the curvature of our planet. It could not have been faked. It could only have been taken from the Heavenly Court."

Sima Yi's words race in circles through my head, spinning off into implications. Everything the gods do betrays a little more about themselves. They showed Sima Yi a different video than the one they showed me—that of Shimin suspended in a fluid-filled tank—to prove they weren't scammers. But of course, that video wouldn't have convinced Sima Yi when he wasn't there to hear Qieluo's story of the hovercraft appearing out of thin air and taking the remnants of the Vermilion Bird's head. Without that context, that video could've been filmed in any room. A view of our world from the Heavenly Court, though? That's irrefutable. Yet it might also divulge clues about what the Heavenly Court really is.

"Did you save that video?" I ask, unable to suppress the urgency in my voice.

"It, unfortunately, vanished from my device soon after it was sent." Sima Yi regards his tablet as though he's longing for a lover. "But I have no doubt it was a view from the eyes of the gods. It was the most beautiful sight I had ever seen."

I curse in my heart.

It's telling, however, that the gods resorted to revealing themselves to a third party in order to contact me and Qin Zheng.

"How did the gods communicate with you in your time?" I tip my head toward Qin Zheng, speaking quietly.

"I would get cryptic telegrams," Qin Zheng mutters. "I never confirmed if they were truly from the Heavenly Court, but their threats never failed to pan out."

So they've always contacted us through tangible devices, never appearing as apparitions or anything mystical, like in the legends. Well, nobody sends telegrams anymore, and Qin Zheng has been meticulously keeping digital devices away from me and from himself.

Could it be that the gods can *only* send messages to us through technology, so he inadvertently forced them to involve Sima Yi? You can't threaten someone who can't receive your threats. This would mean that, whatever the gods are, their reach isn't supernatural. It's limited.

"What would happen if we just killed him?" I say, pointedly louder, my eyes on Sima Yi.

"They would simply choose another envoy," Qin Zheng grumbles. "And we would be direly punished."

Sima Yi lets out a bellowing laugh, raising his arms at his sides. "Indeed, I have no fear of whatever you wish to do to me. My spirit will rise to join the gods in the Heavenly Court. Until then, I shall go ahead and fulfill my duty."

He turns on his tablet, the light bathing his face. After several swipes and taps, muffled audio plays from it.

"*When you're in battle, don't you feel what the Hunduns feel, how complex their emotions are?*" It's my own voice coming through the speakers. "*Doesn't that ever make you hesitate?*"

I go cold below the neck.

"*That's just a defense mechanism, like a bee stinging you as it dies.*" Qieluo's response is much clearer. This must've been recorded on a device she was carrying.

Qin Zheng's hand tightens on my shoulder. So does my armor over my whole body. I choke for air, spots seeping into my vision.

As the tablet plays the rest of the conversation I had with Qieluo, Sima Yi saunters over to me.

"As the envoy of the gods, this is the first message I am delivering to you." He stands over me, backlit by the amber lights. "It would be good if you stopped discussing matters like these, Lady Wu."

I don't know what scares me most: the fact that the gods can listen in to this extent, the thought of Sima Yi having free rein to watch my every move, or the prospect of turning to face Qin Zheng's wrath.

CHAPTER TEN

LONG LIVE THE EMPEROR

If my coronation weren't tomorrow, if my absence wouldn't ruin all the plans in place, I suspect Qin Zheng would have conjured a blade again and slit my throat on the spot.

His silence is more foreboding than if he were screaming at me. He wheels me back to my residence himself. Unsure if Sima Yi actually knows the full truth of the Hunduns, then wary of talking about it in the open air, I don't speak until we're in my room.

Right as I'm about to argue my case, Qin Zheng hauls me out of my wheelchair and hurls me onto the bed. I land hard against the mattress in my armor, terror shooting through me as if I've been tossed into a winter lake.

"I-it's not like I actually revealed the truth to Qieluo!" I push myself up.

Qin Zheng slaps a hand on the bed and leans over me, forcing me back.

"Address me correctly," he says, his voice and gaze depleted of warmth. Not that he exuded any warmth to begin with, but I now see the stark difference between being a game piece to him and being the target of his world-consuming fury.

"Your Majesty," I make myself say, my mouth moving against the veil of my mask. My body trembles on its odd angle, unable to move higher but also unwilling to collapse.

Qin Zheng hovers over me like a tiger that's pounced upon prey, staring at me with bloodshot eyes. Is he going to . . . ?

No. He said he wasn't attracted to me.

But sometimes it has nothing to do with attraction and everything to do with imposing power.

I shiver when he touches my bottom lip through the metal strings of my veil. His fingers go ice-cold as the network of meridians on his face blackens with Water qì, but they swell and shrink in pulses, as though he's desperately holding his power back.

"There will not be a next time," he says.

I nod.

"*Say it!*"

A sharp breath slices into me. "All right, there won't be a next time! I get it, Your Majesty!" I stammer out through chattering teeth, sounding nothing like myself. I hate it. I hate what he does to me.

His other hand flexes in and out of a fist. Paradoxically, the sight calms me, bringing me to a numb acceptance of the worst to come.

"Does Your Majesty want to hit me?" I say. "Go ahead. Prove you're no better than the men you look down on."

He shuts his eyes and breathes in a deliberate rhythm, inhaling for a few beats, holding for a few beats, then exhaling slowly. After a few repeats, his fist loosens. He lingers for a few more stifling seconds before whirling away, taking my wheelchair with him.

"No one is to speak to her," he says to the guards outside. Then he slams the door with a force that quakes the walls.

I swing up on the edge of my bed, grasping my freezing mouth beneath my veil, shaking uncontrollably. Then I flinch at the sight of my armor, remembering the sensation of being caged in by it. Instinct screams at me to take it off and throw it as far as possible, yet that would mean giving up on the power it could grant me and the protection it gives.

Protection against anyone who is not Qin Zheng, that is.

Tears gather in my eyes, burning hot. Tomorrow, I have to marry this man.

I swear I'll find a way to learn all his powers and put him back in the ground where he belongs.

My imperial wedding is a much more somber farce than my Match Crowning with Shimin.

Even though every electronic device carries a danger of being hijacked by the gods, Qin Zheng and I accept the convenience of watching the symbolic bridal procession on a mounted screen in the Chrysanthemum Room, where so much has happened. I wonder if he keeps dragging me to this room specifically because he's seen my memory of dealing with Gao Qiu in it, and he wants to make me uncomfortable. I wouldn't put it past him.

My body double sits still as a statue as cameras follow her across the bulletproof windows of her electric carriage. She's wearing a spray-painted replica of my Yellow Dragon armor and a gold-dusted red bridal veil that matches her red cape. Her masked face is barely visible beneath the translucent silk. I have the same veil in my lap for when I'll need to put it on. Other carriages trail after hers, carrying Qieluo, Liu Che's partner Wei Zifu, and the female pilots of the other Chrysalises we brought to Chang'an. It's like the way the daughter of a prominent family would bring her childhood servants into her marriage, except I never actually got a chance to meet most of these ladies-in-waiting.

Overall, this feels more like a ritual than a wedding. The musicians along the street don't play chirpy tunes on brass *suǒnà* but drums and cymbals in a menacing rhythm. No firecrackers go off. No one cheers or heckles from the buildings on either side, unlike the procession during my Match Crowning with Shimin. We were paraded that day in the reverse direction, from the Gao Estate to the Golden Lotus hotel. The carriages prowling after ours had been plastered with ads. Qieluo and Yang Jian's carriage flaunted an airbrushed image of her holding a tube of eyeliner from Gao Enterprises' Mirror Flower makeup line. Xiuying and

Zhu Yuanzhang's carriage—I wince extra hard at the memory of them—displayed a dynamically posed shot of a Black Tortoise model kit.

It all seems so silly now.

No ads taint my body double's procession. No ads survived anywhere. The soaring skyscrapers of Chang'an used to be covered in digital promotions for the latest commodities or entertainments. Now, their oversized screens display military posters and the revived Dragon Head Flag. Many slogans accompany them:

Fight corruption until the end!
The Yellow Dragon descends once more!
His Majesty will lead us to victory!

Portraits of Qin Zheng appear on many posters, either pointing into the distance or looming over Chang'an like a disappointed father. One big screen transitions between a newly taken photo of him and a grainy historical one I've seen in army promo videos and Wan'er's history textbooks. Little things like this smack me with a fresh reminder of how bizarre it is that he's here, defying logic, defying gods, defying time. The persistent drumming and cymbal clangs resound deep into my bones. I keep an eye on him in my periphery. The production crew failed to conceal his lack of sleep. It only makes him look more unsettling, like death itself walking in mortal light. He hasn't spoken a word to me since last night. It's been the best I could've hoped for.

When the procession reaches the winding mountain roads that lead up to the estate, that's our cue. He gets up, chair screeching against the floorboards. Instead of traditional wedding clothes, gold-embroidered red capes hook to our armor's shoulder guards, a phoenix sewn across mine and a dragon sewn across his. His cape whispers over the floor as he marches to the door ahead of my wheelchair.

The screen on the wall blacks out.

"*Wu Zetian*," a mechanical voice drones from the speakers.

We whirl around.

"Go be a dutiful wife, Wu Zetian. Be a dutiful mother. Rein in your renegade husband and restore the balance you destroyed."

"Show yourself!" Qin Zheng lunges toward the screen.

It flicks to an image of Shimin in the fluid-filled tank, his shattered body suspended by thick tubes and wiring.

The sight hits me like a bolt of lightning, stopping my heart, my breath, my mind. A sickness rushes through my blood. Yet I can't look away. Can't let go of the hope in the shuddering signs of life in his heart and lungs.

I have to kill this hope. I have to set us both free. I have to, I have to, *I have to*.

"Stop trying to trick me!" I yell with the same vigor as Qin Zheng. "I know you're dangling a corpse! I know he's as good as dead!"

The voice gives no response, but the glow of the tank changes from spectral blue to alarming red.

Horror stretches within me when Shimin's eyes flutter open above his heavy black oxygen mask. They scan around, sluggish at first, then awareness and panic surge into them.

"No—" My hand flies to my mouth.

Bubbles gush around him as his limbless body thrashes in place, shifting the tubes and wires attached to him.

Stop! I try to say, but the plea tears out of my throat as an incoherent sob. The room sways. I double over in my wheelchair. I can't breathe. There's not enough air to breathe.

Qin Zheng's voice comes muffled, as though I'm drowning. He's yelling at me, shaking my shoulders and clutching my face to scrub away the tears leaking out of my mask. He says something in warning. I don't process what I hear until his hand leaves my cheek and then flies back in a slap.

I seize his wrist before his palm makes contact.

"Don't you fucking dare," I say between wheezes of breath.

Drumbeats pick up outside, as harsh and relentless as my heartbeat. We have to go. The cameras are expecting us. Huaxia is expecting us.

But Shimin is still on the screen, warping my every sense. Can he see me as well? How useless I'm being?

A large vase near the door wobbles in my vision. With an anguished cry, I use both hands to hurl it at the screen. It shatters against the image, creating an avalanche of gleaming glass and porcelain shards.

A muted pink glow recedes from my gauntlets, a blend of Metal white and Fire red.

Qin Zheng and I both gawk at my hands. But if he's impressed by my first successful conduction of qì through this armor, he stops showing it the next second.

"Gather yourself together," he commands before shoving my wheelchair out of the room.

The drumming gets louder in the hallway, numbing my ears. Regret wells up inside me as we leave the screen behind. I should've demanded more answers from the gods. I should've looked for more clues about the Heavenly Court in the video feed. Yet all I want to do is vomit.

Qin Zheng stumbles slightly. I didn't expect him to be so affected as well.

I can't believe we'll have to convince Huaxia to bow to us like this. I throw the bridal veil in my lap over my head. The translucent red silk tints my world.

Upon spotting us, two maidservants pull apart the bead curtain at the throne room entrance. One of them makes a quick gesture to alert someone inside. The drums cut off by the time we enter, blocked from public view by the throne and dais.

"Introducing the Chairman of the Council of Sages, Sima Yi!" Yizhi's voice broadcasts through the grand chamber.

I can't see past the dais, but I hear the susurration of silk. I picture Sima Yi strutting in front of the dais in his dark purple Sage robes. He starts giving a speech. The words barely stick in my brain. Something about Huaxia having gone without guidance for too long. The corruption and decadence we've fallen into. The miracle of Qin Zheng returning to lead us again.

"Now, on behalf of the new Council of Sages, I hereby proclaim the restoration of His Majesty's rule!"

The drums resume with the force of a thunderstorm, vibrating into my chest.

"Breathe," Qin Zheng whispers while pulling me to my unsteady feet.

From the back of my wheelchair, he unlatches and passes me a ceremonial scythe he made from the Yellow Dragon, its dull, curved blade hovering several heads taller than me. It's meant to let me represent the rural peasant class, though I used a scythe only a few times in my life before my family learned not to allow me near sharp objects. I did more threshing and milling during our harvests. Qin Zheng himself morphed out a sledgehammer to represent urban workers. Apparently, he used to work in a factory as a small boy before becoming a pilot, then he outlawed child labor after coming to power. The Peasant Empress and the Worker Emperor. That's what we're supposed to be.

Using the scythe like a staff, I take a tentative step on my half-healed feet. I will not be sitting through this coronation in my wheelchair. I can't kneel in a wheelchair, and kneel I must.

Qin Zheng slaps a hand on the small of my back to push me around the dais and into open view. At once, two blocks of the central court officials—the top scholar-bureaucrats in Huaxia—drop to their knees on either side of a long carpet and kowtow with their palms and foreheads to the floor. Near a pillar to our side, Yizhi and Sima Yi do the same.

"May my emperor live for ten thousand years, ten thousand years, ten thousand upon ten thousand years!" the court chants in sync, the words echoing and layering through the hall until it's as if the entirety of Huaxia has gathered to this one chamber. And that may as well be the case. This is being broadcast from every screen and radio in the empire.

The production crew handling the cameras, microphones, and lighting equipment lower their postures as much as they can without messing up their jobs. Only I remain standing with Qin Zheng, keeping myself upright with my scythe. It's not my time to kneel. Not yet.

"You may rise!" Qin Zheng stamps the long handle of his sledgehammer against the ground, facing a camera on the carpet running from the dais to the doors. Through my veil, I see vague figures of ourselves in a monitor beneath the camera, our ceremonial tools held to our sides the way Qin Zheng dictated during the rehearsal. The crew looks as though they might pass out at any moment from the direct force of his scrutiny. They'd better not. If I can't, they can't either.

The shifting of silk robes cascades through the hall as the twin blocks of central court officials get up. Metallic footsteps ring through the silence that follows. Qieluo and Yang Jian stride in my direction in their smooth White Tiger armor; Liu Che and Wei Zifu approach Qin Zheng in their skeletal Azure Dragon armor. They all wear capes the color of their most dominant qì.

Although Liu Che keeps his head especially low, that doesn't stop my hackles from rising when he gets closer. My mind feels as shattered as the screen Shimin was on, my thoughts like grinding shards. I force myself to focus on getting a proper look at Wei Zifu, the only Iron Princess I haven't formally met. Qin Zheng didn't let them come to the same rehearsal as me. She looks younger than her thirteen years, her cheeks soft with baby fat. Her feet are bound, though not in the extreme way mine were; they're just unnaturally narrow. She can walk without a cane on the wide soles of her armor. I wish I could speak to her, figure out if she hates me as much as Liu Che, and if I can do anything about that. Though, after Xiuying's betrayal, I know better than to bet on one half of a Balanced Match being much different from the other.

Once the four of them stop on either side of me and Qin Zheng, they snap their left fists up near their ears in what I've learned is the "laborist salute." Qin Zheng and I return their salutes. Then they pivot into military stance, hands clasped behind their backs. With that, Qin Zheng's intended tableau falls into place. The six strongest pilots in Huaxia united before the throne, a visual declaration that pilots are back in charge.

Qin Zheng steps ahead of us and speaks. "When I awakened in the Yellow Dragon and discovered that I had slumbered for two hundred and twenty-one years, I expected to see a much greater Huaxia than that which I left behind." His voice comes out raspier than usual, but his pronunciation remains carefully controlled, every syllable wrestled close to modern radio-standard Hanyu. "I expected the war effort to have thundered beyond the Kunlun Mountains and reached the western ocean of our legends. I expected humanity to have liberated itself and restored the great heights we once achieved, heights to rival the gods. Yet the reality I found brought me utter disappointment."

The temperature drops several degrees. I'm not sure if I'm imagining it or if he's causing it with his Water qì. Many officials lower their heads further, like reprimanded children.

Qin Zheng goes on. "Instead of a society thriving in freedom, what have I found? An inequality of wealth hundreds of times worse, a larger amount of resources concentrated in even fewer hands. You have developed the technology to produce food and construct housing on a scale we could only dream of in my time, yet you would sooner destroy edible food than give it to the starving, and rather leave homes empty than shelter those on the streets! Where is the sense in this?" A microphone on a long pole above our heads conducts his words like mountain echoes. "Worst of all, you have forgotten that we are at war for our survival, and that war is not *entertainment*! You worship my name, yet you have betrayed every ideal I fought for!"

Even my own face burns as if slapped. To be honest, growing up on the frontier, I was too busy hating everyone in my immediate vicinity to think much about rich oligarchs and corrupt officials. They were too far off in the cities, too abstract, and anyone who got more than a little money or power absconded as well. People do not stay at the frontier if they have other options. No one wants to be the first to be crushed by the Hunduns. We mostly made our own things and grew our own food, sharing among the village and going hunting and gathering in the woods if needed. The things we ate may have been bland as cardboard compared to what I get nowadays, but at least we didn't have to smell anyone having a feast next door. I imagine it's different for those who grew up impoverished in the cities, where the rich flaunt their wealth in front of them every single day.

"From this point onward, there shall be a new order in Huaxia!" Qin Zheng declares. "There shall be *revolution*! My citizens, you have been deceived into thinking the richest among you *deserve* their fortunes for so-called hard work, when the truth is that there is a level of wealth impossible to achieve without exploiting those working far harder for far less! I am not opposed to prosperity, but one must not prosper by keeping others in desperation! According to this principle, basic sustenance and shelter shall be guaranteed for every citizen. Individuals who own multiple residential properties must select one for personal use and relinquish the rest for public housing. You shall be eligible for compensation depending on investigations into the funds with which you acquired the excess properties. Turn in your ill-gotten gains like Imperial Secretary Gao, or prepare to face justice!"

He points his sledgehammer at Yizhi, who gives a deep bow.

An increasing stir runs through the officials as Qin Zheng goes on, talking about nationalizing banks, natural resources, and health care. This is getting a lot more specific than I expected. He didn't give this full speech during the rehearsal. I thought he was just a fan of killing rich people. What is this about canceling all medical and educational debt?

"May no more talent languish from a lack of access to resources!" he shouts, almost hoarse. "This includes women, who must no longer fester in unproductive existences! They have bodies capable of work and minds capable of thought. They ought to put those to use in service of Huaxia. This means the opening of public education and careers to them, and the banning of the degenerate practice of foot-binding, effective immediately!"

I swear my spirit momentarily leaves my body. Can Qin Zheng really stop the horrors and change the very anatomy of the world with a few commands?

He tried before, but that was different. Huaxia didn't have the shame of failure hanging over us. Maybe, just maybe, families will listen this time.

"Working people of Huaxia, you have forgotten your power. You have let your outrage grow dull while numbing yourselves with mindless consumption. Gather your dignity!" Qin Zheng strides closer to the camera, pointing his sledgehammer. "The profitizers have fooled you into thinking them generous for providing you with work, but it is in fact *your* labor that moves the world and sustains *their* luxuries. They are nothing without you. So stand together! Your enemy is not the Rongdi willing to accept lower pay out of greater desperation. It is not the colleague campaigning for higher pay for a job you consider less worthy than yours. There is no sense in fighting each other for scraps while the true hoarders of wealth laugh at your in-fighting from their gilded storehouses!"

He falls silent for a moment, breathing hard, dragging a look of contempt over the trembling officials. The first few rows are in purple robes while the rest are in red, colors of the highest ranks of Huaxia's bureaucracy—ranks that take considerable connections and resources to reach. When he speaks again, there is a dark, low challenge in his voice.

"The parasites will not part with their extravagances willingly. They will resist any change to the old order they benefited from. So teach them that mercy is no longer theirs to give, but *yours*. You have my blessing and protection—gather in councils at your workplaces, produce a list of demands for your employers, and do not work until those demands are met! Yes, I declare a general strike! Furthermore, report the misdeeds your authorities have gotten away with for too long! Rise against the profitizers. Rise against the corrupt. Rise against those who have everything in the name of those who have nothing. Rise, rise, rise, *rise!*"

His sledgehammer momentarily turns into a sword as he pulls it back and thumps it down at his side. Tingles spread in waves down my scalp. I imagine his words rippling through laborers with aching backs, factory workers with cramping hands, servants and clerks with sore faces from false smiles, and so many others barely getting by in Huaxia. I picture them looking at Qin Zheng on their screens as though seeing the sun for the first time.

Many officials have gone ghastly pale, yet they have no choice but to drop to their knees at the production crew's cue. "May my emperor live for ten thousand years, ten thousand years, ten thousand upon ten thousand years!"

Qin Zheng turns to extend a hand to me, gaze smoldering with a determination to wage war and win. War on multiple fronts, against the Hunduns, against the greediest among ourselves, and, secretly, against the gods.

My heart pumps fast and hard, my blood feeling electric-charged, incandescent.

I've gotten too used to thinking of Qin Zheng as the guy who comes into my room every few days, insults me, and then leaves. But he is more than a man; he is a force that bends destiny, capable of toppling empires or raising them, and two hundred years of existing as a legend have only amplified his power over the minds of the masses. Now I understand why Yizhi chose to give me up to swear loyalty to him. If I put aside my conflict with Qin Zheng regarding the Hunduns, I do agree with the rest of his ideas. It'd be nice if people could stop wondering where their next meal will come from or where they'll stay for the night. If every little girl after this will be spared the pain I lived with. I'd make those happen myself if I could, yet if I tried . . .

Something breaks inside me as I face the truth that the public would sooner worship his corpse than accept me as their leader. I don't need to guess at how quickly I'd get put down for being hysterical, delusional, and dangerous for uttering the same words Qin Zheng just did.

They hate me for every reason they love him. I'd have to spend so much time and effort to fight against that, and I might never succeed. I told myself I crushed the Sages to bring change to Huaxia, but truthfully, I wasn't thinking of much beyond the necessity to kill the Sages before they killed me. I had no concrete plans for afterward. Ultimately, I did it for myself. I want to take Qin Zheng down for the same reason, but how much will that delay progress for the masses, who he actually has plans for? I don't know if his plans will work. But he certainly has more experience running a country than me.

I close the distance between me and Qin Zheng, put my hand in his, and bow my head. I shudder at how his armor contour emerges in my senses. Instead of unveiling me like a regular groom, he makes a thread of spirit metal unspool from the back of my collar to yank the veil off. The silk drifts behind me to the floor. The throne room's full colors fill my vision.

"This woman is the one who reawakened me from my slumber!" Qin Zheng lifts our joined hands, squeezing mine so tightly I have to suppress a wince. "Through this union between a son of urban workers and a daughter of rural peasants, we liberated the Zhou province, and she shall continue to fight at my side as my empress!"

He turns us toward each other.

Kneel, he mouths, looking at me with as much disdain as he aimed at the officials.

A jumbled concoction of feelings washes over me, nausea the most potent of all.

"*Go be a dutiful wife, Wu Zetian. Be a dutiful mother.*"

I shake the gods' words out of my head. I won't let Qin Zheng render me into that. This is just a formality, a show for the masses. I won't stay so far behind him in capability forever. Anything he knows, anything he can do, I can learn. Even if it takes me years.

He's a good shield while I build myself up, at least. Yizhi had a point in that I'd have a lot more to worry about if Qin Zheng weren't standing invincible before me. I can't imagine having to deal with these seething officials myself before I'm ready.

I lower myself to my knees, the greaves of my armor thumping against the center carpet. My wedding cape pools behind me. I rest my scythe on the ground. Qin Zheng morphs his sledgehammer into a tall antlered crown that matches his own. Unlike all other pilot crowns, his was never designed to be split in two.

My hair has been pulled into a topknot so the crown's cylindrical base has something to pin to. When Qin Zheng holds it above my head, I get a flash of Shimin doing the same. My heart seizes up, but maybe this is worth pushing through for him as well. Qin Zheng must have a plan to confront the gods. I know it.

"Wu Zetian, may our hearts—"

His sudden pause stretches for too long.

I look up. His eyes are shut, and he's biting down on his lip, as though he's struggling to hold in a breath.

Before I can react, a cough rips out of him. He rushes to cover his mouth, but not in time to stop blood from splattering onto my face and the crown that's supposed to be on my head by now. We lock eyes for a bewildered instant, then another cough rattles him.

Then another. Then another, more blood spurting from his mouth each time. He collapses to his knees and falls toward me. I barely manage to catch the weight of him. My crown slips from his hand, the bead veils at its front and back splaying across the carpet. Still coughing, he clutches his chest like he wants to dig his fingers in and hold his lungs in place.

"Cut the feed! Cut the feed!" Yizhi screams, bolting toward the main camera crew.

Everyone else reacts a second later.

"Your Majesty!" the officials cry out. A few lunge out of formation to come help him, but most don't.

Qin Zheng continues to cough and shudder in my arms. A flat screeching noise goes through my mind, accompanied by a single thought: *You've got to be fucking kidding me.*

There goes any hope for change in Huaxia.

No...

No, not yet! During the rehearsal, Yizhi said the livestream would have a ten-second delay.

I hurl Qin Zheng off me and pick up my scythe and blood-splattered crown.

"Generals, get His Majesty onto the throne!" I call to Qieluo and Yang Jian while pulling myself to my feet with my scythe. "Chairman Sima, get over here and do a closing speech! Camera crew, get a close-up on Chairman Sima. Capture His Majesty in the background, but out of focus so he's blurry! Officials, stay in formation! You're not helping!"

Like a whirlpool suddenly stopping before spinning in another direction, everyone dashes to do what I say. With my crown under my arm, I scuttle after Qieluo and Yang Jian as they carry Qin Zheng up the dais to the throne, his arms slung over their shoulders.

"Can you look normal long enough for Sima Yi to close this off?" I whisper to Qin Zheng, wiping smears of blood from his mouth with my cape. At least it won't show on the red fabric.

His eyes stay tensed shut, but he nods and shifts into a more solemn posture on the throne. I pray that the stream cut off before his collapse. If my plan works, it should give the impression that the feed simply glitched out during my crowning.

Much less gracefully than planned, I crown myself, fumbling its tall hollow base over my topknot. Once I connect the thread of spirit metal from my collar that Qin Zheng used to unveil me, the crown sits weightless on my head. At last, I'm officially the Empress of Huaxia. I wipe his blood off my face and armor and straighten beside his throne, holding my scythe at my side.

I hope I look powerful. One of us has to.

PART II

HEAVENLY EMPRESS

天后 Tiānhòu

The false ruler Lady Wu has an unpleasant personality and a lowly birthright.... She has the heart of a snake or lizard and the nature of a wolf. She favors the insidious and murders the righteous and good.... She is hated by both men and gods, and heaven and earth cannot allow her to exist!

—Luo Binwang,
from *Denouncement of Wu Zhao On Behalf of Xu Jingye*

CHAPTER ELEVEN

OUT OF TIME

Behind a wall of glass, Qin Zheng lies in a harshly lit sterile room, his hair loose and his armor replaced by a hospital gown. We took him to the medical school of Chang'an University, built on the mountains as well, a short electric carriage ride from the Gao Estate. The coronation meant no classes were in session today, no gawking eyes to question who was under the sheet-covered, heavily guarded stretcher being rushed through the halls.

Sima Yi, Yizhi, and I sit in a dark observation booth facing the sterile room. We can't confirm what's wrong with Qin Zheng until the lab results for his blood come back. The obvious guess is poison, and so the first suspect was *me*, the last person to be alone with him. Accusations spewed from the officials as soon as the cameras shut off. If Qin Zheng didn't maintain enough lucidity to deny I had an opportunity to poison him, they were ready to have me tortured for a confession.

Bastards. As if it's not more likely that one of *them* did this to protect their dirty fortunes.

Snippets of noise elapse beside me as Yizhi and Sima Yi scroll on their tablets, trying to keep up with the videos being uploaded across Huaxia. Spontaneous worker rallies in every major city, crowds chanting in front of the homes of local menaces, walls being spray-painted with slogans condemning the rich and corrupt. The army has orders to stop any looting, assaults, and excessive property damage, but I've glimpsed many clips of luxury carriages getting turned over and set on fire.

Huaxia had been a pile of ash that hadn't known it was gunpowder until Qin Zheng threw a match at it.

Yet these common people unleashing their long-repressed grievances have no idea the savior who swore to protect them is slumped here, hooked to an infusion drip to stave off the fever he's been hiding for days. I *knew* I wasn't imagining it. Men, I swear . . .

Thankfully, the livestream's ten-second delay worked to prevent anyone who wasn't in the throne room from seeing him collapse, resuming, as I'd hoped, with Sima Yi's concluding speech. Our official story is there was a network failure due to literally everyone in Huaxia watching the broadcast at once. I'm sure there are people questioning that narrative, but the riots in the streets should be a bigger distraction now.

We can't erase the memories of the officials at the coronation, though. I recall the way most of them made no move to help Qin Zheng. They'll probably breathe a sigh of relief if he doesn't make it. Then they'll exact retribution without mercy from the masses who dared to rise up. I can't believe I'm saying this, but I hope Qin Zheng pulls through.

There's an urgent knocking on the door behind us.

"Come in!" Sima Yi calls over his shoulder.

A soldier outside lets in Doctor Hua Tuo, a medical professor at Chang'an University and a family friend of the Gaos. I heard from Yizhi that he's the one who's been overseeing Qin Zheng's flowerpox recovery.

"Your Majesty." The out-of-breath doctor bows, his topknot and long beard as white as his lab coat. He shuffles past us to an intercom in the glass wall. A piece of paper quivers in his rubber-gloved hands. "It's not poison, Your Majesty. It's infection. Two of them, with no relation to flowerpox."

"Two infections?" Yizhi launches to his feet. "Doctor, are you sure?"

Doctor Hua passes the lab results to Yizhi. "Yes, and I'm afraid both are opportunistic infections."

"But His Majesty's immune system measures have been normal!" Yizhi checks the results.

"What does this mean?" Qin Zheng's hoarse voice emerges through the glass, barely audible. He scoots up in his bed, scars visible on his unmasked face.

"It means..." Doctor Hua sinks into another bow, gulping. "It likely means that, being two centuries removed from the rest of us, Your Majesty lacks immunity to many of our modern pathogens."

"Fine. Then cure me."

Sweat beads at Doctor Hua's temples. "We can certainly treat the current infections, but I'm afraid... I'm afraid Your Majesty risks catching a deadlier infection at any moment if you continue mingling among others. To be safe, Your Majesty must stay in sterile quarantine."

"For how long?"

The doctor, still bowing, appears to hold his breath for several seconds before saying, "For good."

His words are quiet, yet they strike like a thunderclap. Sima Yi lurches out of his chair, glancing between Qin Zheng and Doctor Hua, whose aged body trembles with its effort to remain bent. Yizhi grips the lab results with both hands, crinkling the paper as he reads it again.

Qin Zheng sits with his eyes glazed over, expressionless, but the rigid set of his shoulders betrays the explosive reaction he's holding in.

"Surely, you jest," he says, without lifting his head.

Yizhi scans the lab results over and over, then slowly lowers the paper. "Your Majesty... the science makes sense."

"You're saying I must stay in this room for the rest of my life."

Doctor Hua drops to his knees, bone impacting the floor with a cringe-inducing sound. "I am truly sorry, Your Majesty, but every time you leave a sterile space, you risk catching a disease we cannot treat! We already gave you every vaccine theoretically safe for you to receive, so it's evident that there's no cure for this condition, since Your Majesty's very existence in this century is meant to be impossible. There are consequences to defying the natural order, and this is one of them."

"Get out."

"Your Majesty—"

"Out!" Qin Zheng raises his cough-ruined voice. "Get out!"

The four of us exchange wide-eyed looks, then Sima Yi, Doctor Hua, and Yizhi file backwards out the door. Yizhi keeps it propped open for me. I shake my head. Concern crosses his face, but he lets the door close.

"I meant you as well," Qin Zheng snaps when the lock clicks shut. He presses the heel of his hand to his forehead.

"No." I roll my wheelchair toward the glass wall's intercom. My armor glistens under the pale light from his side. "What did you want to do alone, lie there and sulk? There's no time for that. You set Huaxia on fire with your little speech—*literal fire* in many cities—and now the people are counting on you to back them up as they go after their bosses and governors. You can't rile them up and then leave them fending for themselves!"

Qin Zheng barks out a scratchy laugh, sounding on the verge of losing his mind. "Since when did you care about the people?"

"You convinced me to!" I knock on the glass with my armored fist. "You made me and everyone on the streets right now believe Huaxia can be less rotten, less unfair, because you're Qin Fucking Zheng and you defy impossibility! I was ready to put up with your shitty personality for the rest of my life because I saw the value of what you want to do!"

He regards me in stunned silence, then shakes his head and throws his hands up, jerking the infusion line attached to his arm. "How do you propose I do anything while confined to this single room?"

"You can still make speeches. You can still go on camera. You can call officials here or talk to them over the networks. Plenty of women live their entire lives confined to a handful of spaces. It's what *you* were doing to *me*. Surely you can handle the same."

His glare turns murderous. It fails to faze me. What is he going to do, come out and risk another infection to choke me?

"Get yourself together, Qin Zheng," I say. "Huaxia needs you to keep your promises. I've heard a lot of stories about you since I was little. None of them ever mentioned you were pathetic under pressure."

He crosses his arms, eyes falling shut. Medical equipment blinks and beeps beside his bed.

Right as I'm about to insult him some more, he flips his covers aside and swings his bare feet onto the white-tiled floor. He pulls himself up with his drip stand and wheels it toward me. Along the way, he picks up a metal chair. His loose hair sways and his long, pale legs wobble with each step, flashing beneath his hospital gown. He should seem vulnerable, being so exposed, yet the unnaturalness of his movements is unnerving instead, as if I'm facing a nightmare creature beyond prediction. I fight down the urge to wheel backward.

He sets the chair across the glass from me and takes a seat, gripping his drip stand like he's still holding his ceremonial sledgehammer. With him in the fluorescence-bathed sterile room and me in the dim observation booth, it's as if we're in a real-life version of the yīn-yáng realm. I see his facial scars more clearly than ever, how they streak across his brow and cloudy right eye.

"Go tell Doctor Hua to return with the medicine to treat my infections," he says, some composure back in his voice.

"Okay." My fingers drum on my knee. "Then can you . . . write down the old ways of pilot training or something? I don't want them to be lost with you if the treatment doesn't work."

He gives a start at my bluntness, then lets out a humorless chuckle. "The old ways cannot be conveyed by words alone. Stay the night with me. I will show you."

He reaches behind his shoulder. Metal-white qì rises in his irises and meridians. Using its precision boost, he weaves a golden, glinting thread of spirit metal out of the spinal brace he kept on his back. He presses the tip of the thread to the glass. A second circuit, bright green, lights up across his skin—Wood qì for speed. The thread whirls like a drill through the glass. Tiny shards splatter like frost around the puncture.

I'm not sure what its purpose is, but I take the thread with my armored fingers. The shape of his spinal brace emerges in my awareness, floating like a sixth sense across the thread.

"The most effective pilot training is done through a mind link," Qin Zheng says. "That is why only a pilot can truly mentor another pilot."

"Mind link? Should you really risk going out to the Yellow Dragon with me?"

It hits me that he can only pilot the Dragon if absolutely necessary now, when its omnipresent threat should've been this revolution's strongest defense. The public *cannot* find out about his condition.

On the flip side, this is a good excuse to make him train me for the prospect of piloting the Dragon without him. He can't complain about me stealing his Chrysalis if leaving quarantine to use it might kill him. Though my eagerness about learning from him cracks when he gives me a look so condescending I consider tugging him face-first against the glass with the thread.

"Let this be your first lesson," he says. "Empty your mind of preconceptions about Chrysalises and spirit metal. Popular understandings of their properties are either grossly simplified or deliberately kept enigmatic to prevent the crafting of rogue Chrysalises. The truth is that spirit metal itself is all that's needed to conduct a mind link." He glides a finger along the thread. "We simply need to fall asleep while sharing this connection."

"That's it?"

"Indeed. Less human engineering goes into a Chrysalis than one would expect."

"Huh." I thumb the thread, feeling another level of reverence for the material. No wonder the gods trapped us in an eternal war to have a steady supply of it. It makes me wonder more intensely about what the Hunduns truly are, to be made of this, though I quickly snuff out the thought. If Qin Zheng and I are to share a mind link again, I can't let him catch me thinking these things.

I hate the idea of opening my mind to him, of course, but I can't turn down this form of training if it's as effective as he says. Aside from when I threw the vase at that screen, I haven't figured out how to conduct my qì through this armor. I can't turn this situation from a *calamity* to an *opportunity* if I don't have the skills to back myself up.

"All right," I say. "Let's start tonight."

CHAPTER TWELVE

WHAT ARE YOU?

The world smells of soot and smoke. I stumble up a fire-ravaged mountain between charred, fallen trees. Cinders drift like gray snow through the hazy air, landing warm on my skin. My lungs burn, and every muscle in my body strains to the brink of tearing, yet I can't stop, or *they'll* get to me.

I can hear them crawling behind me, their fractured, exposed bones scraping over the ash-coated ground. Voices swarm around my head like hornets.

"*... how could you ...*"

"*... we raised you ...*"

"*... heartless, rotten girl ...*"

"*... now reap what you sow ...*"

Tripping over something, I tumble into ash. I flail to keep going, but loops of a glowing golden thread tighten around me, binding my arms and legs. I can do nothing more than writhe in place as mangled bodies reach me.

"*You did this.*" My family digs their skeletal fingers into my flesh, speaking out of sync with one another. "*You did this. You did this. You don't care about anyone but yourself.*"

"That's because no one else does!" I cry. "You didn't care about me first!"

"*I did*, Mei-Niang." Shimin's voice flutters like summer heat into my ear. He's beside me with only half a body, dragging along tubes and wires like entrails. "*Make me whole. You have to make me whole.*"

I scream louder.

"I see," says someone above me. Metallic footsteps clink to a stop. "Having a guilt problem, are we?"

I snap into reality—or the fact that this *isn't* real.

I glare up at Qin Zheng, who appears full-armored in his spirit form. So this dream link thing actually works...

The golden thread around me connects to his wrist. He winds it a few times around his hand and yanks me up, dangling my bound arms above my head.

An indignant noise escapes me. I squirm against the thread. "Let me go!"

"This is a dream realm manifested by both our minds. You can free yourself if you truly wish." He lifts my chin with his free hand. "Or do you enjoy being tied up before me? Because I can make much more pleasing bindings than this."

I'd spit in his face if I could figure out how.

"I assure you, I did not do this to you," Qin Zheng says with an edge of amusement. "You imposed this on yourself. Do you feel you deserve to suffer for what you've done?"

Ignoring him, I concentrate on the winding path the thread takes around me. I compel it to loosen. It shines brighter as it does. The moment I can move my legs, I find my footing and push away from Qin Zheng.

"There, see?" He unravels the thread from me. It shortens to a direct line between our wrists.

I jerk at it, trying to dispel it altogether, but I freeze when I look down and catch sight of the crushed bodies again. They haven't gone away. Just gone still.

"You made the correct call." Qin Zheng peers down at them as well. "Morality is a luxury those of us born to be chewed up and spat out simply cannot afford."

A violent wind stirs the ashes. I wish I could shove him out of my mind and rip this scene out of his memories. I don't want him to know me, to look at me like he can see through to my deepest depths. And maybe that's exactly what he's doing. If this dream link works the same as a battle link, he could be trawling through my memories as we speak. Nothing in my head is safe from him. Yet I can't seem to delve into him in return.

"*Your* mind realm is an ocean of hungry ghosts coming for you," I say. "Are you also haunted by the things you've done?"

He looks momentarily winded, but recovers with a shrug. "I do not let it stop me. Any so-called power obtained without a bloody fight is but a tranquilizing mirage. This is why I was not entirely resistant to making you my empress. You showed adequate resolve, at least." He indicates the corpses around us. So many of them, overflowing down the mountainside. And not just human. Hundun husks litter the ashy slope as well, in a warped memory of the scorched valley where Shimin and I piloted the Vermilion Bird for the last time.

I turn away from the sight. "What would you have done if I'd chickened out on crushing the Palace of Sages?"

"Oh, I would've agreed to execute you upon the third complaint I received. I still might, if you prove to be a *liability*," he says with a snarl, his eyes burning with the same hatred he's been directing at me since he found out I tried to talk about the Hunduns with Qieluo.

I could kill you with a nick in your quarantine glass and a wet cough, I want to say, though I think better of making threats I can't fulfill just yet. The officials would pounce on me at once if he died. Like what happened two centuries ago to General Mi. I need to be better prepared.

I need to absorb his abilities first. Let's see if they'll dare pounce if I can summon the Yellow Dragon on them regardless of whether Qin Zheng remains alive.

"Liability? Says the great emperor whose own immune system can't handle the tiniest modern germ," I say, a more subtle reminder of his vulnerability.

With an even more venomous glare, Qin Zheng wanders to a tree stump at least five paces wide and twice as tall as him. "A lot can change indeed in two centuries. Funny to think that these trees sprouted from seedlings and perished at such sizes wholly within the span of my slumber. In my time, this stretch of the Kunlun Mountains was much too close to the front lines to grow extensive vegetation."

He splays his hand outward. The dream realm shifts, tree carcasses blowing away as ash to reveal a mountainside drained barren of qì by unseen Chrysalises stationed nearby. Brick buildings and canvas tents spring up in the valley below. By some sort of dream intuition, I know he's showing me a military base from his era. The buildings look as rugged as those in my village, not like modern training camps built from smooth concrete. Vague blurs of people weave between the structures like phantoms, their weathered clothes not holding much color.

"It still feels as if I simply woke up in a faraway place." Qin Zheng gazes upon the scene. "That I could find my way home if I headed in the right direction. If only . . ."

Rage flares from him, hitting me as physical heat, cut through with a twinge of bitter regret. Images flash in a deeper layer of my mind. Long tents full of pox-infested patients groaning in agony. Qin Zheng rushing bundles of linens between rows and rows of pallets. Chrysalises digging mass graves and sweeping in piles of corpses. Heaps of clothes and belongings set on fire. Qin Zheng frantically discovering a pustule on his own arm.

The force of the memories knocks me a step back. I don't think he shared them intentionally, since he doesn't appear to be waiting for my reaction. Plus, he wouldn't show me he was foolish enough to go into a quarantine zone while being the ruler of a whole empire.

So *this* is what it takes to get a spillover from his mind. He needs to be vulnerable.

I step closer to him than I'd ever like to be. Gently, I touch his shoulder.

"So what's our plan against the gods? We're not letting them get away with reigning over us, right?" I lower my voice and my lashes, resonating with his rage as I think of Shimin, held captive, on that screen. Although we entered this dream realm for training purposes, it's not lost on me that this is also a great place to discuss something in complete secrecy. It'll do good to remind him there are way more prudent targets to seethe about than me.

Qin Zheng glances at my hand, but doesn't push it away. With a wave of his arm, the mountain landscape darkens and gives way to a night sky salted with infinite stars. Our spirit forms float as if we've risen to the heavens themselves.

"There." He points at a bright speck sailing a path through the night. The scene zooms in, stars streaking past us. The speck expands into a humongous structure made of two metal rings attached around a long central shaft, with many panels and parts protruding from the other end.

I gape at it. "Is that the Heavenly Court? What it really looks like?"

"Indeed. An image taken by a scholar who could not restrain his curiosity. He had crafted increasingly sophisticated lenses to peer into the cosmos, despite that being a field of study forbidden by the gods. I had to sentence him to death. Before I condemned him, however, I confiscated his findings." Pages of handwritten notes flutter into existence near Qin Zheng's outstretched hand. Writings and calculations drift off the papers in shining scrawls, organizing themselves against the starry view. "This is what I remember."

"You *memorized* all this?" The numbers dizzy me. Yizhi's math homework was the one subject I never wanted a second glance at.

Qin Zheng peers at me with a trace of smugness. "I can memorize anything I put my mind to."

"Of course you can," I grumble.

"Regardless, I had no other choice. I could not keep the notes."

The pages go up in flames, but their contents remain shining before us. The Heavenly Court becomes a two-dimensional sketch with arrows around its twin rings, indicating that they move in opposite directions.

"The scholar hypothesized that the Heavenly Court is a massive artificial structure with rings that spin to generate rotational gravity, which would take effect around the perimeter of the rings." Qin Zheng traces his finger around them. "This means the gods are subject to the same physics as us, instead of existing in a mystical form as in our legends. They would not build technology of such scale to supply gravity simply for the tribute girls they take from us."

Right. Shimin is far from the first person to have been whisked up by the gods. Every new year, they make us leave nine girls for them along with our usual tribute of spirit metal. We don't know why or what happens to the girls, but, assuming they're not killed for sport, they'd be living among the gods in the Heavenly Court.

I drift closer to the rings. "So are the gods just . . . regular humans?"

"We would have to see for ourselves."

The sketch of the Heavenly Court fills with realistic detail again while rapidly expanding. On and on it grows, reaching a size that sends terror swooping through me as I tip back to take it all in. From the side, the rings are as wide as earthbound cities. From the front, their diameters must be thousands of meters across.

"The Court moves extremely quickly, orbiting our world once every hundred and eighty minutes," Qin Zheng says. "However, theoretically, it should be possible to intercept it with the correct timing based on precise calculations."

A tremor runs through my spirit form at what he's suggesting. "Were you planning on doing that two hundred years ago?"

"I held the thought in the back of my mind, though I seldom entertained it, for it would almost certainly be a suicide mission. Now, I have nothing left to lose. I see the truth that nothing I do for Huaxia will last through the ages as long as the gods lord over us."

Another wave of his anger assails me as physical heat. But this time, I feel a sense of dread for him. For *us*.

"You really think we can reach them in, what, the Yellow Dragon?" I question.

"It would take an unparalleled effort. We would get but one chance. And we must betray no outward hint of planning it until the moment we depart."

The Heavenly Court's twin rings spin before us in opposite directions, impossibly large. I feel reduced to a speck, a flea gazing upon a colossus, paralyzed with the same helplessness as when I stared up at the Black Tortoise in my regular human body.

Yet somewhere in this metal monstrosity is Shimin, ensnared as a plaything between life and death, along with the tribute girls taken each year. I can't imagine they're living well. Forgiving the gods is not an option.

"I'm in," I curl my fists and say. "When do we go?"

Qin Zheng rubs his chin. "We would need to refine my calculations. Mathematical instruments and knowledge of physics have surely improved since my time. The issue is seeking what we need without rousing the gods' suspicions. Now that I am stuck in a quarantine chamber . . ." His jaw tightens.

"A quarantine chamber in a *university*. Everything we need should be right on campus. Yizhi would know who or what to find, and what excuses to justify contacting them."

"Do not speak of this to Secretary Gao unless you can do so as discreetly as possible," Qin Zheng warns.

"I could just enter a dream link with him, couldn't I?"

"No. The disparity between your spirit pressures is too great. Head deep underground instead. That worked for me to evade the gods' surveillance in my time. As I understand, there exists a network of tunnels beneath the palace."

"What if their surveillance tools have since gotten better?"

"If even the depths of the earth cannot grant us secrecy, we have no hope of keeping this from the gods."

I sigh. "So it's a gamble."

"The biggest of our lives," Qin Zheng says. "Hm . . . Let's hope you can recall the feeling of Pilot Li's spirit signature when we ultimately make our move. It could be an asset in tracking the Heavenly Court's exact location."

My chest clenches as if he punched me. "I'd never forget."

His gaze softens, going misty. "You'd be surprised by how quickly your memory of someone can blur once the world no longer carries any trace of their existence."

"But—" An electric shock of an inkling streaks through my mind. An idea so absurd my first thought is to laugh it off, yet it just might make a difference. "But there *are* traces of Shimin left in Huaxia."

"*Half a liver and one kidney.*" Yizhi's voice echoes by my ear. "*That's what they take from every healthy death row inmate. For anyone who needs a transplant.*"

"The kidneys—" I say. "Each holds half of someone's primordial qì, right? Shimin was forced to donate one of his. Would it still give off a spirit signature that feels like his, even in someone else's body?"

Qin Zheng's face seizes up in bafflement. He opens his mouth, looking ready to call me ridiculous, but the insult never makes it out. He slips into a vacant frown before saying, "This is . . . worth looking into. Find the person who received Pilot Li's kidney. Visit the locations he once frequented, as well. That could strengthen your spiritual bond with him."

"Will do." I make note of his every word, weaving them into a plan of action. "And what about my training? I'll have to be as skilled as possible with spirit metal if we're to attack *gods*. Don't tell me you're planning on handling everything yourself. Let me be useful."

"Very well." Qin Zheng waves his hand. The stars wink out. A different section of the Kunlun Mountains returns through the darkness. The Great Wall of two centuries ago rises beneath our feet, piled up with rough bricks instead of concrete, marking what must've been the Zhou province's frontier. We look out across the Xihuang Desert, which separates us from other human strongholds in the west.

Qin Zheng leaps onto the Wall's edge, armor clattering. "As I've mentioned, you first must liberate your mind from restrictive preconceptions about spirit metal, Chrysalises, and the world itself."

A Water-black Chrysalis materializes outside the Wall like ink gathering shape, almost as tall as the Wall itself. It steadies into the form of a crow with three legs, its sharp eyes shining Fire red.

"Which class is this unit?" I climb to join Qin Zheng on the Wall's edge. The drop to the bottom doesn't look as steep as at the modern Great Wall, but it's hard to tell by how much, and thus hard to judge the Chrysalis' weight class. "Prince class? King class?"

"Queen class." Qin Zheng gives me a pointed look. "This is the Three-Legged Crow, my mentor's Chrysalis. We used feminine terms for a unit if the commanding pilot was female."

Ah. So this is what he meant by not clinging to assumptions.

"I take it she wasn't part of a Balanced Match," I say, feeling a ripple of grief at how, with no one to pilot it, this Chrysalis must've been destroyed during the fall of Zhou. "Then who served as her secondary pilots?"

"Condemned men, mostly. Criminals."

Something sours in me as I think of Shimin in his bright jumpsuit and chains. Yet I don't know what other policy I'd wish for the army to follow. Would it really be better if they manipulated regular boys into signing up as concubine-pilots the way they do the girls, calling it a noble sacrifice?

Well, I guess that's what they already say when conscripting boys into the war. It's just not enough to get them to proudly die in service of a female pilot.

"What do you think Chrysalises are?" Qin Zheng goes on before I can muse further. "Why do they take the forms they do?"

"Uh . . ."

When I think hard about the question, a spilled-over memory belonging to Shimin surfaces in my mind: him and his previous partner, Wende, manifesting the Vermilion Bird out of a King-class Hundun husk. As if I were there myself, I feel their mutual excitement and uncertainty as they plugged into the mind link, then how their shared desire for freedom spread expansive wings out of the Fire-red spirit metal over the course of hours.

"The forms reflect the pilots' minds," I answer.

"But why are they always an animal or a figure of legend?" Qin Zheng points at the Three-Legged Crow, without a doubt a manifestation of the creature that resides in the sun in our myths, carrying it across the sky every day.

"That's just how things . . . are?" Admittedly, I've never given this much thought.

"There is, in fact, no reason other than that someone, at some point long ago, determined that animal forms provide an efficient framework for conceptualizing Chrysalises. The Standard Form on all fours for easy balance, then increasingly humanoid in more advanced and controlled forms. The truth, however, is that Chrysalises can be anything." Qin Zheng lifts the glowing thread between our wrists. "Just as I morphed this thread out of my spirit armor, a pilot can manifest any form out of a Hundun husk. And they can completely reshape an existing Chrysalis if they wish to. The issue lies in whether their mind can inhabit that form without breaking."

With a swing of his arm, the Yellow Dragon lunges into existence beside the Three-Legged Crow. Wind gusts across my cheeks as the Dragon curls itself into a massive mound taller than the Wall.

"To embody a Chrysalis is to embody a new identity," Qin Zheng explains. "If that identity is weak, the pilot's control of it shall be weak as well."

The Dragon melts into a golden blob like the Emperor-class Hundun it must've been made from.

"I could morph the Yellow Dragon into a shapeless mass, but I would not be able to pilot it well. On a subconscious level, my mind would not make sense of existing in such a vague form. As with the details in this dream realm, Chrysalis manifestation relies a great deal on the subconscious. For example, I see that you once brawled with a Chrysalis called the Headless Warrior."

Qin Zheng makes it appear, slightly smaller than the Three-Legged Crow. I jump at the reminder of how deeply he can dive into my memories.

"I would guess that it initially failed to form a head during its manifestation," he says. "However, this then reminded the pilot of the headless warrior of legend, which used its nipples as eyes and its navel as a mouth, and so the Chrysalis developed further in that direction, because the pilot's mind could accept it as a strong identity. In this way, preconceptions provide convenient guidance to manifesting and advancing Chrysalises. What you must be wary of is letting the framework restrict your imagination."

A small subunit emerges from the blob that used to be the Yellow Dragon. It looks like Qin Zheng in his spirit armor, except it has an actual dragon head and bat-like wings on its back. With a few beats of its wings, it flies to the Three-Legged Crow and drops down on one knee on its head.

"You were surprised by the Yellow Dragon's second form. This was because you were bound by the idea that a more advanced form ought to be larger and taller. It did not occur to you that there is no reason you could not go smaller if the situation called for it."

"Right." I study the subunit's every detail. "Is it possible to do simulated battles in here? Now that you can't jump into the Yellow Dragon willy-nilly anymore, I should learn how to use it, right?"

Alarm flashes across his face. "The Dragon was never a unit to be used 'willy-nilly.' Its recuperation period is a full month, rather than half a month, and thus it must be reserved for *my* most important battles. I deployed my first Chrysalis, the Black Bird, for more casual purposes."

Another Water-type, bird-form Chrysalis springs up beside the Three-Legged Crow, almost its twin, except without a third leg. In a storm of dark feathers, Qin Zheng's spirit armor changes from the Yellow Dragon's to a skin-tight black one with a feathered crown framing his face and gauntlets tipped with sharp claws. I swear his eyelids gain a dusting of smoky pigment. For some reason, I can easily imagine him sauntering his hips in this look.

"What?" He squints, probably noticing how I'm holding back a laugh.

"Is this what you wore while convincing people to bow to your rule?"

He flexes his black-clawed fingers near his face. "It worked."

"Well, I'm assuming the Black Bird got destroyed with the rest of the Zhou province, so the Yellow Dragon is all we have. It's just a matter of time before people question why we're not flying to the frontiers to . . ."

I mean to say, "destroy the Hunduns," yet I can't get the words out of my mouth, even as the map of the relentless attacks on our frontiers flashes in my deeper consciousness. *If we don't do something soon, more concubine-pilots will die*, I tell myself. Yet it doesn't get any easier to speak.

"The Yellow Dragon is not an effective unit for combating Hunduns," Qin Zheng snaps with more than a little possessive reluctance. "They can sense it coming from too far away, and they run to avoid it. The battle at the Zhou frontier only worked in our favor because we were able to ambush them from underground. The Dragon is meant for inter-Chrysalis warfare."

"That won't stop people from expecting us to act if things get worse at the frontiers!"

The idea of rebuilding the Iron Widows nudges at my mind again. Even disregarding my agenda to pry the secrets to piloting the Yellow Dragon out of him, if any of the frontiers fall, so will the revolution, because there's no justifying this new order if we can't keep our people safe.

Rebuilding them is also the most efficient way to develop my own power base. After all, what kind of powerful allies can I count on to be more loyal to me over Qin Zheng if not fellow Iron Widows, especially if I take them under my wing?

"How about we do a sweep for girls with high spirit pressures and give them their own Chrysalises to command?" I say, swallowing all bitter, confounding thoughts about the war itself. "If we double the number of pilots, there'll be less scrutiny on why *you're* not deploying."

He stares into my eyes as if trying to read my thoughts. Can he actually do that in a dream link? I hope not. I focus on thinking about the frontiers' safety. Nothing else. Certainly nothing about building a power base independent of him.

"Your era has not seen female commanding pilots for two centuries," he says, with a cautious slowness. "I faced quite the resistance from the central court simply to restore the pilot seat calibrations to equal levels."

"Didn't you tell them about Iron Widows like General Mi?"

"I did. They still blame those female commanding pilots for the fall of Zhou."

"That's ridiculous!" I grasp my head. "Then—then all the more reason for me to go show them it'll be fine! That letting a girl command a Chrysalis won't be the end of the world!"

Technically, I already showed them when I seized control of the Nine-Tailed Fox from Yang Guang, but given the drama and grief his death caused, it's probably not the best example of "fine."

"You are getting far ahead of yourself." Qin Zheng suddenly advances in on me, forcing me backwards. "You have much more to unlearn. Answer me this: What are you?"

"Huh?" I trip a little before resolving to stand my ground.

He presses closer. "Answer the question. What are you?"

I push against his shoulders to keep him at arm's length. "I'm a human girl! What kind of question is this?"

"What makes you who you are?"

"What do you mean by—"

His clawed fingertips strike my chest. My dream form peels apart from the point of contact, flesh and tissue flaying away in layers. I scream. The sound cuts off when the carnage reaches my throat, shredding my voice. My bones crumble to powder and fly off on the wind.

"What are you?" Qin Zheng asks again. "I strip away your skin, your flesh, your bones, and what are you? What makes you who you are?"

I plunge into darkness as I lose my eyes and ears as well. I can no longer see, hear, or feel.

This isn't real! I remind myself, but it does nothing to get my senses back. His control is impossible to resist.

You are a collection of nerve impulses believing themselves to be a singular entity named Wu Zetian. Qin Zheng's words come to me like thought, not substantial enough to be sound.

Somewhere in my consciousness arises the idea of a brain and the nerves that trail from it in branches, a storm of electrical signals firing within them. It's like a diagram out of Yizhi's biology notes. The outlines of the brain and nerves then fade away, leaving nothing but the dazzling signals.

What you are, what we all are, is an illusion. Accept the pretense of your own existence, and you can extend the illusion. You have always been the pilot of a vessel. You simply became accustomed to thinking of the cells that make up your body as yourself, even though you could lose much of those cells and still exist. Once you understand that spirit metal is not so different, you can unlock its true potential.

The storm of electrical signals stretches onto a diagram of the Yellow Dragon, streaking like lightning along its long form.

In your human body, your will can only conduct in predetermined ways. You can consciously hold your breath but not intentionally stop your heart, for example. This is a necessary system of order to bind together the chaos of elements that assembled to create you. Spirit metal, on the other hand, has no inherent restrictions. Subconsciously, you limit yourself so this does not overwhelm you, but as long as you find the balance between order and chaos, you can achieve more control over spirit metal than you ever imagined.

The signals disperse from their lightning-like paths, filling the Yellow Dragon so the entire diagram glitters with activity.

I want to react, to ask questions, yet I can't find a way to speak. I try to fight out of the oblivion, yet I have nothing to fight with. Soon, the Dragon fades away, and no more thoughts come from Qin Zheng.

I'm alone in the void. In some way, it makes me understand what he means by chaos without order. That's how I am now, existing everywhere yet unable to act, like mist that can't gather into form. I am free, yet I am nothing. Is this what it'd be like to be dead? To be untethered from a vessel that can interact with the physical world?

This must be a test, a challenge from Qin Zheng to reshape myself out of the vast everything. But am I supposed to become my human self or the Yellow Dragon?

Just as I aim for the latter, a loud, pounding noise jolts me out of the dream.

Reality bombards me with sensation. Even though the room is dark, it takes me a solid half minute to readjust. Being human feels much more intense than I remembered. I pat myself all over, astonished to have a body again.

I sit up in the bed a soldier wheeled into the observation booth for me. My breaths come short and quick. My feet give their usual dull pulses of pain.

Across the glass, Qin Zheng stirs awake as well, his bed parallel to mine. Medical machinery hums in the darkness, its scant lights tracing his contour out of the gloom. I yank off the thread of spirit metal connecting us and toss it away like a snake, though I realize a second too late that it makes my unease too obvious. Qin Zheng gives me a knowing look. I can't help but feel that what just happened was not merely a lesson in piloting, but a lesson in not getting any ideas about replacing him.

The pounding noise sounds again.

"Your Majesty," a soldier calls through the door of the observation booth, "Chairman Sima and Secretary Gao wish to speak to you regarding an urgent matter."

"Let them in!" Qin Zheng shouts, his voice much hoarser than in the dream realm.

The door unlocks. Yizhi and Sima Yi shuffle in, accompanied by a spill of daylight. We slept for longer than I thought, while they look as though they haven't slept at all, their robes wrinkled and hats skewed. Yizhi turns on the lights.

"What is it?" Qin Zheng winces against the blast of fluorescence. He looks marginally better after a night of intravenous antibiotics.

Sima Yi hurries forth with a tablet in hand. "Your Majesty, you need to see this video released by Chief Strategist—no, my apologies. I mean this video released by the *rebel leader* Zhuge Liang."

CHAPTER THIRTEEN

THE REACTION

"Citizens of Huaxia, I implore you to cease this descent into anarchy and see that you have been fooled by a theft of our realm!" A weary-looking Zhuge Liang, the strategist who officiated mine and Shimin's Match Crowning only to give the secret order to kill us, declares on the screen Sima Yi holds out to me and Qin Zheng. The defunct White Lotus Flag hangs in the video background. "I represent the survivors of the tragic events half a moon ago. Although we are grateful His Majesty the Emperor has risen from his two-century slumber, we have realized in horror that he is being fed lies by the thieves Sima Yi and Wu Zetian! His Majesty's heart may be with the people, but if he had any true understanding of modern Huaxia, he would know that so many drastic reforms cannot be enacted at once! Yes, there is much about our society that begs for improvement, but if it is not done in careful increments, our economy will collapse and we will be plunged into chaos! Violence is never the answer!"

I peek over my shoulder at Qin Zheng. He practically vibrates with tension on the other side of the glass, his eyes like hollow pits.

"We place no blame on His Majesty for this," Zhuge Liang continues on the screen. "Evidently, the Temptress Wu has seduced the Thief Sima, and together they have conspired to impose their reckless dominion over Huaxia!"

I gag and back up against the glass, as far as possible from Sima Yi, who grimaces so hard he gets a double chin. This is the grossest accusation I've ever been hit with, and that is saying something.

"These thieves are holding the Son of Heaven hostage in order to subjugate the masses!" Zhuge Liang shouts, raising his arms. "See how Sima Yi has become the Chairman of the Council of Sages, despite never having been on the council! See how Wu Zetian has become the Empress of Huaxia, despite any passerby knowing she has no virtue worthy of a mother of the realm! She has slaughtered heroes and lain with murderers!"

The video switches to footage of me laughing maniacally with my foot on Yang Guang's corpse, then a few of my provocative shots with Shimin, then the suspicious way Qin Zheng's crowning of me cut off. I dig my nails into the edge of my bed to keep myself from snatching the tablet from Sima Yi and smashing it on the floor.

"Your Majesty, if you are listening, I implore you to think thrice about what you've been told by these thieves. They have taken advantage of your abrupt awakening to lead you astray! They spew lies and spread divisive conspiracies to further their own agendas! Do not be fooled any longer! I am fully aware I risk death by speaking out, but I fear for nothing except the well-being of the people, who are the ones who suffer most when the stability of society is shaken. I vowed to give my life in service of Huaxia, and I shall bend to the task until I am worn out and not stop until my last breath! For this reason, I must speak to return the peace. I beg of Your Majesty: denounce these thieves, recognize the truly virtuous officials in your court, and pull back these unrealistic reforms!" Zhuge Liang gives a deep formal bow, thrusting his hands out with one set of fingers cradling the other. "May my emperor live for ten thousand years, ten thousand years, ten thousand upon ten thousand years!"

The video ends.

I clutch my mouth, not trusting myself to speak without yelling.

"Economy, economy, these fucking reactionaries always going on about the fucking economy!" Qin Zheng says through clenched teeth, his street dialect slipping through. "Easy for them to say. They're not the ones starving as it is! How far has this bloke's message got?"

"It keeps getting uploaded onto the networks from an untraceable location, Your Majesty," Yizhi says. "I have a tech team taking down any copies that appear, and they're working on an algorithm to prevent further uploads, but Zhuge Liang clearly has some very skilled technicians on his side. It has also played a few times on the radio."

Qin Zheng massages the bridge of his nose. "Here I thought it was plenty annoying when the reactionaries dropped leaflets all over the bloody place."

"Zhuge Liang must think I betrayed him and the others," Sima Yi mumbles to himself, head hanging low. "Well, I suppose I did. I just couldn't tell them I had a divine-ordained reason."

"Where is he?" I endeavor to keep my composure. "Where did you and the other strategists run to when . . . when . . . you know what I mean."

It is very weird to ask someone how they escaped your attempt to kill them.

To Sima Yi's credit, he answers earnestly. "When we realized you were coming for us, we packed onto a shuttle and headed for the Han province at full speed. We then used our connections to settle into hiding." He looks to Qin Zheng. "Your Majesty could send soldiers to search our hideout, but Zhuge Liang and the Sui-Tang military command are likely elsewhere by now."

"Where could they have gone?" I ask. "Do you have an idea?"

Sima Yi shakes his head. "They could be anywhere in Han. It's Zhuge Liang's home province. There's not a house that wouldn't open its doors for him, even at the risk of death."

"Put out a national warrant and find him," Qin Zheng says. "I want his head on a pike."

An idea comes to me, one I bite back at first, but then I realize all four of us are in on the knowledge that the gods can send messages to us. This is it. Here we are, the innermost circle of power in Huaxia.

Skies help us. Literally.

"Could we try asking the gods where Zhuge Liang is?" I say.

Yizhi and Sima Yi both go still, as though they short-circuited.

"I . . ." Sima Yi swipes hesitantly on his tablet. "Their messages always vanish. I'm not certain how to send any in return . . ."

"O gods on high!" I call toward the device. "Would you kindly tell us where to find Zhuge Liang and the other rogue strategists?"

Sima Yi jerks his tablet against his chest, looking ready to reprimand me. But then the tablet goes *ding*.

No way.

With wide eyes, he checks the notification. But then his shoulders slacken.

"My sincerest apologies; it's just my wife asking if I'm coming home for dinner tonight." He scribbles on the tablet with his stylus. "I swear I told her I'm dealing with a major crisis!"

"Someone married you?" I sneer.

"I have four children, *Your Highness*!" he says, somehow making my title sound like a slur.

"Poor her. Poor them."

He visibly holds back from retorting. I crack a grin, but it fades at the thought that I nearly made his wife a widow and his four children fatherless. And they're the lucky ones. There's no doubt I *did* shatter many families during my rampage.

I shut out the memory of the mountain of corpses in my dream realm. I can't let myself think about it. The enemies I'm up against don't crumple under the weight of their actions. If I do, I'll never best them.

We wait a while longer for a response from the gods, but nothing comes. Of course. Why would the gods make our lives easier instead of ever more difficult?

"Your Majesty," Yizhi speaks up, "it's best that you give a firm response to the video as soon as possible. We can get a green backdrop in here and then edit you into the throne room. The average person won't be able to tell the difference."

"Very well." Qin Zheng gives a grave nod. I bet he doesn't actually understand what Yizhi is talking about, because I don't. But I trust Yizhi to know what he's doing.

"What about the officials?" I point out. "The ones who saw what happened with their own eyes? What do we tell them?"

"That it was poison," Sima Yi says. "They're all assuming it was an assassination attempt anyhow. Your Majesty, I would suggest recording a separate video assuring them of your survival but forbidding them from discussing the incident to avoid 'upsetting the masses.' And please emphasize that you are *not* being deceived by us."

Yizhi studies the glass confining Qin Zheng. "If I may, I would also suggest building a quarantine chamber in the throne room itself so Your Majesty can keep holding court there. I've consulted with engineers. It's possible. The officials can be told it is bulletproof glass to guard against further assassination attempts. They won't question that."

"Won't they?" I say. "So many of them clearly resent the reforms—"

"The *revolution*." Qin Zheng cuts me off. "Do not associate me with the impotency of *reformism*!"

"Okay, same problem, *Your Majesty*." I copy Sima Yi's way of saying a title as though it's a slur. "Your top officials hate what you're doing, and now they have a resistance leader to rally behind. How do we stop them from leaking what they saw to discredit you?"

"We could execute them all."

"Your Majesty!" Sima Yi splutters. "I would strongly advise against that course of action, especially now that you are in a . . .

less optimal position. Your officials have already seen many of their peers crushed by rubble. Another mass purge, with seemingly little reason, would alienate the literati and further contribute to rebel sentiments. Your Majesty's heart may be with the working class, but only educated men have the ability to run your government."

"Educated men are working class as well if they make their living from wages instead of property ownership," Qin Zheng says dryly. "Labor is labor, whether manual or intellectual. Pitting them against one another only divides the masses and distracts them from the truth of their common struggle, Chairman Sima."

Sima Yi flushes bright red. "Your Majesty knows what I mean."

I sigh, cradling my head. "Even if we can't kill them all, we need to scare them a little."

"A fine idea, empress." Qin Zheng rubs his chin. "I must admit, this technological ability you have in the future to broadcast footage to the entire nation at once will make it much easier to deliver the visual impact."

"Wait, the visual impact of what exactly?"

Qin Zheng flashes a smile that raises all the hairs on my body.

CHAPTER FOURTEEN

EYE OF THE STORM

When the men in my village weren't watching Chrysalis battles on their tablets, they'd be watching *cùjū* games, shouting in unison as sweaty men in loose, cropped clothes and frayed topknots kicked a ball around a massive arena. I've glimpsed Chang'an's Phoenix Nest stadium many times on various screens, overflowing with bright lights and fifty thousand cheering spectators.

The seats are full tonight, though no one is cheering. The blocks and blocks of people don't speak any louder than murmurs. Through a random draw open to low-income Chang'an households, they received an invitation to witness what's about to happen.

From a dark passageway at the ground level, I keep an eye on the audience. If things go off the rails, I can turn my wheelchair around and escape at once. And so can Yizhi, if he needs to.

"Keep yourself safe, okay?" I say to him across the passageway.

"I will," he says, maintaining as much distance from me as possible. It's a beat later that he remembers to add, "Your Highness."

I'd rather he didn't.

He checks his wristlet, then adjusts his earpiece and says a cue. A floodlight in the stadium switches on with a loud sound, blanching a booth above the audience stands.

Yizhi raises a microphone and announces, "The Emperor and Empress of Huaxia have arrived!" His disembodied voice broadcasts through the stadium speakers. He's not meant to be seen just yet.

Everyone hushes and pivots in their seats to kneel as best as they can toward the booth. Body doubles of me and Qin Zheng step into the light in their replica spirit armor, their respective masks disguising their features.

"My citizens!" Qin Zheng's voice fills the stadium. A close-up of him plays on several jumbo screens, prerecorded in his quarantine chamber and edited over a shot of the booth. With his body double matching his gestures as he denounces Zhuge Liang's message, even I have a tough time remembering it's a stitched-up illusion.

"The reactionaries fear the economy will collapse if we change too much too quickly. The same economy that has *been* collapsing into crisis every few years? Do they believe me incapable of reading reports of the regular recessions since my disappearance? How many of you, the common folk, lost your savings and livelihoods when the residential property market imploded a mere three years ago?"

Scattered cries of outrage rise around the stadium. Then more join in, increasing in density and volume.

Three years ago . . . that was about when Yizhi and I first met. I vaguely remember him talking about this, remarking that while everyone else in the cities was panicking over going bankrupt, his father made *sixty million yuan* from the crisis by "shorting" the market, whatever that means. Honestly, investing doesn't sound much different from gambling.

"It was the irresponsibility of the banks that caused the implosion, yet what did the old order do?" Qin Zheng's recording continues after a pause, as if he anticipated exactly how the audience would react. "It bailed them out with taxpayer money—*your* money! *You* paid the price for decisions made by the grotesquely wealthy, who learned no lesson besides that they can act without consequences! *This* is the system the reactionaries wish to defend?"

The audience roils more fiercely, many shouting while pumping their fists in the air.

Qin Zheng's voice carries on over the turmoil. "Violence is not the answer, they say! But what do they count as violence, pray tell? Do they count it when landlords buy up all housing with their existing wealth and then grow even wealthier off of tenants they would not hesitate to throw into the cold? Is it not violence when a hospital turns away a patient for being unable to pay for treatment? Is it not violence when a laborer breaks his body in a factory, only to receive a mere fraction of the profits from his work? Where was the concern, the horror, of the reactionaries against *these* everyday acts of violence? In the name of stability and security, they condemn only the violence that challenges the status quo, never the violence that perpetuates it. Yet those of us born of the streets know full well that stability and security have only ever existed for the elites! Violence is indeed the answer when the *question* is whether we ought to endure exploitation so others can live in luxury!"

The audience grows close to boiling over the stands, rising to their feet while yelling in agreement.

"Enough with these excuses to do nothing so a minority among us may cling to comforts built on the backs of the less fortunate! I heard the same fearful rhetoric about revolutionary upheaval two centuries ago, yet what has their beloved *incremental progress* brought upon Huaxia? A future that's become more incrementally corrupt! Clearly, there is no path forward for the humble within the comfort zone of the elites. To them, I say: This is no longer a world that caters to your delicate sensibilities. As I was reborn, so shall Huaxia be!"

Qin Zheng's body double spreads his arms in rehearsed sync with the video on the screens. Goose bumps sweep across my skin as fifty thousand voices erupt into screaming cheers and chants for him to live for "ten thousand years, ten thousand years, ten thousand upon ten thousand years."

I have to admit to a sense of awe at how he can captivate an audience without even being present. This is power beyond having the biggest Chrysalis or being the most skilled with spirit metal. This is the kind of power that makes a leader.

I know from Shimin's case that becoming the strongest pilot doesn't automatically get you the respect and adoration of the masses. If I'm to build my own power base to push the changes *I* want in Huaxia—changes that will free women and girls from destinies they don't want—this is yet another skill I need to master.

I swear, the list never ends. But I have to catch up. I have to.

Qin Zheng can't terrorize me into reining in my ambitions.

The floodlight aimed at the booth shuts off, leaving our body doubles as backlit silhouettes. Other lights switch on to illuminate the stadium's packed-earth base, covered in markings for *cùjū* matches.

Yizhi cradles his microphone. This is his cue. He nearly gives me a look, but stops himself before his head fully turns. Instead, he leaves me with nothing more than a slight nod before walking out into public view. Light bathes him, turning his purple robes several shades paler. A metal gate slams down on oiled tracks in front of me. It's meant to protect me if things go wrong, yet I can't help the anxiety that flutters through me at not being able to rush out and protect Yizhi.

"My fellow citizens," Yizhi says into his microphone after reaching the center of the stadium. He raises his left fist, his words and image broadcasting across Huaxia. "My name is Gao Yizhi. However, it is not a name I am proud to have, because my family's legacy was built upon deception, coercion, and exploitation."

With his raised left hand, he pulls out the long pin securing his hat, pushes his hat to the ground, and unties his topknot. His hair falls free over his back.

My anxiety rises. What he's about to do will be controversial.

"For too long, I watched my father and his associates live outside the law, amassing their fortunes by exploiting the common folk without mercy. The crimes of my bloodline run deep, too much for me to atone for in one lifetime. But I will certainly make an effort!"

Yizhi tucks his microphone into a leather belt at his waist. From another side of the belt, he whips out a dagger that glints in the stadium lights. He gathers his hair and puts the blade to the bundle.

A collective gasp goes through the stadium. It takes several drags for Yizhi to slice through his hair. The surviving locks fall beside his neck in uneven lengths. He swaps the dagger for his microphone once more and raises his severed hair like an offering toward the booth with mine and Qin Zheng's body doubles.

"From this moment on, I shall take the family name of my mother, a humble-born concubine who died by my father's whims! I, Zhang Yizhi, pledge my utmost loyalty not to my crooked kin, but to His Majesty the Emperor, who will free Huaxia from its corruption!" Yizhi turns in a circle, showing his severed hair to the audience. "Other sons of criminals, I urge you to join me before it's too late!"

He opens his hand. His hair scatters away. Turning some more, he points at a passageway in the stadium opposite mine. "Bring in the accused!"

The gate of the passageway lifts up. Soldiers usher in three shivering men. Their robes are of the finest embroidered silk, yet they're chained at the wrists and ankles. Earlier today, Yizhi named them to Qin Zheng as three of Chang'an's most notoriously corrupt men. Judging by the jeers that swell through the audience the moment their faces appear on the big screens, he wasn't exaggerating.

Three more people emerge from a different passageway, wearing tunics and trousers of much rougher fabric. Witnesses to the men's crimes. Although we guaranteed safety for them and their families, they don't look any less nervous than the captured oligarchs.

The soldiers spread the three accused men across the stadium grounds, then they give Yizhi a raised-fist salute before forcing the men to their knees. Yizhi walks over to one of them, a lanky, gray-haired man in emerald-green robes adorned with complex embroidery. On the big screens, the venom in Yizhi's eyes is unmistakable. I have a feeling this man is one that Gao Qiu sent Yizhi to as a child.

Yizhi speaks with no emotion. "Cai Jing, owner of Huashi Construction, do you admit to embezzling millions from government building contracts, cutting costs with cheap materials and dangerous work conditions, and bribing the officials of the old order to look the other way?"

Yizhi angles his microphone toward Cai Jing.

"I did no such—!" Cai Jing lurches up, but a soldier pushes him back down.

Now Yizhi calls on one of the witnesses. "Miss Qiu. Your husband worked on a project of Cai Jing's, where he and many other workers developed a debilitating lung condition from inhaling toxic dust. Is this true?"

The woman scuttles over to Yizhi on natural-sized feet, evidently from a family that never considered the possibility of her marrying rich. After giving a hesitant raised-fist salute, she takes out a folded piece of paper, wrinkled and yellowed with age. "I—I have the doctor's report . . ."

"But Cai Jing's company refused responsibility, didn't they?" Yizhi asks. "And the courts sided with him?"

Miss Qiu nods, eyes squeezing shut.

Yizhi takes a baton from a soldier's hip holster and offers it to Miss Qiu. "Citizen, I'm deeply sorry the old order failed you. But in the new Huaxia, you don't have to swallow this injustice any longer. Now, you can be the first to finally punish Cai Jing for his crimes."

The stadium goes so silent I can hear wind whistling through the seats. I drive my wheelchair up to the gate of my passageway, nearly pressing my face against the metal grid in anticipation of what she will do.

For a long spell, she makes no move, her attention bouncing between the baton, Yizhi, Cai Jing, the soldiers, and the booth up high. It's understandable. I'd suspect this is some sort of trap, too.

Cai Jing's face reddens with strain, then he bursts out shouting, "Gao Yizhi, release me! You have no proof of what—"

Miss Qiu grabs the baton and swings it into Cai Jing's jaw. Shock explodes through the audience, many hands flying to mouths. The wrath on Miss Qiu's face vanishes by the next second. She staggers backward, dropping the baton on the dusty ground.

Some part of me expects the soldiers to lunge for her, because that's what happens when the powerless strike against the powerful. Yet they don't move. Not even as Cai Jing shrieks and curses, clutching his jaw. Blood dribbles from his mouth, staining his pristine robes.

Gulping down air, Miss Qiu double-checks everything around her, confirming the lack of consequence to her act of vengeance. Then fury crawls back onto her face like a twisted mask. She picks the baton up and swings it into Cai Jing's face a second time, knocking him over. This time, the audience's gasps come charged with glee. Cheers and applause break out. People call for her to do it "Again! Again!"

She does. Fifty thousand cries of jubilation drown out the sounds of her baton smashing into Cai Jing's flesh and bones. Several blows later, she stumbles and pants with exertion, yet her eyes are wild and bright, like she's coming alive after walking around half dead for years. I recognize the feeling. I felt the same when I came out of the Nine-Tailed Fox and dumped Yang Guang's corpse at my feet.

As if heaven and earth have switched places, a change ripples through the air. No doubt everyone watching across Huaxia can feel it.

"Gao Lian!" Yizhi heads over to the next accused: his own uncle, kneeling in crimson scholar-bureaucrat robes as the governor of Chang'an. He was at the coronation, a witness to Qin Zheng's collapse. His fate will serve as both a testament to Yizhi's resolve and a warning to other officials. Sima Yi should be watching this with the rest of the Sages right now, observing their reactions.

Gao Lian, on his knees, screams something at Yizhi, inaudible over the audience's heckling. He thrashes against the soldiers as Yizhi's amplified voice lists the crimes he's accused of: selling government positions, taking staggering amounts of bribes, and forcibly evicting families to make way for new development projects. The second civilian witness stares at Gao Lian with the hunger of a predator. Before Yizhi finishes confirming that the witness' family was beaten by thugs so they would sign over their property, with the witness' elderly father dying from his injuries, the witness snatches a baton and unleashes his fury onto Gao Lian.

The audience's delight roars toward the stars as bones snap, skin breaks, and fine silk soaks with blood.

The third accused shivers as though he's in a rainstorm, though any pity I might've felt for him evaporates when Yizhi announces that he was in charge of a company that used toxic chemicals in its foods to falsify flavors and nutritional content. Despite independent journalists finding evidence, the company faced no real repercussions, and instead the journalists were jailed for "incendiary activities." The third witness is a young mother whose baby died from kidney stones related to tampered formula produced by the company. Her wrath is just as bloody as that of the wife who lost her husband and the son who lost his father.

My head spins. The energy in the air is too feral, too infectious.

Two weeks ago, I'd have been cheering the loudest. Except now that I'm empress, whatever this leads to will be *my* problem. And I can't shake the feeling that we've unleashed something we might not be able to control.

Yizhi stands in the middle of it all like the eye of a violent storm, short hair blowing on a breeze, expression unreadable.

CHAPTER FIFTEEN

DOOMED TO SECRECY

I don't return to Qin Zheng's quarantine chamber for the night. I need to start getting Yizhi's help with our plan to reach the Heavenly Court.

At least, that's my best excuse to meet privately with him.

"Tunnels, midnight, don't bring electronics," I whispered to him under cover of the stadium noise. I didn't add what I wanted to talk about, just that Qin Zheng approved of the meeting.

Once I get back to the palace in a heavily guarded carriage, I go to Gao Qiu's old residence, a grandiose single-story manor that was supposed to serve as mine and Qin Zheng's imperial quarters. On the lantern-lit stone porch, a pair of soldiers opens the double-doored entrance. This leads to a receiving room that bombards my vision with red: red candles, red cloths on the table and chairs, jade pendants hanging from red strings, and red draperies everywhere. A bloody husk of an imperial wedding cut short.

In the lavish bedchamber, bigger than all the rooms in my family's house combined, an intricate gold and crimson carpet leads to a round, absurdly large bed on an elevated platform. Translucent red silks stream down over it from a circular bronze frame on the ceiling, the ends of the fabric secured around the platform edges. I grimace. Would Qin Zheng have demanded we consummate the marriage despite our mutual disgust? I'm glad he's the one bound to a prison now, no matter how it's made us both more vulnerable.

I try not to imagine the gross things Gao Qiu once did in this bedchamber. I would not have chosen to move here if not for its one key feature: easy access to the tunnels beneath the estate.

While waiting for midnight, I ask Wan'er for a writing lesson. We moved all our study materials to a desk in the bedchamber. My reading might be improving briskly under her tutelage, but writing remains a different beast, like trying to draw faces from memory. Which is frustrating, because if I could write fluidly, I could pass Yizhi notes instead. That would pose less risk than saying things out loud.

On Wan'er's advice, I practice the names of the Huaxia government's six ministries and the titles of the hierarchy of officials in charge of them. It's a bit embarrassing, how little I know about how our government actually works. I can't let that stay the case if I'm to seize any sort of real power.

We have a saying at the frontier: "The mountains are high and the emperor is far." It means the squabbles of politicians are so distant we don't give them much thought beyond when government clerks come to yell about taxes or spirit pressure testings. Now, my head spins as I sort out the system: scholars qualify to become bureaucrats through civil service exams, then they work their way up from their municipal government to their provincial government to the central government to perhaps the Council of Sages. Theoretically, the advancements are based on merit, but the old order was so dependent on connections that most scholar-bureaucrats never made it past the municipal level. The revolution is supposed to change this, but who knows how well that will work?

I remember Shimin once dreamed of breaking into these rings of power. I wish I'd spoken with him about politics more. Handling this precarious situation I'm in would be so much easier with him here.

Wan'er is a good teacher, though. It feels better than learning from Qin Zheng, or even from Yizhi back in the woods. Call me cautious, call me paranoid, but I never fully trusted Yizhi until he showed up to help me at the Great Wall. I was always wary of a hidden agenda within him whenever we met up, especially since he knew how dangerous it was for me. I took the gamble because I desperately craved the knowledge he brought. In reality, on his part, I suppose he assumed he could simply buy me from my family if they ever caught us.

"Ugh." I grimace at my latest attempt at writing "Ministry of Finance." The characters look like they're wobbling in fear, much as the actual ministry must be after the policy changes Qin Zheng ordered.

Wan'er manages a polite smile at my writing, dimples curving in her round cheeks. "No need to press so hard, Your Highness. Keep your wrist light and free, like this."

She takes her own pen and inscribes much more elegant characters beside mine. I have no idea how it's possible to write so prettily while gripping a pen, not an inkbrush designed for traditional calligraphy. She and Shimin would've been great friends.

I wish I could practice writing with Wan'er all night, but midnight soon approaches.

Having also moved into the manor, Wan'er retires to her own chamber on the other end of the building. A few minutes after she's gone, I find Gao Qiu's closet, where Yizhi said the tunnel entrance is. At the flick of a switch, golden hues light up around every shelf and cabinet. The closet is the size of a whole other room, though it's mostly been emptied. There's only a rack of spare conduction suits, for both me and Qin Zheng, and a selection of casual robes.

I search the dark wood floorboards until I see the small gap Yizhi told me to find. I get down from my wheelchair and use the gap to lift a floorboard like a lid. There's a lock and chain in a concrete nook beneath, a key already in place. I unlock it and use the chain to haul open an entire section of the floor. Cold, stale air gusts into the walk-in closet. A light turns on by itself over a concrete staircase spiraling deep into the ground. A crevasse beside it holds a bare-bones elevator, made of little more than a rusty metal frame, wire mesh, and a panel with two buttons. I unlatch my cane from my wheelchair and, bracing myself for some pain, make my way down the stairs until I can cross into the elevator. I hesitate when it sways under me, but if this were dangerous, Yizhi would've warned me. And I'm certainly not taking the stairs to the bottom.

I press the down button.

The scent of mildew rushes up at me as the elevator plunges through a dark shaft. I drop to the floor and brace against it for dear life. A single light bulb in the elevator illuminates the rough stone streaking by. I shiver in my armor as the wind whooshes colder and colder. The drop continues for so long that I start getting outraged that this—of all the ways, after everything I've been through—is how I'll die. But eventually, the elevator slows to a stop.

I wobble out into a tunnel, almost vibrating with residual motion. A long stretch of darkness looms before me, but there's a shifting light at the other end. Yizhi—confirmed by his familiar spirit signature—shuffles toward me, wearing a pale cloak and carrying a swaying electric lantern. An urge to call his name catches in my throat, throttled by caution.

Light bulbs automatically flicker alive on the rough concrete walls ahead of his brisk pace. I itch to rush toward him, but my healing feet force me to wait in place as the darkness between us shrinks shorter and shorter.

"Your hair—" is the first thing out of my mouth once he gets close. He's disguised as a maidservant again, his hair fastened in twin bundles at the sides of his head. But how is that possible after what he did in the stadium?

"Clip-ons, Your Highness." Without meeting my eyes, Yizhi detaches one of his side bundles, revealing how it was clasping an elastic-tied stub of his real hair.

I can't help but laugh. I didn't know they made things like that. "Well, you still look good."

"Thank you, Your Highness." Yizhi gives a small bow.

My attention wanders to a half-open metal door beside us, thick and tarnished. "These tunnels ... did your father build them?"

Yizhi shakes his head. "They're a remnant of the Warring Era, when people had to go underground regularly to avoid flight-capable Chrysalises from other human nations, like the Yellow Dragon."

Curious, I push at the door. It swings back with a whine that echoes way louder than expected.

I snap alert, activating my spirit sense, though there are no signatures this deep underground aside from Yizhi's. Judging by the way sound travels through this tunnel, it'd be pretty impossible for someone to creep up on us, anyway.

I slip past the door. No automatic lights switch on inside. Yizhi follows me, his lantern glowing like an ember through the shadows, illuminating cobwebbed equipment, rusted chairs, and empty shelves. A chill settles over my bones, as though I'm intruding into a tomb.

"Your father could've hidden here from me," I whisper, feeling like louder words might disturb vengeful ghosts. "He could've saved himself."

"He was never the type to cower," Yizhi says, equally hushed. "He didn't even maintain the bunkers in these tunnels properly. He took a gamble. It didn't work out. It happens when you play games of power."

There's so much I want to say to that, yet nothing I dare speak.

I find myself scrutinizing Yizhi as Qin Zheng would, trying to discern his motives and judge his loyalty. From now on, his short hair will be a constant visual declaration that he's willing to shed anyone's blood in service of Qin Zheng, even that of his kin. No one will cross him as long as Qin Zheng lives, but neither will they trust him again.

The question is—how much of it was an act?

I didn't miss the intensely personal hatred in his eyes for the three men he condemned today, now languishing in prison infirmaries while on standby for proper trials. They were corrupt, no doubt, but Yizhi didn't choose them entirely out of righteousness. He saw an opportunity for vengeance, and he took it.

"I'm sorry, Your Highness," Yizhi suddenly says.

I jump. "For what?"

"For whatever's making you look at me like that."

Something within me comes undone. With a huff, I lower myself to the ground and place my cane beside me. "I'm just . . . worried," I say, rubbing my arms.

"Are you cold, Your Highness?" Yizhi sits down as well, setting his lantern between us.

"Uh—" I thread my fingers together. Although my armor gives my body good protection and support, it does nothing to keep me warm.

Yizhi goes to unfasten his cloak.

"Don't!" I blurt.

At his confusion, I take a deep breath and say, in a more composed manner, "Don't do things like that for me anymore, Secretary . . . Zhang." I remember to use his new name.

His hand falls away from the buckle at his collar. A fresh wave of hatred for Qin Zheng roils through me.

Once again, as in the mountains, Yizhi and I are sitting across a small yet insurmountable gap from one another, forced to keep our feelings under lock. Except it is so much harder now that we know what it's like to breach that distance. We should be holding each other, grieving for Shimin, yet there's no shelter to do so as long as Qin Zheng can access my memories every time we link up. My mind itself is not safe. If Yizhi betrays even the slightest hint of crossing the line with me, Qin Zheng won't hesitate to kill him.

How is it that our relationship will always be doomed to secrecy?

The silence between us stretches for so long that the tunnel lights switch off outside, leaving only the lantern glow to paint us out of the darkness.

"Are you angry with me for what I did today, Your Highness?" Yizhi murmurs.

"Of course not," I whisper. "What I am is scared for you. You've stuck a huge target on your back."

"The target was on me the moment I traded my family's fortune for His Majesty's favor. I might as well make the most of it."

"Those men today . . . they did terrible things to you, didn't they?"

There's a small pause before Yizhi answers, "They did terrible things to a lot of people. You heard the cheering, Your Highness. Huaxia was overdue for a cleanup."

I don't press further. I don't know why I pried in the first place. What I need to believe is that Yizhi is unyieldingly loyal to Qin Zheng's cause. Only then will Qin Zheng believe it as well.

At least the three of us will always have one common enemy: the gods.

How do I ask Yizhi for help with the plan without sounding suspicious? Although we're as far from the gods' scrutiny as possible, I don't want to risk talking explicitly about what Qin Zheng and I are aiming to do.

"Speaking of corruption," I say, "do you happen to know someone really, really good at calculations? There's a lot to be done if we want to win against it."

While pretending to scratch my head, I point firmly upward.

Yizhi's eyes widen in the lantern glow. I hope it means he's realized which enemy I'm truly plotting against.

"Uh, my second oldest sister Taiping might be of help, Your Highness. She's a genius with numbers."

"The one who refuses to get married?" I think he's mentioned this sister a few times.

"Yes, Your Highness. She was a top logistics manager for Father's enterprise, so good at it that he kept agreeing to delay her marriage. And now..."

I smile. "Now she's free to do what she wants."

"Indeed. She wanted to meet Your Highness when you stayed here before, but Father wouldn't let her."

"Typical." I snort. I'm not new to being isolated like a plague source.

"*Stay away from the Wu family's second daughter*," the parents in my village would warn their children. None of them let their daughters be friends with me. Especially not after I got caught kissing Xu Hui, a girl who lived a few houses down, when we were seven or eight and playing on the edge of the woods. We weren't really old enough to understand the significance of a kiss, but it added an infestation of panic on top of my existing infamy as a "difficult child."

"She sounds perfect for the job," I say. "Can't wait to meet her."

Yizhi cracks a faint grin. "The feeling is mutual, Your Highness. I can assure you of that."

"There's something else, though..." I think of how to phrase my next request subtly, but there's no way to get it across without being blunt. I blow out a long sigh. "Do you think you can find the person who received Shimin's kidney after it was harvested out of him?"

Yizhi's smile fades. A crease forms between his brows, but he's too careful to voice his confusion.

"He's been haunting me," I say, which isn't a lie. "I can barely sleep. I think knowing what happened to this last trace of him on the planet might... help."

Yizhi nods, his eyes gaining a wet sheen. I don't know if he can deduce the full depth of my intentions—using Shimin's spirit signature as target practice to pinpoint the Heavenly Court is *pretty out there*—but he says, "We own the government databases now, Your Highness. I'm sure we can find out."

CHAPTER SIXTEEN

MOTHER OF THE REALM

The next morning, I sit in for Qin Zheng at my first court assembly, positioned on a second, smaller throne behind his empty one on the dais. From the rafters of the high ceiling, a bead curtain streams down in front of the thrones, preventing the officials from seeing me clearly. It's such overkill when my mask and veil already hide my face, but this is the traditional setup for when the wife or mother of a ruler sits in for him. Qin Zheng is all about smashing tradition until it provides a convenient excuse to keep other men away from me. He certainly has ... issues.

I go along with it because it's a sensitive time. Whatever helps keep the central court in line. Wan'er stands beside me, holding my ceremonial scythe. She must seem like mere decoration to the court, but I know she'll have good political advice when I need it. I mean, she managed to unionize the palace workers despite being one of the newest hires. "Staffers" they now demand to be called, not "servants."

"I wish to reiterate once again that every decision I make is by my own will," Qin Zheng says on a livefeed from his quarantine chamber. It plays on two screens, a small one affixed to the back of his empty throne, for my eyes, and a big one dangling in front of the dais for the officials to gaze up at. "With our pilot bond, my empress cannot deceive me. She shall be my eyes and ears until I am well enough to return to the palace."

My gauntlets give a metallic squeak as my fists clench. Across the bead curtain, most officials get visibly less tense at his declaration.

However, a particularly old one in the purple-robed front row speaks up. "Your Majesty, if I may: it would be much wiser to depose Lady Wu so Chief Strategist Zhuge may return to serve you. Lady Wu will—"

"Governor Chu, we have been over this," Qin Zheng cuts in wearily from the throne room speakers.

Shockingly, the official fires back with more ferocity. "Lady Wu may not be able to deceive you, but she is a mere peasant girl, with a mind filled with childish fallacies! She knows nothing of the true complexity of political and economic matters. Whatever Your Majesty has heard from her cannot possibly be more than a bastardized truth!"

"Who the fuck is that?" I whisper to Wan'er. "Do you know?"

"That's Chu Suiliang, the new governor of the Tang province," Wan'er whispers back. "He used to be the vice governor, but got promoted after . . . the, um, incident."

Ah. He must hate me more than he likes his promotion.

"Governor Chu!" Sima Yi raises his voice, standing a few spots over from Chu Suiliang. "Who are you to question His Majesty's judgment?"

"And who are you, *Strategist* Sima, to speak against this matter when you have the most to lose once Chief Strategist Zhuge returns? Your jealousy of him is no secret!" Governor Chu retorts. The officials between him and Sima Yi stand stiffly in place, wide eyes aimed at the floor.

"That is slander! I respected him greatly!"

"Then why are you here, posing as our new Chairman, while Chief Strategist Zhuge has been forced into hiding?"

"Because I respect His Majesty more, while Zhuge Liang does not! He thinks himself so righteous that he can interfere in His Majesty's personal matters! If anything, *he's* the one holding His Majesty hostage—with his pompous rhetoric!"

"The choice for the mother of the realm is no personal matter!" Governor Chu yanks out the long pin securing his bureaucrat hat to his topknot and hurls the hat to the ground. "For over forty years, I have served Huaxia, and I vowed never to do wrong by my duty. Thus, I beg of Your Majesty: heed Chief Strategist Zhuge's warning!"

"Generals, remove Governor Chu from the court," Qin Zheng commands on the livefeed, massaging his temples.

Qieluo and Yang Jian march toward Governor Chu from either side of the dais.

"Chief Strategist Zhuge is the single most respected scholar among us, and he is correct about the Harlot Wu!" Governor Chu points at me. "She is unhinged of mind and tainted of body! If she is allowed to remain the empress, it will be the undoing of all order in Huaxia!"

As Qieluo and Yang Jian approach him, he drops to his knees and smashes his forehead on the ground over and over in violent kowtows. Blood spreads across his forehead. Qieluo and Yang Jian seize him by his arms, but he resists.

"Get him out of here already!" I can't help but shout.

"See how she speaks out of turn!" Governor Chu thrashes against Qieluo and Yang Jian's efforts to drag him away from the other officials. "See past her vixen charms! She is dangerous and vile and unfit to be your empress!"

While Governor Chu spews more accusations, Yizhi breaks from his position near the dais. He's dressed in a new kind of purple robe, more in the style of a guard's than an official's, tight-sleeved and bound at the forearms with leather braces. A silver-studded belt fastens beneath its crossover top, and its pleated bottom cuts off above black boots. A golden ribbon ties back his chopped hair, pointedly visible without a hat to cover it.

Nervous glances follow him. He uncaps a syringe from a holster in his belt and stabs it into Governor Chu's shoulder.

Governor Chu's insults trail off. He slackens in Qieluo and Yang Jian's arms, eyes rolling back.

Yizhi faces the rest of the assembly. "Order before the throne!"

"Well done, Secretary Zhang," Qin Zheng says, though he looks deep in thought. Like he's genuinely weighing the pros and cons of keeping me alive. And the cons just might be winning.

With a raised-fist salute, Yizhi returns to his position while Qieluo and Yang Jian drag Governor Chu away. I resist the urge to smother my face with my hands. I cannot look weak right now. That might tip Qin Zheng over to "find an excuse to be rid of me" territory. He could go along with the officials' accusation that I poisoned him, for example. If he releases the footage of him collapsing before me, no one would think he's callously backstabbing the girl who brought him back to life.

"If I may . . ." Sima Yi steps forth. "Those like Governor Chu are failing to consider how the empress will be critical in one matter: providing heirs for Your Majesty. Think of it—a pilot lineage revived from legend! How could we throw this opportunity away?"

I freeze up on my throne.

"Indeed," Qin Zheng says. "I had no surviving children in my time due to repeated miscarriages among my concubines, but I look forward to witnessing the advancements in reproductive medicine since then."

Sima Yi eyes the officials to his left and right. "A mother with a spirit pressure high enough to match His Majesty in a Chrysalis surely has a much better chance of carrying strong, healthy sons of his to term."

Fury rushes like boiling water through my veins at how smoothly they're flowing through this exchange. Qin Zheng and Sima Yi clearly discussed this—this *use of my body*—before the assembly, without me present. I bet they even figured out how to do it with no physical contact between me and Qin Zheng. There are ways.

Skies, is this the real reason he's keeping me alive, even though he despises me? He wants to *breed me*?

The worst part is, it's actually pacifying the officials. Many nod absently to each other, postures relaxing. I fantasize about crushing them all in a Chrysalis as I did their predecessors, but I've learned the painful lesson that this creates a whole new world of problems.

"If I may also speak—" Yizhi joins in, making my heart miss its next beat. "I propose that it would be wiser to leave this matter until at least a month from now, so there will be no doubts as to the child's parentage. We would not want to leave any room for slander and gossip."

Acrid heat swoops up and down through me. I know Yizhi's trying to help, but his words cut like knives, deeper than everyone else's, because he's the one person I trusted never to hurt me. Yet here he is, talking as if all that matters about me is my womb, and that it ought to be subject to the judgment of these sleazy men.

He's playing a role, I remind myself. *He's acting his part.*

If Yizhi were being his true self, he wouldn't dare bring attention to my hypothetical baby's parentage issue. While the officials are no doubt imagining what Shimin and I did in our last days together, Qin Zheng knows the hidden other possibility—that I could be carrying *Yizhi's* child without knowing it. What a mess that would be. I'm pretty sure I'm not pregnant, given the precautions we took and the timing of my last bleeding, but who knows? If fate and fortune wanted to play a joke on anyone, it'd be me.

Qin Zheng says nothing against Yizhi's proposal, but he does not look happy on the livefeed as the officials mutter among themselves. I can't let the risk Yizhi took be for nothing. I need to . . . I need to . . .

I need to return to the war front.

The realization leaves me cold, but no way can I stay in the palace just reading books all day with Wan'er. There's practically nothing that bothers men more than seeing a woman they think is sitting around "mooching" off her husband. If I don't go busy myself with pilot duties, Qin Zheng and the central court will never drop the idea of making me do *maternal* duties.

Not to mention that if I don't take a lead in the war effort, how could I expect to rebuild the Iron Widows as my personal power base? More girls than me need to seize power in this revolution, or we'll all stay the playthings of men, fearing their every whim and trapped with no choice but to totter on bound feet and birth baby after baby.

"Who's the new Minister of War?" I ask Wan'er under my breath.

She leans toward me. "It should be Xu Jingye, fourth from the left in the front row. He was a senior strategist in the army's Central Command, like Chairman Sima and Zhuge Liang."

Fighting down shame I shouldn't be feeling, I open my mouth.

"I concur with Secretary Zhang!" My voice rings through the throne room, which goes quiet. I do my best to copy the pretentious way everyone speaks here. "However, I have no intention of sitting idly while waiting for a month to pass. Minister Xu," I address the wide-faced, square-jawed man Wan'er pointed out, "Yesterday, Captain Liu and Captain Wei returned to the Han province in the Azure Dragon, correct?"

Minister Xu bows. "To answer Your Highness: yes, they did. The captains said they wished they could have stayed longer to be sure of His Majesty's well-being, but the war dynamics at the Han frontier are too dire for them not to return to action."

"And those dynamics became dire in part because they broke from the strategists' scheduling to come attack me and His Majesty, correct?"

Minister Xu clears his throat. "Well, yes, and they were disciplined severely for the transgression, including being fined six months' of their wages. But I am certain they acted due to a misunderstanding, Your Highness. It was a chaotic night. Many rumors and lies were spread."

"Many indeed. And since *I* was the subject of most of those rumors, it seems I should head to the Han frontier myself to dispel any lingering misunderstandings and get its war dynamics back to a secure level."

"Your Highness—!" Sima Yi bugs his eyes out at me like he's trying to beam his thoughts into my head. "Have you forgotten that His Majesty is not yet well enough to pilot?"

"Tell me, Chairman Sima," I say, "what does a male pilot in a Balanced Match do when his partner can't go to battle? Such as when she's heavily pregnant?"

"He would take a concubine—but it would be the utmost insult to His Majesty for another man to touch you or the Yellow Dragon!"

"What if I didn't go in the Yellow Dragon?" I clutch my throne's lacquered armrests. "What if I took the Nine-Tailed Fox? It's sitting unused at the Sui-Tang frontier, correct?"

Hushed gasps flutter through the assembly. On the livefeed, Qin Zheng straightens in his chair, watching intently through whatever cameras are in the throne room. I hope he's thinking of that conversation we had about doing a sweep for girls with high spirit pressures. He should be realizing that there'll be fewer doubts about it if the public gets their minds blown by seeing me deploy independently of him because he's too busy with, I don't know, restructuring the health care system or something. We'll make up an excuse. It'd be a powerful statement that customs can be broken as long as it keeps Huaxia safe. No matter how much denial he's in about his condition or how deeply he wants me gone, surely he can recognize that me taking the Fox is a good strategic move when this frontier crisis is demanding that we act.

Sima Yi's mouth moves uselessly a few times before he says, "That would still be highly improper!"

"Since when do you care about propriety when it comes to war, Chairman Sima?" I snap. "Might I remind this assembly that *you* were the one who campaigned the hardest for me and Pilot Li, infamous as we were, to lead the recovery of Zhou?" I eye Minister Xu, who was surely there for the discussions. He stays rigid as a statue.

"Your Highness, the situation then is incomparable to now!" Sima Yi whines. "If we're talking about reinforcing Han, then Prince-General Yang and Princess-General Dugu should go in the White Tiger, now that they have also recuperated their qì!" He gestures to them, who've returned from wherever they dragged Governor Chu to.

"And how do you propose they get the White Tiger to Han if we can't deploy the Yellow Dragon to fly it there? Let them trek it there manually, at the risk of destroying everything along the way? I doubt our roads and bridges were built to withstand the weight of a Prince-class Chrysalis."

"If we clear the roads and let other flight-capable Chrysalises assist with the airlift—"

"Enough!" Qin Zheng grunts in his livefeed. "My empress makes a worthy point in that letting the Nine-Tailed Fox sit unused is a grave waste. I am sick of hearing this court argue against allowing woman a greater role in the war when we should be utilizing all the talent we can. My empress may have a spare co-pilot, so long as his manhood is removed."

Every official in the assembly goes as pale as they did when he told the workers across Huaxia to rise up in revolution.

"Your Majesty, I—I beg your pardon?" Sima Yi's voice shoots up in pitch.

"You heard me. Find a young man with a reasonably high spirit pressure and castrate him." Qin Zheng makes a slicing motion. "Then my empress may pilot the Nine-Tailed Fox with him."

CHAPTER SEVENTEEN

THE REST OF THE VOICELESS

I get into a screaming match with Sima Yi after the assembly, with Yizhi catching some fallout, but then I waste no more time and proceed to look for a ... eunuch-pilot, I guess. I need to get *out of here* before anyone gets any further ideas about deposing me or breeding me.

The fairest way to choose a guy for certain doom and suffering would be to pluck one out of the Tianlao, the highest-security prison in Huaxia, where every inmate is on death row anyway. But I waver when I realize Shimin had been held there before he was conscripted as a pilot. I decide that I can't rely on the Tianlao's files. I need to go there and judge the prisoners myself.

Not wanting to draw excessive attention, I take the most understated electric carriage in the estate's collection, stored in a cavernous lot in the mountain. For the Gao family, though, "understated" still entails a glossy black exterior embellished with pearlescent fragments arranged like cranes in flight among wind-stirred plum blossoms.

"Hope Your Highness realizes the Tianlao isn't a tourist destination." Qieluo helps me into the carriage, serving as my bodyguard.

"Obviously," I grumble, taking one of the four white leather seats that face each other in the carriage. I put my crown in my lap so its antlers won't smack anyone in the face.

Wan'er gets in after us, coming along for general assistance. Right as she moves to pull the carriage door closed, an elevator nearby opens with a *ding*.

"Wait!" a voice calls out.

The sound of a cane clanks into the parking lot. Someone emerges in a male-style robe of exquisite orange silk with blue lapels and a leather belt around the waist. For a second, I think it's Yizhi—except the person has bound feet.

A few guards block the cross-dressing woman who looks uncannily like Yizhi. She gives a dramatic groan. "Guys, it's me! Your *Èr Xiǎojiě*!"

Gao Qiu's second daughter?

Oh. She's the math genius sister Yizhi talked about.

I lean out of the carriage. "Hey, are you Gao Taiping?"

"Yours truly!" She waves. "Mind if I tag along, Your Highness?"

"Let her come," I tell the guards.

Taiping puffs out her cheeks when the guards move aside. "To think I was one of your bosses a few weeks ago, but now that I'm living paycheck to paycheck, you act like you don't even know me."

As she climbs into the carriage, Qieluo gives her a hand while saying, "You know no one's going to believe you're a man when your feet are bound, right?"

"Oh, I'm not trying to fool anyone. They can think whatever they like." Taiping sits down beside Wan'er and rests her cane against the inside of the carriage. Her hair is pulled up inside a black *fútóu*, something else usually worn only by men, its round top almost grazing the ceiling and its two long ends trailing past her shoulders.

"If you say so." Qieluo pulls the door shut.

Taiping studies me up and down, eyes crinkling. "Your Highness sure is a busy woman. Zhi'*er* told me you couldn't meet me today because you're going on this expedition, but I thought I could just join you instead of—" She does a double-take on Wan'er. "Wait, have we met?"

Wan'er tenses up. "I am an estate staffer, Miss Gao. You've probably seen me around."

"No, no, it was somewhere else." Taiping's gaze drops to Wan'er's chest. "Weeks ago, at . . . the club? Didn't I do a jelly shot off your—"

"I do not frequent such establishments!" Wan'er's cheeks go bright red. "You must be mistaking me for someone else!"

"Ahh . . . I see." Taiping nods repeatedly. "You're not open about it. Okay, I guess it was *someone else*."

"What?" I blink at this incomprehensible turn in the conversation. "What's a jelly shot?"

"A very fun way to consume alcohol, Your Highness." Taiping winks.

"Oh." Alcohol has never been associated with "fun" for me, but to each their own. This sounds like some city folk nonsense that's none of my business.

Qieluo and Taiping simultaneously reach for a narrow compartment beside their respective seats.

"I can do the honors." Taiping unfolds a screen out of her compartment first, steadying it before herself on metallic joints.

Qieluo scowls. "I know how to operate a self-driving carriage."

"I don't doubt that, Princess-General Dugu, but I've taken this baby out for a spin many times. And it's *my* city."

"Fine. Whatever." Qieluo drops her own screen back into its compartment.

Neon colors shift over Taiping's face as she works her screen. The carriage rolls forth, the hum of its electric engine echoing through the parking lot. Incredibly, it steers *itself* through the Gao family's vehicle collection, many bedazzled with gold and silver filigree. Each is probably worth more than what the average worker makes in a lifetime. It boggles my mind sometimes, the technology the ultra-rich have access to.

A gate lifts up on steel tracks with a resounding rumble, then our carriage speeds out of the mountain through a tunnel. Making the occasional swipe on her screen, Taiping asks Wan'er more mundane questions, like what her name is and how she came to work for the estate. The tension leaves Wan'er's shoulders as they speak no more of "the club," whatever that is. I find an opening to ask Taiping to join Wan'er in tutoring me so I can understand economics and "do math better," to which she enthusiastically agrees. I'm not yet sure how to hint to her that the math is for attacking the Heavenly Court in the Yellow Dragon, and how she'll react once she realizes, but that'll have to wait until we have more privacy.

Spiraling mountain roads take us down to Chang'an proper. Although the carriage windows look black from the outside, they offer a clear view from the inside. And what I see makes my jaw drop.

The double doors of many walled estates have been smashed up, splintered gashes exposing the furniture barricading them from the inside. Elaborately carved window frames have only fragments of glass to hold on to, like broken teeth. Shards glitter on smoke-stained stone porches. Soldiers with rifles slung around their shoulders patrol the area half-heartedly, most scrolling on digital devices.

"Wow," Qieluo exclaims under her breath.

"I heard there was a lot of looting and killing around here last night." Taiping presses against her window.

Beside her, Wan'er frowns. "Nobody was killed."

"N-nobody was killed?" Taiping's attention whirls around.

"There are a lot of people determined to make the demonstrations sound much worse than they were, Miss Gao. It's what they always do to discredit protests. I'd be careful about where you're getting your information from. Yes, things got messy, but ultimately, anyone who can afford an entire servant-staffed estate in West Chang'an is definitely involved in some exploitative business."

Taiping makes a troubled face. "'Exploitative' is a bit strong of an accusation to make, don't you think? Most families here simply inherited their estates. It's not their fault there are people starving over in North Gate."

"Nothing bad is their fault, yet they have no problem indulging in the luxuries their inherited fortunes make possible?" Wan'er's voice loses all warmth and shyness. "How did your ancestors amass so much if not by paying workers next to nothing for sixteen-hour days in factories, and by criminally sabotaging other competitors?"

The air in the carriage goes still as ice. None of us missed her switch from "*their*" to "*your*."

"Why are you bringing my family into this?" Taiping splutters. "His Majesty already took all our property and nationalized our company. I have to go back to work as a regular employee right after this trip. I didn't even get to relax that much in the general strike because His Majesty approved the company's new work terms in, like, two hours." She shakes her head. "We should've asked for more vacation days."

Wan'er returns her attention to the barricaded estates. "The very fact that you think a strike is supposed to be relaxing tells me all I need to know."

Qieluo and I exchange a stupefied look from the corners of our eyes. What is happening? They were having a friendly conversation two minutes ago!

"Okay, sorry I'm not some sort of benevolent deity!" Taiping cries before I can say something to de-escalate. "Most humans aren't! You're being so ... Look, if no one's allowed to get richer than anyone else, how would society advance? What would motivate us to make better and better stuff, like technology?" She indicates the control screen before her.

"Oh, please, most components in Gao Enterprises products were originally developed with government-subsidized research for military and surveillance purposes," Wan'er fires back. "So, by researchers who *weren't* driven by profit. Don't assume I don't know that. Also, now that you've cornered the tech market, you're deliberately making your products plummet in functionality just past the warranty to force people to buy a new device every few years. The companies that actually make enduring products don't survive. How is that producing '*better stuff*'?"

"That's just good business sense," Taiping says with a flick of her wrist. "If you hate big companies so much, why did you apply to work for us?"

I shrink against my seat, expecting the question to fluster Wan'er, yet she breathes in and out and keeps her composure, as if she was waiting for it. "Because I need to work to survive. I criticize all of this *because* I'm forced to partake in it. Not all of us have the luxury of going on joyrides in the middle of the day and dressing however we want without being harassed or fired from our father's company."

Taiping peers down at her male-style robe. "Do you want to wear this?" She tugs her blue silk lapels. "Is that what this is about? Because I can give it to you. We can swap right now." She starts undoing her belt.

Now Wan'er gets flustered. She smacks Taiping's arms down. "I don't want your clothes! That was not even close to my point!"

This is going to a weird place. I wave my hands. "Hey, let's, uhh . . . take it down a notch."

Wan'er jumps like she's just remembered I'm here. "My sincerest apologies, Your Highness." She bows her head, which is suddenly uncomfortable to witness, as if I'm smothering something wild and majestic. "I got carried away."

"Has our dearest emperor been ranting to you?" I say, half a joke to lighten the mood.

She raises her eyes with no humor in her gaze. "With all due respect, Your Highness, His Majesty didn't invent these ideas. Laborists advocated them for hundreds of years before His Majesty, and in the hundreds of years he slept."

"Laborists?" Taiping scratches her temple, right beneath the edge of her *fútóu*. "Like the terrorist group?"

I have never seen a human make a more incensed expression than the one Wan'er turns on Taiping.

"*What now?*" Taiping throws her hands up. "Are laborists not those people who set buildings on fire and plant bombs under people's carriages?"

"That was only *one* sect of—" Wan'er pulls a small tablet out of her maidservant uniform and flashes a code at Taiping. "Add me on Central Chat. I don't want to keep yelling in front of Her Highness."

"Uh, okay." Taiping scans Wan'er's code with her own tablet.

They continue their argument in message form, styluses flitting across their devices. Every so often, they make weird faces at each other.

Qieluo raises a brow at me. *What just happened?* I can tell she wants to say.

I shrug. I've known Yizhi for long enough that I can't be surprised by the way rich people think. And, honestly, I have no ground to stand on in a debate about morality.

I decide not to ask if Wan'er and Taiping still want to tutor me together.

After we cruise past the extravagant estates and roll deeper into the city, the streets grow more cluttered and filthy. The buildings rise higher and get duller, trading intricate wooden architecture for rain-stained concrete studded with steel-barred anti-theft windows.

Just like how I dispelled Yizhi's fantasy of the frontier as a pristine paradise where humans live at one with nature, he in turn showed me photos of Chang'an that revealed the grit beneath its glamor. Photos of people sleeping in cramped rooms divided into what are essentially cages, the sum of their worldly possessions hanging along the metal grids. Trash-filled slums in the shadows of gleaming skyscrapers. Men with thinning topknots and tired eyes squatting in damp alleyways, slurping bowls of noodles near hotly glowing ads for luxury handbags. Yizhi stopped showing me pictures like those after he started trying to persuade me to go to Chang'an with him, but it's not like I could wipe them from my memory.

The energy in Chang'an today, however, is vastly different from those photos. We run into bustling crowds on the streets, vibrant as a New Year's festival. They play drums and gongs and light up firecrackers. Poles in hand, dragon dancers undulate a massive puppet of the Yellow Dragon. Taiping hits a button to spin her seat around so she can manually steer past them.

Hawkers peddle heaps of the Dragon Head Flag for people to wave and hang from every window. Overnight, many folks have cut their hair like Yizhi and joined a trend of tying yellow sashes around their heads or waists. Rongdi women who didn't grow up with the Han tradition of keeping long hair have set up camp behind signs advertising their haircutting skills. Their lines of customers stretch on and on. Every snip of their scissors brings a skip to my heartbeat.

The number of women out in the open is remarkable in itself. I didn't fully believe Yizhi about how different things are in the cities until now. They all dance on natural feet, cheering just as wildly as the men around the burned wrecks of luxury vehicles. But, of course, women with bound feet wouldn't be let out in these circumstances when they're the wives and concubines of rich men, as Taiping, Big Sister, and I were meant to be. Funny how we're from the very top and bottom of society, yet we suffered the same way, packaged to be bought and sold.

On some streets we pass, people wait in line with small burlap sacks in hand and a personal device at the ready. After a soldier scans their device, they each receive a big scoop of rice from a giant vat.

"Is food really free now?" I squint at the long queues of mostly women mingling with their children in tow.

"Just the essentials," Wan'er says. "Everyone's guaranteed a basic ration of rice, flour, and vegetables."

"Oh, yeah." Qieluo raises her tablet. "The Ministry of Welfare developed a platform called Citizen Central before the coronation. We all had to download it and log in with our identification numbers. Every day there's a list of rations you can redeem from the government. Though if you have to wait in these lines...eh."

"What matters is that the option will always be there for those who need it," Wan'er says, sounding quite fed up with the amount of privilege in this carriage.

Huh. Qin Zheng did more preparation ahead of announcing his revolution than I thought.

Still, the bolder the people get, the more unease feeds into me. They think they have him as their invincible guardian. They don't know they're wrong. It's like they're playing with fire while having no idea the bucket of water next to them has only a thin layer left.

I flex my gauntlets on a pulse of panic, trying to see if I've miraculously developed the ability to channel my qì as well as Qin Zheng. I haven't. If a militia organized by disgruntled corporations suddenly bursts onto the streets to beat these people back into submission, I would not be able to defend them.

I only get big breakthroughs in my skills when I'm in a Chrysalis. There's a reason strategists think pilots learn best when thrown into battle.

Why is it that every problem in my life has to push me toward the battlefield?

"I... worry about the shortages and inflation we might face," Taiping mumbles while turning a pair of steering handles, inching the carriage away from the crowds around street vendors and food carts. "If more people have spare money to buy things, yet fewer are willing to work as much, supply won't keep up. This could get...messy."

"Will you not be happy unless the common people are kept on the brink of starvation?" Wan'er deadpans.

"That's not what I said! I was just expressing a realistic concern! Sure, everyone's all pumped up and excited right now, but how long do you think this enthusiasm can feed on itself once shelves start going empty and prices shoot up? How do you think this will end? It can't—"

Suddenly, half the street stops and looks in a certain direction. I hear it a second later: a whirring noise drawing nearer.

A young man with a helmet and goggles rides in overhead on a hovercycle like the one Yizhi has, silk robes buckled around his limbs so they don't tangle in the spinning rotors extending from either side of the vehicle.

"Wang Zhong!" screams a woman pushing out of a ration line. "You owe my daughter her purity!"

A dazed second later, the masses explode with outrage. Cursing and shouting, they pelt the young man with everything from rocks to fruit peels to crumpled paper. Something trips his hovercycle's rotor blades. It dips in the air. He steadies it clumsily and then glares over his shoulder, goggles throwing a flash of sunlight, his face fuming red.

"I'm not Wang Zhong!" I think he yells, though it's barely audible over the commotion.

Rather than backing down, the people take more deliberate aim. The rage on his face cools into fear. Before he can pull into a sharp climb to get away, a long roll of firecrackers flies very high and lands on one of the hovercycle's rotors, tangling the blades.

The hovercycle plummets with a sputtering noise, lopsided.

The mob backs away in a circle to clear space for its landing. Then everyone swells toward it.

There's so much shouting I can't hear if the young man is screaming. I can't tell what they're doing to him. It all happened so fast I can barely react. Neither can the soldiers managing the nearest ration line. Their hands go to their guns but bounce away immediately when the women react with yelling and pointing. Some help themselves to the rice, taking multiple scoops. This causes several arguments among the shifting crowd. People push and shove like a swarm of hornets, but most can no longer get near the hovercycle or the rice. Some turn around and point—

Toward *us*.

Fuck, we're in a luxury carriage!

A whole section of the mob stomps right at us. Taiping grasps her steering handles, but it's too late. More bodies press up behind us. We're surrounded. We hardly have time to look at each other before people start slapping our windows and shaking our carriage. Shouts for us to "come out!" fog up the glass. Qieluo grips my arm. I hug my crown tighter in my lap.

"Take off the silk!" Wan'er snatches Taiping's lapels.

Taiping spins her seat to face inward again. "You were saying about *nobody getting killed*?" she shrieks while unbuttoning her robe with shaking fingers.

"Nobody *yet*!" Wan'er flushes. She helps Taiping strip down to her white inner garments and stuff the gaudy robe into a compartment beneath her seat. Then Wan'er turns a pleading look onto me. "Your Highness!"

The carriage wobbles more violently, rattling us against its innards. I smack my window. "How do I open this?" I cry. To think I was worried for these people a minute ago!

Taiping braces against Wan'er and presses something on her control panel. The glass rolls down. The raw sound of the mob pours over us, accompanied by the smell of smoke. Hoping no one snatched a gun from a soldier, I stick my head out. Several arms nearly hit me in the face.

"*Stop!*" I demand.

Silence falls in a wave as people recognize me. My golden mask, the stringed veil dangling in front of my mouth.

Hands leave the carriage. Feet scamper backwards. Soon, even those around the hovercycle and the rice vats stop what they're doing. The young man slumps to the ground, goggles cracked and robes torn, one shoulder bared and bruised. His slight resemblance to Yizhi in that riding gear sends a twinge through my chest, but speaking up for him would rile this mob back up for sure.

"May my empress live for a thousand years..." some mumble the greeting they're supposed to give me. None do it with conviction.

The street goes dead quiet and dead still. No one seems to know what to expect from me in this situation. But of course, I was just a subject of gossip to them for months. I deliberately played up a controversial image to profit off their attention. The only reason they're not dragging me out by my hair is because I'm Qin Zheng's empress.

My hands tighten on the edge of my window. I can't let them think that's all I am. Some are *filming*, devices streaming to heaven-knows how many more eyes across Huaxia. The way I handle this could make or break my new image.

I recall the way Qin Zheng roused the audience in that stadium with his words. How he sent them into ecstasy by telling them things that made them feel hopeful, feel *seen*.

"Power to the laboring class!" I yell, pumping my left fist in the air.

Something shifts in the mob immediately.

"*Power to the laboring class!*" a good portion of them echoes.

"Down with the old order!" I throw out another slogan.

"*Down with the old order!*" more shout after me.

Oh, wow. Talking shit about rich people really does work.

I lean farther out the window. "They need us; we don't need them!"

"*They need us; we don't need them!*" The mob is fully back to life, almost jittering with energy. Now to direct this energy somewhere else...

"Citizens, let us not succumb to the same instincts of greed that corrupted the old order! Let us be better, and take only our fair share!" I call out. Those around the rice vats drop the scoops, looking guilty. "At the same time, let no more parasites escape justice!" I point to the beleaguered young man. "Let's escort him to the Tianlao!"

The mob cheers louder than ever.

"Hey, hey! Ho, ho! These parasites have got to go!" I shout out the carriage window through a megaphone someone in the crowd gave me.

"Hey, hey! Ho, ho! These parasites have got to go!" The long rally behind the carriage echoes my words as a world-shaking force while we move at a steady pace toward the Tianlao, situated on the outskirts of Chang'an. More people join us on every street. I'm pretty sure most have no idea what's happening, just that they want to be part of it. Arms tied behind his back, the unlucky young man gets shoved forward ahead of the carriage. But at least he's not being beaten to death.

Taiping focuses on driving the carriage, knuckles as pale as her undergarments. Qieluo sits perfectly still in her seat.

Meanwhile, Wan'er brainstorms more slogans on her tablet and labels them with phonetic markers so I don't embarrass myself by reading them wrong. I'm so glad to have her, because I would've run out of these ages ago. There are only so many ways to say "I hate rich people and think they should die."

"There is only one solution—working-class revolution!"

"There is only one solution—working-class revolution!" the masses repeat after me.

There's a delicious power in hearing thousands answer my every call. In some moments, I genuinely feel like we could accomplish anything by acting as one.

But then I remember I'm lying to them. In so many ways.

Even if Qin Zheng were fine and we took out all the rich and powerful, what's next? The common people will work together and provide for each other and live in harmony ever after?

No fucking way.

"The people, united, will never be defeated!" I keep going nonetheless, because I can't give up this opportunity to win the hearts of the masses. If I want power beyond the battlefield, I do actually have to get people to like me. I need to gain the kind of influence that will make Qin Zheng wary of deposing me. I want to be so revered that crowds would riot in the streets for me if I were being wronged.

Becoming likable. Now that is the most daunting challenge I've ever faced.

When we finally spot the Tianlao—a fortress of concrete, barbed wire, and armed soldiers in guard towers silhouetted against the cloudy sky—a painful sense of familiarity breaks over me, even though I've never been here. I'm several seconds slow to shout the next slogan, and my voice wavers. I hope no one thinks much of it.

I power through until we reach the prison gate, where a very confused warden receives his unexpected thousands of visitors. He wears the pale-red robes of a fifth-rank official, decently high but not enough to be part of the central court. He's a different warden than the one from Shimin's memories.

Good. I don't think I could hold back from punching that one if I saw him.

"Just so we're clear," Qieluo says in the carriage while a circle of yelling people presents the young man to the warden, "I never got my money by doing anything shady, okay? All I did was take the standard wage for a pilot of my caliber and advertise a few products for Gao Enterprises."

Taiping watches the crowd coalesce in front of the prison gate, looking like she's processing fear for the first time in her life. "And I, uh, straight up don't have money anymore. I swear."

"Stop flaunting your luxuries, and maybe people will believe you," Wan'er says dryly.

Taiping whirls toward Wan'er. "You still think your revolution isn't violent?"

"I didn't say it's not violent! I said any violence by the common people always gets exaggerated! The old order would've gunned down that mob and then condemned them in the news without a word as to *why* they were angry. But Her Highness gave them hope that the new order actually cares, and so they backed off from hurting us, didn't they?" Wan'er looks at me like she's seeing me in a new light. "It goes to show that the people won't be unreasonable if they're given even one reasonable way out to what they want."

Her gaze makes me feel a strange, hefty responsibility. As if what I did wasn't simply swindling thousands of people into escorting a random guy to a prison I was heading to anyway. I force a smile.

The crowd bursts into cheers and applause when soldiers take the young man and the woman who accused him through the gate, along with several others. Seems like multiple people have grievances with him, if he's even who they think he is. I thought better of verifying his identity in the streets. If it'd turned out this was all for nothing, the mob would've simmered in dangerous dissatisfaction instead of scattering while laughing and singing.

"Your Highness . . ." The warden approaches my carriage once the masses have gone on their merry ways. He puts his fist to his open palm in a martial salute. "I, your humble servant, am Lai Junchen. May I ask why—"

I clear my throat. "Warden Lai, the people came to you because they expect the Tianlao to be the highest standard of justice in Huaxia," I say in my window, doing my best impression of someone who knows what they're doing. "Whether or not investigations are your jurisdiction, bring in the relevant personnel to do a thorough inquiry into the young man and his accusers. If he isn't the one who wronged them, find the real culprit. Do not disappoint the people, or that mob just might come back." I narrow my eyes.

The warden gulps, then bows. "Your Highness' wish is my command."

On foot, he leads our carriage through several more gates and checkpoints. While crossing the prison grounds, flashes of memories hit me, of being forced to assemble products while chained to other inmates and watched by guards who whip out their guns or cattle prods at the slightest hint of defiance. The images fill me with the urge to run, even though I destroyed the powers that used to control the prisons.

"Whoa, you okay?" Qieluo steadies me by my shoulder.

"It feels like I've been here before, even though I haven't," I say, quietly enough that only she can hear.

Her features soften with a certain understanding. She lets go of my shoulder. "Yeah, stuff like this happens all the time with me and Ah-Jian. The more you pilot with someone, the more your lives blur together."

I smile a little at her slip of using a pet name for her partner.

Although this may be far from a happy place for Shimin, I decide to cherish the sensations it stirs up within me. In some way, it's like he's on this trip with me.

After we get out of the carriage at the prison camp's main building—with me in my wheelchair and Taiping fully-clothed again—Warden Lai guides us into an observation booth that looks into another room. Kind of like Qin Zheng's quarantine chamber, except the walls are dull concrete instead of smooth white tiles.

"Rest assured, those on the other side cannot see through to here, and they cannot hear us unless we allow them to." Warden Lai sits down at a microphone on a long table in front of the observation window. He pulls out his tablet and props it up. Sima Yi appears on the screen, calling from his new office in the palace.

"Your Highness," Sima Yi says in front of a shelf full of thick tomes, looking close to popping a vein. "What in the *skies* did you just do? Can you please explain why you're trending on the networks for inciting mob violence?"

"I was *stopping* mob violence!" I hiss. "They were fully ready to kill that guy on the spot! And us, too, maybe! You had to be there!"

I realize the reactionaries will have a field day with this as further proof of how dangerous and devious I am.

Whatever. The elites' opinion of me is already at rock bottom, while a lot of common people might start liking me for this.

"I . . . Never mind." Sima Yi rubs his hand down his face. "Warden Lai, just get to the candidates."

"Of course." Warden Lai offers me a file folder. "Your Highness, I have three inmates under twenty years of age who showed a spirit pressure of over five hundred in their latest tests."

I pass the folder to Wan'er in a way that I hope comes across as authoritative instead of self-conscious about my reading abilities. "Let's see the first one."

The warden holds down a button on the microphone. "Bring him in!"

A thick metal door opens in the room we're looking into. A guard leads in an inmate in orange prison garb, with a prisoner tattoo on his cheek and chains rattling at his wrists and ankles. He's a gut-punch reminder of Shimin at first, but then their many differences sharpen out to me. He's nowhere near as tall or broad as Shimin, his physique being more lanky and frail. And his hair hasn't been cut, so he's sporting a typical topknot. His cheekbones are high and sharp, and his eyes are long and thin, reminding me of a fox, while his eyebrows flare up at the ends like flames.

"This is Di Renjie, the candidate with the highest spirit pressure by far," Warden Lai says. "An interesting case. The other two were conscripted into the army reserves as children and committed their crimes before they were called on as pilots, but this one didn't break five hundred pressure units until he was incarcerated. His latest test result was one thousand six hundred and thirty, pretty close to the Iron Noble threshold. I was expecting him to be fast-tracked as a pilot against usual protocol, just like—"

Warden Lai stiffens, guilt overtaking his expression.

A pang spears through my heart. Again, Shimin has been rendered an unspeakable pariah, never to be mourned as a hero for his part in the retaking of Zhou. And not even because he was a criminal, but because no one is comfortable talking about how I was basically married to another man before Qin Zheng. As if that somehow emasculates their dearest emperor.

The sound of Sima Yi flipping through papers fills the silence where Shimin's name should've been said. "Ah, I've heard of this rascal."

I pull myself back to the mission. "What did he do?"

"Treason, inciting subversion of state harmony, participating in illegal gatherings, resisting arrest, assaulting law enforcement personnel, contempt of justice . . ." Sima Yi glides his finger across a page. "The list goes on and on."

Warden Lai sneers. "He thought he knew better than the Sages. Could've gotten a nice degree from Chang'an University, but decided to run a newspaper and radio show that spread inflammatory messages against the government. Riled up a bunch of other students to make trouble at the Palace of Sages three years ago. It turned into quite the situation."

"Oh, *he's* the one responsible for that mess?" Qieluo remarks.

Di Renjie's narrow-eyed stare pierces across the glass, making me wonder if it's true that he can't see or hear us.

Wan'er flips through the folder with her mouth pinched tight before saying, "Warden Lai, I followed the events described here in real time, and the students weren't 'making trouble.' They were peacefully protesting how the old order bailed out the irresponsible banks after the real estate market collapsed. It was the soldiers who escalated the situation by tear-gassing them, and then they started shooting into the crowd when all the students did was throw some rocks back."

Warden Lai glances up and around like he's looking for a buzzing fly. "Why is this servant girl speaking to me?"

"Warden Lai," I raise my voice, "you will treat my assistant with respect."

"My apologies, Your Highness, but this little girl—"

"*Woman*," I cut him off. "She's twenty-four."

"Yes, be careful, Warden Lai," Sima Yi says. "Her Highness gets prissy if you say anything remotely negative about women."

I don't dignify that remark with a reaction.

Warden Lai's attention bounces between me and the screen with Sima Yi, as though he's unsure which of us he should suck up to. "Well, regardless, this young woman has no idea what she's talking about. Those rascals simply had too much time and energy on their hands. There are proper channels to make one's complaints heard. You don't cause a ruckus at the Palace of Sages, never mind assaulting our brave troops with stones!"

Wan'er shoots Taiping a look that screams "*I told you so.*" Taiping flashes a sheepish grimace.

I give a huff. "Warden Lai, if you care so much about proper channels of complaint, shouldn't you be arresting me and our dearest emperor for rendering the Palace of Sages *nonexistent*?"

The warden pales. "I wouldn't dare, Your Highness! That's not what I meant!"

"Should we even be keeping the prisoners in for protesting the old order when the old order is gone?"

"With all due respect, Your Highness," Sima Yi says, with no respect at all, "we're getting beyond the scope of what we came here to do. Just begin the questioning, Warden Lai."

"Yes, Chairman, right away." The warden activates the microphone. "Di Renjie, I am here with representatives of the new government. They are offering you a chance to serve Huaxia in exchange for a pardon of your death sentence, but it would require the castration of your manhood. What do you say to that?"

Warden Lai's finger leaves the button. There's a long pause where I expect Di Renjie to blow up in bewildered outrage. Yet he doesn't. Calmly, he says, "If the task is to become a backup pilot for Her Highness the Empress, I am willing to undergo the procedure."

I slap Warden Lai's table. "You weren't supposed to tell him what he's being recruited for!"

The warden waves his hands wildly. "No, Your Highness, I swear not even my guards know! Di Renjie just ... notices things! Yesterday he figured out my wife and I had a fight with no clue other than that I came in with my robes wrinkled!"

"Maybe that's a sign you should learn to iron your own robes," Qieluo says.

"Please, see for yourselves!" Warden Lai activates the microphone again. "Di Renjie, explain why you think this has anything to do with Her Highness!"

Di Renjie's eyes shift side to side like he's scanning something no one else can see. "Something happened to His Majesty near the end of the coronation. He was not the one present in the Phoenix Nest Stadium last night. The shadows in close-up shots of him did not match the shadows of him in far shots."

"I assembled the prisoners to watch the broadcast to put some respect into them," Warden Lai hastily explains to us before turning back to the microphone. "Shadows? You are on a special level of nonsense today, Di Renjie!"

"It was a mere suspicion until you summoned me here with those two other inmates," Di Renjie says. "The only traits we have in common are our Chrysalis-capable ages and high spirit pressures. Until a minute ago, I thought we were about to be formally recruited as pilots, but there's no reason that would entail castration—unless we're partnering with a co-pilot we must avoid any intimate contact with. That, coupled with how His Majesty appears to be out of commission, leads to the obvious conclusion that we are being recruited for the empress herself. Breaking piloting tradition seems like the exact sort of move she would make. I heard the tinkling of spirit metal on your end, Warden Lai. Her Highness is with you, isn't she?"

"Whoa," Taiping breathes out. "This guy is brilliant."

"Which makes him dangerous," Sima Yi says. "Especially with his history of insubordination."

I let out an aggressive sigh. "Again, that was against the previous government, which we have literally destroyed. If we—"

"Your Highness, if you're there," Di Renjie lifts his eyes, "I am willing to endure mutilation to become your co-pilot, but you must promise me one thing: that you'll fight for the rest of the voiceless as hard as you fight for yourself. That includes the prisoners here. No matter what they might've done, surely you can see how broken this system is, how it exists to punish the downtrodden and benefit the wealthy. You have to dismantle it. You *have* to."

I bite my lip. Why is he imposing this expectation on me? I already have so much to worry about! Just getting more power for women and girls is a daunting enough goal!

"Insolence!" Warden Lai shouts into the microphone. "You've got no right to make demands, Di Renjie!"

Sima Yi flips harshly to another file. "I think it's time to look at the next candidate."

I say nothing to keep Di Renjie from getting escorted away, yet I can't stop thinking about him as we review the next two inmates, evaluating their reactions to the possibility of escaping their death sentence on the condition of being castrated. They both react a lot more predictably—immediate outrage and refusal, followed by bargaining attempts and perplexed questions about what kind of task would require them to lose their genitals. As for the crimes that landed them here: the second inmate committed a series of armed robberies that ended in the murder of a store owner, and the third was caught producing pornography so heinous, we groan in united disgust when Warden Lai describes it.

"I don't care if you choose him or not, castrate him anyway!" Qieluo yells. "Actually, I'll go do it myself." She storms toward the door.

Warden Lai chases after her. "Princess-General, please do not make a mess!"

"I do not want to ever link with this guy's mind." I block the inmate's face from my view. "Get him out of my sight!"

"So the choice is between an eerily intelligent rebel and a homicidal robber," Wan'er muses as a guard ushers the third inmate out of reach of Qieluo's wrath. "Di Renjie has a much higher spirit pressure and would probably survive more battles with Your Highness, but Feng Xiaobao committed the worse crime, so technically he's more deserving of the risk of dying in your Chrysalis. What's Your Highness' verdict?"

I realize what this choice boils down to: *Will you use your power to change or to punish?*

"I'll take both," I say. "Di Renjie as my main co-pilot, Feng Xiaobao as a secondary option. If I rotate them, the risk can be spread across the two of them."

Sima Yi makes an indignant noise on the screen. "Your Highness, you can't—"

"Can't *what*, Chairman Sima? If male pilots can have multiple concubine-pilots, why can't I have multiple eunuch-pilots?"

Sima Yi's mouth curdles. He slaps down his papers. "We'll see if His Majesty approves."

CHAPTER EIGHTEEN

A PRICE WORTH PAYING

Qin Zheng, who's unusually commendatory about the rally I incited, doesn't care how many men I pilot with as long as the world doesn't consider them men anymore. The surgeries happen by the afternoon.

It's so weird when I think about it, how people act like genitals are all that matter when it comes to being male or female. What's fundamentally changed about Di Renjie and Feng Xiaobao besides their ability to have children or pee standing up? They still have the same minds, same appearances, and same attitudes and ideas shaped by their upbringing as men. Anyone who meets them after this without knowing what happened would continue to treat them like men. So how can it be said that their masculinity was dependent on those organs they no longer have? If it were that simple to shed one's gender, I would've stabbed myself in the womb long ago.

In any case, Qin Zheng makes sure no one in Huaxia remains in the dark about this concept of a "eunuch-pilot." Sima Yi goes on a new government-directed talk show, broadcast to every screen and radio, to spin a cover story about why Qin Zheng is sending me off to war in his stead while he "focuses on Huaxia's rebirth." During a conversation with the eagerly nodding host—a famous battle commentator who used to yell over livestreams from Gao Enterprises' camera drones—Sima Yi explains, with diagrams and old military records, how the Yellow Dragon isn't actually an effective unit against Hunduns and should therefore be saved for thwarting "counter-revolutionary campaigns."

It's not a perfect excuse, but it'll have to do for now. Then after I rebuild the Iron Widows, hopefully the security of the frontiers will never become so worrying that people would clamor for Qin Zheng himself to fight.

There was a dark, venomous time in my life when I would've felt triumphant about this turn of events—finally, boys getting mutilated to serve a girl instead of the other way around. Yet no sense of victory stirs in me. Their pain doesn't alleviate mine or that of any other girls. I'm not going to lose much sleep over it when Di Renjie and Feng Xiaobao both agreed to the procedure in exchange for getting out of the Tianlao, but it doesn't feel productive, either. It's just another show of Qin Zheng's ownership of me, intended to emphasize *his* boundaries, not mine.

The night before I take off for the frontier, despite my disgust for him, I ask for another training session so I'm as prepared as I can be to put on a show that'll convince the masses to accept the idea of female commanding pilots.

Once we're in the privacy of the dream realm, though, he reveals something unexpected.

"You think I truly care about having children?" He laughs. "Hardly. I went along with Chairman Sima's nonsense as an act for the gods."

"*The gods* want us to have a baby?" I gape.

Then again, why am I surprised? *"Go be a dutiful wife, Wu Zetian,"* they told me. *"Be a dutiful mother."*

"A man with no loved ones left to threaten is an unpredictable liability," Qin Zheng says. "Since they knew I would resent having this forced upon me, Chairman Sima brought the matter up to me as if it were his own suggestion. But I saw through it. The gods wish to give me a son to give me a weakness."

"They can't 'give' a son to you," I snap. "Children don't pop out of nowhere. I'm the one who'd have to grow it in my body for nine months."

"Precisely. On my end, I'd have to expend more effort to defy this plan than to go along with it, so if you insist on keeping your womb unused, you'd better prove you are worth more as a pilot than as a mother."

I wish I could kill him. I really do.

Unfortunately, he's a great teacher when it comes to wielding power.

For our training this time, he challenges my understanding of qì, urging me to see past the surface differences between its five types.

"Whether Wood, Fire, Earth, Metal, or Water, all qì is composed of the same primal particles." Qin Zheng turns the dream realm pitch-black and manifests a swarm of lights like fireflies between his hands. "What gives rise to their different qualities are the particles' different configurations."

The swarm of light shifts across several formations, each arrangement vibrating at a different speed and giving off a different color.

"Spirit metal operates by the same principle, being simply qì in crystallized form, the way vapor can gather into frost."

The lights condense into a golden lump, which then expands above his palm, revealing its microscopic structure of densely packed particles.

"However, like frost, spirit metal is inherently unstable. I assume you're aware that raw particulates from the ground cannot be forged into useful constructs. But do you know what is different about spirit metal from a Hundun that gives it the properties we desire?"

I scrutinize Qin Zheng's glowing diagram. "Something at the microscopic level?"

"The bonds," he says. "The bonds between its primal particles undergo a change that strengthens its structure and makes it capable of conducting qì with spectacular effect."

A current of Wood-green qì crackles through the golden particles, making them vibrate faster.

"Observe how the conducted qì can influence the spirit metal's primal particles. When under the multiplied pressure of a dual-person link in a Chrysalis, the particles can even temporarily transmute into another type."

Another stream of qì scurries through the golden particles. They vibrate to the point of slipping into a different arrangement, turning green.

"So it has to be two inputs?" I ask. "It's not possible for a person to transmute spirit metal on their own?"

"I would never say 'impossible' when it comes to spirit metal, but I found no records of such in the latest scientific literature. Neither did I find any progress in artificially replicating the bond change in Hundun-derived spirit metal."

He drops a bitter look at his diagram, the first time I've seen him conflicted about the fact that his power comes from the very enemy he swore to defeat.

"Alas." He lets the diagram vanish. "Let's move on to the channeling of qì."

Suddenly he's behind me, sliding his hand up my spine. Before I can protest the touch, Wood qì—which I've never wielded before—surges into me. It races like electricity through my dream form, lighting me up in green meridians, conducting so quickly it feels like it might burst from me, the way leaves rupture from trees in spring.

"*Feel it.*" Qin Zheng's voice rebounds from everywhere at once. "Feel how differently qì can behave from what you're used to, how the difference arises from a simple rearrangement of particles. It is a misconception that each individual has but one or two set types of qì inside them. In the way that an impulsive person can learn restraint, we all have the capacity to channel qì types we have weaker affinities toward."

The sensation overwhelms me, so much that everything turns inside out and I am within the qì instead of the other way around. Microscopic particles now look as large as lanterns, rushing past me in green streaks. Then they shift in color and speed and density as Qin Zheng makes me experience the other four types of qì.

I lose myself in the space between these primal particles, aware for the first time of how everything in the world is shaped by the same fundamental units in eternal motion, even in something as rigid as Earth-type spirit metal. Its particles can hone into Metal type, loosen into Water type, agitate into Wood type, or rouse into Fire type. Change is all there is.

It's no wonder Qin Zheng is so much more capable than us modern pilots. There's no way an ordinary strategist could invoke this sort of understanding through words alone.

When he grounds our dream forms again, I find myself sitting across from him in the courtyard of a historical military base. Between us is a large basin of drifting iridescent vapors.

"I noticed you pilots nowadays must channel your most familiar qì before you can access other types." He swirls his hand in the vapors. "That is a wasteful and unnecessary crutch. You should be able to reach for any type of qì and channel it independently." He teases a trail of pure red vapor out of the iridescence. "I know Metal is your most dominant affinity, and Fire is your secondary. Now work on channeling Fire without drawing along Metal."

"Okay." Thinking of how Fire qì feels—its heat, its explosive power—I try to copy what he did.

It's a lot harder than it looks. The vapors aren't tangible enough to be picked up. After waving my hand inside the basin for a bit, I feel a slight coolness that I'm able to coax out by mental will, but what emerges is Metal white. Which is the problem. I churn the vapors some more, feeling for a hint of hotter qì, yet I can't get any red to emerge without first pulling out a substantial amount of white. It's as though the overpowering sensation of Metal qì prevents me from feeling anything else until I get it out of the way.

Qin Zheng leans with his knuckles against his cheek, looking bored.

"You know," I say, partly out of remembering Di Renjie and partly so we're not both fixated solely on my failures, "after visiting the Tianlao, I was thinking we should release all prisoners in jail for protesting the old order. Don't you think it's a little hypocritical to keep them locked up when we overthrew the same government they fought against?"

Qin Zheng's eyes slide sideways in thought. Two seconds later, he says, "You're right. I shall issue a pardon order tomorrow."

"Oh." My latest attempt at isolating Fire qì drops from my hand.

He frowns. "You sound disappointed."

"No, it's just . . . a big move to make. And tomorrow is very soon."

"Why delay? You raised a good point. This is honestly an oversight on my part." He scratches the edge of his antlered crown. "On my first day awake, I decriminalized laborist activities and freed those detained on such charges, but of course anyone held on other anti-establishment felonies would more likely be a comrade of ours than not. If they prove their understanding of laborist principles through a written test, they could become a vanguard of the revolution."

Guilt squeezes my heart. "Then Di Renjie will have missed that by only a day . . ."

I'm not sure if Di Renjie identifies as a laborist, but I can't imagine him struggling with a test.

Qin Zheng squints as if reading something on my face, then says, "He agreed to his fate, and he may prefer having a direct line to you over being another organizer on the streets. It appears he wishes to influence my policies through you. I mind it not, as long as his ideas are sound."

Oh. It was my memories that Qin Zheng was reading.

I shake off the prickle of discomfort. "I guess this just feels . . . too easy. Too good to be true, that we could talk about mass-pardoning prisoners and have it start happening the next day."

"Then why propose it? How slowly did you expect me to take this? Or is it that you secretly wished for me to say no so you could tell yourself you made an effort to bring change without having to face the consequences it might entail?"

"That's not—what I—" I trip over my words at the worst time.

Qin Zheng smiles. "You are unused to wielding power, I see."

I stir the vapors more harshly and compose myself before speaking again. "Aren't you at least a little concerned that if we change too much, too quickly, all of this will fall apart? I know Your Majesty doesn't want to hear this, but you're pretty easy to kill now."

"Oh?" He leans over the basin. "You're worried about me?"

I bite my lips together to hold in a flash of fury. "Qin Zheng, the hopes and fates of thirty-four million people are tied to you."

He makes a *tsk* sound. "Insolence! Do not call my name directly. Also, thirty-four million? Why merely thirty-four million?"

"What do you mean, 'merely'? That's how many people . . ." I trail off when another mocking smirk rises on Qin Zheng's face.

"That is closer to the population in *my* time," he says. "Did you miss a digit wherever you got that number? The latest census of Huaxia shows *a hundred* and thirty-four million."

"Fine, a hundred and thirty-four million people. Same point."

"I am not taking pointers from someone who does not even know the correct population of her nation."

As I ponder whether it'd be worth the drama to dump this basin over his head, he turns more serious. "I jest, but I am fully aware of the fragility of life. All the more reason to release political prisoners as soon as possible so they can aid in community organization. The revolution cannot hinge on me alone." He falls silent, looking deep in thought, then regards me with a renewed intensity. "If something happens to me, throw open the armories and tell the masses to arm themselves before the reactionaries come for them."

My hand goes still in the vapors. "You mean give everyone guns?"

"The workers and peasants, yes. Do not make the same mistake my allies made in my time and assume the parasites will ever give up on the idea of striking back."

My dream form sways at the thought of dealing with the upheaval in Huaxia without him. Something Taiping said comes back to me: "*How long do you think this enthusiasm can feed on itself once shelves start going empty and prices shoot up? How do you think this will end?*"

My attention drifts to the glowing thread between me and Qin Zheng. I imagine it severed and dangling uselessly.

"Do you have any idea how powerful modern guns are?" I say, unable to hide the quaver in my voice.

"I've witnessed demonstrations. In an ideal world, I would confiscate and destroy them all, but since there is no realistic possibility of keeping these weapons entirely out of the hands of counter-revolutionaries, I'd rather the masses have the capacity to fight back. I aim to put every civilian through basic firearms training so they'll know what to do if they must utilize one."

"That sounds like the quickest way to guarantee a terrible civil war!"

"Empress, we are already in a civil war. You began it the moment you crushed the Palace of Sages with all those elites inside."

He says it matter-of-factly, with no air of blame. But, even knowing he would've made the same decision if I hadn't, the weight of the rubble descends on my mind, bringing flashes of flesh bursting through skin and eyeballs popping out of skulls.

"On the path to true change, some battles cannot be avoided," he adds. "I was not the one who incited my unification campaigns, you know. The other six nations declared war on me first."

"They . . . did?"

"I came to power in the chaos of a worker uprising. It terrified the other nations. They labeled me a 'pariah regime,' lamented a 'humanitarian catastrophe' under my rule. Four coalitions, they formed to take me down. Funny how none of that concern came when thousands wasted away in factories, only when we began stringing industrialists up on lampposts." He shakes his head. "Anyhow, the solidarity among the owning class transcends borders, and they tolerate no challenge. So I, too, transcended the borders."

"You're saying the other six nations *forced you* to conquer them?"

"Yes, when they refused to coexist with me," he says, with no trace of irony. "Do you understand what a revolution is? A revolution is always a tragedy, a destructive force unleashed by those stripped of every last option for peace. There's not a revolutionary in history who doesn't wish they could've gotten what they wanted within the world order they knew, but you cannot reform a system designed to keep power out of your hands. I learned this lesson long ago. So have some faith in my judgment, will you?"

"Your past judgment got you knocked out of the regular stream of history in the prime of your life."

I regret the words as soon as they're out. It's his turn to look like he wants to dump the basin over my head.

"Okay, that wasn't fair," I say before he can act on the urge. "Not like you could've fist-fought a virus. I'm just worried this will spiral out of control and implode on us. How do we know when to stop before we go too far?"

"Too far?" He scoffs. "We've hardly enacted any changes, and you're worried about going too far. What has gotten into you, empress? This was not the attitude you had when you dragged me into crushing your government while I was half awake, or when you incited that street rally."

Slowly, I raise a dumbfounded look upon him.

He doesn't see it? He doesn't realize?

"I learned that drastic actions have drastic consequences," I say, hollow.

You, I can't help but think. *You are consequence enough for a lifetime.*

Mercifully, he doesn't appear capable of hearing my exact streams of thought, or he would've killed me many times over by now.

"I mean," I add, "after your first revolution, the world literally got worse than you ever thought it would."

"Not all of it!" he says, somewhat sheepishly. "I may wholly condemn your era in my speeches, but I have in fact had some pleasant surprises. Imagine my relief when I discovered we no longer need to print millions of ration booklets for families across Huaxia, because a digital platform is sufficient. The improved production techniques and transportation methods also mean we can fulfill the rations without much difficulty. Have you any idea what game-changing miracles these would have been in my first reign? There is much we can fix by simply repurposing such technology to serve the masses rather than the elites."

"Serve the masses," I echo incredulously.

He tilts his head. "Yes?"

"You sound so idealistic sometimes despite being . . . *you*."

"That is false; I am a materialist," he says with a scowl. "Do not confuse me with the idealist laborists, who do nothing but fantasize about the perfect bloodless revolution while criticizing every attempt in reality for failing to match their vision."

"What about our reality makes you think we could actually make a government that *serves the masses*?" A sudden despair comes over me, like water up to my neck. "Yes, we can tell the masses to rise up and destroy the current elites—but then what? People will rush and shove to become the new elites squeezing everything out of everyone else, because that's what humans always do!" I say, thinking of those in the ration line who scooped themselves more rice at their first opportunity. I clutch my head. My voice is small when I next speak. "What is the point of all of this if it'll fall apart the moment we're not vigilant enough? We're going against human nature itself."

Qin Zheng watches me in heavy silence, then pushes to his feet and turns around. "Come with me."

As he walks ahead, our surroundings transform into a street full of ghostly people marching in ratty clothes. I step over the forgotten basin of vapor to follow him. This new scene is much less vivid, the low buildings on either side of the street hazy in detail. The people, blurry at the edges, hold up tools, wooden poles, and signs made from paper or cloth. They pump their fists toward the smoky sky while chanting in sync.

Everything is too indistinct for me to make out exactly what's on their signs or what they're chanting, but I don't need to. They are fed up, and they want better for themselves. That much is clear.

"You believe human nature consists of greed and selfishness," Qin Zheng says, while weaving to the front of the rally. "I do not disagree with you regarding that, but I do disagree on where it leads. If the fate of society is sealed by human self-interest, how is it that a minuscule fraction of our species can control all vital resources and compel the wider majority to toil for them?"

The rally slows to a standstill, though the people don't stop shouting. A line of soldiers yells back at the crowd, rifles raised.

Qin Zheng keeps speaking over the incorporeal voices. "When someone stomps their boot on us and tells us to labor for them while they sit and reap most of the value, our instinct is to resist. There is nothing natural about this arrangement. It requires considerable, constant force to maintain."

The rally swells a few steps forward.

The soldiers open fire.

In spite of the unreality, I cry out and lunge to pull down a woman next to me. My hand goes through her, useless to stop a bullet from striking her chest. Her body jerks violently, splattering blood. She crumples to the street along with many others in the front rows. Phantom screams echo through the air.

I draw back my hand, feeling slightly silly for reacting. Yet, at the same time, I can't shake the bone-deep intuition that this really happened at some point in the past.

As the woman's blood soaks through her protest sign in a red triangle, like the one on the Dragon Head Flag, the scene shifts again. The bodies on the ground fade away, and another mass of people confronts another line of soldiers. The street is different, and so are the soldiers and their uniforms, but the grimy, ragged crowd chants with the same vigor. They beckon to the soldiers. A few begin to lower their rifles.

Then a loud noise goes off behind us.

I don't see what caused it. It sounded more like it came from an alley than from the crowd. It doesn't injure any of the soldiers.

They reposition their rifles and fire back anyway.

More blood. More screams. More death.

Before I can catch my breath and demand to know why Qin Zheng is making me watch this, the scene resets yet again. Another street. Another time. Another line of soldiers, another crowd of people.

"If to exploit is an element of human nature," Qin Zheng lifts his arms as the clash repeats over and over, "then *this*, to resist exploitation, is *also* human nature. No exploiter has ever lived in peace without their weapons, their soldiers, and their propaganda and lies. And I have enough faith in human self-interest to believe that those who do the true labor of society will rise for their own sake until there are no more exploiters to combat, however many eons it may take. Every oppressor, through their denial of humanity, sows the seed of their own destruction."

In the next manifestation, the soldiers nod at each other before turning their rifles around and charging as one with the people.

"Of course, it will not be easy," Qin Zheng adds as the rally streams past us toward whatever powers once kept them divided. "But every attempt is worth something, even the failures, because they can teach us what to avoid the next time. Dare to believe the world can be better than this, empress. That would be the true manifestation of collective human interest. After all, a society that takes care of its own does not produce children who grow up dreaming of burning it down."

He looks at me as though he's telling an inside joke between us. A shiver travels through me when I see my own all-consuming rage reflected in his eyes.

I have never hated someone so much and yet not wanted them to die.

CHAPTER NINETEEN

HOW CURSED, THIS CYCLE

I remember sitting numbly by Yang Guang's corpse in the Fox's cockpit, drained of anger and purpose after boasting to Huaxia about killing him, while other Chrysalises carried the Fox back to his watchtower. It hasn't moved since, awaiting the next pilot powerful enough to inherit it. Which should've just been me immediately, but the old order was more committed to keeping power out of women's hands than acting logically.

After landing on a hovercraft pad on the Great Wall with Wan'er and Qieluo—who's just here to be my bodyguard, as the White Tiger is still stuck in Chang'an—we're received by someone who freezes my blood like the sight of a ghost.

Auntie Dou, the senior maidservant who supervised my spirit pressure test before letting Yang Guang carry me away.

Really, I shouldn't be surprised to see her. Although this stretch of the Wall is no longer a frontier, but a transportation hub that relays supplies to Zhou for reconstruction efforts, it's staffed by the same people. Where were my fellow enlistees reassigned after Yang Guang's death? I never gave it much thought until now. I wince at the memory of how I yelled at that one girl, Xiao Shufei. I shouldn't have blown up at her like that. What did it accomplish?

At the same time, I'm glad I never made friends with those girls. Any girl I had a remotely positive relationship with would've ended up as a hostage at the Palace of Sages with my family.

Because that's how the old order kept us powerless—by turning any bonds we shared against us.

I'm pretty sure the Sages got Xiuying to convince me to reconcile with my mother and grandmother just so they'd have more effective hostages. And Xiuying would've never done something like that—nevermind attack the Vermilion Bird in the Black Tortoise—if the Sages hadn't threatened her children. Perhaps my mother and grandmother could've forged a better relationship with me for real if they'd gotten to experience more life outside the stifling environment of our village. But I'll never know now.

Auntie Dou falls to her knees before me on the launchpad. "May my empress live for thousands of years, thousands of years, thousands upon thousands of years!"

"Get up," I mutter in extreme discomfort.

She shakes like a tree in a storm as she gets to her feet. I have so much to say to her, but not in front of others.

Soldiers carry Feng Xiaobao out of the hovercraft on a stretcher. He spent the flight strapped to a gurney at the back, sweat beading across his ashen face, unconscious from painkillers. I'll be using him for the grunt work of transporting the Fox from the Sui-Tang frontier to the Han frontier, while Di Renjie is being flown directly to Han to be saved for real battle.

If it was Shimin I had met in the Tianlao, I wonder if I would've let this happen to him.

You would've had to, I insist to myself. There's no right or wrong when it's survive or succumb. I can't torment myself for putting my own interests first, or I will lose to those who do it with ease.

Auntie Dou leads me, Qieluo, and Wan'er across a short bridge to the watchtower's elevator. I tell Qieluo and Wan'er to go up first, using the excuse that we won't all fit when I'm in my wheelchair. They don't question me.

"Wu Ruyi," I say once Auntie Dou and I are alone. A wind sweeps across the Great Wall, grazing us with dust. "That was my big sister's name. She was a girl you helped settle into this watchtower. Yang Guang killed her while throwing a fit. He did that a lot, and you knew, didn't you?"

A sob rips out of her throat. "Your Highness, I—"

I catch her by her elbow before she can drop to her knees again. "How many girls did you watch him hurt? How many bodies did you clean up?"

Her mouth convulses with gasping breaths. Tears shine on her cheeks. Suddenly, I see a flash of my mother showing the same terror, with my father seizing her elbow in the same way.

I let go at once. Auntie Dou collapses with her hands on the concrete ground. I take a few seconds to shake off the reminder of my parents.

"Listen," I say more softly, "I don't blame you for the things *he* did. I know no one would've listened if you'd spoken out. You would've been punished while making no difference. But from now on, you can no longer watch these things happen in silence. If anyone hurts a girl under your care again, you let me know, however you can. I will listen, and I will make sure justice is served. The world has changed, and you must change with it. Do you understand?"

"Y-yes, Your Highness," she chokes out between sobs.

When I go to press the elevator button, I find my own hands trembling as well. There's no doubt I killed innocent girls myself when I destroyed the Kaihuang watchtower and the Palace of Sages. Maidservants just there to earn a living, crushed to death by me, who fantasized about setting them free. I know what it's like to push those lives to the back of my mind, not letting myself dwell on what their names might've been and who might be weeping for them. If I did, I wouldn't last a moment without shattering.

It was because of the decisive actions I'd taken, this revolution *I* started, that I could even have this conversation with Auntie Dou.

There's no way to make up for the lives I've taken, but if I break down, their deaths will mean nothing at all.

Getting the Nine-Tailed Fox to the Han frontier is a matter of physically trekking it there by following the Great Wall. At dawn, I swap into the Fox's spirit armor—the exact suit stripped off me after that first ride—while a drug-dazed Feng Xiaobao gets shoved into the armor Yang Guang died in. Feng Xiaobao should have a decent chance at avoiding that fate when we're only going to be traveling, not battling, but I also don't really care. I take off with him in the yīn seat, which should hopefully be calibrated equal to the yáng seat now. His spirit pressure is so much lower than mine that I don't meet him in any kind of metaphysical realm. His mind merely thrums in the back of mine like music through a thick wall.

Light spreads up from the horizon as my journey goes on, gold blooming into pink then into blue. Far from a perfect circle, the Great Wall meanders around the outer edge of the Qin Mountains, looking over barren plains and rocky hills. I pass defunct watchtowers whose owners are now stationed at the Zhou frontier. The air gets hotter and damper the farther south I go. The experience of temperature and humidity is generally duller in a Chrysalis, but having the sun bear down on the Fox's metal surface brings a dizzying discomfort nonetheless. Mine and Feng Xiaobao's human bodies must be disgustingly sweaty in the cockpit. The hours melt into one another, increasingly sluggish, until, at last, I spot the ocean for the first time.

It takes all my restraint not to race toward it with no regard for safety, considering that Hunduns could emerge from its red waves much more unexpectedly than across open wilderness. A cautious buffer zone is maintained between the Wall and the Southern Ocean to provide leeway for battle. Watchtowers, and the Chrysalises parked beneath most of them, are spaced much closer together than along the Sui-Tang frontier.

"The buggers can survive underwater, but not at too great a depth," Sima Yi said while briefing me about the war conditions in Han. "They're crowded in really close to the shore. That's why they'll always be fighting to get back to land."

A certain heaviness weighs down on me as I run the Fox parallel to the distant shoreline. At the same time, I don't slow my pace. This frontier needs my protection, and I need to protect this frontier to prove my right to be the empress, just like the pilot rulers of centuries past. The Fox's four paws stomp deep imprints in pink dirt, different from the gray I'm used to thanks to the increase in Fire-red spirit metal particulates in the south.

In total, it takes over fourteen hours to arrive at the Han watchtower assigned to me. I'm so exhausted by the time I disconnect from the Fox that, after confirming Feng Xiaobao survived the bumps and jolts of the journey, I fall asleep right in my pilot seat.

I'm shaken awake by Qieluo, the cockpit hatch open behind her. She and Wan'er rode here with a bunch of soldiers who escorted the Fox in trucks on top of the Great Wall. I'm barely conscious of them veiling my face and helping me out to the docking bridge. The Han frontier's head strategist introduces himself as Strategist Huo while soldiers climb into the Fox to deal with Feng Xiaobao.

After Strategist Huo finally shuts up and bows out, Qieluo and Wan'er support me up to the watchtower's loft. It's as pristine as we found Yang Guang's yesterday, scrubbed clean of any hint that someone once lived in it. How many pilots have come and gone through these lofts, dazzling Huaxia like shooting stars before fading quickly from memory? There's something grotesquely poetic about how these boy pilots drain the lives of their concubines for power, yet once they fall in battle themselves, their surviving concubines will erase the traces of their existence. I imagine Xiao Shufei and the other girls who enlisted with me were saddled with the task of throwing out Yang Guang's belongings. How cursed, this cycle, and for what?

A world built from lies. A reality that isn't real.

An impasse I can only break by growing strong enough to kill gods.

As soon as my head hits a pillow, I plunge into a deep, dark sleep.

CHAPTER TWENTY

NO MORE WEAKNESS

I don't like being at the frontier and worrying about the war that much better than being in Chang'an and worrying about getting impregnated, but I aim to make every second productive while waiting for my qì to recuperate for battle.

I lend the Fox's second set of spirit armor to Qieluo to try and go into a dream realm with her. It turns out to be far less vivid than what Qin Zheng and I usually manifest, no more than vague shapes and colors. He wasn't lying about dream connections being less stable between two people further apart in spirit pressure. I don't think I'll be able to generate a coherent realm with anyone with a lower pressure than Qieluo—which is basically *everyone else in Huaxia*.

I do my best to pass on what I've learned from Qin Zheng so far. It's not much, given I've only had two lessons, but what's important is reviving the practice of pilots imparting experiences to each other instead of relying on strategists. Dream sharing is one of those things someone can't really learn unless they get a demonstration, though after they go through it once, it's easy for them to replicate. In the following nights we're here, Qieluo can spread the ability to other pilots at the Han frontier, starting with the handful of female pilots in Duke-class Balanced Matches, who can relay it to Count-class Balanced Matches, and so on. Those girls can also pass it to their partners, who can then pass it to other male pilots.

It makes me wonder how the existing Balanced Matches processed the revelation that the seat inputs were unequal in the old order, and therefore they aren't actually balanced with their partners. What kind of conversations did that spark? Qin Zheng exempted their Chrysalises from recalibrations to avoid throwing off these already rare Matches, but it must've changed something between every pair to know the girl is stronger after all. I call one such girl in a Duke-class Balanced Match over to my watchtower to talk—Dou Yifang, her name is—but I fail to get anything more than awkward, overly formal answers out of her. Personal connections were never my strong suit, and my new status as empress makes things infinitely worse. I'm almost jealous to see Wan'er constantly messaging people on her tablet in her downtime, including Taiping, who she hasn't given up debating. They certainly have plenty to argue about, with everything going on in the revolution.

For some reason, the thought of the two of them makes me wonder something else: If Qieluo and I can successfully connect into a dream realm, what's stopping two people of the same gender from piloting a Chrysalis together?

I can't see a technical reason it wouldn't work, though I can't find an easy excuse to test it, either. Chrysalises aren't things to be activated on a whim; they always carry the danger of death. I don't want to risk any more girls' lives, and male pilots would sooner let themselves be crushed by a Hundun than pilot with another boy.

I banish the curiosity to the back of my mind, along with any thoughts about the Hunduns themselves. I distract myself with lessons from Wan'er, practicing my reading and writing every day until I struggle to keep my head up. Whenever my eyes fall closed, if it's not nightmares that come for me, it's memories of Qin Zheng's desk full of open books and his ability to counter the officials' every doubt with data and theory. It always fuels me with a scorching drive to read a few more pages or write a few more characters. I want the power to sway millions with my words as well, a power I could rely on even if I can't get to a Chrysalis. Wan'er's slogans worked for that one rally, but it takes more than that to truly push Huaxia in the direction I want. I have no intention of abiding by the choice of being either a mindless brute or a baby-making vessel.

In addition to tutoring me in history and politics, Wan'er reads me her favorite pieces from female-edited journals that circulate among literate women. I had no idea there were publications like that. She tells me women used to be able to go to universities, but after reactionaries blamed the loss of "traditional values" for the fall of Zhou, the government found excuses to expel them from higher-level schools. Gangs then went around attacking any woman who didn't act as they saw fit, from those walking alone on the streets to those who showed too much skin to those not having bound feet.

When Wan'er shows me grainy photos of corpses dumped naked in the streets with their breasts cut off, my brain can't even process the images in a way that summons rage. I just feel empty, mourning the destruction of a world I never knew.

A world that can't be born anew unless I can safeguard the revolution.

The big screen in our loft is constantly on in the background, updating us with policy changes and revolutionary activity across Huaxia. Things happen so fast, it's like we're waking up to a different world each morning. Every day, there come explosive investigations on the richest men in Huaxia and reports of peasants forcing their landlords to burn their land titles.

To Wan'er's dismay, people have definitely gotten killed by now. I admire her faith in humanity, but we've both experienced how a crowd can get carried away. Watching her scroll on her tablet, I've seen at least one video of a mob parading a dismembered body around. Qin Zheng condemns these spontaneous killings as the work of "counter-revolutionary provocateurs" and calls on the masses to not fall for their tricks to make the revolution look bad, but he also never encourages soldiers to crack down hard on the common people. Those deemed to have used excessive force to subdue crowds get severely penalized and shamed.

I've realized that the military's loyalty is the single most important factor to make or break the revolution, and it's hanging in a very precarious balance. The military was built to defend the interests of the rich and powerful, after all. Qin Zheng's return superseded all chains of command for the time being, but the instinct they honed for years was to point their guns at the masses to herd them in line. If I were an average soldier, I'd be pretty confused right now. If I were an officer from an elite family, I'd be tempted to believe Zhuge Liang's assertion that Qin Zheng didn't quite come back right and is being manipulated, and therefore it's okay to plot against him.

What I must do is convince them it's not okay to plot against *me*, either. That even if they suspect something is wrong with Qin Zheng, I am also a force to be reckoned with. Although my skills are underdeveloped, I know I have raw piloting prowess on par with the likes of Yang Guang, Shimin, and Qin Zheng. People made up supernatural conspiracies in their refusal to believe it, but after I go to battle independent of a legendary male pilot, we'll see how much denial they can still summon.

Soldiers bow to strength. Despite all my studying, sometimes it really does come down to showing everyone how big your Chrysalis is.

After a stretch of pleasant weather that spares me from the battlefield for longer than expected, Hundun sirens ring out for my area on a cloudy night.

I lurch to attention at my desk, shaking my sore wrist. Wan'er, in the middle of another digital argument with Taiping, drops her tablet and helps me to the loft's descent pole. Although my feet are getting better by the day, they need another few weeks to heal completely. Carefully, I nudge open the circle of metal plates around the descent pole. A sharp ocean wind blows in, smelling of salt and algae.

"May Your Highness return in glorious victory!" Wan'er shouts over the wind and sirens.

I grip the pole tighter. The drop to the docking bridge suddenly seems steeper, the wind howling louder through the opening. I imagine my body landing in a contorted heap on the gridded metal.

No. Enough of that.

Pushing through the stiffness in my limbs, I hook one leg around the pole and leap through the opening. My armor screeches against the metal, sending sparks into the night. I raise my knees and angle myself so I land on my behind instead of my feet. It couldn't have looked graceful, but thankfully the camera drones haven't flown up to me yet. With one hand on the bridge railing, I make my way toward the Fox.

A minute or so later, an elevator opens at the back of the bridge, revealing Di Renjie and his soldier escorts in a spill of light. It's my first sight of him since the Tianlao. I told myself I was letting him heal in peace, but honestly I feel a little bad about what he went through, especially since the technicalities of his plea deal prevented him from being included in Qin Zheng's mass pardon. My first memories of Shimin come rushing back at the sight of Di Renjie's reflective orange jumpsuit. I compel myself to pick out their differences: Di Renjie isn't collared or muzzled, and no guns point at him. No reluctance weighs down his limbs. He strides toward me with such determination that it looks as though *he's* leading the soldiers instead of the other way around.

"Your Highness, remember what I asked of you?" he says while climbing into the cockpit with me, the frailty in his voice the only indication that he's been through major surgery.

Ugh. His words ring in my ear: *"You must promise me one thing: that you'll fight for the rest of the voiceless as hard as you fight for yourself."*

"Haven't you heard about the mass pardon of political prisoners?" I whisper. "That was my proposal."

"That is not enough."

A twinge of outrage shoots through me, but I don't argue with him. I just plant myself in the yáng seat and look away as he takes the yīn seat in front of me and unzips his jumpsuit. Once the soldiers leave the cockpit and slam its hatch shut, I mentally feel for the section of spirit metal that's touching Di Renjie's back. I pierce the hair-thin connection needles into his spine. A grunt jolts in his throat. His qì surges into the Fox, the same Metal white as mine.

Interesting, I think as I let my consciousness fall into the Fox like a drop of ink into water.

Curves and edges of spirit metal sharpen in my senses until my human body fades and the world flickers back to me through the Fox's massive eyes.

The barren terrain outside the Great Wall stretches before me under the cloudy night, transitioning to pink sand before crashing into roiling ocean waves. Swarms of Hunduns skitter out from the shoreline like bedbugs, already making alarming progress across the beach. The battle leeway is truly tiny compared to what we get at inland frontiers. Wasting no more time, I bound toward them on all fours in the Fox's Standard Form. Its paws land like muffled thunder in the sandy soil. Di Renjie's consciousness lingers as a mere phantom at the back of my mind, leaving me alone in my piloting efforts.

Soon, camera drones fly up, buzzing like mosquitoes around the Fox's head. I become piercingly aware of how thousands and thousands of eyes must be about to judge every move I make, and that their judgment will decide if girls in general can command Chrysalises in their own right. As far as I can see to either side of me, the Chrysalises parked at adjacent watchtowers remain dormant. The Han strategists are trusting me to handle this whole stretch of the coastline by myself.

Or perhaps they want me to fail.

Up closer, the ocean foam curls like paper before fizzing out on the dim pink shore. Each heaving wave brings a tumble of more Hunduns onto the beach. They funnel into a tight formation and come for me.

I know what I'm supposed to do: meet them and smash. Kill, kill, and kill until they retreat. Yet the more I prepare to do it, the worse my nausea grows. Is it possible to vomit in a Chrysalis? I don't think I want to find out.

"*Humans . . . Scourge of the universe . . .*" the Metal Emperor's unnatural voice repeats in my head.

Just before I collide with the Hunduns, something snaps inside me. I take a sharp turn, racing the Fox parallel to the besieged shoreline.

"*Your Highness, may I inquire as to what your strategy is?*" Head Strategist Huo asks through the Fox's cockpit speakers.

I have no idea is the answer I cannot give. Hunduns and camera drones swerve after me, giving chase from above and below. More Hunduns splash out of the ocean, their six insectoid legs kicking up sprays of sand and foam. I leap the Fox over them, but they're emerging too quickly for me to avoid them much longer.

"*Your Highness, not vanquishing the Hunduns in your vicinity will only draw a larger swarm around you!*"

"I'm aware!" I shout through the Fox's mouth, as if I have an actual plan.

Everyone awake in Huaxia must be watching this, my first battle as empress. How must the masses be judging me?

What is she doing?

She's clueless.

A woman, after all.

With a hoarse shout, I turn around and smash the Fox's front claws into the Hunduns. As several shatter, their dying rage shoots up the Fox's limbs like the pain in my every human step. I stagger backward, right into another wave of Hunduns assailing me from behind. They crawl up the Fox's hind legs while the swarm chasing me presses in from the front, parting around the remains of their kin. They have me surrounded. I keep stomping at them, but each burst of death stabs at something deep in my core, making me want to scream. Which is something I must not do. I can't look like I'm scared or panicked.

No more weakness! I berate myself. I've toppled a government, killed my family, and sacrificed countless innocents for power. What would've been the point of all that if I falter before I can make as substantial of a change as rebuilding the Iron Widows?

I smash and crush and trample the Hunduns, imagining them as the invaders I'm supposed to believe they are. Yet the anguish and fury surging into me from their collective dying moments make the lie impossible to slip back into. I kill them while screaming apologies in my heart, as if that makes any difference. I kill so many that gleaming fragments of spirit metal pile up around the Fox like a new, coarser layer of sand. It does nothing to deter the Hunduns. They don't stop coming my way, pouring over the carcasses of their fallen. I shake the Fox's body and thrash its nine tails to keep from being smothered in Hunduns.

"Your Highness, transforming to Ascended Form will allow you to wield a weapon!" Strategist Huo's voice sieves through the overwhelming sounds of Hundun legs scratching against the Fox.

"Don't tell me what to do!" I yell.

The gawking red eyes of camera drones, enclosing me as aggressively as the Hunduns, become too much to bear. I charge toward the one place I can be free from their scrutiny: the ocean.

I splash through waves, deeper down the seabed, ever more sluggish, until the Fox is entirely submerged. I reinforce the cockpit to keep it airtight. I don't know where I'm going, just that I need a moment to hear myself think. I prowl along the mushy ocean bottom, movements slowed by pitch-black water and a bunch of very persistent Hunduns clinging to the Fox's legs. Strategist Huo's frantic shouts crackle into static, then into silence.

I let the Fox go still in the crushing darkness. Its massive body, insignificant compared to the ocean, hits the seabed in slow motion. I remind myself of what's to come if I can't get back up and dazzle Huaxia: the fall of the Han frontier, the end of the revolution as blame gets thrown around, the women who danced around burning luxury carriages and marched in my rally getting beaten back into the slums, corpses with their breasts cut off, girls with crushed feet. Even if I don't die here, Qin Zheng would execute me for showing anything less than overwhelming might. He wouldn't tolerate an empress who chokes during battle. Is there really no way out of this war unless we take down the gods first? The stars are so far away.

Shimin is so far away.

Hunduns float around me in nearly every direction, illuminated from within by their cores of qì. Unable to make the Fox talk underwater, I can only think the things I wish the Hunduns could know.

I'm sorry.
They lied to us.
We didn't know.
None of the common people know.
I found out, but they won't let me tell the truth. They'd kill me and brand me a liar.
I'm sorry, I'm sorry, I'm sorry . . .

It takes me a few seconds to realize the Hunduns aren't simply being hindered from attacking me by water pressure. Many linger on the Fox, yet none of them make an effort to burrow inside.

Can you understand me? I think as hard as I can.

I hear no response, yet I swear a fresh wave of emotion rushes into me, the kind of bitter sadness that remains after anger burns out.

Wait—if pilots can feel the Hunduns' emotions when in a Chrysalis, can Hunduns feel ours as well?

Before I can seek an answer, many Hunduns suddenly swing around, alert. A whoosh of water heaves our way, swaying smaller Hunduns off balance.

I activate my spirit sense. Beyond the thick gathering of Hunduns, a large spirit signature—at least Duke class—speeds toward us from the shore. For the Hunduns to react like this, it must be a Chrysalis.

They hurry away from me to go confront it, thin legs swimming furiously through the water. Particulates scatter in their dim auras.

No! I yell in my head. *Don't go fight it! Just leave!*

I crawl after them in the Fox, water dragging at my movements. Through the darkness comes the green shine of two far-set Chrysalis eyes. Enormous black wings flap in slow motion at the unit's sides, yet its head is that of a whale. It has to be the Whale Bird, a Water-type Chrysalis evoking the *kūnpéng* of legend.

The Hunduns gather in a writhing sphere around the Whale Bird. It pushes them back with hefty whirls of its wings and transforms to Ascended Form in a rupture of green light. Its whale head bends forward while the rest of its body swings vertical, becoming more humanoid. Wood-green lines trail down its belly from the wide line of its mouth. Thick arms separate out from its wings, each gripping a green-striped mace. It smashes Hunduns between the maces, producing sparks like firecrackers.

Stop! I mentally scream.

Neither side does.

Wood-green qì pulses along the stripes on the Whale Bird's body, yet the speed boost the qì type grants is hardly effective underwater. The Hunduns wade past the currents fanned up by the Whale Bird's wings and dig their sharp legs into its head like a swarm of hornets.

I can't let this happen. The Whale Bird's pilots can't die because they came to help me. This battle would be seen as an utter catastrophe. Because of me, no girl would be allowed to command a Chrysalis again.

Pushing off the muddy seabed on the Fox's front paws, I transform it into its own Ascended Form. Except, keeping in mind what Qin Zheng said about Chrysalis forms having no inherent rules, I don't let it expand in size, so it's not further encumbered underwater. Metal-white highlights edge in around the Fox's individual pieces, refining them into shapes more intricate than what Yang Guang's Earth-type qì used to produce. Its nine tails fan out into exceptionally sharp lances. I rear up on its straightening hind legs and reach over its developing shoulders to pry off one of the lances.

Swinging the lance as swiftly as the water allows, I clear a path through the Hunduns until I reach the Whale Bird. I loop the Fox's arm around the Whale Bird's much burlier elbow and drag it toward the shore. It beats its green-lined black wings to propel us faster. I continuously swipe Hunduns off its head with my lance.

Get away! I keep shrieking in my mind. *I don't want to kill you!*

Our movements get looser and easier as the water gets shallower. The moment the Fox's head breaks from the surface, I retch out the seawater in its vocal cavity.

"Why did you come?" I yell at the Whale Bird. "I had things under control!"

Not even a lie.

"I-it was an order!" the Whale Bird says out of its wide mouth, its voice unnaturally deep.

"*Apologies, Your Highness*," Strategist Huo says, connection returning to the Fox's cockpit speakers. "*We weren't sure what was happening with you.*"

"His Majesty trained me in ways of piloting lost to the centuries!" I declare while wading toward the beach, knowing the rest of Huaxia will hear the excuse via the camera drones whirring overhead. "My methods are beyond your understanding, and you ruined them!"

As Strategist Huo apologizes profusely, I wonder if Qin Zheng is enduring his hatred of electronics to watch this battle live, or if he plans on evaluating it through my memories the next time we link up. Either way, he won't be happy with me.

The Whale Bird's lower half splits in two, tail fin reshaping into a pair of sturdy legs as we splash onto dry land. The pink sand looks much farther down than it did when the Fox was on all fours. I pivot back-to-back against the Whale Bird.

Unrelenting in their pursuit, Hunduns flood out of the waves.

Dread, frustration, and rage twist and tangle into a trembling knot within me. For a moment, there in the silent depths of the ocean, we achieved some sort of understanding. There's a way for humans and Hunduns to communicate, if we would only stop killing each other long enough to figure it out.

But that's no longer possible for the rest of this battle. Not as long as the Whale Bird is with me and the cameras are watching. If I shouted about what happened, no one would believe me. And even if they did, who would accept the idea of peace?

The Whale Bird smashes at the Hunduns with its maces. Not letting myself look slow to react, I pry off another lance to fight with both the Fox's arms. The only way to salvage my performance in this battle is to outshine the Whale Bird.

"Out of my way!" I roar.

How did I think I could run from this? It's not just my own fate on the line. I'm representing all the girls of Huaxia. I can't fail them. I can't die as pointlessly as my sister did.

I leap and stoop and spin through the Hunduns, not really that graceful, but it hardly matters when my lances are so sharp they slice through spirit metal like parting water. Though, as I fight, I realize there's a much better weapon for this scenario. I connect my pair of lances perpendicularly at the ends and reshape them into a scythe. Qin Zheng will appreciate the imagery of this. The Peasant Empress, literally waging war with a scythe. I swing it low to shear apart whole swaths of common-class Hunduns and arc it high to deliver precision strikes to noble-class ones, so they can be easily reconstituted as Chrysalises. I push through the recoil of emotion from my kills by thinking of the kind of life that awaits millions of girls if I can't seize power for us all. Of every time the world belittled me, abused me, failed me. My family breaking and binding my feet in hopes of selling me for a high price. My father striking me for the slightest disobedient look or retort. No one coming to my defense except Big Sister. Learning of Big Sister's death. Realizing Yang Guang would not be held accountable. The Black Tortoise attacking me and Shimin on the Sages' orders after we gave our everything to take back the Zhou province. The gods dangling Shimin's life in their untouchable court in the skies. Qin Zheng imprisoning me. Qin Zheng in general. Qin Zheng. Qin Zheng. *Qin Zheng*.

When Hunduns finally stop coming out of the ocean, I double over in the Fox, leaning on my scythe to keep from collapsing. There's no sand visible near me anymore, just a wide stretch of metallic carnage. It feels like I should be covered in blood. Instead, there are merely glinting shards of spirit metal caught in the Fox's fur-like texture. A dusting of a pristine massacre, cold as the stars watching above.

CHAPTER TWENTY-ONE

NONSENSICAL

Although Strategist Huo praises my kill stats and apologizes for not seeing my "intricate strategy," I don't sleep well after the battle. Not even with my body exhausted of so much qì. My nightmares churn together, Hunduns closing in on me while speaking with the voices of those I killed, Qin Zheng choking me while I'm suspended in a dismembered body like Shimin.

When Qieluo shakes me awake in the morning, I stare at the ceiling for a long while before dragging myself up. I gaze out the loft windows at the ocean sparkling peacefully in the daylight. Because of what I did, the Han province isn't a chaos of refugees fleeing like my ancestors in Zhou two hundred years ago. I proved there's no sense in hindering girls on the battlefield. That has to count for something.

"There's about to be an address from the throne." Qieluo gestures at the big screen in the loft. It displays the Dragon Head Flag, which takes over all screens in Huaxia before Qin Zheng's speeches.

I maneuver into my wheelchair and let her and Wan'er help me over to the couch.

The sound of drums picks up when the feed cuts to Qin Zheng. He appears in full armor and cape at a podium with his throne dais blurred in the background. I honestly can't tell if he's there for real. It's surreal to experience these broadcasts like an ordinary citizen after witnessing the technical chaos behind the scenes.

"Good morning, my citizens," he speaks, his voice echoing in a way that may or may not be artificial. "Through the spectacular battle last night, my empress has shown you the untapped potential of female pilots, how they are perfectly capable of commanding Chrysalises in their own right. For this reason, I hereby announce that conscription to the Human Liberation Army shall no longer discriminate by gender! Every girl between the ages of twelve and twenty-four who demonstrates a spirit pressure over five hundred units is now eligible to be called into service, the same way her male counterparts are."

Noises of surprise escape from Qieluo and Wan'er. My blood slows, chilling in my veins. This isn't what I meant when I said to do a sweep for girls with high spirit pressures! Whether those girls would enlist was supposed to be voluntary!

"No longer shall we waste the potential of our worthy girls!" Qin Zheng continues on the screen. "In addition, every non-Chrysalis-capable young adult between the ages of eighteen and thirty, regardless of gender, shall now serve a minimum of one year in our army's infantry units! You do not have to be a pilot to fight for the revolution, and Hunduns are not the revolution's only enemies. To defeat all who would oppose the working people, we all must do what we can to the best of our abilities. Only when we rise as one can we win true liberation. Strength in solidarity! Glory to Huaxia! Freedom to humanity!"

The broadcast ends.

"Well." Qieluo is the one to break the silence. "That *is* equality."

"Is it?" Wan'er frowns. It's the first time I've seen her look conflicted about one of Qin Zheng's policies.

"Let's fly back to Chang'an," I say as calmly as I can manage. "I need to have a word with our dearest emperor."

Once we're back at the palace, I discover that, in the weeks I've been gone, construction has finished on the throne room's quarantine chamber. Qin Zheng moved there from the university's medical school. Yizhi tells me the entire hallway behind the throne room, along with the private rooms there, has been incorporated into the sterile zone, so no one can enter from that end anymore. I go in from the balcony instead, pushing through its paper screen doors.

I wince as sunlight ricochets off a massive wall of glass in the middle of the chamber, spanning up to the high rafters and sealing off everything surrounding the throne and dais. I breathe in, breathe out. Talking to Qin Zheng about the war will always be dangerous.

He looks up from his desk high on the dais when I wheel down the center carpet.

The fury brewing inside me evaporates at the absurd sight of him. He has apparently given up on maintaining his appearance, ditching his armor for a simple black robe and wearing his hair in a messy bun instead of a neat topknot.

"Welcome home, empress." His voice comes through speakers on the ceiling. He wobbles as he gets up.

His robe is alarmingly short.

Hissing, I raise a hand to block him from the waist down. "Will you put some trousers on? I can almost see your junk!"

He looks around his desk with a frown. "I keep my rubbish in the back rooms."

"That's not what I—Whatever. Never mind."

"Oh! Hold on, I understand now. You and your future colloquialisms." He puts his hands on his hips and widens his stance. "Your hypocrisy knows no bounds. Would you tell a *woman* how to dress?"

"I said never mind!"

He picks up a book and staggers down the dais in fuzzy slippers. I cannot tell if he's drunk or sleep-deprived or both. His robe slips looser, exposing a swath of his chest. I nearly yell at him again, but I get the feeling he'd look me in the eye and open his collar even wider. It's what *I* would do if someone complained about me showing too much skin.

Once at the bottom, he plants himself across from me and opens a transparent box built into the glass wall.

"Here." He slides the book into the box. His voice now emerges from an intercom above the box instead of the ceiling speakers. The shadows under his eyes hang deeper and murkier than when I left.

"I see Your Majesty is coping well with life in quarantine." I open the box from my side and take the book. "What is this?"

"*Collected Discourses on Labor and Exploitation*, also known as the *Book of Laborism*, featuring writings by many classic laborist thinkers. I annotated it so even a nine-year-old could understand it. I refuse to have any more political conversations with you while you remain ignorant of basic concepts, such as the difference between private property and personal property."

I scowl, but tell myself not to let his condescension rile me up. I flip through the antique book. His handwriting is so dense and frenzied in the margins that I'll need Wan'er to help decode this.

"Uh." I shut the book. "Thanks."

"So . . . would you like to come to bed with me?" Qin Zheng says in a mocking lilt, though I don't make the mistake of failing to take the question seriously. The icy edge in his gaze is obvious.

He wants to confront me about almost fumbling the battle. I want to confront him about expanding conscription to girls. Neither of us can risk arguing about the war outside the privacy of a dream realm.

"Oh, yes. I've been thinking about it all day," I coo, then peer to the far end of his quarantine zone, where there's a partitioned section and a pair of narrow beds on either side of the glass divider. "Are those for us to use?"

"Obviously. Behold—" He goes to the back of the quarantine chamber and turns a metallic dial on the wall. The glass in front of both beds goes opaque.

"Wow," I say in genuine awe.

"I know." He strides back to the glass wall and leers at me like I'm an easily impressed simpleton.

Maybe I am, but is he any better when it comes to technology?

"How does it work?" I ask.

His face stiffens.

"Science," he says, after an unnatural delay.

I can't help but smirk. "Your Brilliant Majesty has no idea, do you?"

"Do *you*?"

"No. But I'm not bothered by that."

"Of course you're not," he says, like it's supposed to be an insult.

I snort and wheel toward the blacked-out section. "Does Your Majesty have a bedtime at all, or have you just been working until you pass out at random hours?"

He shrugs. "One can never know if their next dip into the void will turn into another two hundred missing years."

He says it like a joke, yet there's a flash of real haunting in his eyes.

"Yes, what a tragedy it would be if Your Majesty's 'next dip' ended up being permanent," I say.

Fighting down the reluctance I always feel when getting closer to him, I push through the door to the partitioned section. A sharp smell of antiseptic washes over me. Aside from my bed, the section holds a bunch of medical equipment, some steel sinks in the back, and a rack of protective gear. There's a transparent door with a complicated-looking locking mechanism in the glass divider separating me from Qin Zheng. This must double as an area where medical staff can sanitize themselves before coming in contact with him. There's something comforting in realizing this section wasn't built solely for me.

Through the divider, I watch him go up the throne dais to gather a stack of papers, then down to stuff them into the box on the glass wall. He pushes a button near the box. A few minutes later, the throne room doors swing open, revealing Yizhi.

My posture goes straight and rigid in my wheelchair.

"Your Majesty, Your Highness," Yizhi acknowledges while fetching the papers from the box. A discomfort hangs over me, as if he's interrupting a game he wasn't supposed to witness.

"Go do your job," Qin Zheng commands him, unnecessarily loudly. "And tell the guards not to allow any disturbance to us unless it's a realm-shattering emergency."

He comes to the bed on his side and yanks a thick black curtain closed behind him, blocking out Yizhi and the rest of the throne room.

I wait for the sound of Yizhi leaving through the balcony doors before I react.

"Did you have to yell at him?" I say near an intercom between the beds, my chest feeling stuffed with something heavy.

"I was not yelling." Qin Zheng shoots me a puzzled look while he sits down and pulls his hair free from its bun.

"You were. Which is interesting to me, because doesn't being rude to your workers go against your entire ideology?"

"Excuse me, I doubled the salary of every staffer here! Without benefiting much from their services, mind you! That assistant of yours drives a tough bargain as their union leader." He shakes his hair loose and combs his fingers through it. "I must do my own laundry and clean my own floors in this preposterous situation."

"Wow. I can't imagine how Your Majesty is enduring such suffering."

"Regardless, I will not be lectured on manners by *you* of all insolent souls." He unfastens his waist sash and throws his robe off his shoulders, revealing his bare back and the golden spinal brace trailing down to his narrow waist.

I almost choke, blocking the sight of him with my hand once more. There are some things I don't need to see. I bite my lip to stop myself from questioning his sleeping attire. Or lack of it. It'll only get worse if I make it a big deal. I just know.

Eyes half open, I take off my crown and mask and place them on a steel cabinet. The rest of my armor I keep on. I'd like to get out of here as soon as I wake up.

Even with the glass divider between us, getting into bed beside Qin Zheng violates every sense of self-preservation that I've honed through my life. As he leans near the glass and burrows a thread of spirit metal through it, my skin prickles and my blood pumps with the impulse to fight or run. Yet I take the thread, because maybe telling him what I saw in the ocean will change his mind in some way.

When I look up, he's staring at me in deep concentration.

"What?" I blurt, keeping my gaze firmly above his neck.

"So it's true that you must receive the laser multiple times to be rid of excess hairs for good." His scrutiny roves over my face. "We ought to get you in for another session. How is it that you grow visible hairs on your upper lip despite being a woman?"

"Oh, fuck off!"

"Insolence! You dare speak to me with such language?"

"What, is Your Majesty going to come over here and discipline me? Because I've got some fresh new germs from the Han frontier hot and ready for you."

I drag my tongue up the glass divider.

This is part of a quarantine zone. It should be clean.

If not, whatever I'm licking up is worth it to witness the combination grimace-shudder that takes over Qin Zheng. I swear he goes red at the ears, though I don't quite confirm it before he smacks the lights off, plunging us into darkness.

"Go to sleep, you vile harlot!"

"I will if Your Majesty would stop being such a massive dick!"

There's a beat before he says, "Well, I'm flattered by that assessment, but what does the size of my manhood have to do with any of this?"

My brain sputters trying to process his words.

After a longer silence, he says, much more quietly, "Colloquialism?"

"*Yes*," I say.

Unbelievable.

I don't notice the exact moment I slip from fuming about Qin Zheng to walking in a dream. I give a start when I realize I'm heading down a busy street with no memory of how I arrived.

"At last." Qin Zheng examines his hands beside me, our golden dream thread trailing from his wrist. His dream form appears in black-and-red robes in the style of his time, the heavy fabric cinched at the waist by a thin belt. A tall headpiece slopes up from his topknot and is fastened under his chin with long, trailing strings.

It's like we traveled back in time. People walk the street in rough, homespun clothes. Smoke spews from brick buildings among wooden structures. Carriages clatter and wobble over the unpaved road, tugged by horses instead of propelled by electricity. The sole indication that electronics exist at all is an absurdly thick screen broadcasting something black-and-white in a shop.

"Where are we supposed to be?" My dream form appears in antique fashion as well, my hair gathered loosely behind me and my robe wrapping several times around my body, like a crimson blanket with wide black hems.

"Handan, where I was born and raised," Qin Zheng answers.

"Oh? Never heard of that city."

"That's because I razed it to the ground."

A colossal crash shakes the ground with the force of an earthquake as a Chrysalis lands in the street, crushing a stretch of buildings. A gale force of dust blasts out from the impact, throwing me backwards. Qin Zheng catches me by my shoulders. Screams erupt everywhere. Footsteps stampede to get away. In the drifting smog, the Metal-white Chrysalis pushes itself up on house-sized hooves, shaking its antlered head. The groan of its spirit metal rings over rooftops. It faces the direction it fell from, rising to a height that rivals the Nine-Tailed Fox's Standard Form, seven or eight stories tall, dwarfing most buildings in this era. Its massive shadow spreads across the rapidly emptying street. It has a dragon's head but the body of a horse swathed in fish scales. It must be inspired by the *qílín*, a chimera of legend.

A second Chrysalis—the Three-Legged Crow—swoops down from the sky, black wings spreading as it lands opposite the *qílín* with another earth-shuddering rumble. Wooden beams fracture in buildings. Handwritten store signs clatter to the ground. Fire-red qì seethes under the Crow's oil-slick feathers, sending ripples of heat through the dusty air. The wind blows hot in my face, stinging my eyes.

The *qílín* charges at the Crow, ramming its razor-sharp antlers into the Crow's chest. The Crow pushes back with fierce flaps of its wings and scratches at the *qílín* with its third claw, situated ahead of the other two. The battle's monstrous shadows waver over the shrieking, fleeing masses. I burn to join them, but Qin Zheng keeps us rooted in place like a boulder in a roaring river.

"In my time, this was not a rare occurrence." He raises his voice over the booming clashes of spirit metal. "The seven nations sent tribute to the gods independently as we sought technological advantages in our wars against one another. Battles broke out constantly, alliances shifted on a yearly basis, and peace was negotiated at bloody prices, but never lasted as long as the roots of division remained. So you see, the only way to end war for good is to win *decisively*."

Buildings burst into flames from the Crow's heat and crumble beneath its brawl with the *qílín*. Fire races across wooden shops and homes as wind tunnels through the street.

Beyond a storm of ash and debris, the Yellow Dragon soars onto the scene, an enormous serpentine silhouette against the hazy yellow sky.

"Wait—if you grew up here, why are you attacking your own city?" I yell.

Qin Zheng's hands dig harder into my shoulders. "My mother was captured in war and made to service the enemy soldiers here. She was not released back to the Qin kingdom until a prisoner exchange when I was nine years of age."

My mouth hangs agape. The only thing the legends mention about Qin Zheng's mother is that she was a prostitute. I didn't know the reality was much worse.

As the Yellow Dragon dives toward the city, disjointed sounds and images flash through a deeper layer of my mind.

A hot, stuffy factory full of industrial looms spinning at precarious speeds. Getting pushed dangerously near them by other child workers.

"*Crawl back to Qin, whore spawn!*"

A long journey on a train guarded by soldiers in unfamiliar black uniforms. A crowded facility. Getting dragged away, screaming for a mother sitting with her arms around her knees among other hollow-eyed women.

"*This one shows metamorphic potential. Enroll in the experimentations.*"

Jolting awake, bound to a bed. Fighting against leather straps. Getting prodded with medical instruments by men in loose white robes with clipboards in their arms and folded black hats on their heads.

"*Test subject two five nine has emerged as the victor. Results are favorable, but subject displays a high degree of emotional volatility. Proceed with caution.*"

Being observed across a glass wall by a pilot king with a red bead crown and his chief Sage, the wealthiest industrialist in the seven nations.

"*Taking the clan name of a woman like your mother is unseemly. From now on, you are a son of Qin. You serve our mighty state. Your name shall be Qin Zheng.*"

Having electrodes attached to the head. Being connected by the spine to a chunk of spirit metal. Struggling to transform it.

"*Conjure a sphere in one minute, Qin Zheng.*"

Spasming with shocks of electricity. Burning alive with crackling pain.

"Conjure a cube in twenty seconds, Qin Zheng."

Forging a spiked ball instead and hurling it at the observation window on a liquid line of spirit metal, shattering the glass. Charging through the jagged opening. Plunging a glass shard into a scientist's throat. Stabbing him again and again, getting splattered with hot blood until soldiers burst in.

"Subject has developed unprecedented abilities, with a spirit pressure level no longer measurable. A successful metamorphosis at last. However, we may have neglected subject's psychological stability. Subject may be too dangerous to entrust with a Chrysalis. An older female mentor might provide pacifying guidance."

Being approached by a stern-faced woman in form-fitting black armor that flares out at the shoulders like feathers. Attacking her. Biting her arm. Getting wrestled under control.

"You will never be free, you will never see your mother again, unless you prove yourself capable of handling your power. Do you hear me?"

Being escorted through a military camp after months in a lab. Blinking at a now unfamiliar sky. Overhearing mutterings everywhere.

"Is that the lab boy? Heard he came out of one of those tainted women. That means he's the spawn of an enemy soldier."

"Have you seen the way he looks at people? No kid with eyes like that is normal."

"Did you hear what he did to Doctor Xia? He frightens me."

Crossing swords on a sparring ground with the black-armored woman. Brawling with her. Training in dream scenarios with her. Learning to read with her. Being regarded with astonishment as her lessons stick with ease. Receiving a faded, nondescript book from her in a dim room. Hearing her speak in an unusually soft yet urgent cadence.

"Let no one discover this in your possession. The Sages may be discussing the prospect of confirming you as heir to the throne because you

are the strongest pilot of your generation—no, among all of us—but every ruler is, in actuality, beholden to the bankers and industrialists, who will not hesitate to arrange for your disposal if you challenge their interests. Bide your time. Read this and understand the necessity of revolution. It is not state borders that divide us, but class. Owners and workers. Exploiters and the exploited. With you on our side, we can win."

Reading more books. Many, many more books. Writing pamphlets under different names. Making speeches in factories in disguise. Talking in secret with other pilots. Convincing a legion of them to defy orders. Defeating an Emperor-class Hundun against all expectations. Manifesting the Yellow Dragon out of it.

"There's no turning back from this point. They already suspect you. Claim what is yours by right."

Stepping over the old pilot king's corpse, flicking blood off a sword. Being pointed at by the industrialist Sage. Witnessing him shout for the soldiers and other pilots at his side to attack, only for them to turn their weapons on him instead.

"Seizing power as someone with your abilities is the easy part. Rulers come and go. It is what you do with your power that decides the true meaning of your reign."

"How could you have been so foolish?" Qin Zheng's real voice slashes through the deluge of memories.

Winded, I reorient myself in the dream realm. The city has been burned and crushed to heaps of cinders and bricks. He's clutching my wrists. Drifting sparks reflect in his wild black eyes.

I don't know if he realizes the scope of what I just saw. That woman—General Mi, I assume—she looks weirdly like my mother, if my mother had ever been so confident . . .

Qin Zheng shakes my wrists. "You could have endangered the entire Han province!"

I fight his grip. He must've peered into my memories as well. "So you saw what happened when I was in the ocean."

"Your behavior was incomprehensible, and you should be very glad you are still alive to—"

"The Hunduns understood me! If you saw my memories, you can't deny that!"

The desire to bring him to the moment pulses out from me. Water crashes over us. The ground gives away, though Qin Zheng doesn't let go of me. The next second, we're floating in the ocean, surrounded by the hundreds of Hunduns that glowed like lanterns around the Fox for that precious span of peace. I marvel at the recreation, surprised by how easy it was to summon.

The same can't be said for breaking free from Qin Zheng.

"They could feel that I didn't want to kill them!" I wriggle against his grasp, my words emerging despite the water. "If the Whale Bird hadn't interfered, things could've gone differently!"

"How so?" Qin Zheng's hold remains iron-tight. "You and the Hunduns would have backed off from one another to go about your merry ways? Are you honestly so naive as to believe such a truce could last? To give up on the war is to spit in the face of every pilot who came before us!"

"But this whole war is based on a lie! It's completely nonsensical! You said yourself that the gods get us to fight it for *their* benefit, so why not try to communicate our situation to the Hunduns and battle as little as we can until we can take down the gods? Why expand the war? Why conscript girls instead of just taking volunteers? However the gods use the spirit metal we give them, generating more tribute will only make them harder to defeat!"

Qin Zheng's grip slackens the slightest bit before tightening again. "Generating more tribute will allow us to maintain the element of surprise as we plan our attack. All war is nonsensical! It is *victory* that gives a war its meaning." Ghostly traces of other pilots drift behind him, replacing the Hunduns. They grow in number until they fill the ocean. "No matter the truth, our predecessors gave their lives for a dream of freedom. Their hopes and yearnings were real. Their resolve was real. If you do not wish for their sacrifice to crumble into history as that of mere swindled fools, you must do your part to bring their dream to fruition!"

The water pressure gets crushingly heavy. Everywhere I look comes the weight of stares from phantom pilots, unavoidable, as if thousands of years—is that even how long we've been on this planet?—are winding up like a trap around me.

The next thing I know, I'm back in the Nine-Tailed Fox, battling back-to-back with the Whale Bird, killing Hunduns so they don't kill us first. With each death I deal, terror and anguish blow back through me like shots of toxin. Except this time, they overwhelm me past the point of fighting on. I can no longer move.

"*Is this what you want?*" Qin Zheng's voice resounds from everywhere and nowhere. "*To torment every other pilot in Huaxia with the truth when there is no way out but to persist until victory?*"

The Fox collapses in the sand. Hunduns burrow through every stretch of its surface. I feel every scrape of their legs and every burn of their qì blasts. A death by a thousand cuts.

"*This war was no fault of those of us born into it. Once both the gods and the Hunduns are defeated, the dreams of pilots past will become reality, and that reality shall be the only one that matters. Let the truth die with us, empress. Falter again, and I shall execute you for treason.*"

The Hunduns puncture the Fox's cockpit. They squash me as easily as a bug.

CHAPTER TWENTY-TWO

BRING DOWN THE SKY

I wish Yizhi never rushed to tell me the truth about our world when his people had found it in the ruins of the Palace of Sages.

I may have begged Qin Zheng to erase it from my mind, to which he may have said it was impossible. It's getting harder to tell dream from reality and lies from facts when he's involved. I don't wake cleanly from the dream link, getting pulled into the nightmare of dying on that beach over and over before I finally break free and stumble out of the throne room.

Qin Zheng made his point.

I think of what I saw from his memories. If he hadn't lived by annihilating others before they could annihilate him, I doubt he would've survived. Maybe I'm the foolish one for getting bogged down with sentiment when our focus should be on ensuring the gods don't get suspicious before we come for them.

After getting back to my palace residence, I find a note on my desk from Yizhi, asking to meet in the tunnels in the evening for "updates."

When I finally see him again, I nearly burst into tears. I want to hold him so badly, yet he inches away whenever I get too close. I can't speak a word of the mess in my head to him either. I settle for sitting beside him, wrapped in an extra cloak he brought.

I breathe in his scent on the cloak as he tells me what he's been up to since I went to the war front. He found the person who received Shimin's kidney, for starters. To my surprise, he says it's an old woman. I assumed it would've gone to a man, but Yizhi tells me there's no difference between male and female kidneys. We all pee the same.

He tracked the woman down using his jurisdiction as an agent of the new Revolutionary Defense Department, also known as the Gewei Bu, established to gather information on corrupt officials, business executives, military commanders, and others who may pose a threat to the revolution. He's not the head of the Gewei Bu—Qin Zheng wouldn't put an eighteen-year-old in that position—but he has extraordinary influence over it because he's also the Imperial Secretary. To kill multiple birds with one stone, Yizhi sent soldiers to snatch the Brotherhood's remaining leaders in the dead of a single night, then he convicted and executed them quicker than they could react. This included his oldest brother, the original heir to the power of the Brotherhood and its underworld activities. Now there's no one left to challenge Yizhi for control of the syndicate. To the startled underlings, he declared that those leaders were never true Brothers because they exploited the ordinary members for profit, and things would be different from now on. He's working on repurposing the Brotherhood as a network of well-paid spies and interrogators for the Gewei Bu, putting their experience in operating in the shadows to better use than selling drugs and extorting small-time store owners.

Although his sequence of moves is breathtaking, I fear for him. But there's no backing down for him at this point. He has tied his fate too closely to the revolution's success.

As much as I wish he could sit with me all night, I tell him to go to bed when I notice him struggling to keep his eyes open. It seems that to be at the seat of power is to be doomed to sleep-deprivation.

The next morning, Yizhi shows up in the palace parking lot disguised as Wan'er, taking her usual place at my side so we can . . . go see the woman who received Shimin's kidney. Skies, that feels so weird to think about. But if it'll help improve my ability to sense Shimin's spirit signature, it'll also help secure my position after I've pissed Qin Zheng off yet again. I must become irreplaceable for a strike on the Heavenly Court to overpower his thoughts about killing me.

Qieluo does a double take when Yizhi climbs into a carriage with us. To her credit, she doesn't question his presence out loud. I left Wan'er at our residence with the book Qin Zheng gave me, to see if she can make sense of his handwriting. I swear she almost jumped for joy when she realized what she was holding. She seemed a little puzzled, though, that I had nothing more to say about his decision to expand conscription to girls.

Really, what is there to say? If girls are to gain the same level of power as boys, I have to admit it's only fair for us to take on the same responsibility for defending Huaxia.

Giant dragon heads have been plastered on the doors of our carriage to mark it as a government vehicle. The last time I rode through West Chang'an, the lavish estates had barricaded their doors in terror. Now they're wide open, revealing people bustling in the courtyards while looking the exact opposite of rich. Shabby clothes cling to their thin frames, yet they work the gardens, carry sacks of rice and bundles of vegetables, and cook in huge vats under the open sky while laughing and singing with each other.

Yizhi tells me and Qieluo that most estate owners fled to the countryside in the provinces, where revolutionary efforts are less organized and investigators are easier to avoid. Hence the checkpoints now on every road leading out of Chang'an. No one can leave without a permit. The ones who couldn't make it out are either hiding deep in the city, or they've turned themselves in to the Gewei Bu in hopes of leniency at a formal trial, preferable to judgment by an angry mob. Their abandoned estates have been reconstituted as community shelters on Qin Zheng's orders.

Further into the city, we come across a rally of people wearing yellow sashes around their heads or waists. They wave the Dragon Head Flag, hold up portraits of Qin Zheng, and wield hammers, wrenches, shovels, and other tools like weapons. Together, they're singing a folk song from the historical Qin kingdom that's been featured in a lot of revolutionary broadcasts.

"How could you say you have no clothes to wear? I will share my robe with you. His Majesty has called his army; I will prepare my ax and spear, and share an enemy with you . . ."

Yizhi spins his seat around to manually drive our carriage out of the rally's way. Closer to the front, soldiers are shoving along handcuffed men who are either dressed in fine silks or scruffy disguises ruined by their pale, pristine skin. Furious gashes of ink inscribe accusations on their faces and clothes. *Thief. Exploiter. Profitizer. Leech. Landlord.*

"Your Highness inspired this, you know." Yizhi keeps his voice at a feminine pitch so Qieluo has plausible deniability about knowing if he's Wan'er or not.

"I did *what*?" I exclaim, sounding more alarmed than I mean to.

"When soldiers in Chang'an arrest prominent figures now, they escort them to the Tianlao on foot like Your Highness did. Tons of people join along the way. They call it an Empress March. His Majesty says it's a great way to encourage people to turn themselves in rather than trying to run or hide. Also keeps revolutionary energy at a controlled level."

"That's . . . excellent." I watch the rally with a cool satisfaction. It's good to see proof that I've developed some influence among the people.

If we weren't on a schedule to meet Shimin's kidney recipient, I might've joined this rally to get more clout.

Yizhi turns the carriage toward a different street. I look away reluctantly—but then I hear a woman's frantic sobs during a lapse in the singing.

"Wait, stop!" I lurch forth in my seat, raising a hand.

Yizhi stalls the carriage.

One particular soldier is pushing a small, weeping old woman with white hair half scattered out of its bun, forcing her to march on her bound feet.

I grasp my door handle. "Who is that? What are they doing to her?"

Yizhi looks over his shoulder in concern, but then his expression goes blank. "Your Highness . . . that's Ye Xingzhen, widow of a former Minister of Finance. The Gewei Bu recently found that she embezzled four hundred million yuán from the Bank of Huaxia through shell companies and proxies."

I jerk back like I was singed by fire only to be dunked into frost. *"Four hundred million?"*

Qieluo swiftly goes scrolling on her tablet, then makes a choked noise. "Look at this." She shows me a video of soldiers going through a walk-in closet full of tiny shoes with intricate embroidery. "Posted an hour ago. They found *three thousand pairs of luxury-branded shoes* in her estate."

Yizhi nods. "She also ran a brothel dedicated to high-level officials to keep them turning a blind eye. She had a whole operation tricking girls from the countryside into working there and then not letting them leave."

"Oh." I slump in my chair. Now I notice the concentration of other women around her in the rally, their eyes red-rimmed but blazing with determination. One of them holds up a sign with not only Qin Zheng, but *me* as well. A depiction of us as silhouettes, him holding his sledgehammer to one side, me holding my scythe to the other, and our joined hands raised between us.

How could I have only seen Ye Xingzhen and not these women?

Four hundred million yuán. That's almost half the assets Gao Qiu had. Impressive, honestly. She must be a genius in getting what she wants. I respect her capability enough to let her take full responsibility for it.

"Let's move on," I say with a flick of my hand.

Our carriage's eventual destination is the kidney recipient's *xiǎoqū*, a kind of gated compound most city apartments are huddled into. Qieluo and I put on veiled hats and hide our armor under heavy cloaks. It's best if no one recognizes us. The carriage is just wide enough that the brims of our hats don't touch. Yizhi slows down near the *xiǎoqū*'s security gate and lowers his window to show his metal identification card to a security guard in a booth.

The guard's eyes go wide. Yizhi raises a finger in a shushing gesture.

"Not a word of this to anyone," Yizhi says, voice remaining feminine. "This carriage was never here."

Nodding too many times, the guard presses a button in his booth. The security gate's crisscrossed metal bars fold to the side to make an opening for us. A sense of awe stirs in me at Yizhi imposing this kind of fear while dressed as a staffer girl.

He reels his window back up and enlarges the neon-bright map on his control panel to see the *xiǎoqū*'s finer details. After driving through several blocks of buildings, he stops near an open garden with a pond in the middle. I assume it was built as a communal space to relax or exercise, but now a semicircle of tiered benches surrounds the pond. *STRENGTH THROUGH SOLIDARITY* reads a banner in a pond gazebo, where a large screen has been set up. In front of the screen is a soldier conversing with a Revolutionary Vanguard—one of the community leaders Qin Zheng encouraged the masses to elect. Marked by the yellow, red, and black tricolor sashes around their waists and the dragon head pin over their hearts, they're mostly union leaders, organizers, activists, or members of the smattering of laborist groups finally emerging into the light after centuries of suppression. When Wan'er and I watched a broadcast about the community elections, she laughed and told me these groups are actually full of petty drama and love to denounce each other based on tiny differences in interpretation of laborism. Everyone agrees that exploiting people's labor is bad, but few agree on what to do about it. And the arguments can get very heated.

"No one hates laborists more than other laborists," she quipped.

I don't understand how they thought it was productive to split their already small ranks into even smaller ranks while getting persecuted by a common daunting enemy, but now, if they want to be leaders in this revolution, they all must accept Qin Zheng's militant, aggressive interpretation of laborism and work together under his directives.

The Vanguard and the soldier glance briefly at our carriage but continue to talk while scrolling on a shared tablet. I guess they have no reason to be suspicious of a vehicle allowed through the security gate. I'm heartened when I realize the Vanguard is a middle-aged woman. The broadcasts said the elections aren't limited to men, but I had to see it with my own eyes to believe it.

Yizhi spins his seat back toward me and Qieluo. He pulls his tablet out of his robes and shows me a file of another middle-aged woman. "Tang Anding and the other residents of her building are scheduled for a community outreach session in about ten minutes."

I take off my veiled hat and clutch it like a shield in my lap as Yizhi lists off more facts about the woman. She's fifty-nine this year. Chang'an native. Unbound. Managed a textiles business with her husband, the kind that's a twinkle compared to the blinding glare of the mega corporations Qin Zheng and the Gewei Bu have been going after. When a degenerative disease struck her kidneys, her family pooled money to buy her a replacement. It's unlikely they know they got it from the infamous Li Shimin. The prisons don't tell people about the inmates they harvest each organ from, just how well they match up with the recipient.

More and more residents gradually file out between the buildings and onto the benches. While we wait for Tang Anding to show up, Yizhi twirls his thumbs, his head hanging low.

"What are we going to do when we see her?" His natural boy voice slips out for the first time on this trip, almost inaudible.

"I don't know," I say. I imagine yanking the woman into the carriage and telling her where her replacement kidney really came from: a boy she likely thought of as a monster, a boy I loved. She'd probably freak out and beg for forgiveness.

But then what? Neither Yizhi nor I have the right to grant that forgiveness. We can't make her return the kidney, either. Not while the gods are holding Shimin among the stars.

Has a transplanted organ ever been returned to its original owner? Could it still function the same? Though, with the condition Shimin is in, he would need a lot more than one kidney back . . .

I shudder at the memory of him being forced into consciousness in that fluid-filled tank. I clutch my face, trying to somehow banish the image.

A hand pats my shoulder. I peek between my fingers at Qieluo, who's doing her best to make a comforting expression. It's not very effective on her face. She gives me two more light pats.

Before either of us can muster something to say, Yizhi straightens in his seat. "It's her."

A muffled barking approaches from behind the carriage. I twist around and, through the back window, spot a small white dog skittering down the road, wagging its stubby tail. At the other end of its leash is Tang Anding, looking older than the picture in her file but much more joyful. The lines on her face crinkle in a laugh as she jogs after her dog, nimble on her unbound feet.

Her joy paralyzes me. She is alive to feel this joy because of Shimin. However unwillingly, he shared his life force with this woman. He lives on within her.

I close my eyes and activate my spirit sense. Qieluo's massive spirit signature hits like a punch at first, then I push past it and feel out Yizhi's, then Tang Anding's, and even her dog's tiny flicker. After concentrating hard on Tang Anding's signature, I can indeed sense two layers to it, as if her soul has an ember at its core, blazing with an agonizingly familiar warmth. I clasp my trembling hands together and press them to my forehead.

It's you. I miss you so much.

When the spirit signature passes the carriage, I imagine it's Shimin chasing after the dog. In my mind's eye, he looks over his shoulder at me and Yizhi, cracking one of his rare yet dazzling smiles.

Tears scald down my cheeks and patter onto my cloak. When I open my raw, aching eyes, Yizhi and Qieluo are watching me with concern.

"I can sense Shimin," I say, sniffling. I think it's the first time I've been able to speak his name since the gods ripped him away. "A piece of his spirit is still alive inside hers."

"Should we confront her?" Yizhi asks softly.

I give a firm shake of head. "No. If we do, she'll be terrified. She'll always be suspicious of strange carriages parking beside her. I want to be able to come back and feel that piece of Shimin's spirit in peace, just like this."

When Qieluo puts her hand over mine, I'm assured that this excuse sounds plausible for someone in grief. May the gods sense no sinister motive when I visit Tang Anding many more times after this.

May they have no clue I'll be training the range of my spirit sense, wider and wider, until I can pinpoint them in the sky and bring them down.

After all, what is the point of a revolution if we don't overthrow those who truly hold the most power over our world?

CHAPTER TWENTY-THREE

THE FLAG OF RIGHTEOUSNESS

"Therefore, we have nothing to fear from the revolution!" ... The Vanguard, who introduced herself as a committee member of the *xiǎoqū*'s residential association, waves a laser pointer at a graph on the screen in the gazebo. "The whole concept of 'middle class' was really created to divide the masses. Ultimately, we have more in common with a street beggar than the one percent of people who own six percent—excuse me, *sixty* percent of Huaxia's wealth. It's in our interests to defend the revolution!"

We end up staying for the entire outreach session, which Tang Anding listens to with her dog on her lap. The Vanguard doesn't sound perfectly familiar with the material herself, tripping over it a few times. Yizhi tells me it's one of many presentations Qin Zheng wrote for the Vanguards to disseminate among their communities.

Qin Zheng was also serious about training the masses to use firearms. After the Vanguard's presentation, the soldier explains the components of a gun and how to handle it. The nervous-looking residents pass an empty gun among themselves, getting chided if they hold it the wrong way. Qin Zheng hasn't revoked the old order's limits on gun ownership, but shooting lessons are now mandatory. In addition to rudimentary introductions like this, everyone will have to go to a military training base at assigned times to practice real shooting. It feels a little absurd, yet, at the thought of what might happen if Qin Zheng suddenly vanishes again, I drop any idea of protesting it.

I spend the ride back through Chang'an wondering how Shimin would've reacted to this revolution. He definitely wouldn't have mourned the old order that crushed his brilliance and resolve at every turn. I can see him becoming a Vanguard and doing outreach sessions, though I'm not sure how he'd feel about Qin Zheng, fire versus ice as they are. I can see them talking for hours about the books they've read, but whether they'd end that discussion as allies or enemies is beyond my guess.

I'm resting my head against my carriage window, daydreaming of leading rallies with Yizhi and Shimin, when Yizhi's and Qieluo's tablets chime at the same time. Qieluo checks hers first with a frown.

Then she goes deathly pale.

"It's the counter-revolutionaries again." She turns her tablet toward me. Three men are on the screen: one at a podium, another on his left, and Zhuge Liang on his right. The rebel White Lotus Flag hangs behind them.

With screeching speed, Yizhi pulls the carriage over to the side of the road.

"Citizens of Huaxia," the man at the podium begins, his words channeling through both Yizhi's and Qieluo's tablet speakers—and maybe more devices across Huaxia? My hand flies to the button that controls my carriage window. The moment I open it a crack, the man's voice echoes from countless directions, carrying on the wind. "I am Kong Zhuxi, a member of the Council of Sages and nephew to the late Chairman Kong." He puts a hand over his heart.

Fuck! A Sage from the old order *survived*?

I fumble my veiled hat over my head and pull my door open. I stumble out onto the busy street. Kong Zhuxi's face is everywhere, speaking in sync on people's handheld devices, on screens mounted in shops, and on displays that stretch down the sides of buildings.

"By chance, I was away from the Palace of Sages during the tragedy that took the lives of my uncle and colleagues. Thus, I escaped unscathed. Through good fortune and a perilous journey, I met up at last with Chief Strategist Zhuge." He gestures at Zhuge Liang. "I share his sentiment of wishing for nothing more than to return to Chang'an to serve His Majesty, but it has become apparent that as long as the wicked thieves Sima Yi and Wu Zetian are whispering falsities in his ear, my life would be forfeit as soon as I showed myself. However, I cannot bear to watch Huaxia descend into madness any longer! I cannot stand by as innocent citizens are robbed of their properties, exemplary men are humiliated and slaughtered on fabricated charges, and the fruits of the hard-working are being pilfered by bandits! These monsters do not spare even our elders!"

Acutely violent scenes of the revolution play while he speaks—including a shot of Ye Xingzhen being pushed along the rally just now, stumbling in her bound feet.

I make an offended noise. "Four hundred million!" I splutter to no one in particular, so incensed I can't form a coherent sentence. "Brothels! Context!"

"Do not believe the wicked thieves' honeyed lies about having the good of the people in mind!" Kong Zhuxi's voice keeps booming through the streets. "They have nothing in their hearts but envy and greed! Their deception runs deep, going as far as to poison His Majesty!"

The feed cuts to a video of Qin Zheng collapsing while coughing up blood at my coronation—footage that was supposed to be erased from existence.

Dread crashes over me like ice water. I turn in a circle, but there is no escape from the secret we tried to bury. It plays out on screens big and small, everywhere my eyes can see.

"Wake up to the truth, citizens!" Kong Zhuxi reappears, his arms held high. "This so-called 'revolution,' these preposterous policies His Majesty was deceived into enacting—they may sound wonderful on paper, but this is reality, where naive fantasies will spell disaster! First they're coming for our best and brightest; next they will come for *you*! No honest man is safe when the lazy and undeserving now have free rein to take your earnings! This terror will not cease. It will plunge us all into ruin, unless we raise the flag of righteousness and banish the wicked from His Majesty's side!"

CHAPTER TWENTY-FOUR

NO WAY TO WIN

"Who leaked the footage?" Qin Zheng slaps the glass wall of his quarantine chamber. The sterile lights overhead cast long shadows under the sharp angles of his face. His scrutiny slashes between me, Yizhi, and Sima Yi.

Yizhi bows, shoulders quivering with tension. "The Gewei Bu will thoroughly investigate the production crew, Your Majesty."

"How do I know *you* were not the culprit?"

A spasm of panic for Yizhi races through me.

"Oh, please, he's the last person who'd leak the footage," I say with feigned calm. "It's *my* blood the reactionaries are calling for. Why would he give them more ammo to push for my execution?"

Qin Zheng paces behind the glass like a prowling predator. After an agonizing silence, he says, "Tell the crew if they do not identify the culprit among themselves, all of their heads will be lopped off and displayed on pikes. And draft an edict for the Ministry of Justice." He snaps his fingers at Yizhi. "From now on, every five neighboring households shall be organized into a collective unit responsible for monitoring each other for counter-revolutionary activities. Those who fail to report the crimes of others in their unit shall be punished along with the culprits. Inversely, those who submit reports with sufficient proof shall be handsomely rewarded."

"Understood, Your Majesty." Yizhi writes with lightning speed on his tablet.

My mouth goes dry. Huaxia has always had extended punishment policies for severe crimes—my family would've been executed with me if I'd murdered Yang Guang in a non-battle circumstance—but this is a new level of intensity. Is this what we have to resort to? The reactionaries' reach is indeed extending further and faster than we expected, and now they have an old order Sage on their side. How can we root them out without using drastic measures?

"How does Your Majesty wish to respond to public concern over the footage?" Sima Yi clasps his hands in deference. "Should we dismiss it as a fake?"

"Would that be believed?"

Yizhi looks up from his tablet. "We could film a recreation of the moment, but with the crowning going right. As long as Her Highness gets fully sanitized and goes in and out of Your Majesty's chamber as quickly as possible, the risk of infection is low. It should be enough to convince most people."

"Most, but not all," Qin Zheng mumbles, looking lost in thought.

"Which is why Her Highness should quit being stubborn and just bear a child for Your Majesty." Sima Yi glares at me from the corners of his eyes. "No amount of posturing on the battlefield will quell public opinion as effectively as becoming a mother."

I choke on my next breath. "How about you worry about your own position first? The reactionaries are calling *you* out, too! Now that there's a surviving Sage, you have no right to be Chairman anymore!"

"And? Do you think I'm in this for power?" Sima Yi says with a whip of his sleeve. "I only want what's good for Huaxia! I'd gladly yield my position to Sage Kong, so long as he turned in the counter-revolutionary leaders. In fact, I'll make a public broadcast stating this! I have no qualms about sacrifice, unlike *Your Highness*."

"Why are you so obsessed with getting me pregnant?" I practically scream at him, though I know it's the gods who are really trying to bring this about.

"Obsessed? I'm being logical! You're the one obsessed with your irrational fears about something your body was made to do, despite it being the easiest defense for your life and position! Some of us *wish* we could sit around with a baby in the belly and let everyone else do the work, but we can't!"

"What reality do you live in that mothers get to *sit around and do nothing*? They only get empty praise for how hard they suffer! Watch how quickly people turn on them when they're anything less than perfect and selfless. And what happens after I give birth? If it's a girl instead of a boy? Will you all drown her with your whining and then force me to try again?"

I think of the age difference between me and my little brother, not even eleven months. A conception before my mother healed from the way I tore her up as I came into existence. My father used to tell me over and over about how other families who shared the "misfortune" of having two daughters in a row would drown the second in a bucket to scare off further female spirits, and how I should call myself lucky that he and my grandparents decided against doing the same.

I wonder if, when their lives flashed behind their eyes as I stared them down in the Yellow Dragon, they regretted that decision more than ever.

"Enough!" Qin Zheng presses his hands to the glass as if he might break it. "Chairman Sima, you will speak to my empress with respect."

Sima Yi bows, a vein throbbing on his forehead. "My apologies, Your Majesty."

"However, it is indeed time to stop being stubborn." Qin Zheng's attention slides over to me.

My skin prickles. A memory intrudes to the front of my mind, of the so-called maidenhood examination I went through when I was first brought to the Great Wall. Of shivering with my legs propped up as an auntie opened me with a cold steel tool and shone a flashlight inside me.

That'll be my fate again as doctors inseminate me.

"What if I faked it?" I blurt.

"Faked it?" Qin Zheng echoes incredulously.

"Your Majesty said your concubines always miscarried, right? So why even put me through that? Let's just *announce* that I'm pregnant so the reactionaries will shut up about me. Then after we root out Zhuge Liang and Kong Zhuxi, we can say I also suffered a tragic miscarriage."

I must admit, some part of me wishes I could be exactly what the reactionaries see me as: a wicked villainess with an emperor as a puppet, doing none of what a woman is supposed to do. Even faking motherhood feels like a concession, an admission that there is no way to win without conforming. But it's a concession preferable to becoming a mother for real. The reactionaries' primary weapon in the war over public opinion has been to blame everything they don't like about what's happening on me. I can't let my pride get in the way of raising the most effective shield I could summon.

Sima Yi smacks his lips. "When we have modern medicine, there's far less chance of you misca—"

"If you put a baby in me for real, I can *guarantee* it won't make it to term," I snap, both to him and to the gods, who are surely listening. "A real pregnancy would affect my ability to pilot, to *generate tribute*." I look to Qin Zheng. "Your Majesty wouldn't want me as the mother to your children. Trust me."

Qin Zheng makes a face like he's tasted something very strange, but then he flashes an even stranger smile. "What do you think of that, Secretary Zhang?"

"I think it's indeed more productive for Her Highness to battle at full capacity than to attempt actual pregnancy at her young age," Yizhi says, with a trace of bitterness I hope only I can hear. "A facade would be enough. Even the hardest of hearts can't stay unmoved by the patriotism of a warrior mother. However, we should still wait a few more weeks before making the announcement. It will backfire if the reactionaries have any parentage doubt to latch on to."

Qin Zheng's smile fades. I almost yell at Yizhi. He needs to stop bringing that up!

"Very well," Qin Zheng says. "Let's announce it after my empress' next battle."

I put my hand to my belly, breathing deeply, harshly.

I'm already telling so many lies to the masses. What's another to gain their love and support?

CHAPTER TWENTY-FIVE

THE WAY TO BE FREE

For the first time in weeks, I sleep alone in the giant round bed in my residence. No Qieluo, Wan'er, or Qin Zheng in the same room. I couldn't bear to lie down next to him for another training session after filming the fake crowning. I had to get misted with antiseptic and injected with some kind of anti-microbe serum before stepping inside his quarantine chamber to kneel to him. There's a limit to how much I can tolerate of him in one day.

Sleep doesn't come easily, too many thoughts warring in my head. As I toss and turn in the red sheets, a soothing glow comes to my side.

"Tian-Tian . . ." Big Sister, luminous as the moon, sits on the edge of the bed beneath its translucent silk drapes. She brushes my hair away from my face.

I don't know if I'm dreaming.

I don't care.

"*Jiějiě*—" I grasp her hand, my voice breaking. "Take me with you."

She gives a slow shake of head. "You can't come yet, Tian-Tian. There's so much you need to fix. Why are you letting them send girls to the battlefield without a choice?"

Something twists in my chest. My grip on her hand goes slack. "Because boys don't get a choice, so we'll never be as respected as them if we don't play by the same rules."

"Since when did rules matter to you?"

"They matter to the public, and that's who needs convincing! It's not like I can get them to magically see girls in a new light without shoving a big change in front of them!" I clutch my face, dragging a breath in and out of my lungs. Then I say, more calmly, "Girls getting to command Chrysalises again is at least a huge step forward. Being held to the same standard of conscription as boys means being recognized as just as capable. Really, the draft exempting us was another way of saying we're weak. Which we aren't."

"Is strength all that matters, Tian-Tian? Only three percent of people have Chrysalis-capable spirit pressures. How does this help the ninety-seven percent of women and girls who don't?"

My mind goes blank for a few seconds. "They'll be . . . inspired. It's always better to see more women with power."

Her eyes turn sad. "Is this really what you want? To take more choices away from girls instead of letting them live by their own wishes?"

"They're not living by their own wishes to begin with! Now, at least these girls won't be stuck in a house somewhere, pumping out babies over and over!"

"Tian-Tian, not every girl wants to make the same decisions as you. There are those who would like nothing more than to be a mother and care for a family. Me, for example. You know I would've been happy with a simple life. Would you make it wrong for women to want that?"

"You're dead because you cared too much about our family!"

"No, Tian-Tian. I'm dead because I was murdered by a young man who got away with too much. I was not the one in the wrong for sacrificing for those I love. Won't you make a world where I wouldn't have been punished for who I was? Or will you only free the women who think and act the exact way you do?"

"Maybe that's all I can do! And it's hard enough as it is! I'm not some all-powerful savior; leave me alone!" I turn over and curl up under my covers.

Big Sister puts her hand over my shoulder, then presses a kiss to my head. "The way to free women isn't by demanding they adapt to the traits men are praised for. Please remember that, Tian-Tian."

It's a long while before I dare to look back. By then, she's gone.

CHAPTER TWENTY-SIX

TO HOLD UP HALF THE WORLD

With my ceremonial scythe in hand, I stand before a line of seven girls in the palace's central courtyard, where I first gazed upon Gao Qiu and his party guests a lifetime ago. It's surreal to think those people are all either dead, destitute, or on the run now. The buildings around three sides of the courtyard have been converted to government offices.

A stinking breeze sweeps my cape against my armor and stirs the white-hemmed black pilot coats the seven girls are wearing. They stand at rigid attention, pressing their palms against the sides of their legs. We collectively ignore the rotting odor hitting in waves from the severed heads impaled on the roofs. None of the production crew confessed to leaking the footage, so Qin Zheng followed through with his threat to execute them all. I can't believe how stubborn the reactionaries are, that they would rather drag their innocent colleagues into death with them than fess up and lead us to Zhuge Liang. Are they *that* determined to topple Huaxia into civil war so people like Gao Qiu and Ye Xingzhen can make the masses their playthings again?

While my fake crowning looks decently realistic, no amount of denouncing the leaked footage can erase the doubt it must've planted in many minds. A breach like that cannot happen again.

The empty stares of the rotting heads don't dissuade some of the girls from beaming with pride. They range from pale to tanned, from half my height to towering over me, from the daughter of fruit merchants to the daughter of a mid-level official. What they have in common are their Chrysalis-capable spirit pressures. They are the first girls conscripted in Chang'an after Qin Zheng extended the criteria beyond boys.

They are the future Iron Widows I'll be shaping into my most powerful supporters.

The days of Chang'an being a hotbed of conscription-dodging are gone. All families with children ages twelve and above have been ordered to report to testing centers to get their spirit pressure values recorded. Off-duty pilots stand by during the tests, activating their spirit senses to ensure the values are accurate. No more paying off testing teams to jot down fake values.

I grip my scythe tighter to keep myself upright for the cameras around the courtyard, operated by a new, carefully selected production team to capture this historic moment. The Empress of Huaxia, speaking to the first girls in modern memory to be conscripted as commanding pilots. Until my fake pregnancy can be announced, I'll have to survive on these grand displays of war contribution.

"My sisters!" I address the girls. "For far too long, you were told that your place is in the home and out of the public eye, and thus you could not join the war effort unless it was in service of a male pilot. This was a blatant, counterproductive lie by the old order to mask its own failures. Such divisions have no place in war! Your tests revealed that you are strong, and that you are more than capable of commanding your own Chrysalises, just like the female pilots they called Iron Widows two centuries ago. Tell Huaxia your spirit pressure values, sisters!"

One by one, the girls call out their numbers while giving a raised-fist salute.

"Five hundred and thirty-five!"

"Five hundred and eighty-nine!"

"Six hundred and twenty-four!"

"Seven hundred and fifteen!"

"Eight hundred and forty-two!"

"Eight hundred and eighty!"

There's a lull before the final girl reports hers. Full-figured and lovely with a wide round face, a small mouth, and slightly downturned eyes, she basks in the moment. Then she takes a deep breath and raises her fist.

"Three thousand four hundred and sixty-three!"

The clicking of camera shutters intensifies. I can imagine the exclamations across Huaxia. Crossing the two-thousand threshold means she'll enter the army as an Iron Noble. An Iron Countess, specifically.

The girl regards me with such bright intensity I almost can't bear to meet her eyes. I must mean something to her. In the same way Qieluo's existence comforted me before I became a pilot, this girl must've seen me on broadcasts and felt a resonance within herself. Guilt eats at me, a feeling of having deceived her. Power is not as easy to wield as it looks on camera.

"What is your name, sister?" I ask.

"Liang Yuhuan, Your Highness!"

"Welcome to the ranks of the Iron Nobles, Countess-Sergeant Liang." I return her raised-fist salute. "The fact that the old order would have let you languish is why they never won the war. In this new era, let us show how women can hold up half the world!"

Wrongness burns the back of my throat. These aren't women. They're girls. None of them understand the carnage that awaits them on the battlefield.

But at least they'll have their own Chrysalises. At least they won't have to serve a man, won't have to leave their lives in his hands. Whatever fate they run into, at least they'll have some power to steer it.

When I lift my chin, keeping my fist raised and trying to look invincible for the cameras, I swear I see a ghostly figure beyond the courtyard, shaking her head before vanishing like windblown mist.

CHAPTER TWENTY-SEVEN

PIECES LEFT BEHIND

While staying in Chang'an for my qì-recuperation period, I avoid being alone with my thoughts as much as possible.

In the evenings, after my lessons from Wan'er—eight hours max, as per laborist principles—Taiping joins us for dinner with a big grin and an agenda to piss Wan'er off. She seems to really enjoy the sight of Wan'er flushed with anger. While we were at the front, Taiping got her own foot-reconstruction surgery in between annoying Wan'er with messages, so she's using a wheelchair as well. Her feet weren't technically "bound," but surgically amputated years ago, diagonally, from her big toes to her heels. That's how rich girls achieve the Lotus Foot look, with much less permanent pain and risk of infection.

Well. It's how they *used to* achieve the look. The same cosmetic surgeons that did those procedures now reverse them with prosthetics at no charge to the girls. The government pays them much less than what they used to fleece from rich folk, but they don't complain. They don't dare.

Although Taiping doesn't wear silk anymore, she wasn't afraid to be sarcastic about the revolution the first few times she visited us. That changes when, one day, she shows up blank-faced and wearing a yellow sash around her waist, like the revolution's most fervent supporters in the streets. She greets us with a raised-fist salute and stays rather quiet through the whole dinner.

It takes me some prodding to find out that Gewei Bu agents arrested one of her friends. Qin Zheng was serious about grouping every five households into a Mutual Responsibility Unit and collectively punishing them for any crimes. Taiping's friend failed to alert the government that her neighbors were missing for over forty-eight hours. Likely, they fled Chang'an without a permit to join a counter-revolutionary cell.

"I can't." I shake my head when Taiping hints at whether I can get her friend a pardon. "It wouldn't be fair to everyone who doesn't have connections to an empress. We're not supposed to be like that anymore. She knew she was expected to watch her neighbors, yet now they're off with their money to do heaven-knows-what against the revolution. People need to take their duties more seriously, or the reactionaries will run rampant. Haven't you been keeping up with what's happening?"

The reactionaries have gotten bolder since Kong Zhuxi showed up. The approval of a Sage has made them feel more legitimate. Guns have gone missing from armories. Factory workers who've reported their bosses for abuse have found their equipment mysteriously broken. Rail tracks have been smashed, and roads have been blown up to prevent goods from reaching cities.

Taiping sighs. "I guess."

"She'll be fine," I say, gentler. "The revolutionary tribunals see cases way worse than hers every day. They'll probably just take all her money and sentence her to community service."

Taiping winces at the mention of money confiscation, but mumbles, "I hope so."

Honestly, no one should be relying on *me* to rein in this revolution. Whatever concerns can be raised, Qin Zheng has talked through a dozen times with his officials.

I focus on my own goals, checking up on the new Iron Widows every day through Wan'er. The Chang'an conscripts have been dispersed across different frontiers. I'd go visit them, except I haven't learned enough from Qin Zheng yet to come off as a good mentor figure. I head to the throne room every night to remedy this.

It's almost become a game between us to see who can hold off going to sleep for longer. Unfortunately, my battle-exhausted qì makes it harder to win.

What's infuriating is that Qin Zheng may sleep at unearthly hours, but he always gets up at dawn for the morning assembly—without waking me up as well, no matter how much I demand it.

"You need your rest," he says, as if *he* isn't in danger of having another stroke at any moment. Fucking hypocrite.

I cannot describe how disconcerting it is to startle awake to the sound of a hundred officials yelling at each other about employment programs. If the side section I sleep in couldn't tint itself opaque from the outside, they'd be leering and laughing at me every morning.

There's also something worse that happens whenever Qin Zheng fades out of a dream realm without me, something I can never admit to him. When I'm not connected to him, nightmares descend on me like monsters given free rein after being held back and starved. Buildings crumbling, Hunduns shattering, people screaming. Those I've killed, those I've failed. My mother, my grandmother, Xiuying. Big Sister. Shimin.

Shimin's memories make up their own class of haunting. Over and over, I'm trapped in the cramped apartment I know by instinct to be his, the home where he grew up with his father and brothers until the day everything shattered into a *before* and an *after*. The discolored walls and narrow rooms warp and shrink, crushing me alive. No matter how I scour its same few rooms, I can never find a way out. Those violent moments that ended the life Shimin had known and began his passage from cage to cage, they come to me again and again, almost seeming to call to me.

And so I answer the call. I decide to visit the apartment for real. Even if it doesn't ward off the nightmares, it'll strengthen my spiritual connection to him, which will help me hunt down the Heavenly Court. None of the misery to do with the war will end, in any way or another, until I end the gods.

Shimin's hometown of Longxi is a three-hour carriage ride from Chang'an. I would've liked to have gone alone with Yizhi, but Qin Zheng refuses to let me leave the palace without Qieluo as a bodyguard.

Our carriage splashes over rain-drenched highways, weaving automatically between heavy-duty trucks transporting goods. But partway there, the trucks ahead slow to a stop in a long, congested lane.

"What's going on?" I peer through the front window, being cleared continuously by thumping rain wipers. In the distance, a column of smoke rises against the stormy sky.

Frowning in his Wan'er disguise, Yizhi scrolls on his tablet, occasionally writing with his stylus. After a while, he sighs. "A bomb went off in a truck ahead."

"Oh." I blink.

Qieluo groans. "Not again."

Even with the threat of collective punishment exposing many schemes against the revolution, the reactionaries still find ways to strike.

"How far is it?" I touch my door handle.

"You want to go there?" Qieluo whirls toward me.

"Are you joking? I can't miss this photo op!"

We put on our cloaks and veiled hats for the trek, with Qieluo pushing me in my wheelchair. Once we reach the burning truck, I reveal myself as the empress to the soldiers already on the scene, give some encouraging small talk to the paramedics tending to the injured, and yell about how the reactionaries want us all to starve while Yizhi films me on his tablet and Qieluo watches for threats in the crowd around the perimeter. Since the reactionaries insist on slandering me at every opportunity, it's only fair I repay the favor. Unlike them, I'm not even lying.

"This is what they do to the food our hardworking farmers toil for!" I shove a handful of charred rice toward the camera. All the disruptions and sabotage have forced us to impose purchase limits on staple foods to ensure there's enough to go around.

It's an unwitting reminder that no matter how well I improve my ability to sense Shimin's spirit signature, we need to take out the likes of Zhuge Liang and Kong Zhuxi before we challenge the gods, or the revolution will fall apart right after we go. And I don't know how we're supposed to defeat them if not by being as ruthless as possible.

After riling up the crowd with cries of "The revolution will persist!" we end up reaching Longxi two hours later than planned. Once we enter the city, an implausible feeling of recognition thrums stronger and stronger within me. It's less overcrowded than Chang'an, with shorter buildings and fewer neon signs competing for attention, their shining shapes hazy through the carriage's rain-streaked windows. Legions of motorbikers weave through the sopping streets in raincoats. Small shops and restaurants operate with their lights on in the storm's dimness.

You've been here before, every sight and sound seems to murmur to me. *Don't you remember?*

I find myself understanding signs with characters I haven't learned to read yet, recognizing stores I had no concept of before. The only sights that ground me in the present are the revolution's impacts. A slogan-filled poster of Qin Zheng shining at a bus stop here, a smashed-up jewelry store there.

When I first proposed this trip, Yizhi did some research and discovered that Shimin's family apartment is no longer inhabited. Which is good, since it means we don't need to barge into an occupied home. The bad news is the reason it's not occupied is because the property firm that used to manage the building turned it into a tourist attraction. Apparently, there's a steady stream of people eager to pay to see Li Shimin the Iron Demon's Original Crime Scene.

"My ladies, I want to stress that very little of the stuff in there is original," Yizhi says once we park beneath the infamous building. "They did a deep clean after the ... incident ... and rented it out again at first. It was only after Shi—I mean, after Pilot Li got drafted into the army that they turned it into a tourist thing. The blood, the kitchen knives, it's all fake."

"The *blood*?" Qieluo questions while hauling my folded wheelchair out of the carriage.

"They tried very hard to recreate the spectacle," Yizhi mutters.

I can hardly bear to keep my eyes open during the elevator ride up to the fifth floor, overwhelmed as I am by a swooping ache of nostalgia. If Qieluo wasn't pushing my wheelchair, I doubt I could've made it into the hallway.

"Your Highness, are you sure you want to go in?" Yizhi thumbs the key in his hand when we get to apartment 502.

I suddenly realize I failed to consider this from Yizhi's perspective. He doesn't have a link to Shimin's memories. To him, this place is a plain mockery.

"Do *you*?" I look up into Yizhi's eyes, even though he won't meet mine in return.

He bows his head lower. "Whatever will help Your Highness."

In my heart, I promise to tell him about every memory that came to me on this trip the next time we're alone.

None of my nightmares prepared me adequately for Yizhi unlocking the door. The moment I lay eyes on Shimin's apartment for real, my head spins, experiencing it from multiple points in time.

The first pool of fake blood is right outside the kitchen, poured over a white-taped outline of a person on the floor tiles. Simultaneously, I see the real sequence of Shimin's father chasing him with a cleaver and slashing him in the chest, then Shimin striking back with his own knife. He was aiming for the arm, yet the blade sank into his father's chest. Afterwards, nobody would believe it wasn't intentional. His father didn't bleed out so cleanly in one place, either. As Shimin frantically tried to help him, he swung his fist into Shimin's jaw. Then he teetered after Shimin, cursing, collapsing, crawling, before finally falling still near the balcony. The forgery pales in comparison to the blood that actually splattered and smeared everywhere.

But beyond the horror, I also see softer, more mundane moments. At the kitchen sink, Shimin's father teaches a toddler Shimin how to scrub chopsticks by rolling them as a bundle between his palms. At the dinner table, Shimin and his brothers laugh and fight with their food as their father half-heartedly scolds them. At the tattered living room couch, Shimin's father relents and plays Shimin's favorite childhood story on the family tablet for the countless time. Much later, in the same spot, he brags to his liquor-drinking friends about Shimin's reading level and tries to figure out a way to send Shimin to a good school.

I'm scarcely conscious of rolling my wheelchair into the middle of the apartment, or how Yizhi is fumbling with the switches near the door, which have turned on eerie shifting lights and creepy music. When I catch sight of a particular bedroom door beyond a corner, it's all I can focus on. The turn is too narrow for my wheelchair to make, so I push to my feet and totter there, bracing one hand against the faded wallpaper. I hear echoes of a girl's muffled screaming behind the door. When I grasp its handle, visions of Shimin's trembling hand flicker over mine. We turn it together with the same tense dread, three years apart in time.

White tape marks out two more bloody outlines in the tight space between a bunk bed and a loft bed suspended over a desk. A fierce struggle flashes behind my eyes. Limbs grappling, a head cracking against a metal bed frame, a knife plunging through flesh and bone. My mind sways. My knees buckle. I drop myself onto the bunk bed's bottom mattress.

"Ze—" Yizhi's hand flies out, but he quickly retracts it. I didn't even notice him following me in.

"I'm okay," I say. "I'm just—"

Blood blooms beneath my armored hand on the bed. It's spreading from Shimin's older brother Jiancheng, half draped over the bed, choking and gasping.

I shake my head. The blood and body vanish.

"You know what?" Qieluo says rather loudly from the doorway. "I've seen enough of this nonsense. Your Highness can take your time, but I'm going to keep watch outside."

She turns around, though casts me a knowing look over her shoulder. I give her a nod in gratitude.

After the metallic crash of her closing the front door behind herself, Yizhi sits down on the bunk bed as well, though as far from me as possible. I lay my hand in the gap between us, dreaming of him taking it without consequences.

"Is Your Highness sure you're all right?" His voice drops out of its feminine disguise. "It's not any bad reaction to the shots?"

"Oh." My hand goes to my hip. He must be worrying about the injections Doctor Hua is making me get every day to keep me as clear of pathogens as possible. A safety precaution for filming more footage with Qin Zheng. "It's fine. Well—I'm not sure. I don't remember what it's like to feel good and normal, so how can I tell what's a symptom of the shots and what's a symptom of . . . existing?"

Rain patters against the bedroom window, dashing speckles of shadows over us.

"I'm sorry," Yizhi says.

"No, no, don't be," I say. "I wish you could see what I can see. The real things that happened here, beyond the murders. The ordinary stuff."

I see Shimin sitting at the desk, writing on his school-loaned tablet, determined to finish an essay despite his older brother throwing rice crackers at his head. I see them laughing at a video together with their youngest brother. I hear the drawl of their nonsensical tangents of conversation as they lie in bed, deep in the night. So many moments in three lives, overlapping in one room.

"I have my own ways to see." Yizhi takes out his tablet. "There are some pictures I want to show you, ones I got from a few of Shimin's relatives."

"He still has family alive?"

"Some distant ones. They were easy to track down with my access to the state databases. It was also easy to get them to hand over pictures when I sent the demand as a notice from the Gewei Bu."

"You are *so* abusing your power."

A brief grin slips past Yizhi's cautious facade. I etch it into my mind, not knowing the next time I might see him smile. I scoot closer to him as he flicks through windows on his screen.

"Is that Shimin with long hair?" I gasp. Seeing a picture of it is different from knowing it through his memories, like looking into a mirror for the first time. Here, his face is much softer and his chin has yet to show any capacity for stubble, but it's undeniably Shimin. He appears about twelve or thirteen, his long hair half up in a style like the one Yizhi used to wear, though no one would mistake him for Yizhi. He's in an ill-fitting robe, the fabric scrunched up near his backpack, and he's standing awkwardly in front of the entrance to his school.

"Yeah, that was his first day at Longxi High School," Yizhi says.

He further explains the context of each picture while swiping through them. Shimin at a sports festival, squinting against the sun. Him holding a trophy he won for his calligraphy. Him jutting out in the back of a group photo with his class. Him standing beside a strikingly handsome older man.

"That's an uncle of his, Li Zhi, who gave me most of these photos," Yizhi says. "He was the only relative of Shimin who still had nice things to say about him."

I zoom in on Li Zhi. I'm not sure why he transfixes me so much. I guess we're pilot in-laws in a way, though thinking about him as such would probably send Qin Zheng into a homicidal rage.

"He should've come to our Match Crowning," I remark.

"If only. But I think he would've had a hard time with the rest of his family if he'd been invited." Yizhi swipes to the next picture.

As we continue through the gallery, one thing becomes clear: Shimin has never been comfortable getting photographed.

"Sorry—" I can't help but laugh at a photo from a Li family trip to a peach orchard, where Shimin's brothers are posing like they think they're cool but Shimin is looking wide-eyed at the camera with clearly no idea what to do with his arms.

"It's okay, I understand." Yizhi nods gravely, eyes squeezed shut. "I love him, but his sense of style is a tragedy, and the wrong camera angles commit actual crimes against his image. Thank heavens he was so much better-looking in person."

"Not everyone spends as much time in front of a mirror figuring out their optimal angles as you, Zhang Yizhi."

"I could say the same to Your Highness."

"Hey, I only started practicing my posing for political purposes!"

We laugh together for the first time in an eternity. Yizhi places his hand beside mine on the bed.

"I miss him," he whispers.

"Me too," I say, bending my head close to his, but not touching. "It's not fair."

"It never has been."

The sound of rain fills the silence where Shimin once existed. It's incredible, how someone could be gone from this world, literally whisked away from the mortal earth, yet leave so many pieces behind. Including me and Yizhi.

I'm not scared of Qin Zheng seeing this moment in my memories. Even if he did, I doubt he'd understand the depth of it.

CHAPTER TWENTY-EIGHT

LIAISONS

In the mornings, Shimin is always the first to wake, diligent as the sun. He untangles from me and Yizhi, brews a pot of tea, and reads in the peace and quiet before we disrupt it with our antics. When he hears me and Yizhi bullying each other to get out of bed, he turns on the stove and makes breakfast, usually noodles or porridge. By the time Yizhi and I finally drag ourselves out, the food is ready. We thank Shimin in kisses.

There comes a thumping at our front door, though I'm the only one who can hear it. Ignoring it, I continue to laugh and eat with Yizhi and Shimin. Something terrible will happen if I acknowledge the sound. I just know.

Once we finish our food, Yizhi does the dishes while I wipe down the table. I smile when Shimin wraps his arms around Yizhi at the sink and kisses Yizhi on the head. I keep smiling despite the persistent pounding at the door—

Cracks splinter across the floor, the walls, the windows.

"No!" I cover my ears as the pounding gets louder, shaking the entire apartment.

There's the sound of something shattering. Shimin stumbles away from Yizhi, red patches of blood blooming over his clothes. Lines like molten lava fracture across his skin.

"Stop!" I exclaim. With impossibly painless steps, I spring out of my wheelchair and wrench open the front door. "*What do you want?*"

The instant I recognize the face in the doorway, disappointment crushes me. Because if *he*'s here, none of this is real.

"Enough indulging in fantasies." Qin Zheng leans his elbow against the door frame. "We have work to—"

Footsteps storm up behind me.

Shimin swings a punch into Qin Zheng's face. Qin Zheng collides with the wall outside, grappling for balance.

My mouth hangs open.

Bracing against the wall with one hand and clutching his cheek with the other, Qin Zheng looks as bewildered as when I brought him back to life and told him he'd overslept for two centuries. Shimin remains at my side, fists clenched.

"Impossible," Qin Zheng utters. "This . . . hurts."

I break into a cold laugh. "Good."

Disgruntled, he straightens himself. "I suppose it bodes well for our mission when your connection to him is strong enough to create such a vivid apparition."

I'm stung by the reminder that, no matter how solid this Shimin feels, he isn't real. I take his hand and run my thumb over his scarred knuckles, cherishing his dream-conjured warmth one last time. How I wish I could shut off the rest of my mind and live in this fantasy . . .

But the real Shimin is out there among the stars, and I must return to reality to have a chance of freeing him from his torment.

"Thank you," I whisper almost soundlessly.

The apparition of Shimin glowers at Qin Zheng, then gazes down at me with a wet shine in his eyes. If the real Shimin learned what's become of me, he'd no doubt look at me with this same expression.

"I'll be all right." I squeeze his hands before letting go.

I don't look back as I step through the doorway to join Qin Zheng, who's still rubbing his cheek in astonishment.

"He could *not* have been that tall," he mutters.

"Well, he was."

"I'll have you know, I was above average height for my time. Our nutrition was poorer back then."

"I didn't say anything about you."

In every training session, Qin Zheng bends my mind a different way, challenging me to rethink my perspectives on everything from reality to consciousness to matter. My progress comes in small bursts, shifting the dense Earth-type spirit metal of my armor a little more each day. I get a pottery wheel and learn to sculpt clay in real life to practice making constructs. I'm nowhere close to Qin Zheng's ability to manipulate it like mercury, but he has over a decade of piloting experience on me. There's no catching up except with patience.

"So far, you have relied on the sheer size of your Chrysalises to win battles," Qin Zheng says in one particular session, manifesting a training ground between brick buildings. "That is rather graceless. With more refined combat techniques, you could use your qì more efficiently. It is easy to crush whole cities with a powerful Chrysalis, but that tends to unite your enemies in outrage and invite allied retaliation on your people. In my time, the better strategy was often to sneak into the enemy's bases and take out specific targets. Behold, this is the Yellow Dragon armor's assault mode."

He gets into a battle stance and forms a sword in his double-handed grip. His bead-curtain crown melts into a helmet with the rough, rippled texture of a dragon's head. It extends in flaps down to his shoulders, protecting his neck. Antlers sprout out from its top, sloping back from his forehead. Guard plates slam together in front of his face, leaving only a narrow gap for his eyes.

Without warning, he lunges at me. I yelp as his sword slashes across my torso, leaving a gouge in my armor.

"*Keep up,*" he growls.

I have no weapon, and forging one is as hard as it is in real life when we're in a dream scene grounded in memory. I scuttle backwards, blocking his strikes with my gauntlets while reaching for my Water qì, necessary for morphing out constructs. I remind myself of its icy, fluid feeling—the sensation that guides me to it every time I practice channeling different qì types.

Qin Zheng's irises beam silver in the shadow of his helmet. The same radiance spreads along the edge of his sword. His next swing, sharpened by Metal qì, hacks through my arm, hitting bone. Blood bursts from the gash, drawing a hiss out of me.

He backs me against a building and drives his sword all the way through my torso. The blade wedges into the brick wall behind me.

I cry out from a detonation of pain. I grab his shoulder guard with one hand and his sword with the other to keep him from thrusting it deeper inside me. The blade cuts through my gauntlets and into my hands. Blood dribbles from my grasp. The awareness that this isn't real does nothing to shake the dream realm's binding effects.

"I could kill you over and over," Qin Zheng murmurs, his shielded face almost touching mine, his eyes half-lidded with an odd tenderness.

Of course he enjoys this. Sick bastard.

He twists his sword. I bite back another scream, refusing to give him the satisfaction of hearing it.

Laughter rolls low in his throat. "How does it feel, knowing you can never best me in anything?"

Venomous hatred courses through me. I imagine it darkening into the black of Water qì.

His shoulder guard softens in my hand. I pry it off while stretching it into a weapon. It breaks free, crooked and uneven, but good enough for stabbing his neck. I sharpen it with my naturally dominant Metal qì and puncture his neck guard. He lurches back, pulling his sword out of me. Blood gushes from my wound. I ignore the illusion and keep going at him with my crude blade.

Summoning what little I can of Earth qì, I reinforce the blade so his counterstrikes don't sever it.

"That's it!" he shouts while parrying my frenzied attacks. "Remember this feeling, this clarity of purpose, and learn to channel it!"

My snarl loosens. I meet his sword with slightly less ferocity, feeling like I've been swindled into improving.

I always wake up from dream training feeling as if my mind has been shredded apart and then crammed back into my skull. Too often, I find myself pausing in the middle of a moment and questioning if it's real. It's hard to keep track when everything I feel in reality can be replicated in a dream realm. There are but a few reliable differentiators: If Qin Zheng can touch me, it's not real. If my body aches after a few moves, it's real.

There's been a learning curve to balancing on my new feet. My hips and legs burn from using slightly different muscles. While I have to admit I feel a lot less pain in each step, I don't think I'll ever be entirely free of it. I practice walking without my scythe or spirit armor in case I have to go without either, and I spar with Qieluo to build muscle memory for the combat techniques Qin Zheng teaches me. I can keep decently steady by expanding the soles of my armor and maintaining a wide stance. I'll never be an impressive fighter in my human body, but I can sure make it as difficult as possible for someone to hurt me.

Throughout my jam-packed schedule of lessons and training, the ultimate goal of taking down the gods and freeing Shimin never stops thrumming in the back of my mind. The big problem is how to get Taiping and her math skills in on the plan without alerting the gods. Her spirit pressure definitely can't sustain a dream realm with me, and randomly asking her to go down to the tunnels with me would scream "Suspicious Activity!"

Though ... not if the gods think we're doing *something else*.

I begin to give her long looks during our dinners, touching her arm more than necessary. I laugh too hard at her jokes. I take a set of bedding down to the tunnels along with a bag of supplies, throwing in pen and paper as if as an afterthought.

Once Taiping is okay to leave her wheelchair for short periods—her surgery was easier to heal from than mine since it involved no bone remodeling—I coyly lead her down the rickety elevator to the tunnels one night, telling her I want to show her something.

"Y-your Highness," she stammers when she sees the bedding. "I am very sorry, it's not that I don't find you attractive, but I cannot in good conscience be with you when you are so much younger, not to mention you used to date my baby brother, which is *way too weird*—"

I give a vigorous shake of head and put a silencing finger to my lips. I'm pretty sure the gods can't see so deep into the ground, but I'm still paranoid they could hear us. Sound travels far in the tunnels. As Taiping stands in awkward confusion, I dig the pen and paper out of the bedding and get to the ground to write *NEED MATH HELP*.

"Is that . . . a euphemism?" She raises a brow.

I gesture harsher for her to be silent, then I write *TOP SECRET MATH. CANNOT TELL YOU WHAT FOR. YOUR LIFE DANGER.*

Her expression shifts into a different breed of concern. She sits down and waits for me to elaborate.

With clumsy writing, I explain the calculations we need and that they must be done without digital devices. In our last dream session, Qin Zheng conjured a diagram consisting of our planet, the Heavenly Court orbiting around it, and the Yellow Dragon, accompanied by giant numbers with units I don't really understand. He made me copy the diagram over and over in the dream realm, literally several hundred times, until I could produce every line and digit from memory.

I replicate them for Taiping now. I don't explicitly tell her our goal is to ambush the gods, but judging by the way all color leaves her face, she has a good guess.

IMPORTANT, I write. *MUST DO FOR FREEDOM.*

I circle *FREEDOM* several times.

Taiping shuts her eyes, chest rising and falling with weighty breaths. Then she nods.

She gets to work on my pad of paper, scrawling calculations while frowning at my diagram.

I'm not aware of dozing off against the tunnel wall until she wakes me up several hours later, looking frazzled, sitting among a mess of ink-filled pages. She hands over her own set of numbers and amendments to the diagram, with many question marks and a written list of things she needs clarification on.

Sneaking the papers to Qin Zheng would be too suspicious, so I once again copy the contents until they're burned into my memory, then I rush over to the throne room to relay them in our dream realm.

Like this, he and Taiping communicate via me across several nights, talking about concepts I pass on without fully comprehending, having debates across the boundaries of reality. Especially about something to do with "matching velocity."

IF YOU DO NOT MATCH THE HORIZONTAL VELOCITY, YOU WILL BE VAPORIZED UPON CONTACT, Taiping writes in huge, bold characters.

The debate ends with Qin Zheng relenting to change the Yellow Dragon's projected trajectory from straight up to diagonal.

I hope the gods don't read too much into this pattern of me spending the first half of my evenings with Taiping and the latter half with Qin Zheng. I hope they're merely entertained by my salaciousness.

The only person I wish didn't misunderstand my liaisons is Wan'er. She had a decent streak of being less harsh on Taiping following her friend's arrest, but after I started fake-flirting with Taiping, she became utterly different around us, too stiff and formal. Finally, I can't stand it anymore and take her along to the tunnels one night so we can tell her it's not what she thinks. That it's too dangerous for her to know exactly what we're doing, but it's nothing decadent.

When Wan'er looks up in astonishment from the paper Taiping wrote this down on, I go farther down the tunnels to give them some privacy to sort things out. I know too well what it's like to be forced to keep a distance from someone you treasure, despite seeing them every day. I can't do the same to them.

I can't help but look over my shoulder every so often. With distance, they become shadowy figures scribbling on a piece of paper they pass back and forth, faster and faster, until Wan'er balls it up and chucks it at Taiping. Taiping surges forward, seizing Wan'er by the wrists. Their silhouettes meet at the mouths.

I turn around very quickly.

A wide grin pushes onto my face, but I also feel a hollow ache in my heart, mourning how I can no longer have the same.

As my recuperation period reaches its end, counting down to when I'll have to head to the war front again, I somehow feel worse than when I was qì-exhausted by battle. One early morning I wake up with the worst nausea I've ever felt and a pinching pain low in my belly. I mean to climb out of bed but end up tumbling to the floor.

"Empress?" Qin Zheng sits up under his covers and palms the glass between us, his shoulders traced out by the barest hint of blue light from the throne room's paper windows. "Are you all right?"

When I let out nothing but a weak groan, Qin Zheng lunges to press an intercom on his wall. "Send in a physician! Quickly!"

I pull myself up by my bed frame, but can't do anything more than rest my throbbing head against the cool metal. Qin Zheng throws on his black robe and marches to the front of his chamber. He gives the glass a frustrated slap, then paces back to the intercom to call for a physician again. After he does so, he leans over his bed, his knees on the mattress, and thumps his fist on the glass divider between us.

"Speak to me," he demands. "What symptoms do you feel?"

My mind is too cloudy. Speaking is too difficult.

"Empress!" He pounds the glass twice more.

I resign myself to the idea of spending the rest of the day in this spot, half draped over my bed. But, seconds later, there's a metallic clatter, followed by the hiss of pressure unsealing.

Qin Zheng slides open the door in the glass divider and storms toward me.

"*Whatthefuck*—" I scramble backwards across the white-tiled floor, shielding my nose and mouth. Has he lost his mind? Even with the shots I'm getting, there's no guarantee I'm not carrying a disease he has no immunity to. "Stay away! I could kill you!"

His momentum hitches, but he drops to one knee in front of me, hand splayed on the ground.

"Tell me what's wrong," he insists, half shadowed in the thin dawn light.

I breathe too quickly against my palm. His proximity charges every fiber in my body to full alert. It reminds me of a time I was sure I heard a tiger growl in the woods near my village, how I stood paralyzed against a tree, mind blanking on what to do. I was supposed to be safe on this side of the glass, beyond his reach, no matter how close he pressed.

"I'm . . ." I shift awkwardly, feeling a dreaded wetness between my legs that suddenly explains a lot. "I think my bleeding's come early."

Qin Zheng goes still. Several expressions twitch past his face before he says, "I see."

The sound of rapid, muffled footsteps approaches from outside the throne room.

"Go back!" I grab a spray bottle of rubbing alcohol from a cabinet behind me and spritz him several times.

He recoils against the stringent mist like a disgruntled cat, but slips back into his chamber and seals the door just as Doctor Hua races in with a few staffers, shouting apologies for the delay.

"Tend to her." Qin Zheng gives a flick of his hand and leans backward against the glass he shouldn't have breached, as if he couldn't care less what happened to me.

CHAPTER TWENTY-NINE

IRON WIDOWS

Doctor Hua determines that the anti-microbial shots wreaked havoc on my body. I breathe a sigh of relief when he discontinues them. With that layer of precaution gone, maybe Qin Zheng will think thrice before coming through that divider again.

Since I'm sick, I put off returning to the war front past a typical recuperation period, but soon the compounding crises in the Han province get too acute to ignore.

"The storm season has come to the south, Your Majesty," Sima Yi says in front of the quarantine chamber one morning, showing an image on his tablet that features a swirl of vivid colors over the Huaxia coastline. "The venerated gods above are warning us about a once-in-a-generation super-typhoon on course for the Han frontier. The pilots will need all the support they can get."

Qin Zheng peers at me across the glass divider. "Do you feel well enough, empress?"

Sitting at the foot of my bed, I drum my fingers on my knee. I could lie.

But what kind of example would I be setting for the newly conscripted girls? How could I convince them to respect and follow me if I'm avoiding a war *they* don't get to run from? Not to mention that this typhoon does sound like a serious threat. The Han province has been plagued with the strongest reactionary activities. We cannot risk anything when it comes to it.

"Yes," I say. "I'll go."

With a look I can't quite decipher, Qin Zheng rests his hand against the glass. "Are you sure?"

I hitch in surprise that he would ask. Then it hits me—is he doubting my ability to battle properly after last time?

"Yes, I can handle it." I push to my feet, decently healed now that it's been almost two months since the surgery. "Your Majesty doesn't need to keep telling me how important it is."

It's his turn to look taken aback. Instead of recovering with some smug comment, he blinks, eyes flicking aside. It's a strange reaction, but I'm guessing he's distracted, thinking about how to prepare communities for the typhoon.

"Very well." He takes his hand off the glass and turns toward his throne dais. "Do not forget to study the book I gave you. I will not tolerate having made all those annotations for nothing."

"Understood, *shīfu*!" I say with fake eagerness.

He hurls me a dirty glare over his shoulder. I fix my face into the very picture of adulation, because that gets on his nerves more than my blatant insolence. This is how he wishes I would act, yet I'm taking all the satisfaction out of it.

After he heads up the dais, giving up on scolding me, I reach for my glass door. I catch Sima Yi looking at me weirdly.

"What?" I snap on my way out.

He ducks his head the moment he's in danger of meeting my eyes directly. "Nothing, Your Highness."

The first thing I do upon landing at the Han frontier again is visit the conscripted girls at the nearest training camp.

When Qieluo and I push through the cafeteria's greasy glass doors, the hubbub inside dies in a receding tide, from the tables nearest the entrance to the very back. Qieluo closes our umbrella and shakes water from it. I survey the rows of tables until I spot what I'm looking for—the Iron Widow table.

Using my scythe like a staff, I make my way toward them.

Qieluo keeps at my side. Our capes flutter behind us, and the clanks of our armor echo beneath the drumming of rain against the building. Although the super-typhoon isn't here yet, the sky is already pouring water.

Metal benches scrape against the concrete ground as pilots, soldiers, and maintenance workers get up and raise their fists in salute. They're all wearing yellow sashes around their waists.

"May my empress live for a thousand years, a thousand years, a thousand upon a thousand years!" they chant out of sync.

Goose bumps spread beneath my Nine-Tailed Fox armor. How many of them are doing it in earnest and how many still want me dead?

I focus on the table I'm approaching. The girls on one side spring up on natural feet, while those on the other side try to rise from wheelchairs. All conscripts with bound feet have gotten priority reversal surgeries.

"No need." I flash my hand to excuse them from getting up, speaking beneath a cloth veil hooked over my ears. I couldn't be bothered to replicate my Yellow Dragon mask with the Fox's spirit metal.

"Power to the laboring class!" Qieluo gives the girls a raised-fist salute, shouting the slogan that's caught on as a revolutionary greeting. She and Taiping have been extra diligent in keeping up with these trends. It's dangerous to come off as an elite nowadays. The lowliest peasant can denounce even a governor for not showing enough enthusiasm for the revolution.

The girls call out the customary reply. "In solidarity we rise!"

"Sisters, may we join you?" I say.

The standing ones shuffle to make room on their bench. I lean my scythe against the wall and sit down with Qieluo. The moment we do, so does the rest of the cafeteria, sending a collective collapsing sound through the air.

This is going to be a very uncomfortable conversation if every eye is on us and every ear is listening.

"Get on with whatever you were doing!" I wave my hand at the other tables.

Hesitantly, they turn back to their food and friends, though their voices don't rise above a murmur. I accept this as the best privacy I'll get and go ahead with confirming the girls' names and hometowns. I've had to make a chart to keep track of all the female conscripts across the frontiers.

For a province that's mostly rural farmland, the Han girls are disproportionately city dwellers, either from the provincial capital Chengdu or one of its few other cities. Which isn't surprising. Urban testing centers can go through hundreds of kids in a day, while rural families have to either wait for a mobile testing team or trek to the nearest town.

In general, revolutionary change spreads more unpredictably in the countryside. After the initial wave of peasants forcing their landlords to burn their land titles, landlords have been fighting back with the help of the elite families that have escaped the cities with their dirty fortunes. They pay people to set fire to harvests, poison livestock, and murder rebellious tenants, often leaving their disemboweled bodies as a warning. Since the countryside is so vast, and extensive tunnels exist beneath them from the Warring Era, it's very easy for the culprits to vanish.

"Guerilla insurgency," Wan'er told me this was called.

They also spread wild misinformation among the peasants, such as that we're forcing people to share everything down to their blankets and toothbrushes, or that we're no longer recognizing marriages and will mandate every woman to sleep around, particularly with Rongdi men. Nonsense like this is turning a concerning number of people toward Zhuge Liang and the reactionaries. I almost feel bad for Qin Zheng whenever I see how stressed out he gets at every report from the countryside.

When I don't have the knowledge to solve these problems, the best I can do for the revolution is to keep the frontiers secure with these new Iron Widows. Yet the more I hear them laugh and talk about how great it's been since they became pilots, how they got to move their families into luxury apartments expropriated from real estate developers, the more I regret coming to face them. Images of them getting crushed in battle flicker behind my eyes.

I make them confirm that, in addition to typical strategist training, they're getting dream training as well. The practice has spread pretty widely since Qieluo and I reintroduced it, with Han pilots going to other frontiers during their recuperation periods to enlighten the pilots there. There was apparently a lot of ruckuses on the boys' part about falling asleep next to each other, but they got over it. During this deployment, I can teach Qieluo the fresh round of stuff I learned from Qin Zheng; then she can pass it down the chain to these new girls, hopefully before their first battles.

While I only know the local Han girls from digital conversations facilitated by Wan'er, two here are from the seven in Chang'an that I presented to the cameras. Liang Yuhuan, the one with the highest spirit pressure, already has her own Chrysalis: the Plum Blossom Deer, manifested a week ago from a Count-class Hundun I'd taken down with a clean strike. Her Metal-white spirit armor covers her torso in solid plates and her limbs in a flower-patterned mesh. Her pilot crown consists of two wreaths of blossoms with four antlers sprouting out like tree branches, further adorned with petals.

"Did you have to pick such a girly form, though?" Guo Anle, the second Chang'an girl, pokes a blossom on Yuhuan's crown after Yuhuan retells the thrill of manifesting her Chrysalis.

"I didn't choose it!" Yuhuan laughs while popping a lychee into her mouth. "I swear, I saw a deer spirit coming toward me in my mind, and then, before I knew it, that was what my Chrysalis was becoming. Besides, 'girly' doesn't mean *weak*." She beams, one cheek full like a chipmunk's. "Wait until you see me in battle. Then you'll eat your words."

Bile rises in my throat. I grab my scythe and pull myself up from the bench. "All right, sisters, this has been a good talk. Work hard on your control over spirit metal. You'll need the skill."

I get away from the table as fast as I can. Qieluo hastens to follow me, glancing back and forth between me and the girls.

Halfway to the doors, a shout from a familiar young voice sends a prickle up my spine.

"Your Highness!"

I turn to see Liu Che running toward me in his Azure Dragon armor. He crashes to his knees before me, cape pooling behind him. His hands splay on the stained concrete, one of them with an unnerving stump where its little finger should be.

"I solemnly apologize to Your Highness for my foolish, ignorant actions." He knocks his forehead against the ground, yet he sounds as flat as the guidance voice in electric carriages.

My skin shrivels at a memory of him standing over me, sword glowing with Fire-red qì, the smell of burnt flesh drifting from the two guards he killed.

The cafeteria has gone quiet again except for the sound of rain. Everyone is staring.

"You're excused," I say, my mouth sour.

He hammers his forehead against the ground a second time. "I deserve a thousand cuts and ten thousand lacerations."

"Okay, calm down! You've been punished already. Just don't do it again."

"In my next life I shall serve as Your Highness' cattle or horse!"

I almost start cussing at him. Scrutiny skewers me from every direction, including from Qieluo.

"I am very busy, Captain Liu," I say. "I'd rather see you serving Huaxia to your full abilities in *this* life than wallowing about what you might do in the next. Take care."

I whirl away.

I don't know who made him do that, but if they meant for it to comfort me, they accomplished the exact opposite.

CHAPTER THIRTY

NO WRATH LIKE MOTHER NATURE'S

"Oh—His Majesty sent another message, Your Highness." Wan'er raises her tablet to get a better signal as Super-Typhoon Baiyue makes landfall. Rain beats down on my watchtower's floor-to-ceiling windows, so heavy that nothing is visible through the water, and we have the lights on in the middle of the day.

I look up from my work on the table. So do Taiping, who used her vacation days to come witness the typhoon, and Di Renjie, who's on standby with me for the Hundun attack expected any moment now. Qieluo is usually with us as well, but she went to prepare for battle at another watchtower with Yang Jian. The White Tiger finally made it to the Han frontier after a very complicated airlift operation from Chang'an.

"What is it this time?" I grumble while returning to the passage I'm copying from the *Book of Laborism*, double-annotated with Wan'er's additions alongside her transcriptions of Qin Zheng's notes.

"His Majesty wants to know if, uh, Your Highness needs the annotations to be further simplified to a seven-year-old's level."

"Ignore him."

"Can we . . . do that?"

"Don't worry; it's on me, not you."

This time during my deployment, Qin Zheng has developed a habit of sending me annoying messages every day. I'm not responding because I don't want to encourage him to keep doing it, except that might've just made him angrier. At the same time, I don't feel like expending the energy to talk to him. I have other things to worry about, like how the Iron Widows are being trained. The weirdest part is that since he doesn't let me touch digital devices and refuses to use one himself, it's really Yizhi messaging Wan'er. I wish I could see Yizhi's face as he transcribes Qin Zheng's increasingly unhinged nonsense.

"But Your Highness, I think His Majesty really wants you to respond." Wan'er scrolls farther down. "Because here he says, 'You do realize the capacity to reply is available to you, right?'" She presses her voice low in imitation of him. "'Tell your staffer to relay your words via her device. I did not wake up in a world where instantaneous messaging has been invented just to have you pretend as if my letters have gotten lost in the mail.'"

She definitely didn't mean to mock him with her impression, yet I burst out laughing. Taiping raises both brows while sipping from a mug of tea.

Di Renjie frowns. "His Majesty seems—"

"Don't finish that sentence, Renjie," Taiping mumbles into her mug. "You might get thrown back into jail."

"I would hope our laws don't sink further in that direction," Di Renjie says with full seriousness. "Speaking of such, I am about finished with my proposed amendments to His Majesty's rewrite of the legal code." He taps his pad of paper. "We ought to focus more on rehabilitation and prevention than punishment. Studies have shown that harsher sentencing does not reduce crime; improving people's material conditions does."

I bite my lips. Di Renjie's proposals always sound so wonderful, so correct.

And so unrealistic in our circumstances.

Like, I don't think Qin Fucking Zheng believes in "rehabilitation." Especially not while fighting a guerilla insurgency. I now understand why he got so annoyed at me for calling him idealistic. Compared to those like Di Renjie, he really isn't. Di Renjie hopes to get the elites to share their wealth and power by appealing to their humanity. Qin Zheng just breaks their necks, loots their estates, and throws the money and jewels to the mobs outside.

Sometimes, I'm glad Di Renjie missed the mass pardon, because he would absolutely be back behind bars for spray-painting "Great Distorter" over murals of Qin Zheng or writing essays about how "the very concept of a laborist *empire* makes no ideological sense."

"I, uh, can't guarantee our darling Majesty will listen to you," I say. "But we can send it."

"How's the new legal code's section on restraining orders?" Taiping takes another sip of tea.

"Taiping!" Wan'er screeches under her breath, making a shushing gesture. Then she turns to me. "Your Highness, can I write a more personable response to His Majesty *for* you?"

"Fine. But don't sound too deferential, or he'll know it's not me." I pause. "Wait, no, he'll find out it's not me eventually if he sees this memory."

I look around the table, at these people I've begun to think of as my companions. Would Qin Zheng be petty enough to punish them for this moment?

"Never mind, I'll write something." I beckon to Di Renjie for a piece of paper.

As he rips a page from his notepad, something rams into the watchtower. The building quakes. Windows shatter somewhere below. We cry out, bracing against the table. The lights flicker out.

"What was that?" Taiping glances around the gloomy gray light persisting from the window. Rain shadows whirl over our faces.

I shut my eyes and activate my spirit sense.

There's a swarm of signatures beneath the watchtower.

"Hunduns!" I bolt up so quickly spots rush into my vision. "Right beneath us!"

"How?" Wan'er gapes. "Shouldn't the sirens have gone off?"

"I don't know, but come on!" I wave at Di Renjie and hurry to my deployment pole.

The sliding plates at the pole's base are harder to budge than usual. Di Renjie kicks them open for me. The instant they give way, the typhoon howls in with a force that blows us backward. I shield my face from splatters of rain. Wan'er and Taiping yelp as papers fly up on the table. Beneath the docking bridge, white-capped waves crash against the watchtower.

The ocean has flooded all the way up to the Great Wall.

I go cold to my fingertips, but I grab the pole with one hand and Di Renjie's arm with the other so he doesn't get buffeted back farther. With no armor to weigh him down, he's more vulnerable than me. His prisoner jumpsuit flaps over his thin frame, molding out his scrawny limbs. Squinting against the wet, roaring wind, we nod at each other. I hang on to his waist and leap into the typhoon.

I used to believe I'd experienced bad storms, ones that kept me up all night as they beat against my family's house, making us shout to each other about whether the walls would hold.

Since coming to the south during storm season, I've realized I am but a sweet northern infant when it comes to weather. These winds, screaming like a mob of demons in my ear, would level my village without suspense. There is no wrath like Mother Nature's.

I hold on to Di Renjie on our trek across the docking bridge. The Nine-Tailed Fox's green surface is barely visible through the rain whipping like white sand against my face.

The bridge and watchtower shudder again from a hard pummel from below. I stumble against the bridge railing. Ahead, the Fox teeters.

My stomach drops as a Water-black Hundun climbs with tentacle-like legs over the Fox's tails, which shield its Dormant Form like a curved cage. It's a common-class Hundun, about the size of my loft, but to face it in my human body is to face a horror not meant to be comprehended with mortal eyes. It goes against basic instinct to keep moving. Yet there's no turning around. There is no way to defeat that thing if I don't get into my Chrysalis, and *my Chrysalis is about to topple over.*

"Brace yourself!" I yell in Di Renjie's ear.

I power through to the end of the bridge and, trying not to overthink it, hurl us through a gap between the Fox's tails.

We collide with the Fox's head as it falls sideways. On contact, I sense the Fox's entire contour through my armor. I use the sum of my mental strength to heave it in the other direction, unfurling its tails against the Hunduns scrabbling over it. Not all of them fall off, but enough for the Fox to swing upright again. I compel its spirit metal to cave in beneath me and Di Renjie, dumping us into the cockpit.

We land in a splash, utterly soaked. I roll over in the puddle and wave my arm at the opening I made. The motion helps me mentally seal it up, enclosing us in darkness. The rain hammering like static against the Fox's metal surface goes muted. I wheeze, my hands and knees aching, and wipe my numb face. Something warm, probably blood, runs from my nose. I don't dwell on it. Instead I crawl and scamper to my pilot seat. I channel some qì light so Di Renjie can find his way as well, then I help open the zipper on the back of his drenched jumpsuit. Thankfully, he was permitted to keep his spinal brace on outside of battle, so all it takes for him to connect is to lean back in his seat. I fuse my armor firmly to my seat and pull our minds into the Fox.

After my senses balloon into the Fox's perspective, I shake off the suddenly much smaller-looking Hunduns like a wet animal. They plop and vanish into the floodwaters, which course up to the Fox's knees. That means the water level is at least three-stories high, deep enough to hide common-class Hunduns beneath its frothy, churning waves.

I propel the Fox into Ascended Form in a burst of white light, craft a scythe, and swing it through the water over and over, pinpointing Hunduns with my spirit sense. Anguish pulses into me with every kill, but there's no room for hesitation when we're right against the Great Wall. I don't know why no sirens alerted me. If any strategists are trying to explain, I wouldn't know; I can't hear a thing over the vortex of sound from the winds. I doubt any camera drone could withstand these forces either. Maybe that's why no warning came.

I reach further with my spirit sense to figure out what's going on. Off to one side, I mentally trip upon a massive spirit signature, at least Prince class, right against the Wall, amidst an alarming cluster of smaller signatures. I'd assume it's the White Tiger—but the army never stations Iron Nobles next to each other. My pilot neighbor over there should be common class and off duty.

A bad feeling quavers inside me. I advance in that direction against rain that whirls so wildly it looks more like roiling mist. The torrential floodwaters shudder with the Fox's every step and drag at its legs. I slice through as many Hunduns as I can without slowing my pace. I stop caring about the ones I miss. The number of them pales in comparison to the growing cluster ahead. I *feel* something happening there before I see or hear it through the storm: a rhythm of colossal tremors in the ground, independent of the Fox's footsteps.

I scream out loud once the scene emerges through wind and rain. An Earth-type, Prince-class Hundun moves as one with piles of smaller Hunduns, ramming into the Wall over and over. Cracks spread from a dent in the concrete with every hit. Fire-red and Wood-green qì spark from some of the Hunduns to do more damage.

I slash through the mass of smaller Hunduns and throw the Fox's weight into the Prince class. It staggers sideways on its six tarantula-like legs before pushing back against me. My scythe snaps in two against the Hundun's hull. Its front pair of legs clamp around the Fox. It's like trying to wrestle an enormous golden boulder that strapped itself to me. I wriggle one of the Fox's arms free and grab another lance from behind me. Channeling Fire qì, I stab the lance into the Hundun. It doesn't wedge much into the dense Earth-type hull. The larger the Hundun, the more spirit metal to get through to extinguish its spark. As I grapple against it, its golden surface wobbling in my rain-slashed view, I wonder if this is just a fraction of what it'd be like to fight the Yellow Dragon. If so, the Fox would be no match.

Too late, I notice no other Hunduns are pouncing on me when they should be. I turn the Fox's head. The smaller Hunduns continue to pommel the Wall as a mass, hammering the dent deeper and wider.

Two different impulses tear my mind in opposite directions. I need to keep the Prince Hundun at bay. I also need to scatter the smaller ones. Is there a way to do both at once?

When I swing my lance at the common mass, the Prince Hundun gets the traction to push me backward and return closer to the dent.

Fuck!

I jab the lance into the Prince again. I can't let it get back to the dent. The Wall can't take another strong hit. I try to dig the Fox's heels into the ground, but it's become slippery muck under the floodwaters. I channel Fire and Metal qì as hard as I can to pierce the lance deeper. If I can kill the Prince—

The next tremor from the Wall feels abruptly different.

I look back just in time to see the common mass smash through the last bit of the dent. Hunduns pour past the Wall on a roar of water, the force of the gush breaking the hole wider.

"No!" I shriek through the Fox's mouth, the sound swallowed by the typhoon. I lunge for the breach, but now it's the Prince's turn to hold me back. Thrashing against its grip, I'm forced to watch more Hunduns stream into the Han province.

When I finally break free, I jam the Fox sideways into the breach, crushing common Hunduns in the process. I cram the Fox's knees against its chest and collapse its tail lances to fit. It stops the influx of Hunduns, though water keeps surging through the gaps in the Fox's fetal posture, coming up to its waist.

The Prince barrels toward me, six thick legs shaking the earth and kicking up foam from the floodwaters.

The instant before collision, I raise a lance out of the water. The Prince impales itself on the tip. It's not much more than a shallow puncture, but I drive spikes out of it like an arrowhead and reinforce it with Earth qì. The Prince can neither pull free to ram at me again nor press forward without piercing itself more deeply.

As we push and tug in our deadlock, cold facts crystallize in the depths of my consciousness. I've already failed in my primary battle objective, done the one thing a pilot must never do: I let Hunduns get past the Great Wall. There are no Chrysalises stationed inside to take them down, because every viable unit is used to *prevent* this from happening.

I can sense the Hunduns that breached the Wall spreading out inside Huaxia. Once they get past the barren grounds near the frontier, they'll reach farmland. Villages. A mandatory evacuation order has cleared those in the super-typhoon's path, but there is nothing to stop the Hunduns from going farther, to where people are. It'll be a bloodbath. The entire Han province might fall like Zhou. And it will be my fault.

I scream while shrugging away smaller Hunduns that squeeze past the Prince to climb toward the Fox's cockpit. There's no room to use the Fox's free hand. One common Hundun crawls past the Fox's shoulder spikes and saws at the base of its head with sharp Metal-type legs. Pain pierces into me. When my concentration lapses, the Prince pulls free from my lance.

I hurl off the common Hundun and lurch partway out of the breach, preparing for another jostle with the Prince. My best bet out of this mess is to kill it and plug the breach with its husk so I can go chase down the intruders.

Yet, as if it can hear what I'm thinking, the Prince trudges away through the floodwaters, vanishing into the storm.

"Hey!" I cry. "Get back here!"

With the Prince no longer in the way, smaller Hunduns swarm me much more intensely. I slot the Fox tightly into the breach again to keep them from wiggling through.

My lance proves too cumbersome for fending them off. I shed most of its length to form a dagger. It doesn't fare much better. The blade constantly slips in the water, and for every Hundun I shatter, two more assail me. I consider fusing my remaining lances into a shield to cover the breach, but given that these Hunduns can amass enough force to break the Wall, they could just do the same to push me to the other side. I can't let them build up like that again.

I drop the dagger and resort to pitching the Hunduns far out, one by one, with the Fox's claws. At first, I sharpen the claws with Metal qì to pierce their hulls, but the extra killing step takes too much time, and the blowback from so many deaths is unbearable. I'll legitimately hold out longer by hurling them out with no damage, even if it guarantees an endless loop of them coming back.

"Requesting backup!" I yell into the storm, but I can scarcely hear myself, let alone have hope that a functioning camera drone might pick it up. I think of Qin Zheng conquering six nations only to be taken down by a virus. I don't know which is a more infuriating way to die, that or *this*.

As my despair crests to a peak, a large, pale shape appears out of the whipping rain. Not a Hundun—it has antlers.

"Your Highness?" its shout carries faintly on the monstrous winds.

Its female voice startles me. Its antlers come into clearer view, wreathed in blossoms. Red eyes glow in its Metal-white deer form, which almost blends in with the storm.

"Yuhuan?" I exclaim. "Is that you?"

Why is she in battle? She barely just manifested her Chrysalis!

"Yes, Your Highness!" She wades laboriously through the floodwaters in the Plum Blossom Deer, submerged up to its belly. Thin red qì lines trace out floral patterns on its sides.

"Why are you here?" I toss the Hunduns in a different direction, away from her.

"I was following the Hunduns! They all started going—" She halts near the riotous swarm around me. "Oh, no, what happened?"

"They breached the Wall!" I make myself admit. "Did sirens ever go off in your watchtower?"

"Of course. Why?" She lurches away from a bobbling Hundun and swats at it with a razor-sharp hoof.

I almost crush the next Hundun I pick up. *The reactionaries.* This must be their doing, a deliberate move to sabotage me. If I survive this, I have some choice questions for the Han frontier's engineers. "Well, mine didn't! So here we are!"

"*What?*"

"Yeah!"

As more Hunduns besiege her, Yuhuan rears the Deer up on its hind legs. Fire-red light cracks across its body. It transforms into a more humanoid Ascended Form, its front hooves splitting into claws, its torso stretching upright, its antlers elongating, and its legs straightening until its thighs are mostly out of the water. Red highlights bleed in around its individual components, including the blossoms engraved on its sides. Yuhuan studies the Deer's arms in awe while backing away from the Hunduns. Then she snaps off the Deer's antlers and wields them like multi-pronged daggers.

"Did any of them get through?" She fights and splashes her way to me.

"Yes!" I hurl a Hundun past her with more force than I intend.

Cursing, she pivots to crouch in front of me like a guard. "What do we do? Shouldn't we be going after them?"

"I can't move from here, or more will flood in!"

"Could I take Your Highness' place so you can go hunt them down?"

An objection rolls to the tip of my metaphorical tongue, but lingers there when I watch how quickly she adapts to battle, skewering floating Hunduns with both antlers in her grasp. She at least got some training before this, while I emerged in my first battle with none at all and managed fine. Why am I doubting her when she's not doubting herself?

As a Metal type, the Plum Blossom Deer is sturdier for defensive purposes. As a Wood type, the Fox is faster. For what we need to do, it makes sense for us to switch places.

"All right," I say. "On the count of three, plug the breach. One. Two. *Three*."

I jerk the Fox out to the inner grounds. Yuhuan backs the Deer into the breach on its knees. It fits better, its smaller stature less cramped. It moves more freely than the Fox could. I place my faith in her and dash away through the storm.

The flowing water spreads out across the open grounds, no longer tugging at the Fox's legs. I collapse into its Standard Form to run faster, the howls of the storm shoving at my back and occasionally heaving me sideways. Following my spirit sense, I chase down the breachers one by one, starting with the farthest. It takes a lot of persistence to catch up to them, but they pose no challenge once I do, being mostly common class.

The rain and wind gradually ease in their lashings. By the time I go after the last breaching signature, the worst of the typhoon has passed. I can actually see decently ahead as I pursue the Hundun all the way to a village.

Or what used to be a village.

The scale of the devastation stuns me. Buckled buildings, fallen trees, ruined crops, tangled power lines, snapped planks of wood, scattered sheets of metal, and random roof tiles and other debris everywhere. I'm not sure what was done by the typhoon and what was accomplished by the final Hundun.

I spot the Hundun on top of a pile of rubble. It leaps down when I approach, putting up a valiant but pointless fight. Once I shatter a claw through its hull, the recoil of its dying hatred flows into a flood of relief. I wobble on the Fox's four legs. I let its head hang low, savoring the peace, the gentler beat of rain against spirit metal.

Then I sense another, much smaller spirit signature in the rubble the Hundun was on. With the Fox's paw, I nudge aside some concrete pieces.

A shivering little girl looks up at me in the corner of a collapsed cellar, arms huddling her head. Two lifeless bodies lie beside her, crushed to contorted positions, fresh blood seeping through their clothes.

Every thought in my head turns to white noise.

CHAPTER THIRTY-ONE

DEFEAT

I wish I didn't have to wake up ever again. Enduring my nightmares is more bearable than enduring reality.

A glass bottle glistens in a slant of moonlight above me, dripping into a line connected to the back of my hand. In flashes, I recall carrying the little girl to the Great Wall in the Fox's cockpit, then being ushered to the infirmary in the nearest training camp and passing out as an army physician examined her.

Why didn't your family evacuate? I wanted to scream at the girl, except they would've been fine in their cellar if I hadn't let the Hunduns through the Wall. This is what happens when they get to humans. How did I think that mercy was mine to give?

When my gaze drops from the bottle, I find not the girl, but Yuhuan sitting in a second bed in the room, her elegant profile varnished by the moon through a window. An intravenous line connects to her hand as well. She's staring at the white-tiled walls, seldom blinking.

A bad feeling bubbles inside me. When I went to park the Fox at its docking bridge, she and the strategists were still figuring out how to position the Plum Blossom Deer to safeguard the Wall breach while it gets repaired. She sounded perfectly perky then, but I wasn't there to see what happened when she disconnected.

"Yuhuan?" I say.

"Your Highness!" She scrambles to get out of bed.

"No need." I hold up a hand while scooting up in my own bed. "Yuhuan, what . . . happened?"

She falls still. Her gaze goes unfocused.

"I killed him," she says, sounding more confused than anything else. "One second I could feel his mind in the back of mine, then the moment I disconnected, he was . . ." She puts a hand to her forehead.

A cold weight sinks in my stomach.

"It wasn't your fault," I rush to say. "These things happen when piloting a Chrysalis. Power comes at a price that's usually out of our control."

"I don't know how it happened. I didn't mean it."

"Of course you didn't. You were defending Huaxia. I couldn't have made it without you, and you couldn't have done such a good job if you'd held back. Your co-pilot volunteered for his role, didn't he?"

Her breathing quickens. "He worked at his dad's bank. They both got charged with fraud after the revolution. He took a plea deal to become a support pilot rather than do ten years of hard labor."

So that's how Qin Zheng is getting boys to volunteer for female pilots like Yuhuan.

I pull myself up with my drip stand and wheel it over to sit next to her.

"He knew what he was getting into. He made the decision to enlist." I reach for the words people use for dead concubine-pilots, saying anything I can think of to keep her from shattering. "He proudly gave his life for Huaxia, and his soul will rest well in the Yellow Springs. His noble sacrifice will not be in vain."

Leaning against me, she buries her face in her hands. "He was twenty-one. He worked at that bank for less than a year."

A lump swells in my throat. I wrap my arms around her and mumble, "Next time, don't ask them so many questions about themselves. It'll only hurt more."

Her shoulders shake. "Why does it have to be like this?"

"Because otherwise the Hunduns will kill us all. You saw what happened."

"Wh-when they said you can feel the Hunduns die if you stab them, I didn't think it'd be so . . . real."

"That's just a defense mechanism, like a bee stinging you as it dies." I parrot the words Qieluo soothed herself with. One by one, I'm discovering the reasons for these platitudes I hated. Why people repeat them despite how meaningless they are to the dead. Why our ancestors, stranded in this world, invented a different reality. Why generation after generation of people in charge continued the lies.

Yuhuan is in this position because I wanted powerful supporters so badly that I brought about her conscription. When she has no choice but to fight, I cannot let her become like me, forever bogged down in battle by the truth.

<hr />

The Han engineers claim my sirens malfunctioned due to the typhoon. It sure is a convenient coincidence for those who want me dead, especially when word about the breach spreads like wildfire on the networks by morning, despite the army ordering it kept secret.

Instantly, the entire scope of devastation across the south gets blamed on me. Then the blame extends to women in general. Then to the revolution as a whole and everything it stands for. It doesn't matter that a once-in-a-generation super-typhoon did most of the damage, and it was the old order that built the buildings that didn't hold up. People aren't interested in facts; they'll believe the spin on a story that best reinforces their existing opinions.

Although I would've liked to spend the rest of my life curled up in the infirmary, I can't cower while the narrative spirals out of control. As soon as the army doctors clear me to leave, I drag myself back to Chang'an to face Qin Zheng.

"You failed to reply to any of my messages," is the first thing he says upon seeing me again, hands on his hips in his quarantine chamber.

I halt in my wheelchair, too qì-exhausted to walk. "*That's* what you're mad at me for?"

"I will not fault you for an equipment failure," he says, more gently. Or maybe he's just exhausted, too, from the countless problems he has to deal with on his end. I didn't know it was possible for the shadows under his eyes to get even darker.

I clasp my hands in my lap, my thumb swiping back and forth on my gauntlets. "I don't believe it was an accident. I think there are reactionaries among the Han engineers."

"Agreed," he says, with a look that raises the hairs on my arms, the look that gets in his eyes when he deals out death as statistics. "I'll be sending personnel for an independent review."

"Good," I say to the floor. I can't stop thinking about that little girl in the flattened cellar, how she trembled as she climbed onto the Fox's rain-slicked paw so I could take her away from her destroyed home and dead family. It's dumbfounding that people would resort to endangering Huaxia itself to frame me, but that's how the counter-revolutionaries are. They'd rather die than accept a changed world that doesn't privilege them as much.

At least I don't have to worry about who will take care of the girl. Orphanages have been getting much better support under Qin Zheng. Since, you know, his executions are creating a notably increased need for them.

I don't notice the silence that fell in the throne room until I hear him take a step forward.

"Are you—"

His knuckles hit the glass. My head jerks up.

He gawks at his hand, looking just as startled, then gives a huff and shakes his head.

"Are you all right?" he says.

"I'm . . . fine." I shift in my wheelchair, not liking the way he's looking at me, as if I'm a broken thing to be pitied. "The villages near the southern coast are the ones suffering. You need to get them aid right away."

"Of course. But first—" He goes up on the dais to his desk and comes down with a thick piece of paper and a pen. He places them in the glass wall's transfer box. "Sign this."

I take it out from the hatch on my end, only to be stunned by the words at its top. "This is—"

"Our marriage certificate. It occurred to me that we neglected to file this document after things took an . . . unexpected turn . . . at our wedding."

"Why would *we* need to sign a marriage certificate?"

"Recordkeeping is fundamental," he insists. "Particularly at the highest levels of government. Every meal you eat is logged and every cent spent on your transportation is deducted from a precise palace budget, or have you not noticed? Legally speaking, whatever an ordinary citizen must file, we must as well. This includes changing our marital status and registering as a new family unit at this address."

"We're not a . . . Okay, fine." I scribble my name as messily as I can, because I think that's what you're supposed to do when signing something. His own signature gives me pause. I run my finger over its ferocious strokes, pressed into the paper. "This document looks ridiculous. Our birthdays are over two hundred years apart."

"How questionable can a difference in age be after the one-hundred-year mark?"

Unamused, I stuff the certificate back in the box. He fetches it with an air of triumph, though I really don't know why this was necessary. He could've gotten a clerk to fake my signature, and I'd have nowhere to complain.

"Stay here. I have something else for you as well." He returns the certificate to his desk before disappearing to the back rooms behind the dais. When he reemerges, he's holding a steaming bowl of something with a spoon in it.

"My *shīfu*'s recipe to aid qì replenishment," he explains. "Lotus seeds, peanuts, red beans, jujubes, goji berries, silver ear, and rock sugar."

A recipe by General Mi Xuan?

"You just randomly had that back there?" I stretch to try and see into the bowl.

"I made it."

"*You* made it?"

"Sometimes it gets rather aggravating to wait for the kitchen to test everything for poison, so I requested some cookware and installed a pantry." He slides the bowl into the transfer box. It quickly fogs up the small space.

"Uh. Thanks." I take the bowl out. It's a dark purple congee, its warm vapors caressing my face when I stir it with the spoon. This is so uncharacteristic for him that it's concerning. It feels like a certain trap, though I don't know why he would poison me when the Wall breach gives him the perfect excuse to execute me in a great public spectacle.

"I must say, automatic pressure cookers are a marvel. You can leave a recipe in there for hours, and it'll stay warm without burning." Qin Zheng hauls a chair up to the glass wall and straddles it in reverse, resting his arms on its back. "Eat it while it's hot."

I guess there's no graceful way to carry this elsewhere in a wheelchair. And he would probably get angry enough to make that execution happen if I refused it.

I scoop up a spoonful, blow on it, then give it a taste.

"It's good!" I look at him in genuine delight. "Like, the perfect level of sweet."

He breaks into a smile he tries to hide, moving his hand in front of it as if he's wiping his face.

I expect him to leave me alone to eat it, yet he soon goes back to watching me with a severe gaze. Does he plan on supervising me until I finish the whole thing? I try to ignore him, focusing on the miracle of Mi Xuan's cooking reaching me across centuries, but halfway down the bowl, I decide to mess with him a little.

"Mmm, this is soooo good." I give the spoon a slow, languorous lick.

He winces, eyes snapping shut, and his whole body clenches against the chair. I fight down a laugh.

"There's more in the back, if you want," he says, voice rougher than usual.

"Oh, yes, *shīfu, please.*"

He buries his face in his hands. The tips of his ears go red. "Will you stop that?"

"Stop watching me eat, then." I shove another spoonful into my mouth. "Go start on getting aid to the south. Oh—actually, let me go personally pass out relief packages. Maybe that'll get the people to hate me less."

He falls still, hand partway down his face. "You realize nothing will salvage your reputation short of making the announcement, don't you?"

My stomach sinks, though I've been prepared for this for a while now. When the reactionaries' strongest tactic for swaying soldiers to their side is to pin everything on *me*, a more acceptable target to rage at than Qin Zheng, becoming a less acceptable target really is an effective counter.

"Yeah. Let's tell everyone I'm pregnant."

I appear silent beside him in his next broadcast, where he announces to Huaxia that "we" are pregnant. He reiterates that pilot titles cannot be inherited—he was the one who banned that two centuries ago—so the child won't automatically be heir to the empire, but he expresses his optimism that the kid will one day test to be a powerful pilot and do great service for Huaxia. He speaks of his pride in my fertility, as if it takes some kind of talent to lie there and let a man (or syringe) shoot the necessary fluid into me, and how I'm determined to keep up the war effort even as an expectant mother.

In reality, I was filmed completely separately from him, and then my footage was stitched onto the same throne room background. A fitting arrangement for two people supposedly having a baby together despite not being able to touch skin to skin. The only ones who know it's a bluff are me, Qin Zheng, Yizhi, Sima Yi, and Doctor Hua, who gives me a guide on how much padding to gradually add in front of my belly to make it look like there's a baby growing in there. Not even Wan'er, Taiping, or Qieluo know the truth. The fewer people who are in on it the better.

Even though I was counting on the announcement to transform my image, I hate how well it works. All of a sudden, I am no longer the conniving yet incompetent vixen who nearly doomed Huaxia; instead, I'm a pregnant girl who did her best. Wan'er tells me that digital comments speak of me with newfound sympathy. Some actually *worry* about me, suggesting I take a break from the war. They yell at anyone who continues to blame me for the Wall breach, especially after Qin Zheng's independent inspection team uncovers evidence of tampering in the siren systems. It implicates a suspiciously large number of personnel at the Han frontier, but what do I know about technology? I feel no rush to beg for their lives. The entire province could've fallen because of what happened.

During my post-battle recuperation period—which the military's existing pregnancy guidelines extend to a month instead of two weeks—I fly across the south with a production crew to get some good shots of me hand-delivering aid to devastated villages. If I'm going to be a motherly figure now, I might as well commit to the bit. The visits are awkward at first, with the villagers staring at me blank-faced after hearing so much about how wicked and devious I am. But the free stuff soon gets them to relax. I convince them the clump of cells allegedly growing in my uterus has compelled me to become an utterly different person. By the fifth village, there's cheering when my hovercraft lands. Peasant women shout to me from behind the lines of my guards, waving little shoes, clothes, or toys they made for my nonexistent baby, from whatever material they could salvage after losing most of their worldly possessions to the typhoon. I truly do not know what to feel about this.

New revolutionary posters get plastered everywhere, featuring me holding a baby bundle up on the Nine-Tailed Fox's shoulder, or in front of a smoldering battlefield, my eyes determined and my cape billowing behind me. They often come with a caption in big block text: *Iron by Birth, Made Steel by Motherhood.*

It always provokes a twitch under my eye, but I never turn down a posing session for the Ministry of Culture, which now funds Huaxia's best artists to churn out posters, pamphlets, plays, games, radio dramas, and screen dramas espousing laborist principles. Whatever works to strengthen my position.

In private, my obvious displeasure saves me from hearing much talk about the baby from Wan'er, Taiping, and Qieluo. Yet they do act more cautiously around me, advising me on what or what not to eat and rushing to support me if I show the slightest unsteadiness. I can't stand it. It's like I'm walking around with a giant bruise of defeat for the world to see.

I keep reminding myself this is a temporary ruse, no longer necessary once we defeat Zhuge Liang, Kong Zhuxi, and their reactionary forces. The Gewei Bu is closing in on them with every foiled plot and uncovered base.

I cannot wait for this fake baby nonsense to be over.

CHAPTER THIRTY-TWO

MORE BEYOND THIS

The smell of rice wine pervades a candlelit room. A woman slouches against the wooden wall in a thin robe, her bare legs tangled in her stained sheets. Loose hair obscures her face, and strands of it are sticking to the glass bottle in her hand.

Mother. I intuitively recognize her.

My small hands nudge at her shoulder. "*Niáng?*"

She shrugs me away, muttering something under her wine-pungent breath.

"*Niáng*, get up. Come on, get up." I tug her arm. "You've gotta eat something."

"Shut up!" She swings her bottle at me. It shatters over my cheek and sends me tumbling to the floor. "Why didn't you die?" She holds me down and drags the broken bottle over my face as I scream and flail. "*Why won't you die?*"

The pain shocks me free. I trip backwards, winded. The room vanishes. What remains is Qin Zheng in a blank white realm, hunched over with his back to me, clutching his cheek. His shoulders heave up and down.

Slowly, he turns around. His hand falls, revealing the jagged scars across half his face.

It's a while before either of us finds our words.

"I suppose you've met your mother-in-law," he says, eyes on his palm instead of me. He appears not in his armor, or neat historical garb, but in the plain black robe and careless bun he usually sports in his quarantine chamber.

Huh. That was the most viscerally I've experienced a memory of his, not to mention one he must've locked deep inside.

What other secrets about him can I draw out while he's vulnerable?

Right as he moves to say something else, I reach up for his face with my gauntleted hand. Being armored has become so natural to me that it's my default look in dream realms. He freezes up when my metallic fingertips graze his scars.

"You keep them in here, when you can look however you want to," I remark. "Why?"

When he had the pox, he certainly didn't let those carry onto his spirit form.

"I hold no memory of possessing a perfect face. I was much too young when I received these scars." He curls his hand around my wrist as if to wrench my arm away, yet ends up applying no pressure. Something about that unsettles me more. I slip my hand out of his grasp, though I keep gazing up into his eyes.

"What happened to her after you rose as a pilot? The stories don't say."

A long, heavy sigh unspools from him, a sound holding years of weariness. He turns to walk away.

I keep up with him. It doesn't feel like he's abandoning this conversation, just that he doesn't want to face me while having it. Rosy sand appears beneath our steps while the Southern Ocean spreads to infinity at our side under illusionary stars. Its waters glow pink as it swooshes and crashes against the beach. I haven't seen it look like that during my deployments. I'm not sure if I'd have to wait for a different season, or if it's a phenomenon of Qin Zheng's time lost to our own.

He walks for a long stretch of silence before saying, "She may have ended up in an enemy brothel following her capture, but after we returned to Qin she had to keep selling her body. She could do nothing else. Her family would not take her back, and no man would accept her as a wife. Once I began receiving a pilot salary, I told her she would never have to do that again and settled her in a residence near the military base."

I shield my eyes against a sandy wind, so real it must've been spun out of a memory. "Even after how she treated you?"

"You believe I should have left her to languish?"

"Of course not. I just didn't take you for the forgiving type."

"It was not forgiveness. It was . . ."

He slows to a stop and faces the ocean. The salt-tinged wind flutters his black robe and stirs the stray strands of his hair bun. "You must understand. For so long, she was all I had. Even in the moments I hated her, I could not stop longing for her to change for the better."

"Did she?"

There's another stifling pause before he answers. "She no longer dared to hurt me, but she never ceased to hurt herself. During one of my final unification campaigns, her staffers found her in her bath with her wrists sliced open. Today is the anniversary."

"Oh," I say, so quietly I'm not sure he heard. The wind blows colder. I wrap my arms around myself, shivering.

He squints at the luminous waves. "She often used to tell me that when she was pregnant with me, she attempted to get rid of me using every method the other brothel women knew. None of them worked. At times, I used to grieve over her lack of success. Other times, I raged over the fact that she tried in the first place. It took me many years to accept that she had very little control over the material conditions that made her who she was. She was fifteen years of age when she had me. I mourn the people we could have been if a different world had shaped us."

He steps forth, one stride after another into the glowing water. The bottom of his robe floats up around him.

"Hey!" I splash after him, reaching out, though I drop my arm when I remember there's nothing to worry about in here. Radiant seawater ebbs and flows around my armored legs. An ache radiates from Qin Zheng, increasing an unnatural pressure in my chest the closer I get.

With cupped hands, he scoops up some water, then lets it spill from his grasp. His hands clench into fists.

"There must be more beyond this." He raises his head. "This ocean, these stars. We were born in a cage, to the amusement of those who imprisoned us here."

I touch his elbow and behold the view with him, the sea and sky stretching into vast unknowns.

"We'll make the gods pay." I peer up at the stars, which we'll have to somehow reach. Taiping and Qin Zheng's calculations jumble up in my mind. I have no idea if they'll work in practice, but it's still the best plan we have.

A small laugh escapes Qin Zheng. "Indeed, we shall."

He turns his gaze to me, the ocean glow shifting under the severe angles of his scarred face. He looks on the verge of saying something else, but then he bends down and fishes something out of the pink waves.

"Show me your hand. I have something to give you."

"What . . . kind of something?" I eye his fist. Is he about to ruin this moment with some dream-spun critter?

"Open your hand," he says with an edge of irritation.

"Tell me what it is first!"

"You shall find out once you give me your hand!"

Having no patience to argue further, I do it. He pulls my hand in and places something hot and radiant in my palm.

"What is this?" I gawk down at a shining spark of light.

"A star," he says, as if it's obvious, still holding on to my hand.

"What do you mean, a star?"

He rolls his eyes. "Imagine I plucked a star from its reflection in the ocean and gave it to you. Is that not poetic? In here, I can do that."

"But why would you? What's the point?"

He blinks a few times, his eyes flicking downward. "Perhaps it was simply an excuse to take your hand."

I snort. "Since when did *you* need an excuse to take what you want?"

A change comes over his demeanor. Heat rises in his eyes, as if someone has struck a match behind them. "You're right. I never have."

He pulls me in by the nape of my neck and captures my lips with his own.

Ah, *fuck*.

CHAPTER THIRTY-THREE

WORSE THAN ANY NIGHTMARE

I can't say I didn't see this coming. I just hoped the signs were all in my head, that I was reading too much into the gradual change in the way he looked at me. The way those looks lingered. I mean, he told me he didn't find me attractive in very explicit terms!

I should not have licked so many things in front of him.

Despite the panic racing through me, his kiss is gentler than expected, his mouth moving languidly against mine. It helps me suppress the urge to lurch away from certain danger. As things stand, I have more to gain from doing this with him than resisting it. What I wouldn't give to unravel him, riffle through his mind the way he does with mine ...

I think of the things I grudgingly admire about him. His unparalleled abilities. His striking intellect. His utter audacity. The fire in his eyes when he rallies the people to rise up.

Before I know it, I've looped my arms over his shoulders. He makes a low noise and clutches me closer by my hips, as if even my chest against his isn't close enough. Desire curls inside me—

No, not *me*. This can't be my own longing. It's *his*, rolling off him like the ocean waves, as overwhelming as his spirit pressure. His hand slides over my rear, then he tips me backward. I brace for a plunge into seawater. Instead, I hit a soft mattress with him on top of me, his arms supporting himself on either side of my chest. My armor gives way to a thin robe. As warmth pools into me from our mingling mouths like melting honey, I recognize the dim new setting as his quarantine chamber. My own bed lies empty across the glass divider that's meant to keep us apart.

"Have you fantasized about this?" I break from his lips to ask.

He tries to kiss me again without answering, but I press two fingers against his mouth and fix a demanding look up at him.

After a brief stare-down, he sighs, sounding almost as weary as when he was reminiscing earlier.

"Perhaps." He picks up my robe sash, playing with it before slowly pulling it looser. "It's indeed a tad maddening, lying beside you every night but being unable to pull you through that glass and touch you like this."

His eyes lock onto mine. My sash comes undone with one decisive tug of his long fingers. My robe falls open, exposing me. I shiver, struggling to keep my head clear. It is very, very hard to think through the ravenous craving taking over me. I don't know what to feel, knowing a need this potent was thrumming under his skin every time he looked at me. If I should welcome it or fear it.

It occurs to me that he didn't need to manifest me with a piece of clothing still on. Maybe that's part of the fantasy. To have me in his bed and undress me.

He grazes his lips from my breasts to my neck. His fingers brush past my stomach and slip between my legs.

"*Ah*—" A startling jolt of pleasure arcs through me.

His mouth curves into a smile against my pulse. I bite my lip. It shouldn't feel this good with so little effort. I think he's *making* me feel it, the way he induces other sensations in me during training. I imagine him caressing a sprawling network of my raw, unprotected nerves, stroking them like the strings of an instrument.

"Not even the gods can hear us in here, empress," he croons near my ear. "Moan for me."

"Fuck off!" I snap instinctively before biting down harder on my lip.

"Hmm?" He withdraws his hand. The pleasure recedes like a tide. "Did you mean that?"

". . . No," I admit, so dismayed by the loss that I arch against him before I can help it.

He laughs and resumes what he was doing.

I make a small whine of frustration at how much I don't want him to stop. He's the last person I should be doing this with. I've had actual nightmares about it. I try to imagine him beheading someone to remind myself of how terrible he is, yet, disturbingly, for a reason I'm not willing to unpack, it makes me move more aggressively *with* him.

It reminds me of the painkillers the army doctors injected into me that time I got shot, how they made pure unnatural bliss course like sunlight through my veins. As with those painkillers, if I'm not careful, this will lead me to ruin.

"Whatever happened to finding me 'mentally childish and physically repulsive'?" My words come out frail and slurred, as if I'm drunk on the overflowing heat between us.

"Perhaps you have grown on me. Besides . . ."—his lips hover above mine—"I never believed you innocent in *these* matters."

He kisses me with renewed yearning.

I stop berating myself for going through with this. If he senses any resistance, I might not catch him so vulnerable again. I remind myself of the words that keep me sane: If Qin Zheng can touch me, it's not real. This is not real. It doesn't count. This is a game, one I won't lose as long as I remember who and what he is.

My thighs tighten on either side of his hips. He pins my wrists to the bed. The golden thread linking us glows softly in the darkness, illuminating the way his fingers slide up to lace with mine. Giving up on maintaining any semblance of pride, I let gasps and moans escape me to the rhythm of sensation rolling through me. I let myself sound airy and helpless. I bet he likes that.

"*Shifu* . . ." I make myself whimper.

It riles him up as much as I suspected it would, driving him to kiss me again and again with a mad intensity.

Somewhere deeper in my consciousness comes a spill of memories I've never experienced. Scenes from two centuries past, rifles and flames and bombs and qì blasts, cries from advancing armies, humans against humans, Chrysalises against Chrysalises. War plans and speeches turning into demolished streets. Workers mobilizing in dingy factories. Finely dressed people getting strung from lampposts. Interpersonal drama with a lot of yelling and betrayal.

The unwinding of his mind into mine delights me more than anything he's doing to me. The more I learn about him, the more I can use against him. I kiss him back harder, hungrier.

"*. . . Go work in the factory down the street, boy. We can't keep feeding you for free . . .*"

"*. . . You were never supposed to crown yourself emperor! You are twisting our every ideal for your personal glory! . . .*"

"*. . . I didn't raise you to butcher thousands! . . .*"

"*. . . If they cannot understand you, eliminate them. They will only hinder the revolution . . .*"

"*. . . Get some rest, Zheng'er. I will come back to you . . .*"

"*. . . Her Highness will never agree to this if we tell her . . .*"

I do a mental double take at that latest voice.

Yizhi's.

I reel back the stream of Qin Zheng's memories. I see Yizhi and Sima Yi in their purple robes, bowing before Qin Zheng's quarantine chamber.

"Will you be the one to tell the empress she now has no choice but to be inseminated, Secretary Zhang?" Qin Zheng says, his voice mocking but sharp with simmering anger. "I believe she would take it best coming from *you*."

"Actually, Your Majesty," Yizhi says, "there's a procedure that can produce a child between Your Majesty and Her Highness without her having to be the one to carry it."

"Is that so?" Qin Zheng's tone turns more normal. "How would it work?"

"We extract her eggs and fertilize them with Your Majesty's necessary material in a lab," Yizhi explains with clinical detachment. "Then we implant the embryos into a surrogate mother."

"Yet that child would still belong to me and her? With no deficiencies?"

It's Sima Yi who assures him, "They'll be no different than if she birthed them herself. A brother of mine did the same procedure with his wife when they struggled to get pregnant. They've got a beautiful pair of twins now, his and hers by blood even though they came out of another woman. Honestly, when it comes to the pregnancy itself, it hardly matters which woman does it."

Yizhi makes a hum of disapproval. "It does make a difference when it comes to maternal age. As I've said, Her Highness is way too young for it. A woman five to ten years older would have a smoother pregnancy. But Her Highness will never agree to this if we tell her, so it's best if we extract what we need without her knowledge. It'll involve giving her shots of hormones for about ten days and then an egg retrieval that can be done under anesthesia while she's asleep. We can build the necessary equipment into her component of Your Majesty's quarantine chamber. I believe this will both appease the gods and spare Her Highness from agony."

I startle awake through several layers of consciousness until I draw in a frantic breath of real air. I lurch up in my bed on my proper side of the glass. On the other side, Qin Zheng rouses as well, blinking blearily at me.

Medical equipment looms in the shadows beside my bed, worse than any nightmare.

CHAPTER THIRTY-FOUR

DARK SIDE

I storm through the palace on my recently healed feet, scythe striking the stone paths, as dawn breaks beyond the surrounding mountains. A sense of unreality hovers around me, making me wonder if I'm still dreaming. In what world would Yizhi betray my trust so grotesquely? It has to be a fabrication by Qin Zheng to mess with my mind.

The soldiers guarding Yizhi's residence freeze up when I advance toward them. They look utterly stumped about whether to stop me as I stumble up its front steps.

"Move aside!" I command.

They do.

I trace the familiar path to Yizhi's bedroom and pummel his locked door with my armored fist.

"Who is it?" His sleepy voice stirs from within.

"*Me*," I say, steady as I can despite the tremors wracking my body.

There's the sound of fabric shuffling, then his footsteps approach at a rapid pace.

"Your Highness?" Yizhi opens the door, his gaze alighting briefly on my masked face before he remembers to avert it.

My chest tightens around my thumping heart at the sight of his free-flowing hair and thin night robe, which he's holding closed with one hand. A sight once reserved for our most intimate moments. I wish I could forget what I discovered and return to that simpler time when it was just us against the rest of the world.

But I will not leave without answers.

"Yizhi, what was really in the shots Doctor Hua gave me?"

I catch the instant he stops breathing, the second his body goes still as stone.

"What makes Your Highness ask?" he says, perfectly plainly.

Spots crowd my vision. Air shudders in and out of my lungs. "Zhang Yizhi, were those shots full of hormones so you could . . . so you could *steal my eggs*?"

It sounds so ludicrous when said out loud. Yet instead of recoiling in confusion, Yizhi opens his mouth for a few seconds, then closes it without a word.

Nausea roils through me at the thought of doctors lying in wait for me to slip into a dream session with Qin Zheng, then sneaking into my chamber to perform procedures on my unconscious body. I recall the time I woke up feeling so horrible that Qin Zheng breached the glass divider in his insistence to know what was wrong. That was the night, wasn't it? He didn't freak out because he cares about me; he was worried the doctors had accidentally broken his favorite toy.

"Zhang Yizhi." I jut the curve of my scythe against his chest and push him deeper into his room. "Zhang Yizhi, please, please, *please* do not tell me there's a woman out there pregnant with mine and Qin Zheng's spawn."

Yizhi trips backward, robe falling open, until he hits a wall of wooden planks where the sliding door to his balcony used to be. A precaution against assassins, I assume. Did he ever consider that *I* could be the one to put a weapon through his chest? That I could use my armor-boosted strength to shatter his ribs with this scythe and leave him choking on his own blood?

"Say something!" I shriek.

"The gods gave us an ultimatum," Yizhi says in a voice so small I almost don't hear him over the pounding pulse in my head. "And I couldn't bear the thought of you being forced to carry a baby."

"So you lied to me? Had a meeting with two other men to decide how to breed me like cattle without me knowing?"

"That is *not* how I think of you." He places a hand on my scythe, but makes no effort to pry it away from his chest.

"No, you just think I don't deserve to know what's being done to my own body! Because I'm too difficult to deal with, right? Too unreasonable? Too unstable?"

This would be easier if he raised his voice to match mine, entered a screaming match with me so we could tear each other limb from limb. Yet he remains impossibly, chillingly calm, as if he were no more than a machine pretending to be human.

"I knew you would've been tormented over the option to have another woman bear the pregnancy," he says. "So . . . I made the decision in your place."

My blood goes boiling hot while my skin chills to ice. "Why did you just *assume* that'd be a discussion I couldn't handle?" I scream. Then, after a hesitant beat, I add, "Did it work?"

His bottom lip quivers. "Yes."

My scythe slips from my grasp. It clatters to the floor with a massive, resonant sound. I brace against the wall to keep myself from collapsing.

There is a woman out there pregnant with mine and Qin Zheng's baby. I will become a mother without having had any choice in the matter. Not even the option to end it by stabbing myself in the womb.

"It's a staffer I trust, Auntie Wei." Yizhi's voice carries over the ringing in my ears. "She's had two children before, so it won't be hard on her. She's being well taken care of. Her family received a new apartment in a prime location."

For a moment, I seriously consider killing Yizhi. I could sharpen the blade of my scythe and lop his head off.

The more rational part of me immediately recoils from the idea. A glimpse of his bed at the corner of my vision sends a splintering crack through my heart and across my psyche. There, beneath his covers, I once felt so safe as we held each other. I laughed and kissed him while indulging in my deepest desires, not caring how the world would condemn me for it, from that awkward, fumbling first time to knowing each other's bodies with practiced ease.

How could that boy from my happiest memories be the same one now ripping me apart?

I'm at a loss, yet the answer is obvious, literally right in front of me in the form of his Brotherhood tattoos. I always knew he had a dark side. I just never thought he'd turn it on *me*. Foolish, foolish me.

Does he even understand why what he did is unacceptable? Or does he think it's all right because he did it to spare me pain?

Numbness spreads through my limbs like I'm bleeding out. I can't stop shaking my head. "Yizhi, you realize what you did, right? You betrayed my trust. You lied to invade my body. You *violated* me. You know that, right? We can't come back from this. Ever."

The worst part is how resigned he looks, as if he's been preparing for this moment for a long, long time.

"I know," Yizhi says, no louder than a whisper. "I knew."

CHAPTER THIRTY-FIVE

ALWAYS PREPARED

"I can't believe him!" Taiping shakes her head beneath the tunnel shadows. With the automatic lights being too unreliable when we're sitting still, a bright white lantern illuminates the pages of dizzying calculations around her. "I swear, I had no idea!"

"I know," I say. "It was all him. All *them*."

"Next time I see Zhi'*er* . . ." She thrusts a punch into her palm.

"Don't," I mutter. "He has our dearest emperor's favor. I don't want anything to happen to you."

"What, to his top-secret mathematician?" She flicks the beads of her abacus, the only aid she can safely use for her calculations. They're pretty much finished, but she likes to triple-check her numbers whenever she thinks of something new to factor in as she reads up on advanced physics.

"The mathematician who's too scared to even wear silk nowadays?" I point out.

"Scared? What is Your Highness talking about? I abandoned silk to repent for the indulgent ways of my past," Taiping says in a solid imitation of Qin Zheng's public announcement voice. "Now I stand in solidarity with my fellow common working folk. No longer shall I don a material they can ill afford."

"*Stop*—" I wheeze, holding back a laugh that breaks through my gloom.

"But fine," Taiping returns her voice to normal, "I'll just give Zhi'*er* a scolding he'll never forget. I swear, he's always been a little strange, but this . . . he is literally playing with lives." She taps on an abacus bead. When she next speaks, it's with a slow caution. "Are you going to track down Auntie Wei?"

My interest droops to the ground. "I don't know."

What could I do? Force her to abort the pregnancy?

"That woman is a proud mother, and she is proud to carry the child within her." Qin Zheng snarled at me when I returned to the throne room to confront him earlier. *"You cannot force your will on her."*

Unsurprisingly, what happened between us in the dream realm changed nothing. Him wanting to fuck me doesn't mean he respects me. In fact, it probably makes him respect me less. Men like him are strange like that, seeing what should be intimacy as conquest instead.

I don't regret what I did with him, though. Who knows how much longer I would've been kept in the dark if I hadn't caught him off guard?

Not that I can do anything with the information. I couldn't even refute Qin Zheng's astoundingly hypocritical argument. I wouldn't forgive a man for demanding a woman carrying his baby to abort it, so what right do I have to do the same to Auntie Wei?

The best I can hope for is that she might miscarry, like Qin Zheng's concubines two centuries ago. But I have no doubt I'll then be pressured to try another pregnancy with my own womb. The gods seem convinced that having a child will be a vulnerability they can exploit in Qin Zheng.

Honestly, I might've gone with Yizhi, Sima Yi, and Qin Zheng's plan willingly if they'd discussed it with me. I'm not unreasonable when it comes to dealing with the gods and playing up a part to pacify the reactionaries.

But they didn't want to deal with the concerns I would've raised at every step.

Sighing through my nose, I tip my head against the tunnel wall. I still don't understand why Yizhi did this. How could it have been worth it? The only reasoning I can think of is that he had to prove he had no more feelings for me in order to keep Qin Zheng's favor. I recall the displeasure that descended onto Qin Zheng's face whenever he was reminded of mine and Yizhi's past relationship, the acridity in his voice in that memory before Yizhi suggested the procedure.

If Yizhi is that determined to draw a line between us, though, I'll respect that line. I want nothing to do with him again.

Taiping flashes a grimace. "Honestly, Your Highness, I don't understand why you ever bothered with men. Too many of them are *not* worth it. Not that I think they're born awful or anything, but getting away with being awful so much more often than us doesn't exactly discourage it. I mean, Zhi'*er*'s my own brother, and I'm not shocked to find out he did something terrible. I am always prepared to be disappointed by a man."

"Through being awful, they have all the power and control," I mumble. "Can't exactly avoid them when they do."

I think of how I ended up with all the men in my life, and how much that depended on them being male. Yizhi wouldn't have been able to take regular trips alone to see me if he were a girl. Shimin wouldn't have been recruited as a pilot, never mind getting paired with me. Qin Zheng would've been erased from history like General Mi. The world wronged each of them in a different way, but being men defined what they could do and where they could go.

Taiping makes a thoughtful noise. "If only you weren't the empress. I know so many *willing ladies* I could've introduced you to. I could've taken you to the clubs."

"Clubs?"

"You know, places like Club Lily, where Wan'er and I first met." She speaks with a glint in her eye. "Gathering spots for those of us who don't quite conform. Women who prefer women. Men who prefer men. Those who like either, or neither. Those who'd rather shake off the gender imposed on them from birth. Anyone who doesn't fit into the neat molds society tries to squeeze us into."

As she describes these "clubs" further, I recall Yizhi mentioning them at some point during our forest meetings. Back then, I knew too little about city life to conceptualize them, but now I can imagine the oscillating lasers, the thumping music, and the outcasts of society drinking away their troubles and dancing with wild abandon.

A flutter goes through my chest. "Places like this really exist?"

"No matter how hard the Sages tried to snuff them out, yes. The soldiers can raid one location, but another will pop up. They'll never be rid of us." Taiping grins. "The clubs aren't open right now because the revolution has everyone extra on edge, but they'll come back. They always do. Maybe I can take you to them in disguise one day."

I manage a smile. "I would love nothing more."

CHAPTER THIRTY-SIX

WORST MISTAKE

Although Qin Zheng played as big a part in the pregnancy scheme as Yizhi, I somehow don't hate him as much for it. It's hard to be disappointed in someone you never trusted.

That makes it easier to stomach climbing into bed just a pane of glass apart from him again for the sake of training.

"I would not be too distressed at the recent revelations." In a dream-spun, candlelit tavern, Qin Zheng sips from an antique-style goblet, the kind with three legs and bestial patterns sculpted into its surface. Unlike the tarnished teal artifacts displayed around Gao Qiu's estate, Qin Zheng's goblet gleams with the rich luster such objects originally had in his time. He often brings me two centuries in the past in his manifestations, teaching me things like horseback riding and taking me to long-gone restaurants and hawker stands to taste food from his memories. He claims it's to make me experience "the ways of a time that produced stronger pilots," but I think he just misses being in a world he understands.

He raises his goblet in a toasting gesture. "It is always a blessing to see the true nature of those around you."

"Like yours?" I sneer, kneeling opposite him at a low table typical of his time, refusing to touch the wine he conjured for me.

"Since when have I hidden my true nature from you? Has this honestly changed your opinion of me?"

I roll my eyes.

He *tsk*s, slamming down his goblet. "Do not roll your eyes at me."

"Or what?"

His eyes narrow. But then a devious smile lifts one corner of his mouth. He leans forward. "Or I might kiss you again. It seems you will only be a good girl when I have you moaning beneath me."

I snatch my goblet and hurl my wine at him. It splashes over his face and drips from the strings fastened under his jaw, which secure his tall headpiece. When he blinks his eyes open with a wider smirk and licks his glistening lips, regret chases my impulse. I've let him know he can rattle me by saying these rancid things. This will just encourage him to keep doing it.

Though not if I throw him off guard as well.

I spring onto the table on all fours and pull him in by the crossover collar of his old-style robes. When his mouth pops open in surprise, I seal it with my own. After the first second of shock, he kisses me back at the ready, hand going to my cheek.

Just when he's most distracted, I bite down hard on his bottom lip.

A muffled cry lurches in his throat. He jerks up, thighs hitting the low table, sending our goblets clattering to the ground. His hand grasps my hair near my temple. Fury flashes in his eyes when we break apart. Pain shoots through my scalp as he tries to yank me off the table, but I wrestle against him, seizing his chin.

"Was that enough to quench your thirst?" I peer down at him with a look fit for the sack of garbage that he is. "Because if you want to waste time fooling around instead of training for our all-important, nearly impossible god-slaying mission—now, *that* would change my opinion of you."

There's a beat before he loosens his hold on my hair. I let his chin go with a hard shove, keeping my face stiff as stone as I shuffle backwards off the table.

He watches me, touching his bleeding lip, before he recovers his smug expression.

"You and Secretary Zhang never made sense as a pair." Qin Zheng wipes the blood and wine off his chin. "He only had eyes for you because you were a prime target for his heroic fantasies."

Pain spears through my chest. "Why are you bringing him up?"

"Because you are moodier than usual, and that is an inconvenience. As I was saying, there is no need to mourn the loss of a facade. I am quite familiar with types like Secretary Zhang. They would come into the brothel heavy with tender sentiment, thinking themselves so refined and enlightened for asking a girl's name instead of prying her legs open the moment they were alone." Qin Zheng touches his chest, voice slow as syrup. "But beneath those kind, righteous exteriors, these boys possessed one common core: they were more enamored with the idea of being a savior than with the women they sought to save. Thus, here we are. He gets to feel like he made the ultimate sacrifice for your sake, while you must deal with the raw, open wound of betrayal."

My entire dream form throbs with feverish sickness. I clench down the urge to douse him with wine again.

"Such is the nature of those who grew up with excess." Qin Zheng picks his goblet up from the ground and gazes into its emptiness. "They never had to worry about survival, so their pretty little minds search desperately for deeper meaning to their lives. This makes Secretary Zhang an excellent campaigner against the corrupt elite he grew up among—do not get me wrong, I appreciate profitizer class traitors; some of my best comrades were class traitors. But as a lover? He will never understand those of us who grew up preoccupied with simply surviving each new day after the last."

"'Us?'" I spit out. "You're not making this an 'us' thing, are you? As if you didn't provide the vital material that made the baby possible?"

"I was thinking about you when I did it. Does that make you feel better?"

"*No!*"

His stifled laugh tells me I have once again given the exact reaction he wanted. I need to stop letting him mess with me. But, skies, is every conversation with him going to be like this from now on?

"Anyhow," he says, "it was Secretary Zhang who insisted on keeping the endeavor secret to spare you pain. I had no qualms about informing you."

"Then why didn't you tell me, huh?"

"Because I knew I would have to deal with *this*." He gestures at me. "I was in no hurry to make my life more difficult."

"You could've avoided *this* for good if you simply told me the gods had gotten serious about forcing you to have a kid. I'm not incapable of compromising. I proposed faking the pregnancy, didn't I?"

A trace of what might be remorse crosses his face, but maybe I'm just giving him too much credit because I can't shut him out like Yizhi.

"What's done is done," he says. "I shall give you some time to get over your emotions, but remember: we have grander matters to worry about than childish notions of romance."

"Oh, you're calling me childish again? I sure wasn't childish when you fantasized about having me in your bed. Or are you more messed up in the head than I thought?"

He grimaces. "Don't be disgusting." His gaze slides down my body, wrapped tightly in the spiraling robe style of his time. "No child has curves like yours."

I push up and storm away through the dark tavern. A burst of his laughter echoes behind me. I bristle. I've never heard him laugh out loud before. It's an unexpectedly boyish sound. But of course, *he's* the childish one. I don't care if my reaction amuses him anymore; I am not staying another second with him.

Dream logic works in surreal ways. There always seem to be other tavern guests at the edges of my vision, yet whenever I look directly at one, they're no longer there. I shove through the front doors and onto a nighttime street, where more hazy people stream through pools of light cast by traditional lanterns. I haven't mastered the art of getting out of these dream realms by will. It's especially hard in manifestations based on real memory. But this has to end somewhere.

Qin Zheng's waning chuckle approaches behind me.

"I jest, I jest—" He pulls at me by my wrist.

"Don't touch me." I thrash against his grip. "I am done with these pointless dream scenarios that are nothing but excuses for you to relive the long-dead past. From now on, I am not doing anything with you that isn't explicitly training. Next time you feel sad and lonely, you can cope by yourself."

Releasing me, he frowns in the soft, fluttering glow of a lantern. Then he sighs. "Empress, do you know why I won my wars of conquest despite the odds being one against six?"

"I swear, if this is leading to a joke about your 'giant dragon'—"

He holds up a hand. "I'm delighted you think my dragon is of a commendable size, but even with it, my enemies could have crushed me if they had banded together. The Yellow Dragon cannot be everywhere at once or operated indefinitely. Yet my enemies were too caught up in old grudges and internal bickering to ally effectively against me. Huaxia's existence is as much their failure as my victory. Let us not repeat their mistake, empress. If we wish to defeat the gods, we must not destroy each other before we destroy them."

"So it's of utmost importance that I stand here and take your perverted quips, or we'll lose to the gods?"

Qin Zheng looks away with a faint grin. "My apologies. I shall try to be less aggravating. It's just that I have so few avenues of amusement in my life. Certainly no one else to make perverted quips to, you know. Though perhaps that adorable assistant of yours . . ." He taps his lips. "She has great respect for me on an ideological level, does she not?"

"That doesn't mean she wants to sleep with you! Don't you dare go after her."

"Oh? Jealous, are we? You can fool around with two men at once, but I can't flirt with another woman?"

The urge to slap him shoots down my arm, but, judging by the anticipation on his face, he might enjoy that. I will not satisfy that kind of depravity. I simply stare at him, blinking blankly, before uttering, "You are the worst mistake I've made in my entire life."

"*So far.*" He points a finger. "The worst mistake *so far*. Though considering we will most likely not make it back from our assault on the gods, I sincerely hope you make no further life-shattering mistakes in the next seven months."

My vivid fantasy of lacerating his skin screeches to a halt. "Seven months?"

All traces of mirth vanish from his face. "I did not agree to producing a child with you solely to obey the gods. It presents an invaluable opportunity. The gods will never expect us to move against them before its birth, so that is exactly what we shall do. About a month before the baby's due date, on a day when the Heavenly Court passes over Chang'an shortly before dusk, we strike."

My mouth hangs open.

Qin Zheng continues, "I have confidence that we can root out the main counter-revolutionary forces before then so we can leave while assured of the revolution's survival. If we don't, we can delay the plan, but otherwise, I truly believe we have no better chance than this."

I shake my head like I'm malfunctioning, fingers going to my temples. "Seven months . . . That's—that's so soon."

"The longer we wait, the more likely the gods will discover our intentions. It is also clear my days are numbered." Qin Zheng studies his hands. "I do not belong in your time, empress. My home was . . . here." He spreads his arms, indicating the wood and brick buildings lit by flickering lanterns. "I am making my best effort at righting the wrongs of your world, but there is only so much I can do when I cannot even step outside without worrying about the pathogens in the air. A living man can never live up to a dead man's legend. I must go while my name can still rally the people to continue the revolution, the way the existence of Huaxia survived my first demise."

I should have no heart in my dream form, yet I can feel every heavy beat of my pulse inside me. Blurry figures pass in slow motion around us on this street spun from his memories. Bittersweet sentiment flows freely from him like blood from an open wound, so tender that, for once, I don't doubt his sincerity. Not when it comes to *this*, the mission he values above all else. The mission that will free Shimin along with Huaxia.

"You're less aggravating when you're saying sensible things," I mumble.

A shine gleams in his eyes. "Dying makes you see things clearer than ever. Coming back from the dead makes you see even more. I will not let myself waste away from disease a second time. That is not the kind of death I desire. If there is one thing I was brought back to do, it is to liberate this world from the gods." He holds a hand out to me. "How about it, empress? Seven months to transform the world."

Sighing, I squeeze his hand with both of mine, which feels more substantial than if I had simply placed my hand in his, in the same way a shared secret can mean more than a shared kiss.

"This doesn't mean I'll tolerate your perverted nonsense," I warn.

He laughs, clear as a bell. "I never expected you to."

CHAPTER THIRTY-SEVEN

REVOLUTION WITHIN THE REVOLUTION

In the end, I decide not to seek out Auntie Wei. Since no one involved me in the conception, it's not my problem. That is Qin Zheng and Yizhi's baby for all I care.

The idea of going to battle gets easier to stomach, knowing I'll endure six or seven more at most. Taking down the gods will have to be my best contribution to stopping the war. *How* it ends will be up to those in the future.

After Yuhuan's frontier-saving performance in the Plum Blossom Deer, more female pilots debut on the battlefield in their own Chrysalises, drowning out the voices of doubt one by one and alleviating the pressure at the frontiers. Even some female conscripts to the infantry are getting fast-tracked into officers. I thought this was what I wanted, that I'd be vindicated to see women make it into positions of power, yet I can't stop thinking about the words that may or may not have come from my sister's lingering spirit: *"Only three percent of people have Chrysalis-capable spirit pressures. How does this help the ninety-seven percent of women and girls who don't?"*

I have to face the facts. What has me becoming empress done for the average woman just trying to get by? Does my rise to power mean anything to them beyond a shock and a curiosity, when they can't replicate what I did?

The revolution is supposed to help them, of course. Everyone can breathe easier with basic levels of food, shelter, education, and health care provided for free. But those are being handled by Qin Zheng's government, with varying degrees of efficiency and sincerity across Huaxia. If I were still a peasant girl in my village, no matter what inspiring slogans hung in my local government, I'm not sure I'd trust whichever guys are now in charge to not laugh in my face and send me back to my family if I asked for help to start a new life in the city.

Through my lessons with Wan'er, I've learned that there are two different types of freedom. Negative freedom is the absence of external interference against doing something, while positive freedom is having the resources to actually do it. Removing the ban on girls going to school doesn't make a meaningful difference to a mountain peasant with no easy way of getting to one.

Maybe it's up to me to create the force that would've given my past self the resources to be free. If I'm really gone in seven months, I need to leave the women and girls of Huaxia with something more substantial than images of female pilots to look up to.

Inspired by the great public response to my aid tour to typhoon-ravaged villages, plus the long tradition of wives of prominent officials making themselves look good with charity work, I entertain the idea of establishing my own organization: the Phoenix Alliance. If I can find a way to fund it independently of the government, it won't have to answer to Qin Zheng when it comes to every little thing.

On the advice of Wan'er and Taiping, I start by consolidating a bunch of existing women-centered nonprofits. They serve as the Alliance's base structure, giving me an idea of how these things work and what kind of support is most urgently needed by which women. Single mothers, old women with no family left, "azure tower women" out of work after Qin Zheng's militant ban on prostitution, young girls being coerced or rejected by their families for whatever reason. Women trapped with men they wish they could leave.

Once we have some solid plans in place, I record a broadcast announcing the Alliance's founding. It's my first formal speech, standing at a podium with the Dragon Head Flag draped on either side of me and everything.

I'm no stranger to studio lights and production crews, but I've never talked at length to a camera. Less than five lines into the script Wan'er helped me write, I become wildly thankful that this can be edited before it goes public. I'm suddenly self-conscious of the way I speak. I mean, I always sound eloquent and sophisticated in my head, but apparently that is not true in real life. Even though I can't hear it myself, everyone says I have a noticeable rural accent. That's not supposed to matter after the revolution, but still . . .

I don't know how Qin Zheng does this *live* for several hours straight without once stumbling over his words. Practice, I guess. And a tragic lack of people willing to tell him to shut the fuck up.

Despite Wan'er's encouraging smile beside the cameraman, with every stutter and pause, I grow closer to dragging her into my place. But if I'm to go down in history as a leader, I must master the ability to rally people beyond just shouting slogans. This, as I've unfortunately discovered, is what ruling is all about. Speeches and paperwork.

Citing the higher poverty rates women face, the amount of our labor that goes unpaid, the number of us who get abused or killed by those who are supposed to love us, and other harrowing statistics, I call for donations to the Alliance. Using my empress powers to *force* people to contribute would make it a government action, so the funding has to come voluntarily.

My script ends there. Yet as I stare into the camera, knowing Huaxia's attention will, for once, be on my words alone instead of a sensationalized moment of me, I keep going. Truths spill like bile out of the depths of my mind. I speak of the way my grandfather used to get drunk and call me and my sister shameful disappointments for coming out as two daughters in a row, products of a weak woman he shouldn't have let his son marry. I tell of how we were made to clean the house and scrub the family's laundry from the time we were little, while our brother got to go out and play with friends before coming back to point out the stains we missed. I recount the time our grandmother fell sick and shouted for us and our mother every ten minutes with a new grievance, keeping us up through the night, never content until our father peeled himself away from a *cùjū* match on his screen for two minutes to bring her a single mug of hot water.

"Sons are more reliable after all," she remarked.

It feels like emptying myself of lifelong rot, turning myself inside out for the world to see. My gaze strays to Wan'er, who's standing with her hands clasped before her chest and a wet shine in her alert eyes. I no longer hesitate to confess my darkest impulses—I admit to enlisting as a concubine-pilot explicitly to kill Yang Guang.

"The truth is that he beat my sister Wu Ruyi to death in a fit of rage," I say, gauntlets pressed against the podium. "A lifetime of caring for others, doing everything asked of her, and this is what she received in return. It made no sense to me. Isn't following the rules supposed to keep us safe? The only conclusion I could reach was that we, as women and girls, are given the wrong manual at birth. The rules taught to us were never meant to guide us to a good life. We follow them out of some blind hope of being rewarded with the same love and effort we give out, but how has that worked out for our mothers and their mothers before them? How many of them got the devotion they deserved for their sacrifices? Have any of them ever *served* their way into true respect?"

The flow of my words amazes me as they run free, charging my voice with a power I thought I could feel only when towering over enemies in a Chrysalis. The fury that used to erupt from me as indignant shouts and violent outbursts weaves into smooth rhetoric with surprising ease, now that I understand why the world is the way it is. I didn't spend months reading all those books with Wan'er for nothing.

"We may stand with our laboring brothers against exploitative profitizers, but even among revolutionaries, there are men who claim to fight wholeheartedly against subjugation, only to become blind to it as soon as women are involved. In the same way that bosses treat workers like dirt, despite needing them to lay every brick and produce every necessity in society, these men attempt to convince women we can't live without them. Except, in reality, it's *they* who can't exist without *us*. At some point eons ago they figured out that if they isolate us, withhold resources we need to live, and call us worthless, they can extract all kinds of labor from us without respecting us for it. Yet if being on our knees was natural to us, why would they have to put so much effort into holding us down? The private home was the first institution of ownership, and women were the first class of people to be exploited as servants. We cannot dismantle the old order without dismantling this foundation on which it was based!

"There is an anger I know we all feel, an anger that tells us we deserve more for the work we do. But this anger too often gets unleashed on daughters, daughters-in-law, poorer women, or women from a different people. Targets safe to abuse without much fear of retaliation. This is a cowardly way of finding false relief. There will be no end to our misery unless we aim *up* at those with true power over us. I took justice into my own hands because the old order wouldn't give any to my sister, but doing it alone was always a fool's errand I survived by chance. Only together can we break the powers that so easily destroy us as individuals. For this very purpose, I am forming the Phoenix Alliance. Join me in this revolution within the revolution, and may it set us free. Power to all laboring women! In solidarity we rise!"

I raise my fist in salute.

After several seconds of no one moving, Wan'er says, "Cut!"

She gives a small clap, beaming.

A lungful of breath goes out of me. The production crew snaps out of their daze to join the applause, though their eyes are directed firmly at the ground. I should assemble my own female crew for future speeches. It's very inconvenient that these men have to work with me without coming near me or meeting my eyes.

The cameraman pulls back from his lens. "Your Highness . . . Well done, but I'm not sure His Majesty will approve of that last portion."

Something deflates in my chest at the reminder that, after all I've said, no one will hear it unless Qin Zheng decides they can. Because he will always be on guard about what I reveal to the masses.

"Send it to him," I say. "We'll see."

Qin Zheng lets the broadcast air, though not without unsolicited critiques once I arrive in the throne room for the night.

"Rely less on your papers. Relax your shoulders. Vary your cadence. Enunciate. Your efforts improved greatly in the second half, but in the future, do try to . . ." He trails off when I lie down sideways on my bed in the sheerest night robe I could get my hands on.

Although he's kept his word to focus on training while in our dream realm, I can tell it pains him to be stuck alone in his quarantine chamber. I have not been above exacerbating his misery. It's very petty revenge after everything he's done to me—and probably doesn't even make sense outside my head—but I do not care.

He clears his throat, eyes flicking everywhere except my body. "Do . . . try to use rhetoric that's less divisive of the working class. You have seen that women of the old order elites are some of the revolution's most fervent opponents. They only bemoan not being able to take part in the exploitation as actively as their male counterparts."

I don't bother arguing that this doesn't mean women's issues don't deserve special attention. I'm certainly not counting on *him* to pay that attention.

"Understood, *shīfu*," I simply say in my sultriest voice while trailing my fingers across the glass between us.

He shuts his eyes and bites his lip. "One of these days . . ."

"You'll come over here?" My breath fogs against the glass. "It's too bad that Your Majesty can only look, not touch." I run my hand over my hip. "That you can never hold or kiss anyone again for the rest of your life."

A chuckle rolls from deep in his chest. When he opens his eyes, they're dark with warning. "Neither can you, my sweet empress."

CHAPTER THIRTY-EIGHT

IN SOLIDARITY WE RISE

I try not to get my hopes up too high about the broadcast's impact, lest I be disappointed. Yet by the day after, so many people have reached out to the Phoenix Alliance that the donation platform crashes for a few hours. A flood of female Yellow Sashes—the revolution's fiercest defenders—take to the streets to campaign for more. In spontaneous mobs, they go door to door to wealthier families to ask if they've contributed.

Huaxia hasn't become equal overnight. Far from it. Even Qin Zheng doesn't think he can dismantle all markets and abolish the concept of money with a snap of his fingers. So far, Gewei Bu investigations have concentrated on the richest of the rich and the most egregiously corrupt, leaving the majority of business owners untouched. Those in the sectors Qin Zheng nationalized merely downgraded from owner to manager. As long as they do real work in running their operations, they continue to fetch handsome pay. However, now the rich fear the poor instead of the other way around. They have to stay on their best behavior. A single report of "counter-revolutionary sentiment" could land them on the Gewei Bu's watch list. A confirmed report gets them paraded to a prison like the Tianlao, where I hear Warden Lai has gotten very efficient at getting inmates to confess and repent.

Let's just say those with the means to donate are highly incentivized to do so.

It wasn't my intention for the Alliance to start off like this, but I'm not going to say no to funding. I do a second broadcast reminding the Yellow Sashes to register as volunteers before taking any action in the name of the Alliance, so we have at least a little more control over them. The Alliance staff organizes them into group chats. When everyone in a group knows each other, it's easier to guard against rebel double agents. A common strategy of theirs is to slip into a crowd and deliberately incite violence to sour people's opinions of the revolution. I can't play into their hands.

Some part of me laments having to urge moderation, though. The chaos the revolution unleashed has long confirmed what I've always believed: that there is more rage simmering within women, barely contained under their strained smiles, than men would like to think. Teenage girls are especially ferocious, starting a trend of carrying rolling pins and bamboo staffs while campaigning for the Alliance in packs.

With the funds they reap, we renovate a building inherited from one of the charities I absorbed and open the Alliance's first official outpost. It's situated in North Gate, the largest slum in Chang'an. On the day of the opening, my freshly hired all-female production crew follows me, Qieluo, the Alliance's management council, and a team of Yellow Sashes as we hand out supply packages to female residents.

Many women show up in hard hats and neon vests, grime on their faces but in high spirits. There are signs of construction everywhere. Instead of bulldozing slums and dispersing the residents, as the old order tried many times—which always led to another slum springing up elsewhere—the revolution is supporting the residents in upgrading the densely packed shanty homes according to their wishes, creating more stable structures with safer utilities. Although some North-Gaters left for opportunities in rebuilding the Zhou province, most would rather not move from the homes they're used to or lose the community ties they depend on. Turns out the best way to lift people out of poverty is to involve them in decisions concerning their lives. Shocker.

I smile and nod and thank my way through not only endless congratulations and pregnancy advice, but also earnest confessions of resonance with the experiences I spoke of in my speeches. It's not the most comfortable thing, realizing every stranger in Huaxia can now picture the ugliest parts of my life, yet this is the one advantage I have over Qin Zheng: the ability to walk among the people. I'd be foolish to not make the most of it. When I peer up through laundry lines and haphazard roofs at a cluster of skyscrapers gleaming in the sun, knowing they can no longer loom without a care as to what's down here, for the first time in a long while, I don't feel like I'm doing something terrible.

I pack my schedule with aid expeditions, including some to mountain villages like the one I'm from, which are critically lacking in medical knowledge and supplies. I grew up thinking every woman used wood ash to absorb her bleedings and that there are no ways to avoid pregnancy. Only after my first trip to Chang'an did I discover anything different. Thus, I show up at villages with trucks or hovercrafts full of better absorbers and silicone menstrual cups in addition to vaccines, antibiotics, and contraception. I am not letting another woman be robbed of control over her body if I can help it, and I am tired of the shame and secrecy around our bodily functions. I talk openly about how these supplies ought to be used as my production crew follows me through my visits.

Naturally, not everyone everywhere is happy to see me. In a village in the Song province—a reactionary-infested headache almost as bad as Han—I'm nodding through an old woman's tale of how she has divined my fetus to be a "girl who will transform the universe" when in the corner of my eye, I catch sight of a man hurling something at me.

"Tyrant!" he cries.

I lurch back just in time to avoid getting hit in the face. The thing explodes on my armor instead, covering me in a thick red liquid that drips to the ground.

The crowd pounces on him faster than Qieluo and my other security staff.

"You make a mockery of laborism!" he cries while wrestling against them, tears streaming down his face. "There's not supposed to be a hierarchy with an *emperor and empress* at the top! Power should be with the working people, not torturers and executioners!"

I fall stunned, my hands hovering before me in defense. That's not what I expected to come out of his mouth.

"You're still taking our grain and making us toil in the factories and mines! You're just calling the boot on our necks 'the people's boot'! You're *worse* than the old order! You're—"

One of my guards stuffs her glove into his mouth, but the damage has been done. The crowd that rushed to restrain him backs away, their arms dangling at their sides and their faces blank.

"Your Highness." Qieluo shuffles back to my side. "We need to get that off you *now*."

I sniff at a splatter of red on my gauntlet. It just smells like tomato.

"*Power to the laboring class!*" the man utters, the words muffled in his throat but obvious after we've all been hearing it as a greeting.

Surveying the dumbfounded crowd, and mindful of the cameras trained on me, I do the only thing I can think of to defuse the tension—I laugh.

"Pretty words! So easy to say!" I shout. "But what are you actually achieving? Stopping me from delivering aid to these good people! The revolution is indeed not perfect, but that's because we keep getting sabotaged by shortsighted fools! Did you think you could cow me? No! I'm staying right here and doing something productive for the revolution, unlike you!"

"Long live the revolution!" Qieluo calls out.

"*Long live the revolution!*" the crowd repeats, because no one wants to be seen failing to do so.

Still, I can tell they're much more relaxed, even revitalized, as a pair of my guards drag the man to the nearest magistrate's office.

"Long live the empress!" some chant of their own volition.

"What do we tell His Majesty?" Qieluo mutters to me while the crowd cheers.

"Nothing," I whisper, suddenly wary of an overreaction from Qin Zheng. If he finds out, I'll deal with it then, but I won't tattle on purpose. "It's not a big deal. Just tomato sauce. That guy probably hid a pouch near his stomach so none of you caught it during the pat-downs."

"So do we . . . let him go?"

I imagine what could've happened if I'd failed to deflect his words. The doubt that could've festered in these people if he'd gone on shouting these things in the village square.

"No," I say. "Keep him locked up."

Despite the occasional negativity, I remain undeterred. The Alliance continues our strategy of converting the offices of the organizations we absorbed into new branches across Huaxia. Out of the locations available for a second Chang'an branch, I realize I can pick one close to Tang Anding's *xiǎoqū*. I then persuade her to work for us as a receptionist by sending a letter citing her "exceptional standing in the community." It gives me the perfect excuse to constantly be in her vicinity so I can hone my spirit sense. Meanwhile, Taiping quits her job at Gao Enterprises and comes to work for the Alliance as well, bringing her logistics management skills and business connections to keep every branch stocked with supplies.

I'm looking through a budget report with Taiping and Wan'er one day, training my sense of the trace of Shimin's spirit signature in Tang Anding outside my office every few minutes, when a commotion breaks out at the front of the building.

"What's going on?" I open my door, scythe in hand. Taiping, Wan'er, and Qieluo follow me out to a scene of a group of Alliance staff standing around a red-faced army officer. A junior lieutenant, judging by the insignia patches on his olive-green uniform. He must be one of the low-born soldiers Qin Zheng has been promoting to replace the old order's army leadership, because his peers entrusted him to be a Revolutionary Vanguard as well. A tricolor sash encircles his waist, and a dragon head pin gleams near his heart.

The staff scoots in either direction to open a path for me.

"Your Highness," Tang Anding glances between me and him, "he said he's—"

"Looking for my wife," says the lieutenant between heavy breaths. "Didn't know Your Highness was also here." He raises his fist in salute. "Power to the laboring class."

His other hand flexes near the gun at his hip.

"In solidarity we rise." I hold up my free hand, gesturing for my staff to shuffle behind me.

"His wife came to take shelter with us," one of them whispers near my shoulder. "Said he beat her and threatened to kill her. I saw the bruises."

"That is nonsense!" The lieutenant points. "Your Highness, my wife must've been exaggerating. She always makes a big deal out of nothing! First they cry, second they make a scene, third they threaten to hang themselves. You know how it is."

"No, I *don't* know." I stamp my scythe more firmly on the ground, making a crisp *ping* against the tiles. "Did you or did you not put your hands on her?"

"It's not what Your Highness thin—"

"It's a yes or no answer."

"She hit me first! Shoved me right here!" He slaps his chest.

"What were you doing when she shoved you?"

He makes an indignant noise. "Right, the whole world gets outraged when a man hits a woman, but when a woman hits a man, suddenly nobody cares!"

"I didn't say I don't care. I'm literally asking you to explain the situation because I want to know more. What were the two of you doing when she pushed you?"

His flushed face goes even redder. "I was just trying to get intimate! Does Your Highness have any idea how long it's been since she's put out, even though I'm laboring for the revolution every day?"

I take a sharp, harsh breath. "So . . . you tried to force yourself on her, she fought back, you beat her up and threatened to kill her, and therefore she ran here?"

His mouth opens, closes, opens. "Don't—don't make me sound like the bad guy! Are men not even allowed to want their wives anymore? I'm sick of these double standards! You don't want equality; you want special privileges! You want to make women a new class of oppressors by controlling men's right to sex and fatherhood! You—" He spots something behind me. "Put that camera away!"

I look over my shoulder. Wan'er is filming him. She takes a step back, but doesn't lower her tablet.

He shoves me aside, hand going to his gun.

Qieluo lunges for him as I stumble, but I sharpen my scythe with Metal qì and swing it.

The curved blade lops off the lieutenant's head, sending a splatter of blood across the staff. Screaming, they back away. His body hits the floor with a heavy *thud*. His gun clatters beside him, sliding across the tiles.

Blood gushes from the stump at his neck, forming an expanding scarlet pool. His severed head rolls near my foot, eyes and mouth still open. Drenched sideways in red, Wan'er blinks blankly a few times, then cleans her camera lens and angles it toward the head. She zooms in with two fingers.

More blood drips from the tip of my scythe. A metallic stench permeates the air.

"Nice." Qieluo is the first to say something. Lifting her cape, she wipes blood off her face.

The staff breaks into confused applause.

One of them retches. Tang Anding helps her to the nearest trash can.

"Sorry," I say, shaking my scythe above the pool of blood. Then I coordinate the cleanup, send Tang Anding to tell that poor woman what happened, and ask Wan'er to upload her footage to support the statement I'll make about this being self-defense.

"Cut the part where everyone clapped," I mumble while heading back to my office with her.

"We need better security." Taiping trails after us, empty-eyed. "At *every* branch."

"Well, the army's too preoccupied with reactionary insurgencies for that." I dry my scythe with my cape.

"I can train the staff and volunteers in self-defense," Qieluo suggests. "A lot of other women in my tribe have fighting skills as well. I can recruit them to help." She looks to Wan'er. "What about you? Know any fighters in your tribe?"

"Uh, my mother and I don't really interact much with the tribe." Wan'er scratches her head.

"That's too bad." Qieluo closes my office door and speaks more quietly to me. "You think His Majesty will be mad about this? That was a Vanguard."

"That was a man who touched *his* empress while pulling out a gun." I let out a bitter laugh. "He'll be mad he didn't get to kill that guy himself."

After the incident goes public, there's some outrage over what I did, but nothing that stops me from recruiting combat trainers for the Alliance.

Interestingly, aside from Rongdi women, a lot of trainers end up being well-muscled women who Taiping tells me used to patrol in front of Club Lily to ward off trouble-seekers. I discover that I have quite the following among these clubs, even before I became empress. I get the Alliance to sponsor the reopening of Club Lily and other places like it, because it feels like everyone who frequented them is in the same struggle. They no longer have to live so discreetly, since Qin Zheng's new legal code dropped the old order's obscenity laws. It was easy to persuade him to do that once I explained Wan'er's and Taiping's different experiences of them, demonstrating how those laws were disproportionately used against the poor. He can be reasonable sometimes.

As the Alliance's ranks grow by the day, we take inspiration from our teenage supporters and issue bamboo staffs to everyone as a nonlethal but intimidating weapon, along with a uniform consisting of a short red tunic, baggy maroon trousers, and a shawl of phoenix feathers lined with gold thread. It makes our members readily identifiable by any woman who needs help. Upon hearing a report of abuse, our people can march in a pack to seize the offender, deliver him to the local magistrate, and make sure no one waves the case away.

I'm not saying I'm building a militia. But it's always better to have a militia than to be caught without one. If Qin Zheng can have his Revolutionary Vanguards and Yizhi can have his Gewei Bu agents, then I can have my Phoenix Ladies.

CHAPTER THIRTY-NINE

HOW MUCH MORE

By the time the green of summer leaves turns into the red of autumn, I can distinguish Shimin's remnant signature in Tang Anding no matter where she is in Chang'an. It's amazing how far my spirit sense can stretch, especially after I visit more places Shimin used to frequent. His school. The underground fight ring he worked at, now repurposed into a club called The Split Peach. If only he could witness how the establishment that used to pit him against other Rongdi men for the entertainment of the rich has been turned into a place where working men do jelly shots off each other's bare chests to resounding cheers.

I turn on my bar stool in my Phoenix Lady disguise to quip about it to Yizhi, only to feel my heart plummet like a stone when I remember he doesn't come with me on these trips anymore.

I don't know if I can ever heal from the wound he left in me. But at least I won't have to bear with it much longer. Plus, I have Wan'er, Taiping, Qieluo, the Iron Widows, and the Alliance. For these last few months of my life, I'll be far from alone.

The Split Peach aside, I think Shimin would've been most excited about the new, fairer civil service exams. There's no shortage of smart, competent people who'd do good governmental work to usher Huaxia into a better future after Qin Zheng and I are gone. It's just a matter of finding them.

Whereas the exams used to be laden with corruption and restrictive criteria, Qin Zheng announces a new round with only one requirement for takers: that they not own any property.

"If you wish to make decisions for the people, you must prove you are more loyal to community than property!" he says in a thunderous broadcast.

Since gender is no longer a limitation, Wan'er and Taiping decide to try their hand at the exams. I discontinue our lessons and redistribute their Alliance duties so they can prepare. Instead, I ask for Di Renjie to tutor me. I may be leaving this world soon, but I'm still interested in learning as much about it as possible.

It hardly takes any convincing for Qin Zheng to agree to let Di Renjie come to Chang'an with me after my monthly battles. No objections from nosy officials either. To them, Di Renjie is no longer a man. It continues to perplex me. Are genitals all that makes a man to them?

Di Renjie is certainly a man in his perspectives, lacking Wan'er's or Taiping's knowledge of women's writings and women's issues. He is also a harsher tutor, unafraid to call me out on mistakes. But I appreciate his no-nonsense attitude, and he's never condescending the way Qin Zheng is. He'd make a great official. I plan on making Qin Zheng pardon him before we set off on our mission so he can take the exams in the future.

It takes a different caliber of person to be an official nowadays. Those who refuse to accept the idea that they must serve the masses instead of the other way around are a high-risk group for defection to the reactionaries. Gewei Bu agents keep close watch on every high-ranking scholar-bureaucrat, rooting out any sign of corruption or treason. It's rumored that officials bid their families a tearful goodbye every morning in case they don't make it back from work. They are so melodramatic.

I can't deny there've been a lot of executions in general, though. They've become a performance, happening every day in the Phoenix Nest stadium, witnessed by thousands of cheering spectators and broadcast on millions of screens. The reactionaries call us cruel and terrible for it, but what they refuse to understand is that *we're* the temperate, orderly force compared to the raw will of the people. It's like how the Red Cliff Dam dampens the primal power of the once flood-prone Chu River that runs across Huaxia, and instead harnesses that energy to fuel twenty percent of our electricity needs. If we fail to diffuse the people's wrath through official channels, it will readily burst past us and drown everything in sight.

Entry to the stadium stands is first come, first served. I hear some old ladies bring their needlework and stay there all day to watch criminals get—depending on the severity of their crimes—hung, beheaded, or shattered by a contraption called The Hammer of Judgment, literally a huge metal block that swings up on a hydraulic system before smashing down. Reserved for the worst offenses imaginable, it guarantees that the culprit won't have a dignified form in the afterlife, if there is one. It was devised as an alternative to older extreme punishments that the central court talked Qin Zheng out of bringing back, such as death by a thousand cuts or drawing and quartering.

I never watch Hammer executions, even though they're usually quite the event, and the list of crimes read out beforehand tends to turn any sympathy to ash. They remind me too much of the crushed bodies in my nightmares.

While The Hammer is reserved for the worst of the worst, the milder methods have taken the lives of some who haven't committed any crimes themselves. Di Renjie criticizes this extended punishment policy harder than anything else.

"Basing guilt on whether someone had 'reasonable opportunity' to report a crime is far too vague and subjective," he says after a particularly bloody day of executions that spiraled out of several Chang'an officials getting caught communicating with the reactionaries. "Extended punishment condemns more innocent parties than guilty. It does not work. You cannot execute one innocent without making ten more enemies."

I shake my head and change the topic. There's no swaying Qin Zheng on this unless we can present a more effective way to root out enemies. Reports from family, friends, and neighbors have nipped so many counter-revolutionary plots in the bud, yet who would've turned their loved ones in if they weren't terrified for their own safety?

At this point, stopping the executions will not magically bring harmony to Huaxia. What the old elites want is to return to power, and they can't do that without retaliating against the common people. I can't bear the idea of people like my brilliant Alliance staff getting dragged into the streets and slaughtered. We *need* to win this civil war before we can go after the gods.

We don't execute children, at least. Though that hasn't stopped the reactionaries from claiming we do.

"This madness, this bloodshed, it must stop!" Zhuge Liang cries in the messages the reactionaries broadcast any way they can.

It's a game of cat and mouse between us and them. We send operatives to infiltrate their ranks; they have informants within ours. There are double agents, triple agents. The most fiery Yellow Sash at a rally could be a rebel provocateur. The most bitter defector who joined the counter-revolution after their family's executions could be funneling information back to us because they never liked their family anyway. The most well-trained Gewei Bu agent planted in a rebel hideout could turn against the revolution for real. No one can be entirely trusted. There's no telling what someone truly believes in until it's too late.

To our endless frustration, the reactionaries have gotten very good at sabotaging supply chains, causing the shortages Taiping predicted and contributing to the economy spiraling out of control. The average person isn't thinking about how Huaxia will have a better future as long as it can ride through this bumpy transition; they just know everything costs ten times more now, if they can even find it in stores. That compels them to either join the reactionaries in thinking we're destroying Huaxia with our far-fetched policies, or to march with the Yellow Sashes and shout about us not going *far enough*. Not enough profiteers and saboteurs being purged, not enough pressure on manufacturers and producers, not enough restrictions on prices. There's no longer any middle ground. The two sides clash on the streets and in the countryside, each act of violence and hatred pushing each other further to the extremes.

Some days I come close to exploding with exasperation. The setbacks and unrest have stalled many issues we're meant to fix. In rural villages, parents still get caught binding their daughters' feet, ingrained as they are with the belief that their daughters won't marry well otherwise. To reassure them, the Alliance organizes events where young boys make dramatic vows to marry only unbound girls in the future. Yet that then makes women with still-bound feet feel repulsive and ashamed, which isn't ideal either. Although reversal surgeries are free, the wait lists are extremely long. It doesn't feel possible to solve every issue like this before I go after the gods.

Then again, isn't that why I created the Alliance? The bonds between the Phoenix Ladies will outlast me. Now that they've experienced the power they can hold when they band together, they won't forget so easily.

It makes me more anxious for Wan'er's and Taiping's exam results. If they can get positions in the central court before I go, the Alliance's future will be even more secure.

The day the national scores are set to be posted online, I await them with the Alliance's central management council at our North Gate outpost, which I returned to working at after I no longer needed to be at Tang Anding's branch to train my spirit sense.

At our meeting table, I make Qieluo refresh the rankings page on her tablet over and over. Everyone else does the same on their own devices. All of Huaxia will find out who the top scorers are at the same time, once an algorithm matches the anonymous tests to their identities.

When we reach the exact reveal hour, the page gets stuck loading. I come close to springing out of my seat to pay the system engineers a stern visit before the rankings finally appear. They're filled with serial numbers at first, then the digits decode into names.

Cries of shock erupt around the room. Taiping screams. It takes me a second longer to read what they saw.

3. Shangguan Wan'er.

Wan'er is the *tànhuā*, the third-highest scorer in the nation.

I join Taiping in screaming. Wan'er gawks at the rankings, looking like her mind has detonated in her skull. Her mother, Auntie Kudi, clutches Wan'er's shoulder, her eyes shining with joyful tears.

"*Tànhuā!*" Taiping shakes Wan'er. "You're the *tànhuā!*"

"And you're in thirty-fourth place, Taiping!" Auntie Fu, another woman on the council, has scrolled farther down her screen. "Congratulations!"

"Oh, shit, really?" Taiping shrieks, checking her tablet again.

"Not bad." Qieluo grins and starts clapping.

The rest of us break into louder cheers and applause. Taiping yells "Group hug!" with almost growling aggression. We maneuver around the table to huddle together. Qieluo stays in place at first, mouth warping in disgust, but I tug at her arm until she relents. She joins the huddle with a roll of her eyes.

An even greater tide of noise rises outside the room. We open the door to find our Phoenix Ladies and the women sheltering with us screaming and jumping. Local North-Gaters are gathering beyond the glass front doors. Wan'er and Taiping get marshaled out into the crisp autumn day and lifted into the air by the crowd. Wan'er squeaks and Taiping throws her arms up, hollering. As I laugh while watching them get paraded through the streets we're cleaning up, I don't think I've been more happy in my life.

This. This is what I'm fighting for.

I just wonder how much more blood I'll have to spill to defend it.

I'm preparing to leave for the palace to discuss Wan'er and Taiping's potential government positions with Qin Zheng when two men enter the Alliance building.

Frowning, I pause my conversation with a single mother seeking help. Everyone in the reception area shifts more alert. Few men have dared to step foot in Alliance branches after the beheading incident.

The two look like typical Yellow Sashes, with shabby tunics and trousers and carelessly cut short hair, yet the armed guard outside the glass front doors stares over her shoulder in terror.

"Can we help you, citizens?" I say after exchanging greetings and salutes with the men.

"Gewei Bu," they say in sync, flashing their badges, which have an emblem of a dragon head in front of a shield.

The air goes still. Qieluo subtly moves her arm in front of me.

"We hope Your Highness will not impede our work," one of the Gewei Bu agents adds.

Shit, are they finally coming to investigate Taiping for being born so rich? I listen carefully to any movement in the back of the building. She's still in a meeting room there. Would it be too suspicious if I sent a signal for her to get out?

To my surprise, the other agent turns to Wan'er, who's at my side. "Are you Shangguan Wan'er, daughter of Kudi Suiye of the Qiang tribe?"

"Yes?" Wan'er tilts her head.

"Where is your mother?"

"In . . . the back?"

The agent marches past the front desk.

"Hey!" I shout, unease building inside me.

Wan'er puts a calming hand on my arm while speaking to the first agent. "What does the Gewei Bu want with her?"

"Did she recently write a short story titled *The Journey of Miss Meng Jiang*?"

"I . . . think so?"

The agent takes a pair of handcuffs out of his trouser pockets. "Shangguan Wan'er, you are under arrest for failing to report Kudi Suiye's counter-revolutionary rhetoric."

CHAPTER FORTY

ENOUGH IS ENOUGH

"You have to let her go!" I slap the glass of Qin Zheng's quarantine chamber. Wan'er and her mother voluntarily went with the Gewei Bu, stopping me—and Taiping, who stumbled out of the back offices with Auntie Kudi—from attacking the agents. But I can't just do nothing on my part.

"Calm yourself." Qin Zheng stands behind the glass, reading a stack of papers about something completely different—there are graphs on the pages. "If your assistant and her mother are innocent, they should be able to clear the matter up."

"What if they can't?"

Qin Zheng looks up from his papers, brows furrowing. His under-eye circles are so severe it looks like he smeared soot beneath his bottom lashes. "Then why was your assistant's mother spreading counter-revolutionary rhetoric?"

"The definition for that is so broad! That short story wasn't even published; she just shared a draft with friends!"

One of whom reported her, I realize in a rage.

But then my fury fades, because what were they supposed to do when *not* reporting would doom them if the story were found to be transgressive?

This is exactly what we've been bringing about. Friends being forced to betray friends.

"Your Majesty can get a copy of the story from the Gewei Bu to judge it yourself," I add. "Please."

Qin Zheng lets out an aggravated sigh. "I do not have time to read *stories*. Your lady friend is not more deserving of clemency simply because she is your friend."

"I'll sleep with you! In the dream realm!"

There's a stunned moment before he drops his arm, crushing his papers. "Is that what you think I would want?" he says, voice as tense as a loaded spring.

"Isn't it?" I hook a finger in my armor collar. "I'll do it. However you like best."

It wouldn't be real, anyway.

"Listen to yourself!" He shouts with a force that turns to static through the glass wall's intercom. "Have you no faith in the revolution's systems of justice?"

I don't answer.

He turns his back on me, shaking. "Leave. Your assistant and her mother will go through an investigation like every other suspect in Huaxia. That is final. Do not interfere."

"Or what?" I snap. "You'll arrest me, too?"

"I will make sure you never see the light of day again," he says over his shoulder.

I scream again and again as I parry swords with Qieluo past midnight, using the gigantic bedchamber in my palace residence as a training space. Qieluo didn't used to use a sword, but she's learning how to fight with one alongside me. We both forged our swords out of an extra bit of spirit metal from the Yellow Dragon and the White Tiger respectively over the past few months.

I feel bad for keeping Qieluo up so late, but I had to take this aggression out somewhere. I couldn't bear to stay with Taiping, who's worried sick about Wan'er. I couldn't concentrate on any books. I couldn't even practice sculpting constructs on a pottery wheel without hurling the whole ball of clay against the wall.

"Hey, slow down!" Qieluo holds a hand out, pausing our sparring. Stray hairs drift loose from her updo. Sweat shines on her forehead beneath the teeth of her White Tiger crown. "Careful! The baby!"

"The baby?" I sneer, remembering the four-month-pregnant padding under my armor. Padding that's supposed to be a *boy*, according to Doctor Hua's latest checkups on Auntie Wei. With a growl, I raise my sword, angling the blade toward my belly.

"Whoa!" Qieluo grabs my arm.

"It's not even—!" I catch myself before the truth escapes me.

Once the tension leaves my body, she loosens her grip. Swaying, I let my sword slip to the ground. It thuds against the long carpet in the bedchamber and skids across the floorboards. Head hanging low, I sink to the carpet as well.

"What are we doing?" I ask quietly, cradling my forehead.

Qieluo squats down next to me but says nothing. I didn't expect her to. Not when any wrong string of words could get her killed.

It's hypocritical of me to only have a problem with this once it implicated someone close to me. I know that. But if the system is harming even Wan'er, who I *know* would never betray the revolution, then clearly something is broken.

I can't stop fantasizing about breaking Wan'er and her mother out of the Tianlao. I can barely hang on to the understanding that it *will* make everything worse. Qin Zheng wouldn't tolerate that kind of rebellion from me.

But what if it wasn't just me?

I extend my arm. Qieluo helps me up.

"Contact as many Phoenix Ladies as you can." I attach my sword to my hip. "Tell them to gather at Unification Plaza first thing in the morning."

Qin Zheng likes rallies? I'll give him a rally.

I fetch my scythe from against the wall and head for the door to find Taiping. I bet she hasn't slept.

"Hold on, Central Chat is down." Qieluo shuffles after me.

Once we get outside, however, something's not right. My residence guards are talking urgently with each other, tablets in hand. They never chat while on duty.

"What's going . . ." I trail off when every lantern in view goes dark, leaving us beneath nothing but starlight.

Hurried footsteps scuff toward us from the distance.

"Your Highness!"

I bristle at Yizhi's voice. My instinct is to turn away, yet he's dashing so feverishly through the estate walkways, dressed haphazardly in his purple official robes, that I give pause.

"You need to get to the throne room right now!" he keeps shouting. "The pilots at the Han frontier have mutinied!"

CHAPTER FORTY-ONE

IN THE NAME OF THE PEOPLE

Liu Che, Wei Zifu, and a row of other Han pilots appear with Zhuge Liang on Sima Yi's screen, standing on the Great Wall with the Azure Dragon behind them. A camera drone's harsh floodlight blanches them out of the night.

Hugging my chest and pinching my mouth, I watch the video in the dark throne room, robbed of electricity after insurrectionists captured the Red Cliff Dam.

"Citizens of Huaxia, enough is enough with this tyranny we're living under!" Liu Che raises the rebel White Lotus Flag. It flutters and snaps in the camera drone's rotor winds. "Look at the world around you—who truly holds the power? How come we have not seen His Majesty out in battle since his return? Something is wrong, and we are being deceived! Clearly, he is not the same emperor of our legends! That emperor would never have let himself get bewitched by a wicked vixen out to ruin all men! He would never have let Huaxia descend into this backwards chaos where degenerates are free to take from honest citizens! Innocents are being tortured into confessing to nonexistent crimes, barbarians are infesting civilized spaces, women are destroying men with false accusations, and family values are falling apart! On behalf of all pilots of the Han province, I declare that we will no longer stand by these injustices! The Han shall not coexist with evil! Tonight, in the name of the people, we take back the real Huaxia!"

When the video ends, Sima Yi turns his tablet back toward himself. "We're trying to reestablish communication lines to receive updates, but so far, we can confirm that a significant portion of the army in Chengdu has defected. They killed the Han governor, opened the prisons, and armed the prisoners. There's all-out war in the streets of Chengdu and an ongoing firefight over control of the Red Cliff Dam."

"So the Gewei Bu's intelligence was partially correct." Qin Zheng massages his temples. "Have the troops from other provinces that I've been diverting near Han's inner borders been deployed?"

"They're on their way in," Yizhi says. "But our current defense plans don't account for the pilots joining the insurrection."

"Your Majesty must prepare to meet them in battle," Sima Yi pleads. "Only you can take down the Azure Dragon."

Qin Zheng's hand stops moving. His gaze remains on the shadow-shrouded floor for a long while.

There's a reason he's hesitating. A reason worth exploiting.

"All right, let's get right on that!" I raise my scythe, aiming its tip at his quarantine glass.

"Oi!" He backs away, arms raised in defense.

Sima Yi grabs my elbow. "What in the skies do you think you're doing?"

"You are not allowed to touch me!" I smack Sima Yi away while not taking my eyes off Qin Zheng. "What is Your Majesty afraid of? You coming out to battle would carry the same dangers as me breaking this glass. Are you ready to die for Huaxia? *Tonight*? Or do you have something more important to do?"

Yizhi and Sima Yi gawk at us in bafflement, but I know what must be playing through Qin Zheng's mind: *"If there is one thing I was brought back to do, it is to liberate this world from the gods."*

His jaw clenches. His hands ball into fists. "You want me to trust you with commanding the Yellow Dragon."

"I want to *defeat the reactionaries*. Do you honestly think I have any sympathy for them, after everything they've said about me? If you don't trust me, what did you train me for?"

Qin Zheng's face remains impassive in the cold light from Yizhi's and Sima Yi's screens, yet his chest heaves rapidly. "So you understand who the most dire enemies are?"

"I do. Have you forgotten who really started this revolution? If I wanted you gone, I could just bring down this scythe. But no. There are those I love who are waiting for me."

Our stare-down pierces across the glass as if electric-charged. The image of the horrific way the gods are holding Shimin captive wedges into my mind. I wouldn't be able to reach him if Qin Zheng were gone. He knows this as well as I do.

I thump my scythe back on the ground. "If you insist on not trusting me to get the job done, then . . ." I do a raised-fist salute. "Huaxia thanks Your Majesty for your service. Don't forget to leave a will."

He shuts his eyes. "Take Di Renjie and go."

"Your Majesty!" Sima Yi cries. "This is not the time to put personal caution before the security of Huaxia itself!"

"Chairman Sima, do not question my judgment. I am better off here, in overall command of the war fronts."

"Her Highness just came back from battle less than a week ago!"

"That was in the Fox," I point out. "The Dragon is fully charged."

"And I can give her some qì." Qin Zheng teases out the thread of spirit metal on his spinal brace that connects us for dream training. His eyes meet mine. "Consider it reimbursement for what you used to bring me back to life."

For the almost six months since my first battle with the Azure Dragon, the Yellow Dragon has stayed wound up around Mount

Ziwei, where the Palace of Sages remains in ruins as a warning to those wishing to bring back the old order.

Guess that warning's not working anymore.

Yizhi lends his qì to Di Renjie while Taiping drives us to the Dragon in a carriage. I'd rather not be dragging Di Renjie into this when he's also qì-exhausted from our recent battle, but I didn't bring my other eunuch-pilot, Feng Xiaobao, to Chang'an. I couldn't have foreseen that I could actually seize command of the Yellow Dragon. Qin Zheng even gave his armor to Di Renjie. For a male pilot, that's on par with sharing a toothbrush.

Technically, I could grab someone else to pilot with, but it's too risky to let anyone outside our inner circle know it's not really Qin Zheng who's in the Dragon. And of our inner circle, Di Renjie's high spirit pressure still makes him the least likely to perish. My brief, mad idea of asking Qieluo to take his place fizzled out when Qin Zheng and Sima Yi decided to send Qieluo and Yang Jian straight to the Han frontier in a hovercraft with reinforcement troops, so they can figure out what's going on there and fight in the White Tiger if necessary. Aside from Wei Zifu, there were no female pilots in Liu Che's broadcast. We don't know what happened to Liang Yuhuan, Guo Anle, and the other Iron Widows. I can't imagine they were willing to join the insurrection when their families gained so much from the revolution. I hope they're alive.

Halfway up Mount Ziwei's curving roads, the Yellow Dragon's head appears in the carriage's front lights like a massive boulder. With a grimace, Yizhi peels his hand off the thin needles Qin Zheng conjured on Di Renjie's gauntlet palm. Taiping slows the carriage to a stop. We rush out. Beneath the mountain, eerie darkness smothers Chang'an. Only the occasional sparkle flares up as backup generators kick in for essential buildings like hospitals.

The Dragon's chin alone is nearly twice my height. For a moment, the memory of my disastrous last battle in it stops me dead. But I've trained for this, strived for this, honed myself on the battlefield in hopes of gaining the skills to wield this vessel of ultimate power. I'm not the same pilot as I was all those months ago. I touch my gauntlet to it to compel its long snout to open.

"Your Highness!" Yizhi calls out.

I peer over my shoulder. His mouth moves again, yet closes without making a sound. Beside him, Taiping gives me a haunted look.

I wonder if she would like me to turn the Dragon around on a government once again.

"Don't worry about me," I say.

"Right." Yizhi sounds short of breath, nodding many times. "Right, Your Highness will be fine. Power to the laboring class." He raises his left fist.

I don't know what else I expected from him. What else he could have said in front of other people.

"In solidarity we rise," I mutter, before climbing up the Dragon's chin by attaching and detaching my gauntlets and knees one at a time like magnets.

Taiping and Yizhi help hoist Di Renjie up, and I pull him into the cockpit after me.

"How tragic civil war is, when kin slaughter kin," Di Renjie says, softly, while we take our pilot seats. "Perhaps we could have driven fewer ordinary folk to the other side if we'd executed fewer innocents."

"I know," is all I say.

"Is Your Highness finally willing to open your eyes?"

I don't respond. I swallow through a lump in my throat before pulling our consciousnesses into the battle link.

The world tips away, the transition much more disorienting than in the Fox. I scatter like a spirit in the oblivion beyond death before finding rebirth as the Yellow Dragon.

Yizhi, Taiping, and the carriage come into view before me, no bigger than ants. Once I get used to the vastly grander scale of the Dragon's senses, I brace its claws against the mountainside and then launch into the sky, unwinding its hollow length. It feels impressively close to Qin Zheng's simulations of our strike on the Heavenly Court, meant to happen in less than five months.

I convinced him that, for the sake of the mission, I wouldn't betray him, but that doesn't mean I'm happy with him. He's not as irreplaceable as he thinks he is. Give me over a decade of experience as well, and my skills could reach his level.

People on Chang'an's dead streets swing their flashlights up at the tremendous *whoosh* of the Dragon's flight. I find and follow the wide highway that leads south to Chengdu. Armored military vehicles come along the same way, speeding between transport trucks that have pulled over between extinguished streetlights.

After I reach the Bashu Mountains south of Chang'an, the highway becomes much harder to see in the moonless night, meandering around peaks and vanishing into tunnels. I keep myself oriented using the stars, thinking back on those nights when Big Sister and I sat in our backyard, pinpointing constellations with a star chart ripped from an old calendar. Like spotting a childhood friend, I recognize the big constellation that points south—the Vermilion Bird, inspiration for Shimin's Chrysalis. I imagine him gazing skyward on the same nights Big Sister and I did, finding some peace in the twinkling cosmos after a long day of school and work, with no idea he'd be snatched up there one day.

The gods must be watching me at this very moment. Are they entertained? I'm not counting on them to help take down the reactionaries when they've made no move so far. Maybe unless Liu Che does something that rivals me at my worst, like crushing the palace with Qin Zheng inside.

The imagery makes me undulate the Dragon faster. But it also keeps me hyper-aware that at any moment, I could turn around and kill him myself. I imagine him sitting at his desk in the dark, hands steepled under his chin, no armor and no Chrysalis, wondering if he just made the worst decision in his life.

Every few minutes, I flare my spirit sense, on alert for a Prince-class signature. I don't know where the Azure Dragon is, but logically it'll intercept me before I reach Chengdu, where I could destroy the insurrection with ease.

Mountains roll on and on in the thick shadows below, so deceptively peaceful in an empire that just shattered in two. My grasp of time scatters on the wind—I could be flying in an infinite loop through an infinite moment—until I sense a massive spirit signature speeding my way.

No, *two of them*.

I nose-dive in the Yellow Dragon and coil it around a mountain with a slow, gargantuan effort, snapping trees and flattening foliage. No point expending more qì to meet my opponents when they're coming for me so eagerly. They're not in visible range yet, but I'd bet my whole empress budget that the second signature is the Whale Bird, the other big, flight-capable Chrysalis in Han. So much for that battle we fought together.

I picture the Dragon's smaller Ascended Form, having a contour similar to its spirit armor except with vast wings and an antlered dragon head. I'll need it, to keep up with two Chrysalises at once. But it doesn't exist within the Yellow Dragon like a premade puzzle piece. Qin Zheng morphed it out on the spot with his ridiculous ability to liquefy spirit metal. Since I've yet to come close to that, I'll have to do this much more gradually.

I channel Water qì as if I'm wetting clay for sculpting. Very, very hard clay—

No, can't think that way. I push past the idea that Earth-type spirit metal must be stiff and unyielding. Instead, I ruminate down to the level of its primal particles, imagining the cold flow of my Water qì wedging into their dense formation, loosening them. I compel layer after layer of particles from the Dragon's head to push toward its front claws, extending them into arms. Using them, I press against the mountain and arch up to form shoulders. I'll have to find the balance between giving the subunit effectual proportions and leaving the Dragon's head thick enough to protect its cockpit.

The spirit signatures race closer. Two winged, bobbing silhouettes enlarge in the distance.

Right, can't forget the wings. The subunit won't be able to fly by undulation. I funnel more particles to sprout wings from its shoulders while stretching its second pair of claws into legs. Skies, why is there so much to craft? No time to replicate Qin Zheng's intricacy. My Ascended Form won't look like a warrior in armor but a beast that pulled itself out of mud. I hope the darkness will keep the pilots from getting suspicious.

As I strain toward a form my mind can comfortably embody, a memory not my own flashes through my head. Qin Zheng, struggling to manipulate spirit metal while hooked up to electrodes zapping him with pain. He wasn't born with his abilities. He also had to work tirelessly, fail countless times under threat of agony, to reach his level. I am not doing something impossible.

It's just unfortunate that I have no room to fail at all.

Wing beats crack above the mountains as the Azure Dragon closes in. With a roaring cry, it transforms to Heroic Form. Red and yellow rays split through its skeletal body and illuminate the mountaintops in a combined orange. Farther behind, what I can now confirm as the Whale Bird goes to Ascended Form in a burst of green.

This is it. I have to fight using what I sculpted so far.

As if I'm detaching from an oversized umbilical cord, I break the subunit off the Yellow Dragon. A hefty weight lifts from my mind, yet the subunit tips sideways. Its head is still out of proportion, and its joints grate like rusted machine parts.

With its four skeletal arms, the Azure Dragon snaps off four of its ribs and sharpens them into blades while lunging at me. I stagger into a wide stance and raise a sword I attempted to construct, which looks more like a paddle. The *clang* of metal meeting metal echoes across the mountains. Tremors travel down the subunit and into the earth. More strikes follow in a dizzying whirlwind of blades and arms and luminous qì. I reel backwards, hearing Qin Zheng's voice from our training sessions, yelling at me never to linger within my opponent's reach. The reaction times and battle instincts I've honed kick in, however clumsily.

"The first order of close combat is to read your opponent's style. Identify their weaknesses and openings!"

Liu Che and Wei Zifu clearly never trained in actual sword fighting. Their slashes are too wide, meant to look flashy against Hunduns rather than to attack and defend with efficiency. I keep my sad, blunt sword firmly in front of the subunit's head, deflecting their blows with movements as tight as possible, while channeling Metal qì to sharpen my blade edge. If we were fighting as humans, I would've had so many openings to stab their organs already. But Chrysalises don't have organs, which is both a blessing and a curse. While I don't have to worry about protecting my core, they don't either. I'll have to get past four moving arms to strike their cockpit and win.

I continuously back away, shedding spirit metal beneath every step as I compress the subunit closer to the Azure Dragon's size and adjust its head-to-body ratio. While stretching my wings wider and thinner, I fan them for balance so I don't tumble down the mountainside. If that happened, there's no way I could keep passing myself off as Qin Zheng. Though this subunit is so rough, I'm pretty sure anyone watching already has suspicions.

I think of what he said about Chrysalises being limited only by assumptions. Does the same apply to the voice that comes out of a unit?

"You insolent children!" I do my best Qin Zheng impression, repelling one blade slash while ducking from two more. "You dare rise against me?"

My voice does come out deeper, but I'm not sure how convincing it is. I really should've done more Qin Zheng impression contests with Wan'er and Taiping.

"Your Majesty, wake up to the truth! You must set Huaxia free again!" Blazing Fire red, the Azure Dragon's swords slice across the subunit's forearms when I raise them in defense. Psychic pain streaks across my mind. I try to will it away, but it's hard to fight the innate notion that a wound must hurt.

"Free to do what?" I keep up my Qin Zheng impression. "Free to starve? Free to sleep on the streets?" I flap the subunit's wings more vigorously, feeling them grow closer to flight capability. Each swing gets less stiff. "Free to bind girls' feet and sell them as brides? To make children work in factories and mines? To cut corners on safety because human lives matter less than *profits*?"

Finally, the wings propel me off the ground.

"*Human lives?*" The Azure Dragon chases after me in an unhinged dance of blades, the clashes of metal punctuating our argument. "The revolution kills people every day!"

I pump my wings through the night, rising and dipping and swiveling to stay out of stabbing range while continuing to sharpen my sword with Metal qì. It's a while before I manage to say what I need to: "Most of those we execute killed far more innocents in their years of holding power, and they would have kept killing if not for the revolution!"

"No, plenty of ordinary people have been tortured and killed just for saying the wrong thing, or because of something their *neighbor* did! People can't trust their own families anymore!"

"Yes, I know! I know that!" I break character in sheer exasperation. "Many have suffered and died! So many things have gone wrong! It's a mess!" I dodge and parry the Azure Dragon's erratic strikes from its four swords. "There've been false accusations, arbitrary imprisonments, and people who've come to power only to abuse it!"

The Azure Dragon falters in the air, making a confused noise. Probably it's wondering why we're fighting if I agree. I imagine stopping this battle, revealing my identity, and fighting alongside the Azure Dragon to take over Chang'an and undo the revolution. All of it.

...As if the reactionaries would ever work with *me*.

"But you know what *also* had all of those things, except worse?" I snap the subunit's wings back to pounce toward the Azure Dragon. "The old order! The fact that the revolution hasn't gone perfectly means we need to do better, not that it's not worth pursuing at all!"

I was about to summon a rally of Phoenix Ladies to protest extended punishment, but that's very different from wanting the revolution reversed altogether. In fact, extended punishment is in place *because* of the reactionaries' vicious sabotage. I won't find liberation with *these* people. Defeating them is the real key to freeing Wan'er.

"But the revolution clearly doesn't work!" The Azure Dragon deflects my sharpened sword. "Everything's falling apart!"

I flick my sword right back for more strikes, looking for an opening through its four swords. "It's only been half a year! Do you think paradise can be built with the press of a button? It's you reactionaries who've been sabotaging crops and blowing up bridges and roads! You're trying to claim a baby isn't capable of breathing while actively smothering it in its cradle!"

"Sorry that we can't stand by as innocents get killed!"

"Your comrades have killed so many people in the countryside! And they're killing more in Chengdu as we speak!"

"That's different! The rebellion is trying to save Huaxia!"

"So is the revolution!"

Our swords cross with a particularly loud resonance.

"You—" the Azure Dragon starts to hiss.

I twist my sword free and drive the now razor-sharp point toward its head.

The Azure Dragon drops through the air just in time to avoid the strike. My sword nicks off one of its antlers instead.

It lets out an indignant growl. "You are not my emperor!"

I'm not sure if Liu Che and Wei Zifu mean they see through my admittedly flimsy ruse, or if they're just being dramatic, but it doesn't make a difference. There's no talking this out. We could list each other's atrocities all day and not produce any change of mind, because this was never really about the morality of who deserves to live or die. This is a showdown between two classes of people with opposing interests. Whoever wins gets to tell the story.

So focused on keeping track of the Azure Dragon's four swords, I almost miss the Whale Bird soaring up behind me. It swings its twin maces at my subunit's head.

I don't duck fast enough. The blow catches me, sending me tumbling out of the sky. I crash-land and roll down the mountainside, instinctively letting go of my sword, before I collide with the Yellow Dragon's colossal husk. How did I ever pilot all of it?

The Azure Dragon and the Whale Bird dive toward me. Grasping the husk, I compel a length of it to split off. Then I channel Fire qì for strength and swing the detached section at the duo.

The Azure Dragon swoops out of the way, but the Whale Bird takes the full force of the blow. It smashes into another mountain, raising a cloud of debris like smoke in the night.

I lunge to retrieve my sword, ready to guard against the Azure Dragon's next strikes. Yet it doesn't go for the subunit's head. Upon reaching me, it banks sharply to my side. The instant I parry its swords, it releases three of them. The sudden lack of resistance makes me spin off balance. Its fourth sword slashes into one of my wing roots. Pain erupts through the subunit's shoulder. I whirl to reorient myself.

Dropping its last sword, the Azure Dragon grabs the wing with all four hands and works with my momentum to tear it right off.

I scream and slash out with my sword, but the Azure Dragon veers directly behind me. Its top pair of arms pinions the subunit's shoulders. Its bottom two arms lock around the subunit's waist. As I wrestle against the double hold, the Azure Dragon hoists me skyward with a blast of qì from its wings.

The world blurs into dark streaks. Wind bears down on us. The blast from the Azure Dragon's wings goes on and on, sounding like a simmering kettle. It's an incredibly wasteful way of flying, but it gets us higher at a concerning speed.

"*Whoever is piloting the Yellow Dragon doesn't seem capable of instantaneous mending.*" Zhuge Liang's voice crackles inside the Azure Dragon's cockpit, faintly audible behind me as we soar higher and higher. Is he watching through a camera somewhere? "*On my signal, drop it!*"

I imagine the subunit plummeting from the heavens, unable to fly with a single wing and unable to sprout another before hitting the ground in an impact that kills me and Di Renjie.

Fire qì roars through me in a last-ditch effort to break the Azure Dragon's hold. I wrench at its arms as best as I can. I sap qì from everywhere its surface touches mine.

It doesn't budge.

When we reach a height I'm no longer sure I can survive, my goal switches to *preventing* it from letting go. Concentrating Fire, Metal, and Earth qì in one arm, I stab my sword through the subunit and into the Azure Dragon. The tip ruptures all the way out of its back. I split the exposed blade and flatten the halves to lock us together.

Cussing, the Azure Dragon sputters in its flight, switching to beating its wings to keep afloat rather than blasting qì out of them. Its bottom hands grope for my sword hilt. This is far from a solution. While squirming to drop us lower, I start mentally carving a wing shape along the subunit's back and side. It should be easier to peel the shape off and shift it into a proper wing than to morph one out from scratch. Though with the Azure Dragon's bottom arms around my waist, I won't be able to test it until the moment I plummet.

When I make the mistake of looking down, dread seizes me, stiffening the subunit's limbs. The mountains await beneath thousands and thousands of stretches of nothingness, the fall too far to survive yet not far enough to give much time for wing adjustments. Maybe if I shed the subunit's whole lower half on the way down ...

I almost burst into irrational laughter. Even if I survive in that way, the Azure Dragon won't be gone. It'll come right back for me and my broken subunit. Maybe the Whale Bird will, too, if its pilots are still alive. Over and over, I see my bones breaking and my flesh bursting through my skin, like the images of Shimin and Xiuying and my family that pervade my nightmares. What was all that for? Slaughter leading to slaughter leading to slaughter ...

Memories jolt me like electric shocks. The new Iron Widows standing together, the delighted women of North Gate, my Phoenix Ladies parading through the streets.

No, everything I've done was not for nothing.

I will not let it be for nothing.

I turn the subunit's head over its shoulder, open its mouth, and disconnect from the battle link.

My mind crashes back into my human body. The worst disorientation I've ever felt hits me like a violent tide. I retch bile over the side of my pilot seat.

"End the tyranny, Your Highness," I think I hear Di Renjie say.

"Yes, yes, come on!" I wipe my mouth and push to my feet. Spots swarm my vision. I wobble to the cockpit wall, slam my back against it, and carve a pair of wings for my armor, as expansive as my mind can handle. Praying they'll work, I leave a second set loose for Di Renjie and stumble ahead through the subunit's open mouth. Wind flutters in my face as I approach the edge. Holding my breath, I flip over the side of its jaw.

There's a stomach-lurching weightlessness, then its shoulder smacks into me. The bobbing from the Azure Dragon's wing beats nearly jostles me down the curve, but I fuse the hands and knees of my armor to the spirit metal. Detaching two at a time, I crawl toward the subunit's neck. I don't want to put my wings to the test unless I have to.

My eyes water in the shrill wind. The Azure Dragon's head is right behind the subunit, one eye shining red through the night and the other shining yellow. Once I reach the blended orange glow they cast on the subunit's nape, I detach my sword from my hip and *leap*.

I hit the Azure Dragon sword-first, my blade ripping through its brittle Wood-type spirit metal. I flap my wings and grapple for purchase.

"*What the fuck?*" The Azure Dragon shakes its head.

Pain singes my shoulder as I endeavor to twist my sword. An extended cry shreds out of my throat, rising to rival the wind keening in my ears. I yank the sword sideways until it opens a flap big enough to squeeze through.

I tumble into the Azure Dragon's cockpit, joints smarting. Liu Che and Wei Zifu's human bodies sit in unnatural peace in their pilot seats, bathed in muted waves of red and yellow from the walls. Pushing through the throbbing aches all over my body, I clamber behind the yáng seat and hold my sword near Liu Che's throat, though not close enough to slit it by accident.

"Get us back to the ground, or I'm killing your human body!" I yell.

"*What the actual fuck?*" The Azure Dragon's voice shoots up in pitch, the sound ringing through the cockpit.

"Azure Dragon, do as she says," Zhuge Liang commands shakily through the speakers above. "There are other ways to win this. Restrain her once you get to safety, but try not to hurt the baby!"

I roll my eyes, though my focus quickly goes to Wei Zifu, out of easy reach of my sword in the yīn seat. Even if I kill Liu Che the instant we land, I'll have to contend with her. I won't make the same mistake I did with Xiuying and assume she's not here willingly.

"Fuck that!" the Azure Dragon bellows.

The lights in the cockpit walls fade out.

We plunge.

Sword narrowly missing Liu Che's jaw, I'm thrown against the ceiling, limbs pinned by an unforgiving force.

"Che, don't do this!" Wei Zifu's natural human voice warps through the tumultuous darkness.

They *disconnected*?

Before I can figure out what's going on, Earth-yellow light returns through the cockpit walls. The Azure Dragon lurches in its fall with a hard heave of its wings, then another, then another, then more in a frantic effort to wrest itself out of its descent. I bounce around the ceiling with every forceful swing in angle until I land hard on the ground on my free arm.

Liu Che dashes toward me, sword raised above his head as if that accomplishes anything except exposing his core. Wei Zifu grips her seat with quivering force, the cockpit light streaming from her gauntlets.

Skies. She's keeping the wings beating by herself, moving them manually.

"Are you trying to kill us all?" I shriek while deflecting Liu Che's downward slash, the sound pinging off the cockpit walls. I should've immediately followed up with a thrust of blade to his eye, but I waver as I stare at this fourteen-year-old boy's true face.

"No, just you!" he yells. "What have you done with His Majesty?"

"Nothing he didn't want me to do! Get it through your head that he's a grown man making his own decisions, and he really believes everything he says!"

"Stop making excuses!"

"That wasn't an excu—!"

"Che . . ." Wei Zifu's voice fades.

Her light dims, receding from her pilot seat.

We pitch into free fall again. This time, I twist to hit the ceiling face up so I can pierce the cockpit with my sword. Straining against the unforgiving force of nature pressing me there, my cheek against the metal, I wiggle my sword to enlarge the cut. It widens at an excruciating pace until, all of a sudden, I slice past a threshold that gets me torn out of the cockpit.

I flash back to Shimin throwing me out of the Vermilion Bird. Just as then, I scream in a tunnel of wind while wrenching my wings against gravity's merciless pull. As I steady myself, bright static popping in my vision, I see that Liu Che shot out of the opening as well. He fights to buoy himself the same way I'm doing, but he then goes into a dive while screeching Wei Zifu's name.

Too late, I realize Di Renjie never followed me to the Azure Dragon.

I join Liu Che in reaching for our falling Chrysalises. Our pleas rend the air.

It's no use.

Our Chrysalises crash into the mountains with our co-pilots inside.

CHAPTER FORTY-TWO

WHAT MUST NOT BE UNLEASHED

On a big screen in Taiping's residence, she and I follow the latest insurrection updates. The broadcaster's booming voice lauds the inevitable defeat of the "vile traitors" by the "heroic revolutionaries." Though quite a few stubborn rebels are still holed up in certain streets and buildings, the army's combined efforts throughout the past night and day have largely killed, captured, or driven the rebel leaders back underground. Shaky footage accompanies the report, from Chengdu, the Red Cliff Dam, and spontaneous uprisings in other provinces inspired by the initial offensive.

I heard the situations on the ground were absolute chaos, with many civilians caught in the crossfire, but this broadcast presents an easy-to-follow story. First comes a montage of the rebels—white scarves over their faces—firing guns and throwing flaming bottles of alcohol through the streets, interspersed with shots of screaming children, crying women, blood gushing out of spasming bodies, and flailing people burning alive. Next come the clips featuring loyalist soldiers, Vanguards, Yellow Sashes, and even my Phoenix Ladies, putting Qin Zheng's mandatory firearm training to use. They're pictured ushering others to safety, firing out of windows or from behind columns, and triumphantly breaching buildings under rebel control. Whenever a revolutionary goes down, the camera lingers, showing their comrades crying out for them and their grimaced yet determined expression as they bear the pain. Whenever a rebel falls, it cuts to the next clip immediately. Because when you're the one who wins, you get to decide how the story is told.

Except for me, I guess. There's much I can't talk about when it comes to my own battle.

"*Is this what you wanted?*" I screamed over and over at Liu Che, shaking his shoulders, once we'd landed and found the lifeless, broken bodies of our partners.

I had to listen to him cry for hours on that mountainside. I didn't know what was going on with the rest of the insurrection, and I didn't have enough qì left to go find out. I slumped near the wreckage of our Chrysalises, replaying what happened in my mind, wondering if this could've turned out differently if I hadn't dismissed Wei Zifu as a lost cause. If I had tried harder to talk to her. She was only thirteen.

This is the kind of stuff the broadcasts don't show.

Eventually, as the rising sun limned the peaks with gold, Qieluo and Yang Jian showed up in a hovercraft, having tracked our spirit signatures on Qin Zheng's orders after retaking the Han frontier.

Now, the broadcast plays a camera-drone video of how they had leaped from that same hovercraft and landed on the Great Wall amid a rain of gunfire, bullets glancing off their White Tiger armor. They told me they then used their spirit senses to locate pilots held in prisons beneath the Wall. Zhuge Liang had been too noble to kill the ones who wouldn't join him. Once Qieluo and Yang Jian broke them out, it was basically over. Yet the rebel pilots fought on, threatening to smash a hole in the Great Wall if loyalist soldiers didn't lift their siege on the watchtower Zhuge Liang was commanding from. Then they followed through on the threat.

"*When laws grow in severity, there comes a point where they become motivational instead of deterring,*" Di Renjie used to say. "*When even the slightest infraction carries the death penalty, why not fight to the bitter end?*"

Warmth stabs behind my eyes. I draw a deep breath and tip my head back, squinting as my view of the broadcast blurs over.

Unfortunately for the rebel pilots, Qin Zheng's conscription of girls meant pilots aren't as hard to replace as they used to be, so Sima Yi, who was commanding the loyalist pilots, didn't hesitate to order killing strikes. The Plum Blossom Deer appears in one clip on the broadcast, driving its twin antler daggers through another Chrysalis' head. I wonder how many people watching this noticed its arms trembling before delivering the blow.

After a qì blast from Guo Anle's One-Horned Boar shot down the last rebel Chrysalis, our soldiers broke into Zhuge Liang's command room. They found him there, dead from a cyanide pill, and the word "tyrant" written in blood on the wall.

This part, they don't show in the broadcast either. They don't talk about what the rebels wanted other than a vague goal of "bringing back the corrupt old order."

There won't be any memorials to Wei Zifu or Di Renjie. She was a traitor, and people can't know he was in the Yellow Dragon with me. I suppose Liu Che found out, but no one will believe him. He's in the Tianlao, awaiting trial for high treason. His age makes it contentious. He might be the first child we execute.

Wan'er is still in the Tianlao as well. Qin Zheng said he'll talk to me after the insurrection gets put down, but for now, he's too busy coordinating the battles. Genuine, good faith complaints from inside the revolution have to wait until the guns stop firing to be addressed.

"End the tyranny, Your Highness."

Those last words I remember hearing from Di Renjie must've been all in my head. He died the moment I disconnected. I found his body in the yīn seat, having never gotten up.

How many more pilots will die like him?

How many will have to feel them die?

Did he ever realize, through our mind link, that the war itself is a lie? Will the truth really die with me?

I think of Liu Che sobbing his throat raw on the mountain. Of Liang Yuhuan staring at the wall after killing her co-pilot in her first battle. Of the Hunduns in the ocean that once hovered for a moment of peace around me.

On the low glass table before us, Taiping's tablet doubles in my vision. I could grab it and ...

No, I can't implicate her.

But I know one person in this palace I wouldn't mind incriminating.

I push up from Taiping's couch with a grip on my scythe. "I have to go do something," I say, my voice still hoarse from screaming for Di Renjie. "Alone."

No one stops me from getting to Sima Yi's office on the floor beneath the throne room. Why would they? I'm the Empress of Huaxia, allegedly free to do whatever I want.

He startles when I shove through his door.

"Your Highness!" he chides, then visibly relaxes. Since when did the sight of me start *relaxing* people? Unacceptable.

I swing my scythe while crossing to his desk. His eyes and mouth spring wide when the curved blade catches behind his neck. With my free hand, I jam a piece of cloth into his mouth.

"Mmm!" He lurches away from my blade.

I launch myself over his desk, scattering documents and stationery, and tie him down with a rope I picked up from the kitchens. It takes the wind out of me, moving so drastically while I'm qì-exhausted, but Sima Yi, who doesn't get much exercise, isn't hard to overpower in spirit armor.

As he squirms against the rope, I snatch his tablet off a metal stand on his desk. My heart pounds so rapidly my breathing turns ragged. There was no way to be more graceful or stealthy about this, since I needed him to have unlocked his tablet recently with his fingerprint.

I pause at what's on his screen: a picture of him and Zhuge Liang at some kind of banquet, bronze goblets raised in their hands. I swipe. More pictures of them at various state events, in war rooms, or concentrating over a game of *wéiqí*.

I give Sima Yi a look. His eyes slide sideways, and color rises on his face. If this were any other occasion, I'd unpack this a little more, but this isn't the time. I keep swiping on his tablet until I find the dragon head icon of Citizen Central, the platform everyone in Huaxia uses to communicate nowadays. Remembering how I've seen Wan'er and Taiping make public posts on Citizens' Plaza, I compose an announcement in Sima Yi's name. With his stylus in my shaking hand, I write the words that have festered inside me for too long:

The Hunduns are the real natives of this planet. Our ancestors were dropped here as prisoners.

Qin Zheng will rush to sweep this away as a lie by a hacker, but it'll create a doubt that'll linger long after our deaths. So much about this world made more sense to me once the truth sank in. It can't die with me. It can't.

I hit the Post button.

A circle spins.

Before it finishes, the tablet blacks out. Harsh white text appears on the screen, line after line.

Wu Zetian, this is an action beyond our agreed parameters.

There are consequences to unleashing secrets that must not be unleashed.

You ought to learn this lesson well.

My hands stiffen against the tablet. Muffled audio comes out of its speakers.

"*I'm telling you to fake the data,*" comes Yizhi's voice, distant and faint. "*I'll infect him with a bacteria strain from the lab to mess him up a little. Then you can convince him his immune system isn't adapted to modern pathogens. It sounds scientifically plausible enough that he'll believe it.*"

"*Why in the skies would I do that?*" says another, much older voice.

"*Because the gods will it. And I'm sure you wouldn't want anything terrible to happen to your family, Doctor Hua.*"

The bottom drops out of my world.

"Don't—!" I clutch my head with one hand as if I could claw this exchange out of my brain. This information can't stay in my memories. The next time I link up with Qin Zheng—

No, maybe if I refuse to do that again until the mission—

"Okay, I get it!" I cry. "Don't send this to him!"

We are past the point of threats, Wu Zetian.

From upstairs comes the sound of a cascade of shattering glass, followed by Qin Zheng roaring Yizhi's name.

PART III

HEAVENLY KHAN

𐰸𐰍𐰣𐱁𐰍𐰤𐱅 *Tengri Khagan*

There is a mighty phoenix spanning its wings at the sun,
Traversing violet mists at dawn, sipping dark dew at dusk.
By fierce winds, it rises, soaring far into the heavens.
Mountains and rivers lose their luster when it heads west;
the sun and moon brighten when it heads east.
It incarnates as a great *péng* in the north;
it pacifies the birds of the south.
It descends to vanquish the era of chaos;
it wields its talents to bring prosperity.

—*Song of the Mighty Phoenix*, by Emperor Taizong of Tang

CHAPTER FORTY-THREE

TO DECEIVE HEAVEN

When I burst out of Sima Yi's door, I hear Qin Zheng bounding down the balcony stairs, wood creaking under his raging steps.

I check Yizhi's office, right beside Sima Yi's. Empty.

Scythe in hand, I race to the stairway at the other end of the building while feeling for Yizhi's spirit signature, more familiar than every other one in the palace. He's somewhere on the premises. I nearly trip down the stairs on my way to the ground floor. The soldiers guarding the entrance startle when I barrel out into the sunset and swivel in Yizhi's direction.

How could he have done this?

It's been nearly six months since the coronation. Nearly half a year, he's kept Qin Zheng prisoner with a *lie*.

If Qin Zheng catches Yizhi, he won't make the death quick.

I dash into a roofed walkway beside a pond blazing orange under the sinking sun. Qin Zheng's crushing spirit signature pulses behind me, closing in faster than I can move. The clanging of his armor sharpens in my ears.

"Get out of my way!" he bellows.

I spin around, pointing my scythe at him.

He skids to a stop, chest heaving, shallow breaths hissing through his teeth. He holds his sword at the ready, and his bead crown has transformed into an antlered helmet. His feral gaze sears a path from my scythe blade to my face. Every hair on my body rises at the sight of him free from his cage. My stomach turns when I remember pulling this suit of armor off of Di Renjie's corpse in order to return it to Qin Zheng.

"You wish to fight me?" He gives a clipped laugh, cold as the temperature dropping around him. In his eyes, pitch-black with Water qì, seethes a wrath that destroyed six nations and burned down the world not once, but twice, across two centuries.

I say nothing. I stand no chance against him. I'm qì-exhausted. I can't wield spirit metal the way he can. I've never beaten him in a single fight in our dream training.

I can't let him get to Yizhi.

Qin Zheng advances through the staggered shadows of the wooden columns supporting the walkway's roof, dragging his sword across the stone floor with a shrill noise that rings in my teeth. It takes every bit of willpower in me to not back away.

"Step aside," he says, his voice like simmering tar. "I would truly rather not hurt you."

He flings his sword at me. It morphs into a long whip of spirit metal that lashes around my scythe blade. I see it coming and channel the dregs of my Earth qì to hold the shape of my armor and weapon.

His face twitches in surprise when nothing on me budges, but he yanks me in by my ensnared scythe, Fire qì surging red through his meridians. I don't let go quickly enough and end up stumbling into his range. His hand darts to my throat as my scythe clatters to the ground. His combat lessons and the moves I practiced with Qieluo flash through my mind. I twist to smash my forearms into his elbow before he can slam me against a column. The instant I spin free, I detach the sword on my hip and slash it at his head on his scarred side, where his vision is worse. He bends backward to dodge it, fury surging in his eyes.

Yizhi's spirit signature approaches.

"Yizhi, *he knows!*" I croak over my shoulder.

He halts, far down the walkway. After a split second, he drops a bundle of papers and bolts in the other direction, rounding a corner hugging the pond. Qin Zheng rams me aside and chases after him.

"No!" I grasp at Qin Zheng, but he throws himself over the walkway railing. The moment his armor boots touch the pond, ice detonates over the surface with a loud crackle. The frozen path expands beneath his every step, letting him cut across the water.

I decide after two seconds of shock to keep taking the long way. This is not the time to brave the odds of slipping and drowning.

As Qin Zheng vaults into the branch of the walkway Yizhi is sprinting through, Yizhi tosses a pair of spheres out of his robes. Thick white smoke explodes when they hit the ground. Qin Zheng charges through it—then his arms start twitching.

"What—" He hardly has a chance to look at his hands before the spasms spread through his body. His legs wobble and buckle. He topples in a loud crash of metal on stone.

More white smoke hisses out of the spheres, building into a fog that reaches me past the walkway corner, faster than I can back off. A potent chemical smell stabs into my nostrils. My muscles lock up and convulse. I'm helpless to save myself from collapsing into a twitching heap, like Qin Zheng.

Out of the fog comes Yizhi, his face obscured by a monstrous breathing mask with black lenses at the eyes and multiple attachments near the mouth. Parting the smoke with a dagger, he crouches in front of Qin Zheng. He jerks Qin Zheng's head up by his chin and puts his blade to Qin Zheng's throat.

Don't! I want to shout, yet I can't make any sound louder than a wheeze. I can barely keep my eyes open, and I can't feel any control over my qì. Qin Zheng's face reflects in Yizhi's mask lenses, his expression twisted with rage but his eyes blown wide. I have never seen him show fear like that.

Yizhi presses his dagger against Qin Zheng's neck, piercing skin. Blood trickles down his pale throat.

I stop breathing.

Yizhi can't do this. Not when we need Qin Zheng to take down the gods.

Yet, if I were free of Qin Zheng...

A tremor goes through Yizhi's arms. I wonder if Qin Zheng can see Yizhi's eyes behind those dark mask lenses, if he's finally, finally gazing into the truth of what goes on in Yizhi's head. I certainly have no idea. I don't think I ever did.

Sounds of shouting and running rise behind us. Yizhi glances up, then leans so close to Qin Zheng that his mask almost touches Qin Zheng's face.

"Remember why I spared you," Yizhi says, his voice low and distorted. "*Remember this.*"

He shoves Qin Zheng aside by the jaw and springs to his feet.

"End the terror." Yizhi points his dagger. "Blame it all on me."

Before he vanishes into the smoke, I swear he looks back at me. But with the smoke's effects dragging my mind into darkness, I'm not sure of anything anymore.

CHAPTER FORTY-FOUR

THE PUSH, THE PULL

When my senses find their way out of the darkness, my skull throbs and pounds as painfully as after I disconnected from the Yellow Dragon in midair. Translucent red silks stream through my vision, flaring out from a circular bronze frame on the ceiling. My foggy mind takes a few dazed seconds to register that I'm lying in full armor on the big bed in my residence that I hardly ever use.

Qin Zheng lies beside me on the massive round mattress, eyes shut, chest rising and falling with a heavy rhythm. Bandages encircle his neck.

I'm vaguely aware of Lingyue, the staffer who replaced Wan'er as my assistant, leaping to her feet at the bedchamber desk, giving a raised-fist salute, and bolting out the huge room's double doors. But I don't take my eyes off Qin Zheng. Every tendon in my body tenses to the brink of snapping, as though I'm next to a live bomb. And he might as well be one, considering the wrath he'll unleash once he wakes up.

I break into a cold sweat, thinking of the full depths of what Yizhi did. Did he make it out of the palace? If he didn't, Qin Zheng will execute him by The Hammer, no doubt.

Did Yizhi weave the ruse to . . . protect me?

I run my hand over my fake pregnancy. Qin Zheng was confident that Yizhi loved power more than me because he went behind my back to deceive me, but Yizhi had been deceiving Qin

Zheng even longer. He played us against each other. An emperor and an empress, mere puppets on his strings.

I can't forgive Yizhi for making me a mother against my will, and yet, if Qin Zheng had been free this entire time . . . I don't want to imagine how different my life would be.

Maybe I should start imagining it, though. No barrier exists anymore between me and Qin Zheng. He can do whatever he pleases to me, and I don't know how I'm supposed to stop him. Especially if my message about the truth of our world actually spread on the networks before the gods caught me.

There's something absurd about being terrified of someone unconscious beside me. He looks so vulnerable with those bandages around his neck. After almost half a year without the sun's touch, his skin is so pale it's nearly translucent. His eyes quiver behind his eyelids, and his brows furrow at whatever he's dreaming about. When he's lying still like this, not making smug remarks or death threats, there's a cold, frail sort of beauty to him. He is a living paradox, so invincible until he's not.

If only Yizhi had pushed his dagger a little deeper. It would've destroyed our best hope of taking down the gods, but . . .

My arm slides across the smooth red sheets. My throat seals up. I reach for Qin Zheng's neck.

His hand seizes my wrist.

As I sit paralyzed in place, his eyes open with agonizing slowness, scanning our surroundings before focusing on me. Without letting go of my arm, he makes a laborious effort to sit up. I resist the compulsion to cower from his gaze. He will punish me for fighting him for Yizhi's sake. I just don't know how yet.

"Your Majesty!" Sima Yi barges through the doors and falls to his knees on the long carpet in front of the bed's elevated platform. "Thank heavens you're awake!"

"Where is he?" is the first thing out of Qin Zheng's mouth. Shivers race down my spine at the chill in his voice.

Sima Yi's throat bobs up and down. "Gone through the tunnels, along with Doctor Hua and the doctor's family. But rest assured that I've assembled a task force dedicated to capturing them!"

Qin Zheng presses his fingers to his forehead. "What did that mutt unleash on me?"

"A nerve gas, Your Majesty. By our scientists' analysis of the residue, it should leave your systems by tomorrow and not leave any permanent damage."

"A *nerve gas*," Qin Zheng echoes.

"It's a neural toxin in the form of—"

"Yes, I inferred."

Sima Yi drops his forehead to the carpet. "Forgive me for not seeing Zhang Yizhi's true nature, Your Majesty! He must've had his escape planned out for months. And the gods . . . they did not warn me," he says, sounding deflated. Guess he's not so haughty anymore, knowing he wasn't the only one in communication with his beloved gods. For the ruse to have worked for so long, I don't think Yizhi was bluffing about it being the gods' will. Was he a second agent for them in more ways than this? Did he hear more about Shimin?

I may never know the answers.

Qin Zheng makes Sima Yi brief him about the developments we missed. We were out for about a day, during which the army captured Kong Zhuxi by tracking retreating rebels. With Zhuge Liang gone and now no Sage as a clear leader to rally behind, the scattered insurrectionists will be easy to isolate and defeat.

When Sima Yi leaves with Qin Zheng's new orders to the government, he shoots me a quick, resentful look before exiting through the double doors. My heart sinks. That glare wasn't venomous enough to be a response to watching me snatch his device to commit *treason*. This means he never found out what I wrote. If he's not jumping to tattle to Qin Zheng, my message couldn't have made it to the public.

"Unbelievable," Qin Zheng says after a long silence. "That opportunist mutt bamboozled both of us with science."

Against all logic, I burst out laughing, though it sounds more like a choked sob.

Qin Zheng's attention whips onto me. "You find this *humorous*?"

I press the heels of my hands to my stinging eyes. "Just the way you said it."

He wrenches my face toward himself. "When I get my hands on him, I will strip the skin off his back and boil him alive. And I will not be so forgiving if you get in my way again."

Coldness seeps into my bones from where his armored fingers meet my jaw.

This isn't happening, some part of me insists. It goes against one of my few anchors to reality: *If Qin Zheng can touch me, it's not real.*

Yet only in reality do I need to breathe, and stars pop in my vision when I struggle to take in the air between us. It's as if he's dangling me off the edge of a cliff, and my next words will determine whether he'll let me go or pull me in.

"I know," I say with all the calm I can muster, my teeth chattering slightly. "If I were you, I'd do the same."

A hint of surprise passes over his features, but he doesn't let go of my face. There's no saving Yizhi from this level of wrath. I can only pray he'll avoid capture until Qin Zheng and I are set to take on the gods in less than five months.

Or is that still our plan, when Qin Zheng doesn't actually have a useless immune system?

I don't dare ask the question out loud. Not after my taste of just how closely the gods are watching.

"Six months," Qin Zheng mutters. "The things I could have done . . ."

His eyes rove over my face, a new intensity heating inside them. He bites his lip, and in this moment I can't tell what he wants more, to kill me or taste me. The fingertips of his gauntlets melt away against my skin like thawing ice. Absently, he strokes my cheek with the bare pad of his finger. My awareness sharpens to the fact that he hasn't touched another human being in nearly half a year.

It might be the only thing keeping me alive.

Fighting every restraining thread of my good sense, I lean in. He moves with me, his mouth angling toward mine.

In the last second before the space between us closes, I jam my hand against his chest.

"You need to host an emergency court assembly," I say softly, my lips almost brushing his. "Right now."

He recoils, blinking, like he's snapping out of a trance.

I continue in a rush, "Tell them Yizhi and Doctor Hua were part of the insurrection and tried to assassinate you. That'll explain why the glass in the throne room is shattered. By walking around on camera, you can also put a stop to the rumors that you're incapacitated. Nothing will work better to crush what's left of rebel morale."

Blinking some more, Qin Zheng releases me. He scowls, yet doesn't meet my eyes. Is he unnerved by how he just reacted to touching me?

He turns, looking as though he's about to push himself out of bed, but then he twists back and grabs my arm.

"You are coming with me," he says.

While waiting for the central court to assemble, Qin Zheng films a scathing broadcast denouncing Yizhi as one of the rebels and announcing a nationwide hunt for him. He smacks his hands on the throne room's balcony railing as he speaks, which should kill any lingering suspicion about previous footage of him being fake. The bandages around his neck add to the realism, being too random a detail to include in a fabrication.

Once the officials arrive, Qin Zheng subjects them to a thorough, menacing petrification in his newly freed state, even stomping down from the dais to prowl among them. I don't know how many have become suspicious about why he never seemed to leave his "bulletproof chamber," but their conspiracy theories won't hold after this. If any of them are double agents, I imagine their last hopes are crumbling into ash.

The hailstorm of broken glass on the floor crunches beneath Qin Zheng's armored soles. He didn't let the palace staff clean it up. I think he likes the imagery of being surrounded by destruction. My side chamber remained intact, though. With its one-way tint activated, I listen to him terrorize the central court until deep into the night. It feels more than ever like I'm tucked away in a box in the corner.

Yet after the officials bow out, shivering like autumn leaves, I'm grateful for the glass and its obscuring tint. It keeps Qin Zheng from seeing me freeze in my chair.

What happens now?

How will I spend my nights when there's no longer anything keeping us apart?

I shake my head. That's not what I should be thinking about. I should be figuring out what to say in my own statement about the insurrection. Just because Qin Zheng is free doesn't mean I have to yield my role as a leader. I should visit Chengdu as soon as it's safe, speak with the Phoenix Ladies hospitalized from the fighting, award them medals and compensation packages. For those who outright gave their lives, maybe I'll commission a memorial and invite their families to the unveiling ceremony. That would be more emotionally bearable than visiting their homes.

Metallic footsteps approach my side chamber. My attention snaps up. Qin Zheng stops before my door, arms folded. He shouldn't be able to see me from the outside, yet his eyes lock onto mine so accurately that I'm hit with a paranoia that he switched off the tint without me noticing. I certainly didn't notice the throne room emptying out, leaving just the two of us. How did that happen so fast? Or did I sit in a daze longer than I thought?

"Come have a drink with me, empress." He touches the glass.

The sight sets off memories of all the times I've been on the other side, mocking him, thinking I'd be safe until the day we launched off on our mission. How naive I was.

No use cowering in this chair. I hoist myself up with my scythe and open my door.

Something shifts in the air, as if I've crossed a boundary to a different world. I look up at him through unobstructed space. He stares back at me with an unreadable gaze.

On the balcony across the throne room, a small table and two chairs have been set up while I was lost in thought. A bronze wine jug and a goblet await us.

"No thanks." I do my best to sound bored. "I still have a wicked headache from the nerve gas."

"All right. Then I suppose we should retire to our quarters."

I bristle.

Right. My residence is now *ours*. Was always meant to be. It's only logical. We'll have to fall asleep beside each other sooner or later to discuss whether our attack plan on the gods is changing. No way around that. Unless I sleep on Lingyue's couch with the spirit thread extending through the manor—

No, that's way too convoluted. I'm not some little girl who can't handle sharing a bed with *some guy*.

In fact, there's still a bed in this side chamber. The more I look at Qin Zheng, the more I'm thinking about its existence. It's not far. Just a few paces behind me. Basically the setting for what we did in our dream realm that one time. Memories flutter through me, of his hands pressing my wrists to the mattress, his lips over my breasts—

"Actually, let's have that drink." I leave the side chamber immediately, twisting my thoughts toward the kind of memorial Chengdu should have. Is a stone slab too basic? Would a statue take too long?

The open night sky beyond the balcony grants some comfort in being alone with him. He can't try anything terrible here. Half the palace would hear if I screamed.

Whether anyone would come rescue me is another matter. I lean my scythe against the balcony at the perfect distance to behead Qin Zheng with one swing. With an amused glance at it, he transforms his sword into a sledgehammer and rests it parallel to my scythe, recreating what we usually wield on propaganda posters.

"Have you ever had lychee wine, empress?" he says once we're sitting down at the small table.

"No." That time with Gao Qiu was my only real taste of alcohol. Since Wan'er, Taiping, and Qieluo think I'm pregnant, they made sure I didn't touch any the few times we went to Club Lily or The Split Peach. They seemed to have fun with it in moderation, though.

Qin Zheng pours a glistening stream out of the jug. "If you'd like any, we must share the goblet. It would not do for the staffers to find two used vessels and deem you an irresponsible mother."

I gasp and palm my fake pregnancy. "But I radiate such maternal warmth."

He laughs, then sets the goblet in front of me with a smile. Now I wish I hadn't made that cheap joke. Under no circumstances should I be making Qin Fucking Zheng smile.

The wine wavers, looking bottomless in the night. I push it across the table. "You first."

"*Empress*," he chides. "If I wanted you dead, I would not resort to poison. Poison is the weapon of cowards. I'd break your neck like a real man."

I stare off into the mountains, regretting all of my major life decisions. "Wonderful."

"Cheers." He raises the goblet, starlight glinting off the metal and in his eyes. He downs half the wine in several quick gulps before passing it back. "My condolences about that liberalist," he says, softer. "Even though he was a liberalist."

The tension goes out of me. He means Di Renjie. A sickness sweeps through my cheeks and eats at my insides. Renjie will never have a statue, even though he cared more deeply about Huaxia than anyone I know.

"I should've . . ." My words come apart like a cloud of breath in winter.

I grab the goblet and tilt the wine past my lips. Sickly sweet and with only a mild kick, it's not as strong as the liquor Gao Qiu made me drink. I almost wish it burned more. Why else do people drink when they're miserable, if not to fight pain with pain?

A breeze sweeps through the balcony, smelling of the damp earth on the mountains. Qin Zheng tips his head back and closes his eyes. "Dwell not on a past that cannot be changed, empress. You'll miss the blessings of the present. The warmth of the sun, the scent of the trees. Things you would not think to cherish until you can no longer have them."

I watch the faint stirring of his lashes. What must it be like, feeling the wind on your face after months of confinement?

"In this world, there is nothing that lasts." His eyes open and turn on me with a pointed force. "What is there one season may be gone the next. Never hesitate to carry out your heart's will while you have the opportunity."

I draw tenser with his every word. Is he talking about our mission? That we shouldn't postpone it?

It's true that just because his fragility was a lie, it doesn't mean he's safe to do as he wants now. The gods got Yizhi to spin the ruse for a reason. They're playing a game of balance, aiming to reap as much as they can from us while smothering any inclination we might have to turn our weapons on them instead of the Hunduns. They took Shimin hostage to control me. They imprisoned Qin Zheng to control *him*. They set him free to punish my attempted rebellion, but it's only a matter of time before they limit his authority in some other way. They'll never let him have unobstructed power.

Ironically, the thought that there remains a time limit on my relationship with Qin Zheng puts me more at ease. We pass the goblet back and forth in silence, refilling it several times.

"You know, lately I've had some thought about how much you remind me of myself." Qin Zheng puts an elbow on the table and leans his cheek against his knuckles. "Neither of us are here because we accepted the destinies levied upon us. We were born to be chewed up and spat out. We broke the teeth instead."

I make a hum of acknowledgment, not bothering with words.

"Yet we are not entirely the same." His voice slows with purpose. "Even if we may share an identical soul, we grew up within different sets of chains that molded our thoughts in different ways, with you being a woman and me being a man. Fascinating, is it not?"

"Fascinating?" I side-eye him.

"Your chains are more numerous and harder to break, it seems. Despite your fierce resistance, you have yet to shed them all."

A bitter taste waters in my mouth. "Is this your way of saying I should stop feeling so terrible about killing a co-pilot?"

"Partly. But not the only matter I had in mind."

"Then what?"

He lands a single finger on my gauntlet. A shiver travels through me from that sole, minuscule point of connection. I gain an awareness of his armor, of how its curves and angles hug his body. I jerk my hand back. He catches it, holding it in place.

"Why does this frighten you?" he questions.

"I'm not fri—I don't like people randomly touching me! Obviously." My voice comes out too high.

"Random? After all the nights we've spent together, my touch is still random to you?" he says with a tinge of mockery.

"Let go!" I tug against his infuriatingly firm grip. "What are you trying to do?"

The mirth leaves his face. "You *know* what I'm trying to do."

My stomach swoops as if I'm back in battle and falling from the sky. Though I'm not sure why I'm rattled. It was obvious, where this is going. What's notable is that he's trying to ease me into it rather than overpowering me without a care. He also got really mad when I outright offered to sleep with him in exchange for Wan'er's freedom. I'm guessing he hates the implication that he's so repellent that climbing into bed with him would be some agonizing act of sacrifice. He needs to feel desired for real. If that's the case, maybe I can get him to do what I want by playing this game more tactfully.

"There it is again. That fear." He observes me like a scientific specimen. "Have you given a deeper thought to where it comes from?"

My heart pounds so heavily against my chest that he can likely feel every frantic beat through my armor. What does he want to hear? I can't just drop my attitude and start begging him to ravish me. That wouldn't feel real enough. "You don't know why people are afraid of you? You're joking, right? You almost killed me less than twenty-four hours ago!"

He gives a slow shake of his head. "You are not cowed by violence or death, or you would not have dared raise a weapon against me. So, I ask: how is it that you show more fear when I touch you gently than when facing down my blade?"

"Wow, I wonder why I don't want to be touched by a man who threatens my life on a daily basis!"

He pulls an offended face. "I do not do that on a 'daily basis.' Monthly, at most. And only when you're thinking about divulging information that could destabilize Huaxia and/or attempting to kill me. The very fact that you remain alive is a testament to my patience."

"Oh, thank Your Majesty *so* much. What an honor."

"Indeed, it is. You deny you want it, and yet . . ." He lifts my hand.

I realize his grip has loosened for quite a few moments now. I could've taken my hand out of his during all of them.

I retract it at once, rubbing my wrist. "Ugh. You disgust me."

"Do I?" He drums his fingers over my side of the table. "You act as if I alone harbor carnal desires, yet I know that to be untrue. You, with an appetite so insatiable you need two men at once to satisfy you."

My vision flares red. I swing my fist toward him.

He seizes my arms and locks my wrists together.

"Are you ashamed of it?" he says with a wild, crazed look in his eyes, the look of a gambler betting everything for the thrill alone. "I've slept with multiple partners plenty of times. You don't see me feeling ashamed."

So much pressure builds in me that I picture myself bursting into flames. "I'm not *you*!"

"You're not a man, you mean. Such is the chain around your mind you have yet to shed." He holds my wrists together with quivering force. "You are not free, empress. Not while you deny your desires out of a shame others have imposed to control you."

I dig my elbows into the table, yet I can't break from his clutches. "Are you seriously suggesting I can't be free unless I sleep with you?"

"If you were a man, would you be this hesitant to act on a mutual attraction so potent?"

"If I were a man, would *you* still be attracted to me?"

Lines crinkle near his eyes. "You truly haven't seen very far into my memories, have you?"

My mouth hangs open. He releases my arms and leans back in his chair, swiping up the goblet to take another drink. His other hand grazes the underside of my hand. Before I can muster my next words, a cold surge of his qì rolls from the last bit of loose contact between our fingers, up my arm and into my collar. The top edge of my collar liquefies and slips, slow as honey, into the conduction suit I'm wearing underneath.

I gasp as the cool sensation trickles down my fever-hot skin, splitting into several languid paths. Frissons of dangerous pleasure arc through my spine. He's caressing me with his mind alone while sipping nonchalantly at his wine. Above the edge of the goblet, his gaze is practically molten.

It's so outrageous for spirit metal to be used this way that it stuns me from reacting for far longer than I should be allowing.

I fling his hand away. The instant our contact breaks, my armor hardens again, feeling almost empty without the pressure of his mind. I need to stay in control. To keep thinking strategically. If only the wine isn't making me feel so funny.

"You are unbelievable." I push out of my chair, but I stand up too quickly. The balcony sways.

Qin Zheng drops the goblet and lurches to catch me across the table, one hand on my shoulder and the other on my waist. His half-masked face doubles in my view before coming into focus, way too close.

"Tell me something, empress," he says in a low rumble, the warmth of his words grazing my cheek. "If you feel no desire for me, why does your breathing quicken when I come near you? Why does your face go flushed?"

His fingers trace my jaw. I snatch his arm to jerk it away, yet I'm shaking uncontrollably, and not entirely from anger. He rounds the table to close the remaining distance between our bodies.

"You are attracted to power. What could be more natural?" He cups my face with both hands and tilts it upward. By his will, my crown peels away and fuses with the rest of my armor. My mask splits apart and rolls to either side. "Look into my eyes and deny that you want me," he says, with the roughness of a warning.

A rebuke surges to the tip of my tongue, but I falter at the last second, afraid I might not sound certain.

That hesitation itself is enough to betray me. When his lips curve into a smirk, I know this is as good of a moment as any to make a believable surrender.

"*Fuck you*," I snap, breathless, and pull him toward me.

"Please," he whispers just before our mouths meet for the first time in real life.

He kisses me back with an aggression that leaves no doubt about whether he's still angry at me for fighting him to protect Yizhi. I match his ferocity by instinct. It's all wrong, rage mixing with pleasure, violence mixing with bliss, but it's the closest I can get to punching him in the face or stabbing him in the chest.

I have never hated anyone more than him in this moment, and hate that burns this hot demands release. We're not so much kissing as we're assailing each other with lips and tongues and teeth. It's like trying to stand my ground against a vicious typhoon, like I'm fighting for survival instead of embracing anything tender. I clutch his shoulders as if I might get swept away if I don't hang on.

He uproots me anyway, edging me backwards until I hit the balcony wall. The length of his body pins me in place, his thigh jamming between my legs. My armor has become soft as flesh under his touch, and I can feel his hands as if they were running down my bare skin, moving with an urgency to make up for months of deprivation. My electric-charged body wars with my wine-clouded mind. I shouldn't have drank so much. *Stay in control*, I remind myself. Yet it's been so long since anyone touched me this way that I struggle to keep my thoughts straight. I miss this, the buildup of passion and desire toward a blinding-hot release. What I did with him in our dream realm has nothing on the intensity of flesh and blood. The medicinal scent of the bandages around his neck and the wine-sweetened slide of our mouths are somehow more intoxicating than the sensations he could flood into me through a mind link. It feels better to drown in this than to let in the pain, the grief, of losing people I actually care about.

"I can make it very good for you," he murmurs against my lips between kisses, his hot breath mixing with my own, "if you tell me you belong to me."

My hands tighten like talons on his shoulders. Skies, *who says stuff like that?*

I might need to gag him to go through with this.

"You belong to me," I say as flatly as I can.

He draws back, frowning, then lets out a low laugh. "Very funny."

My armor liquefies and pools to the floor like heavy gold silk, leaving me in my skin-tight conduction suit.

Cold clarity cuts through the haze in my head. "Wait, not here—"

"Who would stop us?" he says near my ear while palming my chest.

I resist the pleasure tingling through me. "That's—that's not the point—"

The thought of the bed in my side chamber flashes through my head. My mouth opens wider, about to shape the suggestion to go there, except that would be admitting out loud that I want this to happen.

Before I can bring myself to do it, he weaves his fingers into my hair and tugs my head to an angle, exposing the arch of my throat. He drags his tongue over my erratic pulse and suckles my skin like he wants to drink my blood. I go as tense as the time he held a dagger to the same spot after I startled him, every sense in my body driven to the brink between life and death. His other hand slips behind me and fumbles for the hidden zippers on either side of my spinal brace. When I make a noise of alarm, he ravishes my throat with more hunger. This man has no shame. And maybe he's right that this is the crucial difference between us, one that holds me back.

But no matter what, I cannot let this go any further until he bends to my will.

"*Stop.*" I wriggle against him. "Seriously, stop for a second!"

He takes his mouth off my neck and his fingers off my zipper. The night hits cold on the patch of my skin that he left wet. Looking highly inconvenienced, he places his hands on the wall to either side of me. We're both breathing as if fresh out of battle.

I gulp between rasps of air. "Wan'er."

He turns around instantly, hands going to his hips while he heaves a frustrated sigh.

Panting, I push off of the wall. "How am I supposed to sleep with you while you have my friend in prison?"

"*I* don't have her in prison!" He spins to face me again. "The revolutionary law does! Making an exception for her would undermine the very system!"

"Then don't make her an exception. Abolish extended punishment and release everyone who's in for a crime they didn't directly commit."

"It is necessary to . . ." He trails off while staring at my admittedly very large breasts, emphasized by my conduction suit.

"No, it's *not* necessary." I cross my arms over my chest, to his visible disappointment. "Too harsh of punishments end up making people stop fearing them. If they're facing death along with their families and neighbors anyway, of course they'd rather join the rebellion than sit around waiting to get The Hammer."

Qin Zheng huffs, eyes squeezing shut. "We can discuss this later."

"No!" I say, but then I take his hand gently. This is a pretense he'll believe and accept: that I'm indeed attracted to him and want to be with him, only that external factors are making me hesitate. "We've pretty much quelled this insurrection, but more will keep popping up unless we make some concessions to what they're fighting for. You *know* not all of them are in it for unjustified reasons. Your policies are wronging even your most loyal supporters, like Wan'er."

He twists his hand to grasp my fingers. "Are you becoming a reactionary?"

I jerk my arm back. "Skies, not everyone who disagrees with you is a reactionary! Or a revisionist! Or whatever other label you laborists love to slap on each other! I'm not asking you to let profitizers sell human beings again; I'm trying to take the steam out of further insurrections." I slide my hand up his chest. "Now that you're not stuck in a glass cell anymore, there's a thousand new ways for you to die. If you get taken down by an assassin or something without having eased these policies, what do you think will happen to the masses?"

He goes slack all over, biting his lip. He knows what I'm saying:

we don't have enough time or leeway left to push the revolution to more radical heights. Not without risking the implosion of the whole thing once we leave for our mission. Or maybe the gods will kill him before that, if they grow alarmed about how far he's going.

"Fine. I shall consider what you said." He moves to kiss me again.

I block him with both hands. "Not until you actually do it. You should also make Wan'er your new Imperial Secretary once she's free. She's a lifelong laborist who scored *third* on the exams, and she can read your terrible handwriting. While we're at it, Taiping is a great candidate for Minister of Finance. She has experience running the logistics of the biggest enterprise in Huaxia, and she placed decently in the exams, too."

He hovers his lips near my hair while kneading circles into my shoulder. "It's so late in the night," he says in a lazy, whining drawl. "Any policy changes would have to wait until tomorrow."

I gulp, my belly tightening at the way his fingers are moving. I'm pretty sure he's deliberately trying to make me think of how it would feel if he moved his hand somewhere else. "So?"

He pulls back and stares me down as if trying to change my mind through the force of his gaze alone. "You test my patience."

"You like it when I do."

There has to be a reason he constantly provokes me on purpose. He's so sick and twisted that he likes me better when I'm biting back. When I'm a challenge.

Color emerges in his cheeks. A slight grin tugs at the corners of his kiss-bruised mouth. "You are the strangest-priced whore I have ever met. And that is saying something, considering where I grew up."

"I thought you hate it when people call me that."

"Yes, when others do it. You're *my* whore." He pulls me close by my waist. The four-month pregnancy padding under my conduction suit presses into his hips.

I suck a breath through my teeth. "How are you so possessive while being a laborist? Di Renjie was right. You make no ideological sense. You should send yourself for re-education."

"Excuse me, as if I'm not about to perform far more labor than you!"

"Not unless you meet my conditions! Call me a whore all you want—you still can't get with a whore unless you can pay the price. I'm not a cheap slut like you."

I don't actually believe in the concept of "slut" as an insult, but the retort is worth it for the look on Qin Zheng's face alone.

"I'm not a—" His expression freezes, then mellows. "All right, I suppose I did sleep my way across the seven nations. Acquired quite a few pieces of war-changing intelligence from it, actually. Feel free to interpret this as a testament to my capabilities." He rolls a swirl of liquid spirit metal around his fingers.

A flush warms me all over. I clench my jaw shut. What was in that wine?

Smiling, he releases my waist. The folds of spirit metal at my feet swirl up and lock around me as my armor again.

"May this prove I care for you more than you believe me capable of." He steps away from me and returns to the table. "Also, for your information . . ." He lifts the wine jug by its handle with two fingers. "There was no alcohol in this. It's lychee juice with ginger."

CHAPTER FORTY-FIVE

POINT OF NO RETURN

I stumble through the palace with my scythe, my composure crashing after getting away from Qin Zheng on pure adrenaline. The sweetness of the lychee juice lingers in my mouth. Why would he swindle me in such a pointless way?

I make the mistake of looking over my shoulder. He remains half-shadowed on the balcony, one hand on the railing, watching me go.

He's right about one thing: I'm not afraid of him killing me. That would make sense.

This doesn't.

Regardless, I head straight to Taiping's residence to tell her there's hope for Wan'er. She yelps in joy, having been so anxious that she couldn't sleep. Though she raises a brow at my disheveled hair. There are probably bruises on my throat, too. I tell her to not worry about it and change the topic to Yizhi, wanting to know what she heard before Qin Zheng officially announced her little brother as a fugitive wanted for treason. Surely there was gossip in the palace about us getting knocked out.

Her eyes go unfocused. "Everyone was saying he tried to assassinate Your Highness and His Majesty, but . . . that can't be what actually happened, can it?"

"I don't think it'd be a good idea for me to give specifics." I give her a look we've shared many times in the tunnels. The look that tells her there's mortal danger in pressing further, even if it's about her own kin.

Her lips pinch shut. We live with no shortage of secrets.

In the court assembly the next morning, Qin Zheng declares the abolition of extended punishment, issues a mass pardon, and summons Taiping to appoint her as the new Minister of Finance. I watch from my tinted side section as she accepts her set of purple official robes with wide, frozen eyes, as if she's taking a precious artifact into her arms.

She's the first woman in the central court in two centuries. Many officials—even staunch laborists—look like they'd be bursting into protest if they didn't know better than to do that in the open against Qin Zheng. I have no doubt they'll write memos to complain about how her womanly brain can't possibly understand economics beyond how to shop for a family dinner. They'll do everything in their power to goad Taiping into quitting, just like the schoolboys trying to harass their female classmates into giving up. But just as my Phoenix Ladies got those boys to stop by paying menacing visits to their homes and guarding the girls on their way to school, I will be the nightmare of any official who dares to be a nuisance. Society will march on, whether these men are ready for it or not.

Once Qin Zheng dismisses the assembly, Taiping, Qieluo, and I head to the Tianlao to welcome Wan'er and her mother out. Although the mass pardon was only for those implicated via extended punishment, Qin Zheng read Auntie Kudi's short story overnight and personally dismissed her case.

"The mere fact that she mentioned a tyrant in the story does not mean she was alluding to *me*," he said with a snort to me before the assembly.

Thanks to our insider info, we get to the Tianlao before what's bound to be a flood of weeping loved ones reuniting with freed prisoners.

Warden Lai is all smiles and bows while bringing Wan'er and her mother to us in a prisoner processing room. They're wearing suspiciously pristine orange jumpsuits—probably pulled out of storage ten minutes before we arrived, judging by the crisp folds still on them—though there's no hiding the weariness on their faces. Their skin is sallow, and their under-eye circles look as bad as Qin Zheng's. With a choked sob, Taiping rushes to pull Wan'er into her arms.

"Your Highness." Warden Lai clasps his hands near his throat. "I hope you will keep in mind that we of the Tianlao were simply doing our duty."

Wan'er betrays no emotion over Taiping's shoulder. "Let's just go, Your Highness."

It's only once we're in the extra-large carriage we brought to fit all of us does she speak of what she went through.

"They put us in different cells." Wan'er holds her mother close. "Poured vinegar up my nose and kept me awake this whole time with bright lights and loud music. Demanded that I confess to being in contact with counter-revolutionaries."

"Same here." Auntie Kudi sighs, her voice hoarse.

"Everyone who works there needs to be investigated." Wan'er peers outside the carriage window at the flow of people hurrying to the Tianlao. "I had it easy by comparison. There was screaming all down the hall. When I was going in, I saw people getting their fingernails pulled out."

"I'll hold them accountable," I mutter.

Taiping kisses Wan'er's greasy hair, fastened loosely at her nape. "Get some sleep. Things are changing after the insurrection. I'm the Minister of Finance now."

"*There was an insurrection?*" Wan'er exclaims, almost jumping out of her seat. Horror dawns in her eyes as she looks around at us. "Your Highness didn't overthrow His Majesty, did you?"

"No," I say after a pause. "I didn't."

Wan'er slackens in relief. Then a jolt goes through her. "It's not that I don't think Your Highness would make a good ruler! But..."

"But I would've doomed the revolution," I muse for her. "Me seizing power would've made all the reactionaries' claims seem true. So many would've risen with them. The only way to save myself would've been to yield to their interests, return their properties, and let the downtrodden be downtrodden again."

Wan'er breathes deeply in and out. "I'm glad that didn't happen."

"You still . . . ?" Taiping leaves much unsaid.

Wan'er cracks a weak smile. "There will always be cruel people, no matter what kind of system we're living under. I'm not letting them stop me from wanting better for the rest of us."

Taiping drops me off at the Alliance's North Gate branch so I can write and record my statement on the insurrection. By the time I finish my work and return to the palace, Qin Zheng is still meeting with officials.

The moment I step into my—*our* residence, I feel a discomforting ripple of change. Things are not where I put them. My books are stacked differently. There's a pressure cooker in the bedchamber for some reason, and in the bathroom is what looks suspiciously like Yizhi's entire skin care collection, expropriated. The mirrors above the sink have been removed, though. Only a small hand mirror remains on the counter, turned toward the stripped wall.

When I sit down at my desk and leaf through my books, memories of Di Renjie come crashing back. These are mostly his personal copies, well-used and littered with his notes and highlights. Sharp pangs shoot through my chest at every shorthand whose meaning is now lost with him and every sentence he underlined for reasons he can no longer explain. The words blur over.

I did all I could, I want to tell him.

Any attempt at broadcasting the truth, the gods will stop. Any person I tell, Qin Zheng will doom. I can play my little games with him, but I know full well where his boundaries are. Now that he's free, he has even more control over me.

It was a foolish thing to do, anyway. The truth would've destabilized Huaxia further, and we need it to be as stable as possible before we go after the gods. Only when the gods are gone can anyone do anything about the truth.

I hope Qin Zheng never sees those few seconds of memories that prove my attempted treason, though I'm prepared to defend myself. I *did* save the revolution.

I don't hear Qin Zheng come in while I'm taking a bath to clear my head, but when I emerge, the only lights on in the vast bedchamber are the lotus-shaped lamps near the bed. With his usual black robe on and his hair in a lazy bun, he sits on the edge of the round mattress, framed by translucent red drapes on either side, reading a piece of paper by the low lamplight.

"Your handwriting has improved greatly," he says without lifting his attention from the paper. "Now it looks only marginally like a child's."

Warmth rises in my cheeks, though I don't know why I'm embarrassed. It's not my fault I grew up without opportunities to learn. "It'd be way better if I had *started as* a child. Will you put more funding into education for girls in mountain villages?"

He groans. "No more talk of politics for the night. I have grown weary of it." He returns the page to a pile on the elevated platform the bed is on. When he finally takes a proper look at me, the lamplight gleams in his eyes, kindling them orange like a tiger's. He draws a deep breath while going taut as a bowstring. I'm wearing the gold-tinted robe that torments him the most, along with compression stockings, which have really helped with my circulation after the surgery. The fewer functioning brain cells he has, the easier he'll be to deal with.

"Come to me," he says, his voice gaining a charred edge.

"Yes, that's what I'm doing." Scythe in hand, I amble toward him over the long carpet that leads to the bed, feeling like a moth fluttering toward a candle flame. "I went to the Tianlao. You really need to get a better grip on what's going on in there."

"What did I say about no more politics?" He gets to his feet as I approach, towering over me on the bed platform.

"I'm being serious. Don't be more concerned about getting laid than being a good ruler."

Confusion passes his half-masked face, then he recovers with a small grin. "'Getting laid.' Is that what they call it in this era? Because if so, I must say the people will be much more fortunate once I'm in a better mood."

I thump the end of my scythe on the platform, preparing to climb. "I should've turned the Yellow Dragon around on you."

When he helps lift me up, his fingers dig into my flesh a little too forcefully. He doesn't let go of my waist once I'm on the platform with him.

Maybe that was too honest of a thing to say.

His hand drifts over my arm, sending shivers across my skin. "Were you tempted?" he says, the softness of his voice at odds with the intensity in his eyes.

The heaving of his chest against mine makes me realize how quickly I'm breathing. "What do you think?"

He eases my scythe out of my grasp and lets it drop. It hits the floorboards with a loud echo that makes me tense against him, instinctive fear swirling with the *distraction* of looking right at the outrageously low cut of his robe. It's very annoying that my brain isn't functioning well either. Since when have I been impressed by a nice shoulders-to-waist ratio? *Who even notices that?*

He sinks down on the bed again, though his accusatory expression fades when his attention strays to my soft, pudgy belly. He prods it with his fingers. "Sometimes I forget you're not truly carrying my child."

I slide my arms over his shoulders. "I would literally rather kill myself," I say against his lips.

Before he can react, I press our mouths together, kissing him with a viciousness barely contained under my skin. Hatred roars like a wind-gusted inferno inside me. I imagine killing him a dozen different ways—including ripping off his neck bandages and finishing the job Yizhi abandoned—while straddling his lap. He gathers me close, caressing my thighs back and forth before pulling my hips harshly against his own. A gasp breaks our kiss at what I feel through our thin robes.

"Would you like to know why I fooled you with the lychee juice?" He nuzzles my neck, voice rough. "I sensed you were looking for an excuse to cast away your inhibitions, yet what a shame it would be if your mind were clouded." His fingers glide down my spinal brace. I shudder, feeling as if my very bones might succumb to the same liquefying power he holds over spirit metal. "I want you to remember every detail of this," he whispers in my ear.

Wicked heat surges through my veins. From rage or desire, I can't tell anymore.

"I hate you *so much*." I tighten against him. I'm so desperate for the relief of brutal violence that I roll my body against his as the next best thing, again and again, gripping his shoulders for leverage. I want to destabilize him. If I can't have peace, neither will he.

He makes a low, startled sound at the sensations no doubt coursing through him. Then he laughs.

"Yet here you are." His voice slips into a rumble. He palms my breasts through my robe, thumbs swiping over the sensitive tips. "I love the way you *know* I'm an awful idea, yet you can't resist me."

"*As if.*" I hold myself together as the jolting pleasure of his every touch pushes me close to falling apart. "I'm not the one who's been fantasizing about this for months after calling me repulsive."

"This bravado..." He pinches my chin. "I wonder how long you can sustain it. And how different you'll sound when you're lost to desire and begging me for more."

I breathe through the unbearable heat between us. "Right. I wouldn't trust performance reviews by women who can't say no to you."

He frowns. Something clears in his eyes, and he releases my chin. When he next speaks, his tone is much more normal, no longer low with challenge. "Do you truly believe I would do that to any woman after what my mother went through? I grew up hearing her screams through the wall."

I gulp. "You have been *very persistent* at pushing my boundaries."

"Is that what you feel?" He leans back, the warmth of his arms leaving my body. "Because I was encouraging you to question if your self-denial is born of genuine sentiment or societal imposition. The choice to do this remains yours."

Head hanging low, I bunch his loose robe collar between my hands, abruptly cold. "It's not a real choice when you're the most powerful man in Huaxia."

"And you are the most powerful woman. By this logic, who has more of a choice to be with me than you?"

"As if you wouldn't make my life miserable if I chose against it."

He places a hand on my wrists. "I would not. Last night, did I not stop when you asked me to?"

"Because we made a bargain. Would you really have no complaints if I walked away right now?"

"It was not a bargain. I did not—and *would not*—make any political decisions solely to bed a woman. I considered the logic in your proposals, and I agreed. That's separate from what's between us. If you insist on telling yourself I am coercing you into this because you are unwilling to own up to what you feel, then this goes no further. You are free to leave." He puts his hands flat to the mattress, far apart from me.

I suddenly feel very silly, straddling him while going on and on about how much I hate him.

After regarding me for a few moments with the heat gone from his eyes, he shakes his head. "*I'll go.*"

He pushes up beneath me. Clearly, he meant to nudge me out of the way, except it ends up feeling like a firm thrust of his hips against mine. Sparks of sensation loop through me. A mortifying whimper escapes my mouth.

"Wait..." I clutch his shoulders.

His brows furrow, though a trace of his usual haughtiness returns to his features. His gaze flicks from my mouth to my eyes. "Would you like to continue?"

I imagine him moving like that again. And again. And again. A traitorous, aching need builds where our bodies meet. I think I might lose my mind if I have to dwell on this for another day. "Yes. Maybe."

"Is it yes or is it maybe? Be very clear about what you want, dearest. Be honest."

"Fine. Yes."

"Yes to what, precisely?" He shifts beneath me as if to adjust his posture, but the look in his eyes tells me he's reading every little movement in my body. I can't shake the feeling of having fallen into a trap.

"Yes to *this*," I say, face flushed.

"What might you mean by 'this'? I'm afraid I need you to describe exactly what you want me to do to you, in great detail."

The flush spreads to my whole body. "Never mind, I'm leaving!"

He laughs and threads his fingers through my blow-dried hair. "You are like a cat." He pokes my nose. "Defiant for defiance's sake."

"*Did you just*—"

"But I have always preferred cats to dogs." He wraps my hair around his hand, tugging lightly. "Obedience given too easily is worth next to nothing."

"You know, maybe I have so many second thoughts because you say stuff like *that*."

"You speak and do plenty that enrages me. That does not stop me from wanting you."

My mouth pops open, yet no response comes out.

His arms encircle my waist. "How about this: if you ever wish for me to stop doing something, and you mean it resolutely, say the words . . . 'private property.' I will stop. No matter what."

"'Private property'?" I splutter.

He lets go of me at once. "This way, it is absolutely clear. You ought to admit, you give off rather mixed signals. And I will admit I can get a tad aggressive. Let us have no more misunderstandings."

"What's to stop you from punishing me later for denying you?"

"I will not. This I promise you."

My teeth gnash together. "Yeah, right. Why should I believe you?"

Something unnervingly close to hurt flashes in his eyes. He shutters them. His chest rises and falls, almost touching mine again, before he says, "Because I miss you when you're gone. The nightmares return to me. It is . . . not pleasant. My days without you are not pleasant. The only nights I don't fear falling asleep are when you're there with me."

Oh.

Wow. Okay.

It's the same for me when I dream without him. Except I wouldn't volunteer that information under any torture.

When I take too long to respond, he peels his eyes open with an unease I've never seen him show, looking like he's plotting an escape route in his head.

I clasp his half-mask. "Take this off."

"What?" He startles. "Why?"

"If you want me naked, you have to play by the same rules. Take it off."

He blinks a few times, eyes darting aimlessly, before letting the mask roll away. The spirit metal retreats over his ear and into his spinal brace.

I graze his jagged scars with my thumb. His hand flies up, fingers landing on my wrist.

Gently, I press my lips to his scars.

He freezes up against me.

It's a second later that he relaxes, as if he's thawing all over again. I plant another kiss on his neck bandages, then on his mouth. This time, it's different from our every collision before. Our lips mingle with the lightness of whispers rather than the violence of curses.

You are mine. A thought surfaces from the cold core of me. *You belong to me.*

He kisses a hot trail from my chin to my robe collar. His lips nudge at the edge of the silk while murmuring, "There is more between us than hatred. We understand each other like no other. We were bound the moment you awakened me in another era. It was you for a reason." He pulls back and searches my eyes. "Rule the world with me, empress."

My blood thrums in my ears, dizzying. "Okay."

His smile changes in nature. "Good girl."

In one abrupt movement, he flips me onto my back. My cry of surprise is muffled under his mouth. He pins my arms against the mattress, just like that time in our dream realm.

After a throb of reflexive resistance, I let myself melt along with his movements. I give up on fighting it, this monstrous force inside him. Inside *us*. For what? I don't even believe in chastity.

"Just don't get me pregnant," I mutter when his lips stray to my neck.

"Are you sure?" he whispers against my thrashing pulse.

Clarity flashes through my dimming thoughts. I wrench one arm free from his grasp and seize his bandaged throat. He hisses, eyes going huge.

"Yes, I'm fucking sure," I say, much firmer. "Do you want to ruin our whole ruse by getting me pregnant while I'm already supposed to be pregnant? Go put on protection."

He pries my hand off his neck. "Does your organization not stockpile ... pills?"

"Doesn't matter. Do your part," I say, thinking of the cutesy posters in Alliance offices with slogans like this. I can't be preaching about the necessity of taking precautions while neglecting it myself.

He caresses my fingers and puts them to his lips. "But I want to feel all of you."

I fling my hand out of his. "What in the skies does that even mean? Wrap it, or you won't be feeling anything but *private property*!" I shift to get up.

A gruff sigh unfurls from him. "Wait." He stops me with a few fingers to my chest. "They're . . . all the way over there." He rolls off the bed and walks around it to open a nightstand drawer.

I knew it! Lazy bastard. As if he'd let himself get caught unprepared. He just wanted to see what he could get away with. I can't drop my guard for a single second around him after all.

What I don't expect is for him to take an entire pile of foil packages out of the drawer. He slaps them on the nightstand before turning back to me. Eyes like searing coals, he rips one package open with his teeth. There's such a finality to it that my head spins and my mouth waters.

He holds the package out to me between two fingers.

When I catch on to what he wants me to do, I almost roll my eyes to the back of my skull.

"You are so lazy," I jeer.

"This is a laborist state. I shall compensate you very fairly." He smiles. "Once you're ready for *common property*, that is."

"What are you talking about?"

"When you use the stop code, I won't keep going until you say the opposite words."

"Oh." I crawl across the bed and snatch the package from him. Admittedly, I feel a lot better after talking these things out with him, even though I'll never trust him fully. "Well, I'll say it if you kneel for me."

"*Excuse me?*"

"That's what you get for whining about protection. It may be just a matter of pleasure for you, but it's a matter of *safety* for me. You need to understand that."

"Fine." He puts his hands to his hips. "I apologize."

"Not good enough." I cross my legs and turn the package between my fingers. "How badly do you want this?"

He squints at me, but then his stiff expression loosens into something more wry. He drops to his knees in one fluid motion, almost dangling off the edge of the platform.

"Happy?" he purrs, placing his hands on his thighs.

"Yes. Good boy."

A prickle goes up my spine at the forced smile that jumps onto his face. I may have pushed him a little too far. How did he manage to make *kneeling* look menacing?

"Common property," I say, before regret has time to eat into me.

He pounces forth and drags me toward him by my legs. I yelp as my back hits the mattress, sliding. He rips my robe open and pushes my legs apart. His mouth goes exploring between them.

I make an undignified noise at the sensation that laps into me. I slap my hand over my mouth. He reaches up and smacks my elbow until I release myself and let my voice flow free.

At least he can't talk while doing this.

I feel like I'm tumbling over a cliff edge, one that he and I have been wrestling on since I dragged him back to life and into a future he loathes. This time, there are no Hundun sirens to reel me elsewhere, no awful revelations to interrupt. There's just the fall—down, down, down, down into an abyss I should've known better than to stare into.

CHAPTER FORTY-SIX

ONE WAY OR ANOTHER

I've made a huge mistake.

I drift awake alone to daylight through the paper windows, my body throbbing in so many places, I might've aged ten years.

When I make it to the bathroom and pick up the hand mirror on the sink, I let out an ugly squawk at my reflection, particularly the bruises nearly encompassing my throat. Memories flit behind my eyes, of Qin Zheng's mouth on my neck, marking me over and over.

I slam the mirror down, yet, at the same time, an absurd craving pulls at the pit of my stomach, followed by the urge to throw myself off a building.

After getting cleaned up, I flop back down on the bed with my arm draped over my face. I vowed never to shame myself for sleeping with whoever I wanted, but there is no way to be proud of this.

Qin Zheng does intimacy the same way he does everything else: intensely, and with no mercy. I didn't know it could feel so much like a battle for survival, my hands twisting in the sheets as I fought the bombardment on my senses to stay on guard, always on guard, against what he might do next. It does strange things to the mind, to not trust the person literally entwined naked with you. It was something completely different from the tides of warmth that used to fill me inside out with Yizhi and Shimin. Qin Zheng and I didn't so much grow in intimacy as take our frustrations out on each other.

More bruises adorn my hips in a vague pattern of fingers. There were moments last night when I could tell he was thinking of how I'd turned my weapons on him to save Yizhi, and with a flash of fury in his eyes, the brutal rhythm of his body against mine became a punishment for my disobedience.

I could've said the stop code.

At no point did I come close to using it.

I smother myself with a pillow. I'd be less confused if he were like that the whole time, yet he would then slow down and kiss me like he's apologizing, and that's how I learned that the most grotesque punishment is one that turns my body against myself and leaves me wanting more.

When did I become so twisted that I would want more of something like this? I should've ...

No, I can't think like that. Qin Zheng sure isn't. I bet he's walking around not bothered whatsoever, not a single conflicted thought in his head about what happened.

Bastard. Maybe he's right in that I'm still held down by guilt and shame, despite my best efforts at shedding those shackles. Even the way I'm thinking about this—I have got to shake the feeling that he took something from me, that I lost something to him. I didn't. It was a mutual act of pleasure. And a little pain.

Okay, more than a little pain. I hope I left as many bruises on him as he did on me. The state of his back can't be pretty after what I did with my nails.

The door swings open, accompanied by the sound of clattering metal. I jolt up, yanking the covers over myself.

Qin Zheng strides across the bedchamber's center carpet in full armor and cape. When he steps onto the bed platform, I stare him down, even though the look he gives me and the curl of his grin set me ablaze from the inside.

"Good afternoon, kitten."

I fail to stop myself from hurling a pillow at him. He dodges to the side, Wood-green qì flashing in his wide eyes, and draws his sword. With one swift slash, the pillow hits the floor in pieces, goose down erupting around him. I hate the way my stomach swoops at how smooth that move was. Yeah, he can swing a sword—so what?

Laughing, he waves through the drifting flurry and sits down beside me. "Wake up in a mood, did we? Can I make you feel better?" He pets my thigh through the covers.

I slap him away. "Don't touch me."

"Don't play coy." He leans closer and says, "You enjoyed yourself last night. I could see it and hear it. I could *feel* it."

My face goes painfully hot as I recall some of the things I did and said when he had me on the right edge. "I was faking to get it over quicker."

"Now, that is the worst lie you have ever told. You would sooner die than stroke my ego on purpose."

My lips mash shut. He's got me there.

"You missed the morning assembly," he says with a more casual air. "I summoned your former assistant and made her the Imperial Secretary. You were right in that I was in urgent need of a new one."

At the mention of Wan'er, some tension eases off my bones.

"In addition, your mathematician friend showed up with an interesting economic plan," he goes on. "She proposed we repurpose the logistics algorithms of megacorporations such as Gao Enterprises to develop a national management system. Through it, every supplier, factory, distribution warehouse, and other nodes along a supply chain could communicate openly with one another regarding disruptions and respond to real-time changes in demand. The Cybernetic Cooperative Network, she called it."

"Yeah, CyberCo. We've been using it at the Alliance to keep branches stocked. I've been trying to tell you about it for months."

"Perhaps you should have done it with your clothes off."

Wow.

I really slept with this man.

Though I can't deny the relief that fills me at hearing him talk positively about Taiping.

"It's Minister Gao, not my 'mathematician friend,'" I say. "Call them by their titles, like you do every other official."

"Fine. Minister Gao and Secretary Shangguan. Anything for my lovely empress." He moves to kiss me on the head. "Is this what it takes to get you to smile? I should have recruited women to the central court sooner."

"Yes, you should've." I shift onto all fours and climb out of the covers to kneel beside him, resting my arms over his shoulder. Anything to encourage this.

He cradles my face with one hand, stroking my cheek. "The rest of the court inquired extensively about the details of Minister Gao's proposed policies, but she answered them quite convincingly. Perhaps her ideas can get this blasted economy under control."

I lean into his touch. "What about Secretary Shangguan? How's she doing?"

"She's a swift learner. Only needs to be taught once to complete any task. I expected a bigger disruption to my correspondence after my . . ." he snarls, "*changing of secretaries*, but it appears that she can take over the duties of that traitorous snake rather smoothly. Of course, if she betrays me as well, you won't be able to save her a second time."

His hand tenses against my cheek, and his eyes go cold in a way that makes me wonder if he found out that I tried to share the truth of our world on the networks. We did connect in a dream realm last night, *afterward*, to discuss our attack plan on the gods.

My fear scatters when he takes his hand off my face with a wide smile. "Now, I have something for you." He fishes a jade pendant out of his armor. Engraved with gold, a dragon and a phoenix swirl around each other on the round surface. A nudge of his fingers and the pendant splits like the yīn-yáng symbol. He brushes my hair back and strings the phoenix half of the pendant around my neck on a fine gold chain. "This was in the most precious collection of jewelry we've expropriated. I thought it'd make a fitting gift."

The half-pendant falls between my breasts, the translucent jade warm with his body heat. I examine it, tracing the gold outline near its edge. "So, you stole this."

He beams. "It is always ethical to rob the wealthy."

I snort. Maybe I'm just happy about Wan'er and Taiping having an excellent first day as officials, but I don't hate him as much as I did when I woke up. What's the harm in humoring him? Maybe it'll keep him distracted from realizing I tried to commit treason. I take the dragon half of the pendant out of his hands to put it around his neck. Our eyes meet while my fingers work the clasp of its chain at his nape. Even after securing it, I don't move away, breathing the same swirls of air as him. It amazes me, how I've grown used to being so close to *him*, of all people.

He pulls at my lower lip with his thumb. "What are you thinking about, empress?"

"How weird it is that I grew up with a portrait of you above my family's dining table."

He pales, and his hand springs off me. "That does *not* count as me having known you while you were an infant."

"It's okay. The portrait was really greasy. Could barely see your face in it, or maybe it would've conditioned me better against wanting anything to do with you."

"Well," he huffs, "it used to bring me physical pain to look upon *your* face."

"Don't be dramatic. I'm not ugly."

He releases a slow sigh from his nose, eyes flicking down. "No. It's that you bear a passing resemblance to my *shīfu*, General Mi. Once I discovered the fate she endured following my disappearance . . ."

"Oh." I did notice she looked kind of like my mother in his memories. "Is that why you made me wear a mask?"

"Perhaps. Partially."

"But it doesn't pain you anymore?" I touch my face.

A muscle twitches under his eye. "No, you infuriate me far too regularly to remind me of my *shīfu* any longer. You have none of her charm or poise."

"Okay, good. Because it would've been really creepy if you were thinking about her while pounding me senseless."

He winces, then shakes his head. "Case in point."

"So, can I stop wearing the mask?"

"Hmm . . ." His expression turns troubled. "The sudden change would raise unneeded questions."

I sigh. "You just had to make your issues *my* issues."

"Your face is precious to me," he coos, cupping my cheeks. "Let it be all mine to look at."

"I told you to stop being so possessive!" I grab another pillow like a weapon.

Laughing, he catches my arms in his hands and my lips in a kiss. I lower the pillow. When our kiss deepens, stirring cravings of last night, I give up on the idea of it being a one-time thing. I scoot back on the bed. He lets his armor slip to the floor in liquid form.

"It's midday, you animal," I whine half-heartedly.

"As I've said, the people will benefit if my mind is not elsewhere while I consider their woes." He unfastens my robe and pushes it off, leaving me wearing nothing but the pendant. "I've already sent investigators to the Tianlao. See?"

"All right, if it's *for the people*," I mock as I reach over his shoulders for his conduction suit's zippers. It's my first time really seeing him in it. He doesn't look terrible in white.

He cooperates to peel it off himself. While he's distracted, I push him onto his back and wedge myself between his legs.

"Oh—" He makes a puzzled noise.

"I'm still sore." I grasp his knees and loom over him like a hawk. My half-pendant dangles between us. "It's *your* turn."

His eyes go wide, flashing the full circles of his irises. Then his expression loosens into nonchalance, and he shrugs.

"Cheap slut," I sneer at him.

"Needy whore," he fires back with a grin.

After this very healthy exchange, we grasp at each other and collide in another kiss.

I was anxious about getting so intimate with him because I was worried it might make him matter to me more than he should, but that didn't happen. I don't feel any different about him than before. I'm less on edge, even, because there's no more mystery about what it'd be like to cross this line.

I grew up being told I should only do this with the most precious person in my life, that making the wrong choice would ruin me for good, yet . . . it really doesn't have to be that big of a deal. We took precautions. I have a guarantee that he'll stop any moment I want him to, a commitment I *do* think he'll abide by, if he wants this to keep happening. It's like sparring, carrying the thrill of a battle without true stakes.

It's freeing, in a way, to know this is a release, not a binding. He's just a warm body to me, something to take the edge off as we count down toward almost certain death. When I joined him in our dream realm last night, he confirmed that he doesn't think we should delay our god-slaying mission. The longer we stall, the more we run the danger of getting snuffed out before we can strike. Reworking the calculations would reopen risks of the gods discovering our intentions. Continuing as planned is our best option.

Since I'm stuck with him, why should I feel ashamed about having some fun with him? I'll be free in less than five months, one way or another.

CHAPTER FORTY-SEVEN

NOTHING THAT WON'T BE OVER SOON

"*End the terror. Blame it all on me.*"

The more I think about Yizhi's last words to us, the deeper they go. He's giving us a way out of our political conundrums. We can paint him as the villain responsible for everything ugly about the revolution, a trickster who deceived Qin Zheng for power and then went mad with it and edged the government into tyranny. The mass executions: Zhang Yizhi's fault. Unpopular new policies: Zhang Yizhi's fault. Inflation and shortages: Zhang Yizhi's fault. When in doubt, blame Zhang Yizhi and the other Gewei Bu agents.

After sending so many to their deaths with wiretapped secrets and torture-extracted confessions, the agents themselves become the last to be executed on livestream in the Phoenix Nest stadium. Lai Junchen and the Brotherhood underlings, who ran the Tianlao like the eighteen levels of hell, get paraded along the well-worn path from the prison gate to The Hammer. Qin Zheng personally reads out their charges of treason and "crimes against humanity" before condemning them, as if he had nothing to do with any of it. The audience, fully packed after months of waning attendance, explodes into cheers at The Hammer's every fall.

It provides the catharsis of upheaval without us having to give up any real power. Hopefully, this is enough to prevent reactionaries from being able to stoke another insurrection.

However, Yizhi himself has seemingly vanished from the surface of the world. Every single person in Huaxia should recognize his face and know the reward for his capture, yet weeks pass without a single legitimate sighting. Qin Zheng even sends envoys beyond the Wall on horseback—the only means of excursion that doesn't alert the Hunduns—to contact Rongdi tribes, yet none have seen him either. My best morbid hope is that he's dead in a forest somewhere, decaying peacefully into the earth, because if Qin Zheng finds him alive, he's in for a fate that's much, much worse.

When Qin Zheng becomes especially frustrated with the search, he threatens to execute Yizhi's siblings. I have to talk him out of it with logic—if Yizhi could be ransomed with the lives of his siblings, he wouldn't have left them here. Besides, most of them are children, who we didn't execute during the worst of our terror, never mind after our turn to clemency. Even Liu Che was allowed to live after reading a self-criticizing proclamation on camera. Qin Zheng then sent him to a youth reform center far north in the frigid Qing province, where he attends discussion groups on laborist texts with other delinquent kids, writes repentant essays, and does farm work to "learn the value of labor" from peasants.

It's better than getting The Hammer.

Many other big changes come with Qin Zheng's freedom, and we let the masses assume they're in response to the insurrection. Gradually, he starts taking trips outside the palace, beginning with a visit to those hospitalized by the Battle of Chengdu. Then he shows up more and more at factories, farms, large construction projects, and disaster zones to meet with local Vanguard leaders and make speeches. It's better if he goes out with a more positive image among the masses. The fact that he can pilot the Yellow Dragon again is a relief, since I wasn't sure I could reassemble it in presentable condition, but we continue to reserve it for emergencies, such as when heavy storms cause a flood along the Chu River. As we use the Dragon to reinforce levees and rescue families from the roofs of their drowned houses, it's the first time I've felt unburdened in a Chrysalis since finding out the truth of our world.

I maintain correspondence with every Iron Widow who gets conscripted, but aside from spending the night with Qieluo once in a while to relay Qin Zheng's dream training, I don't really have much to do with the war after I'm declared "too pregnant" to go off to battle. The influx of female pilots has taken a lot of pressure off the frontiers, and Qin Zheng doesn't like being apart from me, anyway. He makes me come along on every trip and stand beside him during broadcasts. Wherever we go, though, I arrange at least one solo visit to a local Alliance branch. I always aim to make my own headlines. If the people speak of me after I'm gone, let them not remember me as a nameless accessory.

Since he insists on reviewing every speech I record before it gets broadcast, I force him to listen to arguments for matters such as the need for more paid parental leave and government-subsidized child care. Although I personally cannot be more uninterested in raising a family, I can't ignore how it's an important part of many women's lives and a major obstacle to raising education and employment rates among them. Qin Zheng's not the only one who can talk about something for hours. At least some of my points get through to him, becoming actual policy. I find that the trick is to speak in terms of improving productivity across society instead of moral obligation.

Through the work of Taiping and other new officials, the economy grows steadier. She introduces a new currency, merits, which can only be earned through work and cannot be transferred to others. The tougher the job, the more merits someone can gain. Then they can exchange them for luxuries available exclusively from a government catalog. It's a way to encourage people to do those jobs while fairly distributing what's been confiscated from the old-order elites. It also rescues the luxury industries, which have been floundering since rich people became terrified to look rich. It's no joke that soon the only people who can afford jade bracelets, silk robes, top-grade food, and penthouse condos will be miners, garbage collectors, and scientists. Those will no longer be symbols of wealth but symbols of *contribution* to society.

None of this goes perfectly—there will always be countless problems no matter where we look—but as conditions improve, guerilla skirmishes fade in intensity over the months. No one wants to fight if they can live in some semblance of peace. Regrettably, we've also had to break up and ban Yellow Sash rallies, and workplaces remain far from egalitarian, but we're out of time to let the will of the people burn freely. The world they dream of is possible only if we succeed in taking down the gods.

When the new year approaches in layers of frost and flurries of snow, Sima Yi relays the gods' demands for us to continue the annual tradition of leaving nine girls as tribute on Mount Tai, the most sacred mountain in Huaxia.

In our dream realm, Qin Zheng and I briefly entertain the idea of sending a spy up among the tributes, but it's too obvious a move. We decide not to risk it. We don't even take part in the tribute selection, usually left up to the provinces. And, honestly, I don't want to be involved. I could easily imagine myself as one of them. Maybe in a different universe, there's a version of me being left on that mountain with a hidden blade in my hairpin.

The gods never take our tribute with any camera drones in range, so the offerings always seem to vanish by divine magic once we look away. This year, however, I think back to how Qieluo described seeing an aircraft appear out of thin air to snatch up the shattered remains of the Vermilion Bird's head. As I imagine the girls experiencing the same, an unsettling thought comes to me: What if that's how Yizhi got away? What if he vanished from the surface of this world in a literal sense, whisked up the way Shimin was?

Have they had some sort of reunion?

On the night of the New Year's Festival, as families gather around their best meal of the year and children set off firecrackers across Huaxia, I glare at the stars from the throne room balcony, silently demanding answers I know they won't give. None of the girls taken up ever sent a word back. No inkling about what the Heavenly Court is like. I could stomach it better if I felt sure they went up for a good reason, yet I know nothing except the terrible fact that they'll miss out on being safe by just a month. That's how long is left until the scheduled day of our strike. Now they'll likely die with me and Qin Zheng. And Shimin. And maybe Yizhi. And hopefully all the gods.

"What's on your mind, empress?" Qin Zheng comes up behind me, arms circling above my seven-month pregnancy padding.

"Nine families are missing a daughter at their reunions tonight." My breath leaves me in cloudy blooms. "Do you think they're grieving while having to listen to other families celebrate through the walls?"

Silent, he holds his palm out to the night. Snowflakes drift onto his gauntlet, the crystals brighter than the rest of the palace. All the staffers and guards went home to their families. Only a single building remains lit like an ember on the periphery, where Taiping is hosting a gathering with what's left of the Gao family and her friends from the clubs, who don't have families to go home to. Every so often a burst of collective laughter carries on the frigid air.

"Every family has mentally prepared to eventually give their daughter away since the day she was born as a daughter," Qin Zheng finally says. "I doubt they are much bothered."

I twist out of his arms and glower at him.

He makes an offended face. "I am attempting to comfort you!"

"You're bad at it!"

A hint of color nips at his cheeks. "Which you should not be surprised by! This is not your first day of knowing me!"

I put the heel of my hand to my forehead. "I should've gone with Wan'er to Taiping's dinner party."

He huffs out a swirl of vapor. "Yes, I bet they would have appreciated you intruding upon their family affair."

"They invited me! They just backtracked a second later because they realized I shouldn't leave you to be alone on New Year's!"

His expression goes slack.

"And you agreed?" he says, oddly quiet.

White puffs gust out of my mouth as my brain catches up to what I said. I gulp, fists curling. "Don't read too much into—"

His mouth muffles my words.

Before I know it, I'm catching glimpses of the throne room's high, shadowed ceiling over his shoulder while his body rocks mine against the bed that never got moved out of my side chamber. Sensation rolls through me in waves as he mutters things he can't possibly mean against my skin.

Distantly, fireworks go off. Tears bead at the corners of my eyes when I picture families surrounded by much more warmth and light than what's in this frigid throne room, watching colors erupt in the sky together. My panting mouth finds his, and I drink him in like a drug to chase away everything else I'm feeling.

I understand Shimin more than ever. Self-destruction starts making sense when thinking with full clarity is worse.

I spew curses at Qin Zheng and scratch at his back like a wild animal. These are the only occasions when I can channel my rage at him to my heart's content and have him laugh it off while kissing me deeper. Many arguments and training sessions end with our armor and clothes on the floor when my frustration reaches a peak.

Once we're done, neither of us can be bothered to trek back to our residence through the snow. We settle down on the bed, just big enough for the two of us.

He holds me close and kisses me on the head. "I am glad you stayed with me," he whispers.

"Okay," I grunt.

I roll in the other direction. He doesn't try to keep me in his arms. He's used to me having a bit of an attitude every time we do this.

Sleep doesn't come easily. Fireworks go off throughout the night. I imagine New Year's back at my village, the feast my mother and grandmother would've cooked up with the aunties in our extended family. Roasting one of our pigs in the backyard, braising the biggest fish in our ice cellar, caught by my father in the mountain streams. In the festive atmosphere, even he would burst into loud laughs and commend my mother's cooking after a few shots of liquor. It would be the happiest she'd look all year.

I imagine her telling me how proud she is that I finally learned to compromise and accept a husband as well.

Tears spring to my eyes. I fail to stop my shoulders from shaking.

Qin Zheng stirs beside me in the dark.

"Empress?" He touches my arm. "Are you still thinking of the girls?"

"I'm thinking of my mother," I admit. "My family."

He's quiet for a moment before turning me toward him. "Empress, come here," he says in an almost pleading voice. "You did what you had to do."

I let him gather me to his bare chest, cutting off my thoughts about how, in that moment, he chose to sit back and see if I'd go through with it. I can't blame him for not taking control when I was the one who wanted power. I made the decision to crush them. It's me who has to live with it.

I don't push away from him this time. It shouldn't be possible to drift off to sleep in the arms of someone who represents so much of what I hate, but the throne room is very cold and he is very warm.

CHAPTER FORTY-EIGHT

RISE, RISE, RISE, RISE

Although we've done dream simulations for months, when the night of our strike against the gods comes, I'm not ready. I don't think it's possible to be ready for something like this.

Taiping's entire body trembles as she hands us her calculations after checking them one last time. A lot are estimations at best. The gods don't allow us to look too closely upward. What's sure is that the distance to the heavens is so immense that we have to launch off while the Heavenly Court is halfway around the world to have any hope of intercepting it. Our timing must be precise, or we'll die for nothing. Likely, we will. There's so much that could go wrong, my knees wobble when I think of the possibilities. We don't know what the gods could do to repel us once they realize we're coming. If they could slow down the Heavenly Court, pull it out of its trajectory, or blast us out of the sky. But better to die fighting back than spend a lifetime wondering what could've happened if we'd been braver.

Taiping drives me and Qin Zheng to the Yellow Dragon, twined as usual around Mount Ziwei. Once we get to the Dragon's head, we share a silent goodbye in the carriage. I clench Taiping's hands, trying to convey everything in my heart without making a sound.

Thank you for helping us with this madness.
Thank you for living as boldly as you do.
Thank you for being there for me like Big Sister once was.

I am no stranger to the decision to throw my life away. Only this time do I feel a twinge of regret. I'll miss Taiping, Wan'er, Qieluo, the Phoenix Ladies, and the other Iron Widows, all sisters-in-arms I wish I could've had more time with.

Tears shine in Taiping's eyes. She bites her lip, mouth twisting with a stifled sob.

I could hold on to her for an eternity, but Qin Zheng pats my elbow and gives Taiping an envelope—his last will, packed with instructions on what to do after we set off. For the next five days, she's to tell everyone we're sick while getting Qieluo and Yang Jian—the next most high-ranking pilots—to prepare for their likely ascension to leadership. If five days pass and we're not back, they can announce our deaths and proceed with the transfer of power.

There remain so many problems everywhere that it's impossible to feel secure in letting go, but we did all we could. It was never feasible for us to wait until the revolution was truly *secure* in any sense before leaving. The gods wouldn't have let Qin Zheng live to that point, because they know the first thing he'd do after that is challenge them. The gamble we're taking by abandoning everything so abruptly *is* our biggest element of surprise.

We have broken the old order and uprooted its rotting pedestals of power. Every level of government is filled with scholar-bureaucrats from the lower classes, who only got their chance to rise because of the revolution. Vanguards elected by their peers and educated in revolutionary theory keep every community organized and connected. We'll have to trust them to keep the momentum going. The revolution was never mine or Qin Zheng's. It belongs to the millions of ordinary people who've always dreamed of a better life.

I think of the writings Wan'er and Di Renjie shared with me. So much of it sounded impossible and unrealistic, pipe dreams that would shatter under human greed if brought out of the pages, yet those authors refused to accept despair and dared to imagine more. They burned bright for a future they may not see, fighting and dying and sometimes *winning* despite insurmountable odds.

They came before, and they will come after. I see now that I am part of a long tradition that cannot be extinguished, and this strike against the heavens will be my ultimate act of revolution.

Qin Zheng opens the carriage door. I shiver at the wind that blows over us when we get out. Taiping and I regard each other for one long, final moment before she pulls the carriage door shut. After another reluctant pause, she drives off. With the way we're about to take off in the Yellow Dragon, it'll be too dangerous for her to stick around.

I let out a trapped breath, blinking my vision clear. Tears slip down my cheeks while I watch the carriage disappear down the mountain road. The whir of its engine fades into the ambient sound of rustling leaves.

Qin Zheng moves toward the Dragon's head, but he does a double take looking at the sea of lights beneath the mountain.

"I never got a chance to see much of the city," he remarks.

In his eyes, there is not so much longing as there is confusion. I don't think he ever got over the feeling of being unfastened from time, lost in a world he doesn't recognize. He never stopped calling this "the future."

"It's overrated." I walk past him with my scythe. "Come on."

Once we climb into the cockpit, I split my armor at the front, pull out my eight-month pregnancy padding, and abort it behind me.

"Oh, no, not our son," Qin Zheng says, his tone utterly flat.

"No, that's yours and Yizhi's baby."

"I told Auntie Wei to name him Fusu, you know. Like that folk song. '*There are fúsū trees on the mountain; there are lotuses in the pond.*'" He carries half a tune. "Do they still sing it in your era?"

"No. Never heard it."

He sighs.

Half a step from the pilot seats, the full absurdity of what we're about to do hits me. It's the two of us against *gods*, beings who live in the *sky*. How did we think this was a good idea?

"Zetian . . ."

My head snaps up. I can't remember the last time Qin Zheng uttered my name.

He lifts my hand, running his thumb over my knuckles. His throat bobs. "I'm sorry."

"For what?" I search his face, cradled by the ghostly moonlight coming through the Dragon's open snout.

"For being the way I am. This world has not made me kind."

Something goes off balance inside me. Maybe I'm just overwhelmed by the impossible odds, but a fresh surge of tears loosens from my eyes. Without thinking, I throw my arms around him.

After a slight delay, he holds me tight.

"Same here," I say near the rapid beating of his heart, audible through his armor.

Those like us were not meant to be kind. We were born to rage and burn and destroy all that must be destroyed, so that maybe, one day, much better people than us can live in a world where they're rewarded for their kindness instead of having it twisted to bind them.

When we move apart, our resolve is reflected in each other's eyes. In these last hours of our very different lives, despite all the clashes we've had, here we stand in solidarity. We are no longer an emperor and empress but two mad fools aiming to break out of a planetary prison.

Let it be known that there once lived two mortals who dared to challenge the gods.

With a cold rush of his qì, our crowns morph into assault-mode helmets, antlered and extending down around our shoulders in overlapping, flexible plates.

"One chance," Qin Zheng remarks, as though laughing at ourselves. "One chance and no more."

"Let's take it," I say.

Hands clasped, we head up to the pilot seats. I attach my scythe to the floor. Once we settle in, we shut the Dragon's snout, plunging our bodies into darkness and our minds into the battle link.

After I adjust to perceiving the world through the Yellow Dragon, the yīn-yáng realm steadies in my mind. Qin Zheng's spirit form sits cross-legged beside me like he's meditating. Taiping's schematics appear before us, along with several measures keeping track of everything from time to speed to altitude. I try not to let my mind influence them. Qin Zheng is the one who can better estimate how fast the Dragon is going at any given time.

At least, I hope he can.

The timer ticks down toward zero. Pushing the Dragon up with its claws, we lift its great head and reposition its body so it's coiled like a spring near the mountaintop. Dirt, vegetation, and rubble from the Palace of Sages tumble down the mountainside with our every colossal motion.

When the timer hits zero, there's nothing more to do but launch up with a burst of qì.

It feels like regular flying at first as we undulate the Dragon through the air. We don't go straight up, but diagonally, mindful of Taiping's insistence that we not ignore the "horizontal velocity." The Heavenly Court travels at a breakneck speed around the planet. If we don't match that speed in the direction it's going, we'll splatter against it like a bug into a truck window.

Wind roars in the Dragon's face as we accelerate. The lights of Chang'an pull away below, skyscrapers turning as small as glittering grains of sand. Mountains pass into insignificance. Clouds flit past us as we lash the Dragon's body to build momentum, whipping faster and faster. Higher and higher we go, fighting the pull of the planet itself, the law of nature which decrees that all that goes up must come down.

This is the law we must break to be free.

Despite all our dream realm rehearsals, after a certain height, none of those simulated sensations come close to the true weight of gravity under challenge. It crushes down on us without mercy, punishing us for our insolence.

It's too much.

This is impossible.

What were we thinking?

This is not going to work.

I edge close to giving up, but then the image of us plummeting to our death like Di Renjie and Wei Zifu lurches in my consciousness. We've spilled too much blood to not carry this through for our people. I reorient the world in my mind, imagining us plunging *down* from the earth and into the stars.

When it feels like we can't possibly strain any further, Qin Zheng ignites the Dragon's tail, consuming its own spirit metal to propel us higher. After getting a sense of how he does it, I help him. The Dragon blazes like a meteor in reverse, smoothing out in shape until it's no longer a dragon but a blade tearing through the fabric of reality.

It feels like becoming pure scorching heat, pure blinding light in a vortex of fluttering air. Every fiber and connection that makes up who I am stretches to the brink of snapping.

There is no yīn-yáng realm anymore, just a wild spilling storm of both our memories. His child self screams for me from his lab cell. My child self grasps at him from my village home. Two people who were never supposed to meet, coming together through sheer defiance of fate, for one singular purpose. It's such agony, burning alive, that I regret every choice that brought me here, from crushing the Palace of Sages to resurrecting Qin Zheng to enlisting as Yang Guang's concubine. Everything would've been so much easier if I'd stayed in my village and become a peasant's wife. What about housework and pregnancy and motherhood did I think I couldn't endure? At least I wouldn't be trying to *fly to the stars to kill gods*.

Focus, comes Qin Zheng's most dire sentiment, felt more than heard.

Right. It's up to me to keep us on track with the Heavenly Court.

I reach and grope for Shimin's spirit signature, but the world is nothing but wind and heat and agony. A flash of memory from Qin Zheng shows a man getting torn apart by five horses galloping in five directions. Never have I found such anguish so relatable.

But I cannot give up. I cannot give up. *I cannot give up.* I've come too far to give up. All this pain I feel, all the pain I caused to survive to this moment, will mean nothing if I give up.

I am not a mortal bound to earth. I am a collection of electric signals, pure human willpower concentrated on one objective—

"*Rise*," Big Sister tells me, standing in the stream Yizhi and I scattered her ashes in.

"*Rise*," Xiuying hisses at me, crushed inside the Black Tortoise.

"*Rise*," Di Renjie and Wei Zifu demand of me on a battlefield full of both flesh and metal carcasses.

"*Rise!*" Shimin calls for me in a shower of light as bright as the sun.

There!

It's like bursting into a breath of air after a treacherous climb from the deepest ocean bottom. I can feel an inkling of Shimin's spirit signature. I know I can.

I reel the Dragon sideways, angling into its path.

We are running out of spirit metal! Qin Zheng's concern reaches me. It jolts me into the awareness that the Dragon has burned down to barely more than the mass that made up its head.

Just a little more! I plead. *We can make it. We have to make it!*

Shimin's spirit signature draws steadily closer. At the edge of the Dragon's warped vision—I'm not sure what we're even seeing out of at this point—a silver speck hurtles out of boundless darkness.

I give a primal cry of both awe and terror while curving into its trajectory. The speck rapidly enlarges into a structure of twin rings attached to a long axis—exactly what we expected.

Except it's one thing to imagine it and another to see it coming in real life. Horror dawns on me as its true size becomes clear, like a whole city chasing after us. Even the sides of its gargantuan rings dwarf us beyond comprehension. We really are no more than bugs compared to that thing. Every impulse in me screams to get out of its way, but that's no longer possible.

Before we could ever have been prepared, the Heavenly Court smashes into us.

CHAPTER FORTY-NINE

HAVOC IN HEAVEN

When my consciousness pulls itself together again, the first thing I feel is offended. What do you mean there's *pain* in the afterlife?

It's a long while before I consider the possibility that I may, in fact, not be dead. I peel my eyes open, then immediately shut them when a headache splits down my skull. There's nothing to see but darkness, anyway. I can hear, though: my own ragged breathing, air straining through my clogged nostrils. I taste sticky blood on my upper lip.

A low groan rises behind me. Faint light reaches through my eyelids. When I make a second attempt at opening them, the sight before me shocks me alert.

The cockpit's spirit metal walls, dimly lit with Qin Zheng's qì, are much closer than before and utterly deformed, like golden waves frozen in movement.

"Skies . . ." he grumbles.

We're slanted at an odd angle. I have to keep much of my armor attached to my seat to not fall off when I turn to look at him. He's wiping blood from his nose.

"We're alive," I wheeze, scrubbing my own lower face.

"But no longer in the realm of mortals . . ."

My attention lashes straight ahead, to where the Dragon's snout once was. What's out there is beyond either of our imaginations now.

I flare my spirit sense. It trips upon a dizzying number of spirit signatures, dense as Chang'an, hurrying in all directions.

Chills run down my arms. I go as still as a hunter tracking prey.

"Do you feel them?" I whisper.

"*Yes,*" Qin Zheng says, like a curse.

Whatever the gods are, the Heavenly Court is full of living beings.

Shimin's signature is among them, somewhere nearby. Well, nearer than the distance between heaven and earth, at least. With so many smaller signatures running interference up close, he's paradoxically harder to pinpoint than when I was farther. I sense him in two directions at once, which makes no sense.

Carefully, Qin Zheng rises from his seat, gripping the back of mine for balance. He grimaces at the shrunken cockpit. "We no longer have enough spirit metal for a viable Chrysalis form."

I clutch my helmeted head. "Then ... then we'll have to go out in our armor."

"Perhaps. However, first order of war: survey your surroundings."

Guard plates slam together over our faces, leaving only a gap for our eyes.

Qin Zheng leaps from his pilot seat. He doesn't do it with particular vigor, yet he pitches out so unnaturally far that he smacks into the cockpit's warped wall. He stumbles as he slides to the bottom. We exchange bewildered glances. He tests his steps, jumping and hopping with impossible ease.

"The gravity is lower." He gawks at the floor, voice muffled by his face guard.

I detach my scythe from near my seat, channel my qì to fix the parts where it distorted along with the rest of the cockpit, and make my way down. Everything does feel lighter. I could be walking on vapor, not solid metal. Even my feet hurt less. When I get to Qin Zheng, he stops messing around and presses backwards against the warped wall like a spy. I mirror him.

Our eyes meet for one last moment of tranquility. Then he opens a slash in the wall, between us.

A sound like Hundun sirens wails in, along with distant screams. Very human-sounding screams. We peek through the opening.

I don't know what I expected to see, but it definitely wasn't tall buildings covered in luminous vegetation.

Past a short stretch of rubble and upturned earth in the murky realm, the buildings are strangely but gracefully shaped, playing with curves and geometry. Some twist and fan out in dozens of levels of plants; others have round platforms of overgrowth jutting out from different heights. The plants glow in oranges and greens and blues and purples, like certain rare finds in the mountains near my village. Grass swathes the spaces between buildings. I can match some of the spirit signatures I sense to the structures; the signatures are collectively rushing downward for some reason.

That's all fine. That's all comprehensible after a few seconds.

It's when I peer higher that my sense of reality breaks.

We're on the inner surface of the gargantuan ring we crashed into. The buildings sprawl up its curve and back around, hanging *upside-down* above us. Transparent interlocking hexagons encase this loop of civilization, about the width of downtown Chang'an. Our planet—that mortal realm we just broke out of—looms across the entire visible span of space above, shrouded in the darkness of night but veined with the radiance of man-made lights. It's the kind of view I've seen on helicopter trips to and from Chang'an, except on an arrestingly grander scale, so inconceivably large that my palms break into a sweat within my gauntlets. It feels like that thing should be crashing down on me. This should not be a view biologically possible for me to witness. I recognize the batwing shape of Huaxia's coastline, the concentration of lights along our two major rivers, then the void that must be the Xihuang Desert beyond the Kunlun Mountains. Gently, the planet turns on its axis—or, no, we're orbiting it. When the pattern of lights picks back up on the other side of the desert, a shiver races through me. Those must be the human strongholds beyond Huaxia, which we've had next to no contact with due to how hard it is to get messages across the Hundun wilds. We only have photos and videos from a few expeditions, showing people with very different skin colors, features, architecture, and technology. Have any of them also tried to get up here?

I run out of time for questions when, over the sirens, there comes a sound like buzzing hornets.

Drones flit toward us between the buildings. Larger machines race below them on jointed legs, animallike. Many blinking parts pop out of the wide bulk of their bodies.

The parts start shooting at us.

We duck away from the opening. Qin Zheng seals it shut. Bullets—I think—strike the cockpit with crisp *ping*s, from every direction.

"That has to be the gods' army, right?" I exclaim.

"Cowards." Qin Zheng closes his eyes in concentration, hands on the wall. Despite the pattering outside growing from a drizzle to a storm, nothing gets through.

"The wall can hold." His eyes fly open. "Then so can our armor."

He forms a curved blade in his gauntlet palm, then makes an opening in the wall again and flings the blade out. It remains tethered to his wrist by a thin, unraveling line of spirit metal. Projectiles dart in through the gap. Instead of colliding with the back of the cockpit, they *swerve* to come for us. I shudder when they hit my breastplate. Thankfully, they bounce off our armor with little impact.

Qin Zheng retracts his blade with a sharp *clang* and shrinks the opening to a slit. He peers through it.

"We can damage them, confirmed." A wild energy surges in his eyes.

I pick up one projectile. It's metallic—though not spirit metal—and intricately designed. "These are smarter than regular bullets."

"But useless against us nonetheless." He detaches his sword from his hip. "Let's go hunt some gods, shall we?"

I squeeze the projectile until it bursts. "What else is there left to do?"

"Well, actually, some flight capacity would be helpful when handling those airborne machines." He backs against the wall. Large, bat-like wings carve into shape on either side of him, then he flaps them free.

"Machines!" Qin Zheng laughs as I make a pair of wings for myself. "Excellent. I won't get the complaints that tend to come when I use my full power on *humans*."

He digs his fingers into the wall and forges a second sword on the spot, pulling it free while sculpting it. His irises gleam silver as he sharpens its edges, then he swings both swords with a flourish. "Watch my back, empress."

A breach gapes open beside him. He twists out through it and dashes into the realm of the gods.

Casting the last of my stray fears away, I follow him onto the dirt and rubble outside. The gravity is so light that even I don't have much trouble traversing the mess. Smart bullets assail us as we approach the buildings ahead, which hold no more spirit signatures. The signatures are all deep underground, scurrying away.

The machines gather to blockade us. In sync, they emit a screeching noise that ripples through the air. It buffets us back a few steps, but it's nothing unbearable after I will my helmet to squeeze painfully tight against my ears.

The machines then spew out a white gas. The glow of the plants goes hazy under its cover.

"Oh, *not again!*" Qin Zheng leaps into the air and cracks his wings in quick succession, creating gusts of wind that blow the gas back.

We learned our lesson about heading into strange clouds of gas. We keep going only once our wings are dispersing the mist faster than the machines can produce it.

Qin Zheng reaches the machines first. Mechanical arms dart out of them, grabbing at him with grippers and menacing him with whirring saw blades. He slashes clean through the legs of one machine and stabs it sideways as it falls. Then he spins to yank his sword out and shear more machines apart, exposing wires and electric sparks.

Battle is his natural domain, and he is undeniably brilliant and breathtaking within it. It's impossible to watch him with anything but awe. The airborne drones swarm to disrupt his wing beats, preventing him from flying properly, but he simply springs up off the ground machines to flip and twirl and lacerate the whirling drones. On his drops, he drives his swords into more machines with the backing of his body weight.

I have not understood what he's capable of until now. I'm slightly furious to realize he went easy on me in our training. Memories come to me, spilled from his mind into mine on our way up: Him training in the art of violence since he was a child. In a lab, in rain, in snow, in scorching heat, threatened with electric shocks and starvation. I don't think he knows how to live in any way except unrelentingly and against resistance. He shreds through the legion of machines like a destructive cyclone, fusing his twin swords into a sledgehammer for certain blows. When he catches me staring, he has the audacity to wink at me.

I roll my eyes and swing my scythe into a machine behind us. While turning in nimble circles to take more machines down, or at least as nimble as my feet can manage, I spot a hole in the crystalline hexagons above. That must be where we smashed in. The jagged edges are glowing and . . . shrinking? Is it capable of repairing itself?

With only the radiance of luminous vegetation to rely on, it takes some effort to discern the trail of devastation our landing left. Silhouetted buildings with their tops blown off, a rupture in what I think is an elevated transport rail, and a ruinous gouge in the ground where we skidded to a stop. What's left of the Yellow

Dragon looks even worse from the outside, no more than a melted lump.

Careful to fan my wings in a way that keeps the gas from overwhelming me, I push onward with Qin Zheng, constantly checking over my shoulder and vaulting over the broken machine parts left in his wake. Although adrenaline keeps me going, my head throbs from the strain of the flight up. Bright spots mottle my vision with every big movement. My arms burn from overuse. When the machines come too quickly to handle with a scythe, I attach it to my back, its curving blade high above my wings, and detach the sword at my side for a more agile weapon.

Not for the first time, I wish Earth-type spirit metal could conduct qì blasts. Then again, if we were wearing any other type, we might not withstand the bullets. I grit my teeth through the acidic ache in my muscles and fend off the machines however I can with my sword. This place has the temperature of a mild spring night, but sweat quickly soaks my conduction suit under my armor.

"There!" Qin Zheng points one sword at a building ahead, comprising at least ten floors in a spiral pattern. My heart skips when I feel that it still has spirit signatures crowded inside. We slam back-to-back and fight our way toward the building.

"Brace yourself!" Qin Zheng shouts.

"Brace for wh—"

He attaches his swords to his hips, grabs me by the waist, and hurls me up. I barely avoid stabbing myself as I land on a balcony and tumble through glowing plants. He leaps up after me with a completely unnecessary somersault in the air. I curse at him to give me a clearer warning next time, but I lose no momentum in smashing through the glass at the back of the balcony.

I burst into ... someone's home?

The furniture may be designed in the same strange, sinuous style as the buildings outside, but it's easy to see what they're supposed to be: couches, chairs, a table, a kitchen. Almost every surface is made of a glossy white material inscribed with gold patterns. Digital symbols shine everywhere in vivid neon. Soft light effuses from stylish indents in the walls. The couches and chairs are somehow hovering off the ground.

A small round drone flits toward us, flashing a red light and shrieking in a language I don't understand. With a thrust of my sword I skewer the drone against the ceiling. Its light goes out.

Meanwhile, Qin Zheng flings the couches to make a stack in front of the balcony entrance, blocking off the drones outside. When the bottom couch comes to a smooth stop, it continues to levitate off the ground. The others merely push it a bit lower when they land on top.

Catching our breath through the thin gap above our face guards, Qin Zheng and I press back-to-back again and stalk toward a room with a spirit signature inside. It's faint, but so are most other signatures in the Heavenly Court. Without being familiar with their building structures, it's hard to tell which are genuinely weak and which are just far away.

We pass what appears to be a bathroom full of glass and crystal before barging into a room with a floating bed. The signature takes us deeper, past the corner of another door—

Instead of a god, a small animal backs away beneath racks of strange clothes. It looks like a cat, except its ears are folded, its legs are pathetically short, and patches of green and magenta dapple its white fur.

Qin Zheng lurches toward it, sword raised.

"Wait!" I reach for him, but the creature evades his slashing blade and skitters past us on its puny legs.

He chases after it.

Despite my instinct to stop him from killing a small animal, I waver. Who knows what that thing really is? Appearances can deceive. It could be deadly poisonous. It could be smarter than humans.

"That can't be a god, can it?" I go after him.

As he bolts around the home, failing to get the creature despite channeling Wood qì for speed, I take a closer look at everything else. The furniture is definitely human-sized. When I press down on a hovering chair, I feel an invisible force keeping it off the floor. There's half-eaten food in the slick white bowls on the table. Neon symbols light up on the bowls when I touch them. They're still warm.

Qin Zheng makes a strangled noise from the front door.

"What is it?" I hurry beside him, then air catches in my throat as well.

There are pictures displayed digitally on the wall, and the pictures have people in them. Unnaturally thin and bone-pale, their features are so different from anyone in Huaxia that I can't tell their genders. I'm guessing they're a family, two parents and two children. One adult has golden hair that swoops upward in defiance of gravity; the other has short purple hair cropped at an angle along their jaw; the two children in front of them have different shades of blue hair, and they all have light-colored eyes. Nothing like the statues of gods in our temples.

If they're not human, I don't know what else I'd call them.

"I knew it!" Qin Zheng's hateful gaze rakes across the pictures. "They are no gods. They are ordinary humans, just as we are."

"We . . . we don't know that for sure. Maybe they have special powers."

"Feel the way they're running from us, empress. *We* are the ones with abilities they fear."

The pictures change every few seconds. They show this oddly colored, oddly dressed family laughing with their arms around each other in front of a lake, dancing in a neon-lit chamber, hugging a tree with luminous lines in its bark, and more. Actions that could've been done by any family in Huaxia, if you ignore how the buildings arc upward behind the lake, the utter lack of gravity in the place where they're dancing, and the planet looming over the trees. In some pictures, our cloud-wreathed continents and oceans serve as a pretty backdrop. In others, this curved world appears to have its own blue sky.

I have many questions, and one of these false gods had better answer them.

"Let's keep going." I glare at the front door. Maybe it's not even a front door—we find no handle, knob, or button to open it. But there's a mass of spirit signatures behind it.

Qin Zheng and I nod at each other. In sync, we take a few steps back and turn our shoulders toward the door. Channeling Fire qì for power, we charge forth and smash our way out.

The distorted door flies over a railing and lands somewhere below with a loud, metallic crash. We find ourselves on a wraparound balcony facing an atrium. In the center, a gigantic cylindrical aquarium soars to the top of the building, full of colorful bioluminescent fish. The water's ambient blue light dances over us, marbling our faces.

"*Fish?*" Qin Zheng throws his hands up.

Oh. *Those* are what's giving off the spirit signatures.

With a growl, Qin Zheng peers over the railing at the shadowy bottom floor, then at the nondescript doors lined around the atrium at every level. "No more searching. They come to *us*."

He crouches low before launching himself over the balcony railing, flapping his wings.

I fly after him, sneaking glances at the aquarium while staying on guard. With the Hunduns a constant threat in our oceans, we don't have access to many varieties of fish in Huaxia. Where did these come from? Some are quite big, which explains the human-level spirit signatures.

Once he reaches the top of the structure, Qin Zheng shatters a glass pane in the ceiling and pulls himself through. I dodge the falling shards and emerge after him to a brighter scene outside. High above, a dazzling radiance beads at the edge of our planet, spilling over its curvature. We're orbiting into the side of the sun.

Qin Zheng surveys our surroundings in a battle-ready stance. About a minute later, a lone drone whirs up to us.

"Mister Qin, Miss Wu, we would like to negotiate," it says in Hanyu—*our* language. "If you agree to disarm yourselves, we will grant you refugee status in the Melian Republic. You have seen the marvels of our technology. You will not find a higher quality of life anywhere in the galaxy."

As my brain trips over what they mean by "Melian Republic," a hatch opens on the drone, revealing a screen.

A screen showing Shimin in the tank.

"In addition, we will—"

I swing my sword into the drone, shattering it against the ceiling we're standing on. My pulse pounds loudly in my helmet. I can sense Shimin's spirit signature somewhere above, but I made my mind up about this long ago.

"You hold nothing over me!" I point my sword skyward, if "sky" means the one on our planet, encompassing night and day in the same view. Sunlight spreads over the globe in an ever-widening crescent. White swirls of clouds drift over an ocean I don't know, one that bleeds from blue to scarlet. Another stomach-plunging wonderment goes through me. A tender pressure grows behind my eyes.

Qin Zheng retracts his face guard and smiles at me with what might possibly be pride. He stomps on the broken drone and raises one of his swords as well.

"I am Emperor Qin Zheng of Huaxia, and you have subjugated my people for far too long!" he shouts. "Send no more of these machines, or I shall destroy this building and everything around it! Come out to face the souls you locked in a war you will not allow us to win, heavenly tyrants!"

More light sweeps across the Heavenly Court by the second, revealing the smooth white of its buildings and the vivid greens of its vegetation, adorned with bursts of other colors. No wind stirs the leaves and blossoms. I'd think of this place as peaceful—if

I couldn't feel the frantically moving spirit signatures beneath the ground. Gods, humans, animals . . . who knows?

Something flies in from the distance. We ready our swords.

A message beams across the building in front of us: *DO NOT ATTACK*.

We don't relax. There are two spirit signatures in the sleek flying vehicle, which reminds me of one of the big flat fish in the aquarium.

At last, the false gods are daring to show up.

Qin Zheng clanks his swords together and morphs them into a meteor hammer—the best weapon we can make for ranged attacks. I detach my scythe from my back and forge one as well, shaping the handle into flexible chain links and gathering the blade into a spiked ball at the other end.

We hold our ground when the vehicle drops to a whisper-quiet landing before us. An arc of air flutters past us.

A door falls out of the vehicle's side, forming stairs that lead to an opening.

We brace ourselves for our first encounter with a god. Yet the person who steps out, wearing shoes with absurdly high heels that clank down the stairs, and a red robe that exposes his legs and collarbones, is not a god at all.

"Hello again, Your Majesties." Yizhi plants himself before us.

CHAPTER FIFTY

ENEMY OF MY ENEMY

I throw myself around Qin Zheng as he stomps forth and dangles Yizhi off the side of the building by his neck.

"He knows what we don't!" I cry, the spiked ball of my meteor hammer slipping to the ground with a heavy *clang*.

"There's a bomb on the ship," Yizhi chokes out, raising something in his fist. His loose sleeve doesn't fall to his elbow but somehow floats like red mist. His whole robe drifts around him as if it's under water. "If my thumb leaves this button, it'll go off and level this entire block. You won't survive."

"You have no idea what I am capable of surviving," Qin Zheng hisses, morphing his meteor hammer into a single long sword.

"You have no idea what kind of bombs the Melians can make!" Yizhi glares at him, eyes lined all the way to his temples and painted with graduated shades of red.

"What do you mean by 'Melians'? Is that what these so-called gods are?"

"See? You don't . . . know . . . anything!" Yizhi's face grows redder and his words grow weaker.

Against my shrieking instincts, I let go of Qin Zheng and step back. The more desperate I appear to save Yizhi, the more it might worsen Qin Zheng's wrath. The fact that he's merely dangling Yizhi over a ten-floor drop instead of standing over a headless corpse means his good sense is winning over his rage.

"He's right," I say, as calmly as I can, while reeling in my meteor hammer and attaching it to my hip opposite my sword. "We won't get any answers if you kill him. And don't forget, he didn't come alone." I glance back at the . . . ship, Yizhi called it? Its stairs have retracted, leaving no visible way in.

"Who's in there?" Qin Zheng demands.

"Not . . . telling . . . unless . . ." Yizhi gasps and wheezes louder. His bare legs kick in the air.

Qin Zheng swings Yizhi around and drags him in through the hole in the roof. I give the ship an extra wary look before following them. With careful pumps of my wings, I drop halfway down the building, where Qin Zheng tosses Yizhi onto a balcony.

"How are you here, and what are the gods?" He points his sword at Yizhi, the metal gleaming under the aquarium's shifting blue light.

Yizhi coughs and struggles for air. Everything, from his robe to his makeup to the neon sticks in his hair, glows in the dimness. He pushes to his feet, swaying on his high-heeled shoes. Their sloping arches and pointed tips remind me disturbingly of my own feet before the surgery, though the shoes are big enough that I don't think he had to break any bones to wear them. But they can't be comfortable. I have a bad feeling about why he's dressed like this and what he's been doing in the Heavenly Court.

"I got contacted as a backup to Sima Yi and told to report any sign of 'aggression' by you," he croaks at Qin Zheng. "They see you as a dangerous dictator of a rogue state. After you found out about the plan to keep you contained, I convinced them to take me up here, since they were the ones who endangered my life."

"So are these cretins human or not?"

"They are. Nothing supernatural about them. They just have really advanced technology. The universe is much, much bigger than you think, and there are hundreds of inhabited planets out there. This is a trade station established by the Melian Republic, the most powerful planet. Most people who live here are Melian soldiers or employees of a company called Vivasi Minerals."

My chest draws tight, and my head spins with every bit of information he gives. There are *hundreds of other worlds* besides ours? I can barely imagine the other human strongholds on our own single planet.

Qin Zheng paces in a small circle, looking like he's about to explode. "How dare these pretenders make us worship them as gods!" he says with a lash of his sword.

"Technically, they don't," Yizhi says, gaze dull. "They just never correct our assumptions or the mythology we spin about them. The Melian government's official policy is 'minimal interference with more primitive civilizations.'"

"*Primitive?*"

"Aren't we?" Yizhi raises his glowing, buoyant sleeve. Although the style of his robe looks more familiar than anything I saw in the photos in that home, I can't comprehend the material it's made from. Dragons shaped by shining gold dust move on the drifting flaps as if alive. It reminds me of a proverb: "Heavenly clothing has no seams." Guess we got at least one thing right.

"If they say they don't interfere, why did they take Shimin hostage to demand things of me?" I question, my voice unsteady.

Yizhi meets my gaze, his eyes glistening in the wavering blue radiance around us. After everything that's happened, it's like looking into the eyes of a stranger, a boy capable of deceiving an empress, an emperor, *gods*. Did I ever understand him? I'm no longer sure I want to.

Yet, at the same time, I fear for him.

What did they do to you? What have you been through? Did you find Shimin here?

"The Melians say a lot of things they don't really live by," Yizhi says. "You'll see. Bring me back to the ship and come with me if you want more answers. I know where the armored transport ships are, and those are weaponized and engineered with spirit metal. That means *you* could pilot them if you got your hands on one."

A sharp breath hitches in Qin Zheng's chest.

"Wait, can they hear us right now?" I hush my tone, scanning our surroundings.

"Probably, but it doesn't matter," Yizhi says. "They'd love nothing more than for you to leave the habitat rings. As long as you're here, they can't turn any of their best weapons on you without risking a ton of collateral damage, including civilian deaths."

"Civilians," Qin Zheng spits out like a foul taste. "What have they promised you in exchange for leading me astray? A better position in their little paradise?"

"If all I cared about was my own well-being I would've slit your throat when I had the chance!" Yizhi glares at him with a raw, naked disdain that must've been festering inside him since the first time they spoke. "I didn't spare you just to keep Huaxia from falling apart. Despite how I worked with the Melians, I always hoped you would make it here one day and kick them out. Though I expected that to take years, not this soon. But now you're here, and I have the information you need. Are you going to reject it out of spite?"

"You expect us to trust you?"

"What else will you do? Run around killing at random until you run out of—behind you!" Yizhi points, shock overtaking his face.

Qin Zheng whips around and throws me behind him. We scan the atrium.

There's nothing new in the aquarium's dancing light.

"See?" Yizhi says, casual again. "You don't know this place. You don't even know what to be afraid of. How do you plan on taking it down without guidance?"

Qin Zheng turns back with a loud curse, grip quivering around his sword. "I could end you right here."

"Try it." Yizhi raises the detonator.

"Questionable move, asking me to trust you as you threaten my life."

I side-eye Qin Zheng. "You do that to me basically every week."

"Not the time!" He flashes his palm at me.

"Exactly, we're running out of time!" I move toward Yizhi. "Dawdle all you want. I'm going."

"Fine!" Qin Zheng bars me with his arm. "If you insist, my love."

He pulls me in and kisses me.

I jam my hand against his chest, but relax against it the next second. If I want to keep Yizhi safe, I can't let Qin Zheng think the relationship I used to have with Yizhi matters to me in any way.

When I break from the kiss, Yizhi's face is perfectly still, except his eyes are a little too wide, angled at the floor and unblinking. I keep my demeanor passive as well, despite the acrid heat singeing my face.

What did you expect, once you'd left me with him? I wish I could shout at him.

Not that I blame him, of course. I walked into Qin Zheng's arms by my own will, knowing it was a mistake. One I made many, many times.

"Give me your qì." Qin Zheng yanks Yizhi close like they're dancing, clutching his waist and clasping his hand. It would almost look romantic if not for Yizhi's cry of pain and the blood leaking from their joined palms. Yizhi's meridians flicker aglow, his qì flowing visibly into Qin Zheng, who then launches them both up into the air with a crack of his wings.

I fling myself over the balcony to keep up. Yizhi clings to Qin Zheng with his detonator-holding arm, jaw clamped tight. He almost buries his face in the crook of Qin Zheng's neck, but he jerks his head back at the last second. Their qì-lit eyes meet with utter mutual hatred. After we emerge back on the roof, Qin Zheng continues to siphon Yizhi's qì, holding him in place like they're locked in battle.

"Stop!" I step toward them.

Qin Zheng turns a luminous glare on me.

"Save some for me." I make a gesture of incredulity.

He huffs, but detaches his gauntlet and holds out Yizhi's bloody, trembling hand. My skin crawls at the concentration of tiny holes on it. I had to pierce my palm the same way when I gave my qì to resurrect Qin Zheng, but that was way less messy. He did this poorly on purpose.

I show no emotion as I take Yizhi's hand, something that would've made me feel so warm and safe a different lifetime ago. Even though I have him to thank for that half a year of being out of Qin Zheng's reach, Yizhi's lies to him don't cancel out his lies to me. I don't hate him anymore, but I don't forgive him either.

"Tell me when you feel faint." I puncture his palm with my own needle-thin constructs, not hard to make after months of training.

Yizhi winces. "Will do."

My meridians sting with the flood of his qì, feeling like veins engorged to the brink of bursting. It's not soothing, like when he used to nourish the Vermilion Bird. It's something more unnatural. More unbalanced.

"Did you find Shimin up here?" I whisper while Qin Zheng is distracted keeping vigilant of our surroundings. I might go mad if I hold this question in any longer.

"They let me see him once." Yizhi's painted eyelids droop over his radiant eyes. "I couldn't bear to stay for more than a few seconds."

"So there's no way to bring him back?"

"Not without giving up the chance to destroy this whole station."

In the dawning sunlight, I see Yizhi more clearly. No hesitation exists in his eyes. Although his skin is finer, not a single pore visible, he's also skinnier, the bones of his face more pronounced. However he's lived these past few months, it has taken a toll on him.

"What about the tribute girls?" I ask. "What really happens to them up here?"

Yizhi is quiet for a beat before gesturing at himself with his detonator. "We are liberated from our sexually oppressive cultures and empowered to work at an entertainment center," he says, pointedly loud and as though he's reciting someone else's words. Behind him, Qin Zheng tenses up at what must be a reminder of his mother. "Not just us, but girls from other Orichaean regions, too. That's what they call our planet." He peers up at it. "Orichaea, after orichalite, their name for spirit metal."

Orichaea.

I try to wrap my mind around this name I never knew our world had. Something that unites all of us born under its skies, even though we're isolated from one another.

I clutch Yizhi's hand tighter. "Is there a way to send the girls back safely?"

"Maybe after we get hold of a cargo ship . . . But it'd be a stretch to pick up the girls and fend off the Melians at the same time."

I release a long sigh and gaze up at our planet.

How often must the girls have done the same, mourning a home so tantalizingly close yet an impossible journey away? The sun has fully emerged from behind it, looking like a gleaming diamond against the black void of space.

"Okay, I don't think I can give any more," Yizhi says on a strangled breath, flexing the hand entwined with mine.

I disengage from him at once, feeling more jittery than refreshed, as if I drank too much tea to stay awake. Yizhi waves at his ship. Its stairs drop down with a hiss of air.

"Don't do anything rash," he says to me and Qin Zheng. "Remember, you don't know how to make this thing fly."

Qin Zheng doesn't protest. He no longer moves with reluctance when we make our way up the stairs. If he doubted Yizhi's motives when it comes to the Melians before, I don't think he does anymore.

Low purple light seeps from the ship's inner surface, illuminating two seats I'm almost surprised to see solidly attached to the floor.

In one seat is a bone-pale person with short, fluffy, pink-and-blue hair.

"Nothing rash!" Yizhi shouts as Qin Zheng and I reach for our swords. "This is Helan. Their mother was a Huaxia tribute. They're here to help."

My heartbeat goes off kilter, thudding in my ears. Here is a false god in the flesh. Someone who has peered down on us from the stars our whole lives, untouchable. Yet they look so thin and dainty, even I could probably snap them in half. The strange jacket they're wearing cuts off at their rib cage, exposing the narrow width of their waist. Radiant colors shift at the collar and hems.

"*N-neehow.*" Helan gives a shaky wave.

Only seconds later do I realize that was an attempt to say hello in Hanyu.

"That thing looks nothing like us!" Qin Zheng yells.

"Look at their eyes. Black, like ours." Yizhi points at his own.

"Those are not black eyes. *These* are black eyes." The air chills as Qin Zheng channels Water qì. His irises turn void-black, and so do his meridians, crawling in black paths across his face.

Helan shrieks.

"Stop that, you're wasting qì!" I smack Qin Zheng on the side, though my own skin goes clammy and cold beneath my armor. Watching this false god get flustered is worse than if they were solemn as a statue. It's proof they're as human as us.

So why do they get to live in this paradise above the skies while we have to fight for our survival on the ground?

Qin Zheng powers down with a glower. "Is that a boy or a girl?"

"Neither," Yizhi says.

"Excuse me?"

"Many things work differently here."

"*Woh dwei neemen . . .*" Grimacing, Helan taps a smooth strip on the curve of their ear. A glowing dot appears on their throat. When they speak again, an artificial voice that sounds like their own translates their words into much smoother Hanyu.

"I am sorry for the way my people have treated yours. You have a beautiful culture I adore. It is full of deep spiritual wisdom."

Qin Zheng and I stare at them.

"Kill yourself," Qin Zheng says.

I smack him again while Helan flinches.

"I—I am willing to help you acquire the means to better negotiate with my people!" Helan stammers.

"Helan is part of an organization called the Society of the Friends of the Primitives," Yizhi says. "They have the support of the Unity Party, one of the two big political factions in Melia. The Melians think I kidnapped Helan, but Helan's actually here to help the Unity Party win the next election."

I blink, barely following any of this. "I'm sorry—what? Election? Why would helping us help any of the Melians?"

"Because the Unity Party's chief rival, the Prosperity Party, is currently in power. Every five years, the Melians vote for their leader. Like a worker council, except it's the whole country. The next election is projected to be very close, but this trade station getting attacked under the Prosperity Party's watch could push a lot of voters toward the Unity Party."

"The Prosperity Party is a danger to our democracy," Helan adds, a plea shining in their eyes. "They cannot be allowed to win again."

"You're telling me your leaders must engage in a mandatory power struggle every five years?" Qin Zheng exclaims. "What kind of inefficient political system is this?"

Yizhi shrugs. "Is it really worse than letting the guy with the biggest Chrysalis decide everything, even though there's a constant danger of him suddenly dying in battle?"

"That poses no issue when it's *me*!"

I put my hand to my face. "Qin Zheng, we are literally on a suicide mission."

"It doesn't have to be one if you accept Helan's help," Yizhi says with more seriousness.

Helan turns to Yizhi to say something, but gasps upon noticing his bloody hand, which he's kept clenched until now. Helan's fingers fly to the ship's dashboard. A digital interface awakens, full of neon colors. A compartment slides open with a tap of a button. Helan fishes out a small white can with a red cross on it before taking Yizhi's hand.

The familiarity in the gesture gives me pause. I don't buy that a false god would be sincere in wanting to help us, but whatever kind of person Helan is, whatever role they played in lording over Huaxia, Yizhi trusts them. How did they meet? What's happened between them in the past few months?

Helan sprays a foamy substance on Yizhi's mutilated palm. The perforations fizzle and seal up. A clear layer solidifies above the fizzing.

Unbelievable.

I don't care about floating couches, but *this* kind of technology could have saved so many lives in Huaxia.

"Can that thing be used by anyone?" I ask, unable to keep the bitterness out of my mouth when I think of the festering wounds I saw after floods and typhoons. "You just point and spray?"

"Yes." Helan nods. "It is stem-cell based."

I don't know what that means, but I beckon for it. "Give it to me."

Helan almost drops it in their haste to pass it over. I tuck the can against my thigh by making a pocket in my armor. It could prove useful in battle.

"Where is the bomb?" Qin Zheng inspects the ship's smooth innards. "Keep your guard up against me all you want, but I do not think it wise to keep that onboard while flying into conflict."

Looking him right in the eye, Yizhi takes his thumb off the detonator. My heart misses a beat, but nothing happens. He presses a symbol on the tube and applies a fresh coat of lip gloss with an applicator that spins out.

I have to hold Qin Zheng back yet again as he unleashes a volley of curses so colorful he slips into his street dialect.

Yizhi tucks the lip gloss into his robe and takes the seat beside Helan's. He says something in what I assume is the Melian language.

A voice responds from the dashboard, so natural-sounding that I can't tell if it's another person or just the ship's systems, though I lean toward the latter when the interface proceeds to project a model of the Heavenly Court. Or this "trade station," apparently.

"We need to go up to the central corridor." Yizhi gestures at the long axis linking the two massive habitat rings to a bunch of modules and panels on the other end. "The hangar is on the other side of the station, past the cargo holds. The problem will be getting through the junctions." He spins the projection and zooms in on one of the ring spokes connected to the central axis. "The government has probably locked down every gate leading to the hangar by now. You might have to get out and smash through them somehow, because this ship doesn't have firepower of its own."

A change comes over Qin Zheng throughout the mission brief, as if he's switching modes to all war and no emotion.

"Leave it to me," he says.

Yizhi nods at Helan, who taps another button on the interface. Two extra seats unfold out of the floor. Once Qin Zheng and I sit down, straps dart across our bodies, buckling in the middle.

With a soft hum, the ship rises.

I jump when the walls go transparent, showing an unobstructed view of the outside. Though judging by how the ship's outline remains traced out in neon, this must be a digital illusion.

"Could someone take control of this ship?" I ask, recalling how easily the Melians can hijack devices in Huaxia.

"Helan disabled the components that could let that happen," Yizhi says. "We'll have to fly without some functions, including communication with Helan's allies, but here's hoping it works."

"Go to the Yellow Dragon!" Qin Zheng points toward the melted blob in the distance that really shouldn't be called a dragon anymore. "We ought to give this vessel some additional protection."

Helan turns a steering wheel that seems able to move in any direction, like a cobra's head jutting out of the dashboard. Neon rulers project around it in three dimensions, little lines moving along the numbers with every shift of Helan's hands. The ship cruises off the roof and toward the Yellow Blob.

"Emperor Qin, I have seen serial dramas from Huaxia about you," Helan says, pale cheeks reddening. "I still cannot believe you have come to life again."

"*Our* serial dramas?" I say, while Qin Zheng makes a puzzled face. He never got into modern media. Neither did I, honestly, but those dramas can't have been historically accurate.

Helan nods. "It is incredible, the stories Huaxia can produce despite your rudimentary technology. You are oddly inspiring, Emperor Qin. Many call you a tyrannical dictator, but I think you are misunderstood. You do bad things for good reasons, because you do not want the children of the future to experience what you did."

Oh, no. What was in those drama scripts?

"So you were the one watching my every move?" Qin Zheng lurches forward, straining his straps.

"No!" Helan shakes their head. "Only the government has access to that kind of data. It was through my mother that I discovered stories from Huaxia. Please know I have done everything in my power to advocate for your people."

"Have you?" He lets out a cold laugh. "How gracious."

"If your mother is really from Huaxia, where is she now?" I ask.

"She passed away a few years ago." Helan's real voice breaks while the translation coming from their earpiece remains smooth. "Not every Orichaean adjusts well to life on the station."

My heart sinks. I have many more questions, but the ship lands. The machines still on the ground swarm toward us.

Qin Zheng and I bolt out to defend against them.

While I hack at them with my sword, he lashes a line of spirit metal at the Yellow Blob. The whole thing turns liquid, at which point he hauls it as a molten wave onto the ship, coating its surface. The non-spirit-metal pieces of engineering in the pilot seats slip to the ground. Helan calls to him through the ship's speakers about the parts that must be left uncovered.

Once they confirm we can fly again, Qin Zheng announces he's not going back in, then he vaults on top of the ship. Which is probably for the best, since I don't know if Helan will keep helping us if they speak any longer with the real Emperor Qin.

He crouches down, sword ready. As I'm torn between whether to duck inside or join him in his madness, something stirs in my spirit sense. I whirl in its direction.

"What are you waiting for?" Qin Zheng yells.

"I-it's moving," I gasp. "Shimin's spirit signature is moving."

CHAPTER FIFTY-ONE

VENGEFUL GHOST

There's no time to process this. I knock aside the next machine coming for me and pump my wings to scramble on top of the ship. I kneel next to Qin Zheng, our wings almost touching, and attach my shins and palms to the ship's new coating.

"They must intend on holding him hostage to your face so you can no longer look away," Qin Zheng muses.

"I know! How many times do I have to show that they can't control me with him?"

"They only need you to break once."

"I won't."

"Good."

The ship rouses upward and surges forth, the force of its takeoff pushing the ground machines back.

"Do not fall off!" Qin Zheng shouts over the wind whipping in our faces. "I will not catch you!"

"I don't need you to!" I extend the edge of my helmet above my eyes to shield them somewhat.

In my sliver of vision, glittering white buildings wreathed in greenery reel past us. My stomach sloshes as the ship twists and turns between them, tipping me and Qin Zheng onto sharp angles. I tense my core to keep myself upright. My joints smart from the strain. I can tell Helan is trying to keep us out of open range for drones. Some projectiles ping against the ship anyway, dangerously close to the unprotected parts. I swing my meteor hammer, my movements awkward against so much wind, but I can guide the chain with my mind. I hit at least some drones, smashing them against gleaming walls and windows.

Out of the distance comes a humongous metallic pillar that dwarfs everything else in the ring. Sloping upward, it punctures the crystalline ceiling above and soars all the way to the distantly visible central corridor. It reminds me of a legend about the heavens being held up by four pillars. Well, here's an actual pillar of heaven. Up closer, it's like facing a solid white mountain.

"As we thought, the gates are locked down!" Helan says through the ship's speakers. "But you can try smashing through one!"

"They're those spiral things!" Yizhi adds.

It's obvious what he means. The gates, like spiral engravings in the pillar, are spaced out vertically, and each one is at least five times the size of the ship.

"Aim high! On the count of three!" Qin Zheng swings his meteor hammer in larger and larger circles as the ship slows near one gate. I mirror him. "One, two, three—*now*!"

We fling our meteor hammers toward the gate. They smash through its spiral wedges, embedding themselves.

"Drop the ship, false god!" Qin Zheng commands.

The engines cut out.

There's a weightless moment before we plummet. Our meteor hammers rip through the gate, crumpling metal and severing wires. The ship's engines reawaken in reverse, propelling us down with even more force. Gritting my teeth, I mentally push my meteor hammer as deep as I can through the gate. A sudden give tells me I've punched past its thick surface. Qin Zheng touches his armor wing to mine. Every bit of spirit metal on us becomes a shared awareness. We pry our meteor hammers toward each other, gouging the gate some more, before he joins them with a crossbeam.

"Pull away, false god!" he roars.

Helan obeys. With a thunderous creaking groan, our combined efforts wrench a hole in the gate like opening a can. Once there's enough room to slip through, Qin Zheng and I retract our meteor hammers and press low against the ship. Torn metal and frayed wires narrowly miss our heads as Helan flies into the pillar's hollow innards.

Floodlights beam on at the front of the ship, illuminating a space like an elevator shaft the size of several buildings combined. I attach my gauntlets to the ship's coating to secure myself through the acute climb.

"Beware—the closer we get to the central corridor, the less gravity you'll experience!" Helan says.

I don't really comprehend what they mean until I *feel* my body getting lighter as we ascend. Blood runs in reverse up from my legs. By the time the ship reaches the top of the pillar, mine and Qin Zheng's meteor hammers are floating on their chains like balloons.

The wonder of the new experience quickly dies to how clumsy it makes us.

Getting to the central corridor is a much more complicated business than busting into the pillar. Something about the mechanics of going from a rotating component to a static one. We defer to Helan's instructions, breaking what they tell us to break and breaching where they tell us to breach. Since falling is no longer a concern, we drift easily to whatever we need to tamper with. However, one wrong puncture and apparently we'll suffocate to death, because there's no air outside in space.

While we struggle with a new set of physics and technology we don't understand, Shimin's spirit signature gains on us by the second, coming up the pillar shaft. Yet I can also sense it somewhere *ahead*. What is going on? Did the gods somehow keep different parts of him alive in two different locations?

Don't think about it, I order myself.

I need to keep moving. That's all I can do.

While traversing between modules, Qin Zheng and I grill Helan and Yizhi more about the worlds beyond ours. They tell us the other inhabited planets in the universe are so far apart that only with a technology called "jumpgates" can they contact each other. Before its invention, people had to venture in slow ships across hundreds of years to get from one planet to the next. Things often went wrong, leaving pioneers stranded, without the means to preserve their knowledge and technology. Their descendants were then doomed to start from scratch. Spacefarers became foragers. Data became stories. History became legends.

"That's probably what happened to the first wave of our ancestors," Yizhi says through the ship's speakers.

"Two thousand years ago, right?" I ask while thrusting my sword through a control panel Helan told us to deactivate. That's how long ago the Hunduns supposedly invaded us. The number must've been passed down for a reason.

"Around that time, yes," Yizhi answers. "But there were more waves. The better-equipped ones discovered how valuable spirit metal is in making things. Not just Chrysalises, but spaceships and jumpgates, too."

"But only spirit metal from Hunduns is effective, so the Melians dropped prisoners on our planet to hunt them?" I muse, piecing together the folktales I've heard. The Rongdi stories of being "stricken from the heavens" as punishment. The Yellow Sovereign getting "help from the gods" to craft the first Chrysalis.

"Melia wasn't a country when that started happening. It was a bunch of other galactic powers that dropped their own prisoners on different continents to stake their claim to all the spirit metal in certain areas. But the Melians won the last major war over access to our planet and cut everyone else off."

Finally, after much blundering, we tear our way through to the central corridor. It's so massive it gives me vertigo—countless clear hexagons fitting together to form a cylinder taller than a skyscraper and extending as far as the eye can see. Behind each hexagon floats a mass larger than Helan's ship.

Hundun husks.

"The Melians have a monopoly on spirit metal trade," Yizhi says while the ship flies past husk after husk. "Our whole planet supposedly signed a contract with Vivasi Minerals, a Melian company, four centuries ago."

"So . . ." utters Qin Zheng, who has been uncharacteristically silent for a while. His chest heaves so erratically he looks as though he's on the verge of choking. "All along . . . our existences . . . our ceaseless war . . . it was for these foreigners' *profits*?"

"Basically, yeah," Yizhi says, with an emptiness that can only come from being exhausted of anger over the course of months.

My vision fries black for a moment. Seeing all these Hundun husks lined up for sale makes the truth sink in like nothing else. I think of the colorful family in the pictures we saw, the joy on their faces as they posed in front of the planet where *we* were born besieged by fear. Where wave after wave of pilots, most no older than twenty, fought to their deaths for the belief that they were heroically defending our species from a celestial invader. Every single one of these husks was paid for with our blood and anguish on the battlefield.

I'm glad I can't reach Helan right now, because I would very much like to hear a false god scream.

"Where . . . where are the Earth types?" To my own ears, my voice sounds disembodied from the storm roiling inside me. I push past the haze of my rage to scan the cells of husks. If we found enough Earth type, we could rebuild the Yellow Dragon. Our armor still carries its special property of being able to assimilate other husks.

"Oh . . ." Helan makes a disappointed sound. "I think they ejected all the Earth-type stock to prevent you from using them."

I curse, noticing the empty hexagons that offer nothing but glimpses of our planet or the cosmos beyond.

In my last-ditch effort to find an Earth type the Melians missed, I notice something else: some husks are vivid blue. While

Wood-type spirit metal can look almost bluish, as with the Azure Dragon, I've never seen any as rich as a sapphire.

"Why are some of these so blue?" My eyes follow one until it vanishes far behind us.

"That's a type of Hundun they have in the west!" Yizhi says. "Those strongholds call it Water type, too, but it's slightly different from ours. They also don't have a Wood type or a Metal type, but they have an Air type. Those are the very pale green ones!"

Before I can ask him to explain further, a noise erupts far behind us, echoing through the vast corridor—the same noise our ship made when breaking in.

In my spirit sense, Shimin's signature blazes on a direct line to us.

I double over, chest constricting. My hands dig into the ship's coating.

I can't look behind me.

I need to look behind me.

I don't want to see what's coming.

I have to face it.

"It's another ship!" Qin Zheng readies his sword.

I twist around. A vessel not too different from ours emerges from the distance. Its front window pops open. A beam of red light shoots out.

Qin Zheng and I dodge to the sides. The light hits his wing—and punches straight through, leaving a melted hole.

We exchange a wide-eyed glance. Nothing can destroy Earth-type spirit metal like that except...

Another blast of Fire qì streaks toward us. This time, when we duck, I spot what it came out of: a red palm in a glistening, dark-gray arm.

It takes me several stupefied seconds to parse out what I'm looking at. Shimin climbs halfway out of his ship with a body made of glossy mechanical parts and embedded spirit metal. Only his head is still visibly human. Not even all of it. A mask like a muzzle is clamped over his lower face, covering every feature except his eyes. Red light kindles in his irises, brightening.

Qin Zheng throws himself over me as another qì blast fires from Shimin's spirit metal palm. The ship lurches sharply. There's a sound of glass shattering ahead, then we zip past a hexagon with a melted hole in it.

"We cannot let him hit the ship!" Qin Zheng shouts near my ear. He mends his wings and bats them, poised to take off.

He'll kill Shimin without hesitation.

I shove him back and launch myself off the ship first. My body hurtles through the weightless air, spinning.

"Empress!" Qin Zheng calls after me.

"I'll take care of him!" I heave my wings to steady myself. "Don't follow me!"

"I was not going to!" Qin Zheng's voice fades further by the word.

I watch him leave on the ship upside down. No—it's *me* who's upside down. Yet it doesn't feel like that at all. No blood rushing to my head, no tug on my arms and legs.

A qì blast skims my neck guard, searing the skin beneath. I hiss. Any deeper, and I'd be dead.

"Shimin, it's me!" I wriggle upright in the air while retracting my face guard. What have the Melians done to him? "It's Zetian!"

He charges another blast in his palm.

I detach my meteor hammer from my hip and hurl it at him. By my mental will, the chain stretches then lashes around his mechanical body, binding his arms to his torso.

"Shimin, I'm your partner! We piloted the Vermilion Bird together!" I croak, while beating my wings backwards and winding the chain around my arm to keep it from loosening as his ship draws closer. Wobbling tears blur my view of him. "Remember me?" A growing lump in my throat warps my voice. "Remember Yizhi?"

"Yes, I do," he says flatly while straining against the chain.

I falter for an instant. I didn't expect to actually hear his voice.

The single moment is enough for him to free one elbow and snatch the chain from beneath. Fire qì heats in his grip. I yelp as a burning sensation from the chain reaches my senses as intensely as hot metal on flesh.

"You're the one who left me to die," he says, like the mutilated figment of him that haunts my nightmares. His words crackle through his mask, as if the Melians put a speaker in there to ensure I hear every word. "You and your selfish, petty obsession with vengeance. You don't care who you hurt, who gets in your way."

Bearing the burning pain, I channel Earth qì to reinforce the chain. But I can't hang on much longer. His ship closes in too quickly. I can't flap my wings fast enough to stay ahead. I can't do this. I can't fight him. I can't, I can't, I can't—

He breaks the chain, severing my meteor hammer, and aims his palm at me.

I snap my wings behind me, generating a forward momentum that lets me tackle him. We tumble over the raised front window of his ship and then off it entirely, my shoulder grazing its bulk before we're free-floating through the corridor. I clamp his arms against his hips. A slow, heavy heartbeat startles my ear through his mechanical torso.

He presses a hand to my ribs and injects a direct surge of heat. A cry rips from my lungs. I swing him in an arc and throw him as far out as possible.

As he sails through the corridor, turning a full circle, I spot a red spinal brace in his mechanical back. I draw my sword. If I were to guess at how his artificial body works, I imagine there's a hidden path of spirit metal from his spine to his palms. If I can sever it, I can stop the blasts.

He bounces off a hexagon and continues to skid and drift, but he recovers his orientation with spurts of qì from his palms. Using both hands now, he assails me with smaller, short blasts, as if hurling fireballs. I bend and whirl in wild directions to dodge them. Each flash shatters a hole in a hexagon past me. One blow catches my thigh, igniting a pain that joins the relentless pulsing from my side. I don't dare to look down at the damage.

"I gave my life for you, and what have you done?" Shimin's voice thunders through the corridor. "Massacred innocents. Laid waste to society. Whored yourself out to your tyrant master while I was stuck here, alive, without a proper body!"

Clarity cuts through the haze of pain over my senses.

When would Shimin ever say something like that to me?

I remember the boy who squeezed himself into a narrow space over a cold floor so I could sleep in a real bed for the first time in my life. Who seemed to scowl at everyone he met when he really just couldn't see well because he loved reading too much. Who wouldn't defend himself against insults but risked the most severe punishments to pummel a man on my behalf. Who carried me wherever I needed to go. Who lowered himself to one knee in our red-lit room and pressed a kiss to my knuckles.

This is not him. This is as much a dead husk as what's in the compartments around us.

I shield myself with my wings and swoop to grab his wrist. My other hand jams my blade under his arm. Hooking my leg around his for leverage, I rip my sword all the way through the arm. Wires spark on the stump around a core of Fire-type spirit metal.

He doesn't scream. Before I can do anything else, his one remaining hand seizes my sword-wielding arm and *singes*.

My shriek cuts jagged into the air, warped by the agony shooting through every muscle in my body. I writhe against his scorching grip. I can't get my arm free to use my sword. But since everything floats here . . .

I release my sword. It joins his severed arm in rotation above us. I grasp for its hilt with my other hand. He hooks his leg around mine, copying my technique, and wrestles to keep me from reaching it. His blazing fingers melt through my trapped gauntlet. Bile heaves from my stomach at the scent of my own roasting flesh. Darkness chars at the edges of my vision.

But the wavering sight of his hand, its spirit metal underside so distinct from the rest, gives me a spark of inspiration. I cleave around the gauntlet palm of my free hand and compel the cut-out portion to stretch toward my sword. It wraps around the hilt and reels it back to me. My fingers clamp around it.

I plunge the blade into Shimin's back, right where I can feel his heart pounding.

The sword scrapes past metal and through thick, thudding flesh in a sickening sensation. The tip stops against my chest with a dull *clunk*. A spasm goes through his body. Radiance sputters out of his irises.

No, I want to scream, even though I'm the one holding the weapon. Through it, I feel the hot spillage of his blood, the dwindling of his heartbeat.

"*You*," he says like a curse. Devoid of their red light, his eyes go cloudy and unfocused. "How could you? After everything I did for you, how—Ze . . . tian . . ."

His voice abruptly goes dull and muffled when speaking my name, sounding as though it has switched to a different source. And for the briefest second, I swear the syllables overlapped with the words before. Like when Helan speaks under their artificial translation.

Coldness douses me like ice water.

"Shimin?" My voice comes out small and distant, as if whispered from the end of the corridor.

His eyelids droop. "Make . . . me . . . whole . . ."

He doesn't collapse in my arms. There's no gravity to topple him. There's only stillness, almost calming, until it drags on for too long.

"No . . ." I shake him. "No, no—Shimin, stay with me!"

I can still sense his spirit signature. It's faint, but still there, even though his heartbeat isn't. I can't have killed him when there was a chance his mind wasn't gone. I can't have.

"Shimin, wake up! Wake up!" I touch his cheek, his half-closed eyes, his forehead. Cold.

There's a way to restart a heart—I have to pump my hands against his chest—

I yank my sword out of his back and flap my wings to guide him against a hexagon. Using it for leverage, I thrust my hands against his chest.

Blood spurts out of his wound, lingering in a glob in front of his chest.

Fuck! Why did I stab it all the way through?

The can of healing spray flashes in my mind. I dig it out of my armor, fingers numb and shaking uncontrollably. I spray a thick coating on both ends of his wound.

Nothing happens. No fizzing. I give his chest another pump. Blood seeps right through the foamy substance.

I clutch my helmet and scream.

When I feel again for his spirit signature's weak presence, I trip upon a reminder that there's a duplicate up ahead, somewhere that Qin Zheng's massive moving signature has already passed.

"Make . . . me . . . whole . . ."

Why did Shimin say that?

The corridor's countless hexagonal cells seem to funnel toward a pulsating void in the distance. I don't know if I'm imagining his other signature. I don't know how this makes any sense.

What I can't do is stay here.

Looping my arm around Shimin's cold metal body, I fly toward the unknown.

CHAPTER FIFTY-TWO

THE SPARK THAT CANNOT BE EXTINGUISHED

Traveling along the corridor, I feel shrouded in the same harrowing emptiness I would always feel while trekking back to the Great Wall after a battle. The quiet desolation, discomforting after such violent intensity. The death and destruction lingering everywhere.

Keeping an arm around Shimin's waist, I mentally peel off the melted metal over the various burns on my body. With my free hand, I spray Helan's healing substance on the raw, blistered skin beneath, roasted red, with nauseating patches of yellow and black. The foam fizzes, numbing the pain and creating a glistening layer sealing each wound. Thank the skies I had the foresight to take the can.

Well, I guess it's not the skies I should thank, now that I've broken beyond them.

After flying past so many hexagons that my head throbs from the effort, Shimin's duplicate signature leads me to one cell whose contents are much more scattered than the others.

Vermilion fragments.

I blink back a vision of the Black Tortoise crushing the Vermilion Bird's head. On a surge of adrenaline, I use my sword to shatter through two layers of a substance that appears to be glass but is obviously more high-tech. Its broken edges light up and begin to heal themselves. I stuff Shimin through the shrinking hole and into the cloud of red chunks. Most are bigger than us. The duplicate signature somehow spans *across* them. Our planet looms beyond the other hexagons that make up the cell, wholly bathed in daylight and outlined in radiant blue. I can no longer see any semblance of Huaxia, only unfamiliar land masses and oceans that flow from blue to crimson.

I kick up to a vermilion chunk and maneuver it with both hands against Shimin's spinal brace. I don't know what to expect. I imagine him sparking back to life.

Nothing happens. His spirit signature remains dispersed like smoke.

Do I need to put the fragments together? I ease the chunk toward several more, trying to figure out how they fit. If I could reassemble the head, maybe . . .

I test the fragments' sharp edges against one another. There are so many. Too many. I find what appears to be the beak and work my way out from there.

Every time I move, the pieces drift farther apart. I pull them back toward each other. My heart beats faster and faster as my efforts prove futile, and a pressure builds beneath my skin until, finally, I hurl one chunk against another with a hoarse cry.

Both chunks simply sail out of my reach and keep going.

I fall apart suspended in this wreckage I can't put back together, this puzzle I can't solve. The world I left behind glows softly in the beyond. Instead of rolling down my cheeks, my tears collect in globules around my eyes.

"What the fuck?" I choke out to no one but myself, dabbing at the fluid. Small drops float off like glass beads. I fling more away until my vision clears.

I behold our planet. *Orichaea.* I'm still getting used to it having a name. It looks so peaceful, turning so slowly that I can't perceive it moving unless I pay distinct attention. If this were all I saw of my world, I would never guess that lives were beginning and ending down there. In countless indiscernible points on these massive pieces of land, friends are making each other laugh. Lovers are embracing. At least one person has to be looking right in this direction, with no clue of what's transpiring up here.

Is this how the Melians can live with letting us suffer down there? By being so high up they can't see we're as human as them?

A rage stirs in me, simmering, boiling. The same rage that led me to sharpen a hairpin and enlist as Yang Guang's concubine. That compelled me to drown An Lushan in his own blood. That drove me to crush the Palace of Sages with everyone inside.

This rage is what has kept me alive and rising, rising, rising, rising. There is a spark in the human heart that cannot be extinguished, that yearns for freedom no matter the price, no matter the odds, no matter the weight that smothers it down.

I turn away from the world and back to Shimin. I don't know why I still feel his spirit signature. Maybe I've been fooling myself, imagining it, so I don't have to face the truth that, because of the Melians' trickery, I killed him by my own hand.

I almost shatter again. It's the rage that holds me together, a pure, distilled need to ensure they don't get away with this. I brush his eyes closed and kiss his forehead, leaving a fleeting warmth on his cold skin.

"I'm sorry, Shimin," I whisper. "I'm so sorry. Thank you for giving me the chance to keep living. I'm sorry I couldn't do the same for you. I hope you're at least at peace now. Rest. Please. I love you. I always will."

I let him go. He floats among the fragments of his Chrysalis as if he's simply sleeping.

Flaring out the range of my spirit sense, I feel for the other two signatures familiar to me. Qin Zheng and Yizhi don't move with the speed of a ship anymore. They've reached a destination teeming with other signatures.

I shatter out of the cell to join them.

CHAPTER FIFTY-THREE

SEEDS THAT BLOOM

When I finally see an end to the corridor, I find Shimin's ship stopped in front of a massive spiraling gateway smashed in at the middle. I fly through the distorted hole, just big enough to have accommodated Helan's ship.

I bump into a floating corpse.

My mind goes blank. Red and green flashes catch on an array of floating glassy shards around the body.

Bit by bit, I make sense of the flickering chaos farther ahead. The lights are being emitted by a storm of huge, rotund ships engaged in a wild chase across a vast openness, so vast I momentarily wonder if we're outright in space. Except the pulses occasionally reflect off distant walls.

Helan's ship hovers nearby, entrance popped open. Qin Zheng's and Yizhi's spirit signatures zoom among the moving ships instead.

Those must be the weaponized transport vessels Yizhi spoke of, engineered with spirit metal. The more I stare at them, the more they stir my memories of being surrounded by Hunduns in the ocean. It looks like they're literally whole Earth-type husks fitted with complex attachments, including wide thrusters in the back and long, swiveling barrels that can shoot Fire and Wood qì. All are noble class, at least three stories tall. It's extremely obvious which ship Qin Zheng and Yizhi took—the one every other ship is firing at. However, most flares are faint and puny, barely causing a hitch upon striking true. Their ship fires back with thicker, brighter blasts that tear the others apart on impact. The wreckage hovers in limbo, heaved around by the force of the remaining ships giving chase.

No wonder the gods sent Shimin after me. Their own pilots have pathetic spirit pressures.

I look back to the corpse in front of me. Within a shattered helmet, its blue lips gape in immortal shock at whatever final sight it saw. Pale orange lashes frame its empty green eyes. I didn't know a person could look so colorful and yet so washed out. Globules of dark blood float near its gloved hand, which is infested with tiny holes that make my skin crawl.

The last thing this pilot saw must've been Qin Zheng's piercing black eyes as he lunged to siphon their qì.

Grimacing, I turn the body around. Might as well use it as a shield to get to Qin Zheng's ship.

I pause at the sight of the pilot's spinal brace, embedded over a padded jumpsuit connected to their helmet. It's not just one color, one type of spirit metal. It's multiple. A long stretch of Earth yellow, a shorter length of Fire red, then a small segment of Water black.

Huh.

I once asked Qin Zheng if it's possible to incorporate Fire-type spirit metal into our armor so we can launch qì attacks while retaining Earth-type protection. He told me trying to conduct qì through different types of spirit metal at the same time blows out your spine. Something about the pressure differential.

Was that another lie passed down through generations to suppress our abilities?

I hold the corpse in front of me with no more reluctance and flap my wings toward the racing ships.

"Zetian?" Yizhi's voice comes out of a speaker system when I edge into the flashing madness. "Zetian, over—"

"Over here, empress!" Qin Zheng cuts him off. "Touch the base of this ship!"

Swinging the corpse like a shield, I dodge several qì blasts while pressing closer to their ship. It careens toward me. I reach out over the corpse's shoulder.

The moment my fingers meet the spirit metal hull, I sense its entire contour and the complex parts within. A rippling force tugs me along the bottom to a spiral hatch that hisses open. I toss the corpse away before pulling myself in.

The hatch seals shut beneath me, then a second one swirls open above with a sighing noise. I hoist myself out of the nook, easy with no weight to my body.

My helmet antlers bonk against the ceiling of a dark chamber. Soft lines of light illuminate bundles of piping, clusters of tanks of various sizes, and shelves of transparent compartments with things floating inside. The ship's inner surface isn't spirit metal; it's regular metal, covered in panels and blinking lights. With no room to spread my wings, I use the various items—all solidly secured—to propel myself forward. Everything keeps tilting and bumping into me with the ship's movements as I follow Qin Zheng and Yizhi's spirit signatures to a hatch on a wall. It spirals open, leading into a dim corridor dappled with more light-encircled hatches. Some are transparent, showing shadowy glimpses of beds in pods, plants in incubators, and equipment I can't begin to name. I haul myself through the corridor using the neon-lit handles all over it, their different colors maintaining my sense of up and down. One hatch opens by itself ahead of me. When I pull inside it, I emerge through the floor of what must be the ship's cockpit.

Yizhi, Qin Zheng, and Helan are strapped to seats spaced out along a wide, curved dashboard with vibrant widgets, appearing as if suspended over the zooming ships outside. An illusion of transparency, like in Helan's original ship. A neon framework outlines the rest of the ship's structure. The cockpit seems to be nestled deep within the hull's protection, relying on digital displays to see what's happening outside.

Qin Zheng tips his head toward an empty seat between him and Yizhi. "Come! This is but the first vessel we reached. Our true aim is to commandeer the Hive Queen."

"The what?" I sail forth with a swoosh of my wings.

"The largest ship in this fleet," Yizhi explains, before saying something to the dashboard in Melian. An artificial voice responds, then the display ahead highlights a ship beyond a blockade of attacking vessels. It's so big I would've thought it was the far wall without the special indication. I have a guess as to why it's called the Hive Queen: it's made from a King-class husk.

Yizhi peers at me over his shoulder, mouth open to say something more. Nothing ends up coming out, but I know which question he's holding back. The weight of it grows heavy in his gaze.

"He's gone," I force out of my throat.

Yizhi's eyes pinch closed. A second later, they fly open with a renewed resolve. We've both been prepared for this outcome for a long time.

I reach for my seat.

Qin Zheng jerks the steering handles in front of him. The ship lurches away from a particularly bright qì blast. My scrambling fingers barely snatch hold of a handhold atop my seat. My legs smash into the back of Qin Zheng's.

"Sit down!" he chides.

"Trying!"

Through my gauntlet's contact with the seat, I get another sense of the ship's interconnected Earth-type parts. The bulk of the seats is made of it, extending in long paths down to the hull. But there's a lot more engineering around these than Chrysalis seats, and their connection columns contain other types of spirit metal.

The fear of my spine snapping in half nags at the back of my mind, but when I see another qì blast coming, I swing myself into the seat at once. Automatic straps buckle down my torso and legs. Helan shouts a Melian command. The ship's systems respond in a cheery voice. I wince as a thin line of light from the dashboard scans over me. The voice announces something else, then control panels light up before me.

"Welcome to the crew of the Stinger Dame," the cheery voice says, switching to Hanyu. "I am its intelligent systems, here to assist you on your journey. To call upon me, say my name followed by your command."

A set of steering handles pushes out of the dashboard. A diagram of the battle projects above it, featuring tiny moving models of the ships around us.

"Peel up your spinal brace to plug into the other types!" Qin Zheng shouts, while doing a drastic turn that briefly spins us upside down.

Gripping my straps, I concentrate on where my connection column's Earth stretch ends. I mentally ease away my spinal brace beneath that point, leaving a gap to the bottom part of my spine. My armor instantly strains my mind more with the decrease in contact with my spine, feeling heavier. If there were any gravity, I doubt I could stand up in it anymore.

The rest of the connection column pierces through the gap. A gasp shudders into me as I become aware of more parts in the ship, the different types of spirit metal feeling distinct from one another. I don't think we could embody the ship like a Chrysalis, but I can sense the flow of Qin Zheng's qì through its components. A fainter pressure comes from Helan's seat as well. Yizhi is the only one not connected, though that's not a surprise when he gave most of his qì to me and Qin Zheng.

Heat builds in the Fire-type pathways leading out of the ship's long barrels. I infuse my own qì to strengthen the blast.

Enemy ships rupture and explode in our hot red torrent, shot through with Wood qì like green lightning. The sheer force of the blast makes the ship slip backwards. Qin Zheng shoves against his steering handles. Attached to the seats on movable joints, our connection columns have some give, allowing him to lean forward. The ship's engines hum louder, driving us forward against the recoil.

My own steering handles are locked from turning independently of Qin Zheng's, but there's no such restriction on my mental control of the Stinger Dame. I can feel and influence every tip and turn. It makes for a few awkward stutters in movement when my will clashes against Qin Zheng's or Helan's, but soon I blend with their momentum. Our three minds converge on the goal of breaking through to the Hive Queen.

A flare of my spirit sense picks up on at least twelve spirit signatures inside it. Powerful combined blasts of qì shoot at us from its barrels, but we have the advantage in speed. We dodge the beams and eviscerate a path through the smaller blockading ships until we slam like a magnet against the Hive Queen.

In a sweeping wave, the primal particles in its hull assimilate to the Yellow Dragon's unique configuration, etching into my awareness like a cosmic-sized sketch. The mental strain sends sparks popping through my vision. An ache builds in my nose, on the verge of bleeding again. But we don't need to move the whole thing to win. Once the assimilation reaches the pilot seats at the core, I realize what we can do.

From the connection columns, we drive spikes all the way through the pilots' spines, killing them in an instant.

The Hive Queen slows, gliding on momentum alone.

Nausea rolls through me at how easy it was to take a dozen lives at once. But it's nothing I haven't done before. I think back to something Qin Zheng once said: *"Every oppressor, through their denial of humanity, sows the seeds of their own destruction."*

Here we are. The seeds that bloomed.

"Move to the bottom of the Hive Queen!" Helan points and shouts. "It will be easier to enter through its cargo hatch!"

By our collective will, the Stinger Dame glides along the Hive Queen's hull, narrowly escaping the concentrated fire of the remaining ships. When we get to the hatch Helan means, we blast it open and fly inside. What awaits us is a cavernous cargo hold that could fit half a dozen smaller ships. At Helan's further direction, we lower onto a dock with spirit metal parts connected to the hull. Through it, we mentally seal the hole we made to get in.

Now safe to leave the Stinger Dame, we unbuckle from our seats and maneuver through the ship's cramped corridors until we make it out from the top. Light flutters out of the soles of Helan's shoes, producing a force that boosts them through the huge cargo hold. They link arms with Yizhi to bring him along. Qin Zheng and I fan our wings to follow them, though I quickly lag behind, having not replenished myself with a random person's qì like he did.

Qin Zheng holds his arm out to me. I give it a dirty look. He makes an incredulous expression, shoulders rising. When the Hive Queen trembles from persistent blasts, I loop my arm through his with a grunt. If those ships focus on one spot, they might just melt through the thick hull and break something beyond repair. We hurry to a hatch on the far wall. Qin Zheng and I rip it open with our swords. The corridors inside the Hive Queen are spacier than the Stinger Dame's, but there's a lot more to navigate, practically like going through a maze.

Once we break into the cockpit at last, we find a dozen corpses slumped in a semicircle of pilot seats, the dashboard extinguished before them. Helan grimaces. They touch their fingers to their lips while whispering something, then they put their closed hand to their chest. I quash any budding guilt or pity in my own heart while Qin Zheng and I tear four corpses out so we can take their seats. If these pilots were the ones looking down at us after crushing us, how much thought would they give us?

Qin Zheng reshapes the connection columns so we can safely plug in. The dashboard rouses under Helan's fingers. They swipe through luminous panels and options while speaking commands to the systems. A light scans each of us, then the engines reactivate.

The Hive Queen glides forth, though it's so massive I can't feel it. I can only tell it's moving by the reeling view projected around the cockpit. We build up speed toward the hangar wall. With a blasting stream of qì, we carve a large exit into it. Roaring engines smash us through to the beyond.

The universe opens before us, more stars than I have ever seen in my life. Every racing thought in my head falls still. For what could be a century, all I can do is stare. The Hive Queen keeps sailing forth. If it could go on forever, where would we end up? Is there a possibility we could just . . . leave everything behind?

The sound of a long exhale scatters my absurd fantasies. Helan buries their face in their hands, shaking. I check the battle projection in front of me. The remaining ships have stopped shooting at us. They're fleeing to the sides instead.

Softly, Yizhi says something in Melian to Helan.

"No, I am all right." Helan rubs their temples, their earpiece translating their reply. "This is what I wanted. To give your people the leverage to negotiate."

"When you say 'negotiate,' what precisely do you mean?" Qin Zheng's question slows with each word.

Helan frowns. "A new contract with Vivasi Minerals, of course. With this ship in your possession, you can now demand a much larger sum of knowledge from Melian databases in exchange for further production of orichalite. Although some of the materials required for the most advanced technologies cannot be found on your planet, the wealth of information should still greatly advance your civilization."

"Why should we enter into another contract at all?"

Frown deepening, Helan shakes their head. "Orichalite is too valuable for you to withdraw from the galactic markets. Other planets would come with military fleets to enforce their trading rights, particularly Melia. Believe me, these ships are far from the most powerful kinds that exist. And you would stop receiving technological aid. Why did you come here if not to improve conditions for your people?"

Silence hangs over the cockpit. So *this* is the catch. I knew Helan wasn't helping us out of pure altruism. They want to be the one who convinced us to stand down and go back to fighting Hunduns for spirit metal after supposedly being kidnapped by us. They must think they'll have our gratitude while taking advantage of our attack as a talking point in whatever convoluted political game they're embroiled in at home. I assume this new contract would extend a cut of the benefits to them, as well, for being the one to facilitate it. This *is* the negotiation.

So, do we ... accept?

Almost absently, Qin Zheng turns his steering handles. The Hive Queen creeps around in slow motion, then its engines fade out. We've flown so far that the entire trade station is visible at a glance, hovering off the side of our planet. Its twin habitat rings spin lazily in opposite directions. A halo of tiny specks drifts away from them, spreading out.

I squint. "What are those?"

"Escape ships." Helan gestures to a red panel full of text on their dashboard. "There was a station-wide order for all residents to evacuate half an hour ago."

I sit up straighter. Qin Zheng squeezes his steering handles.

"Careful!" Helan's hand darts out. "If you hit the station from here, you might break it apart."

Qin Zheng's face remains perfectly blank.

Helan's eyes going wide. "Please do not make any rash decisions. You do not understand what you are facing. The Prosperity Party has indeed been awful to you and your people, but once the Unity Party wins the next election, they will treat you on much better terms. It believes in equality and justice for all humans."

"Does it?" Qin Zheng says.

"Yes, I promise. Or why would I have helped you at all? The Unity Party can make sure Vivasi abides by a new, less exploitative contract. You can fly the Hive Queen back to Huaxia as permanent leverage. Whenever you are ready, I can open the communication channels and begin the negotiation. You will give your people much better lives than before."

Qin Zheng and I look at each other. I wonder if we're thinking of the same quote from the *Book of Laborism*: "*As long as the yoke of power remains in the hands of the profitizers, any concessions won by the laboring class can be taken away.*"

I don't understand this Unity Party and Prosperity Party nonsense, but I know this: both want our war with the Hunduns to continue so they can sell the husks to the hundreds of other worlds we never knew existed. Even if one party is "nicer," it's showing no indication of granting us true freedom.

There's no scenario where we fly back to our lives with no consequences. Systems like this don't maintain themselves by tolerating rebellion. Once the Melians catch their breath from the shock of our attack, they'll retaliate one way or another to make an example of us. Either they have the ability to kill us all, or they don't. The only thing we can control is how easy we'll make it.

Qin Zheng and I reach for each other's hands.

Something about it puts Helan on alert. They unbuckle their straps and detach from their connection column before we can kill them with it. "Hive Queen, revoke access of bio-signatures—!"

A whip of spirit metal shoots out from Helan's seat and clamps around their mouth. They tip over, legs floating, hands grasping at their face.

Yizhi springs out of his seat to yank Helan's arms behind them. "Aim for the junctions!" he shouts.

Helan's gaze swings back with the horror of betrayal. Something I'm no stranger to. I almost feel sorry for them.

But I knew Yizhi never intended to compromise either.

Qin Zheng clasps my hand harder. "Fear has never ruled me," he says, like a mantra, a red blaze igniting in his irises.

A matching heat rises through my meridians. "Neither will gods."

Together, we sweep our strongest blast of qì across the trade station.

CHAPTER FIFTY-FOUR

POOR FOOL

Heavenly death is silent.

The station's twin rings fracture in spectacular bursts of flame and debris. Glass, soil, metal, and more fling apart, yet there is no sound.

Helan's arms slacken in Yizhi's grip. They gawk at the destruction, face blanched by the dithering light from the cockpit's display.

Qin Zheng and Yizhi exchange a long glance. Despite all that's happened between them, they've always been excellent partners in deception. What did Yizhi tell Helan to make them think we'd comply with negotiations instead of blowing the whole thing up at our first chance?

Poor, foolish false god.

I aim one of the Hive Queen's barrels at the escape ships, but they're either obscured by debris or right in front of our planet. I don't know what could happen if my beam strays. I hope our tribute girls made it off in those ships.

"How long do we have before the stronger ships come from Melia?" I ask Helan.

They still have a band of spirit metal around their mouth, yet they make no effort to remove it. It's like their brain is stuck buffering, their attention bouncing between me, Yizhi, and Qin Zheng.

"Six months," Yizhi answers instead. "It'll take at least six months for new ships to get here."

"*Six months?*"

"You know how, in the legends, they say a day in the heavens equals a year in the mortal realm? That's kind of real, except not that precise. Time passes differently across the universe. Relative to Melia's base planet, our days move faster. Even if they rush out a fleet the moment they hear about this, by the time it gets here, at least six months will have passed on our end."

I can't really wrap my mind around what he's talking about, but that is way more time than I expected to have. Nothing more will come for us for six months. This particular battle is over. We survived it.

We were not supposed to survive this.

The future I kept myself from thinking about explodes into color in my head, branching into untold possibilities. For at least the next six months, Qin Zheng will have unlimited power over Huaxia. He can do everything he held back from doing before. He can plunge us into all-consuming war, turn the entire nation into a machine dedicated to killing as many Hunduns as possible. Each battle will generate more husks that can be turned into Chrysalises. Each Chrysalis will pull more conscripts into his army. There'll be devastation like never before, and he won't stop until the Hunduns are extinct, even though that can't possibly be done in six months, and the escalation would put us in a disastrous position when the Melians come.

Yet I no longer hold any power to stop him. No leverage to change his mind. Before this, he couldn't kill me or mistreat me too badly because he needed me to navigate to the Heavenly Court, but not anymore. He doesn't even have to keep me around as a co-pilot when any other girl would do. He can strip away my armor as soon as we land back in Huaxia and dispose of me however he wants, so I don't interfere with his plans.

The sensation of him running his thumb over my knuckles startles me. I'm still holding his hand. He gazes at me, eyes weary but mouth curving into a smile.

"We're going to live, empress," he says.

A hot pressure builds in my eyes.

Am I overthinking this? He cares for me, doesn't he? He's done so much to show me that. Even now, the way he looks at me is so different from the way he looks at anyone else. Did he not apologize for the terrible things he had done to me? Tenderness doesn't come naturally to him after the life he's lived. He knows he was awful to me in the beginning. He regrets it. He won't do it again, because things changed between us.

I'll be fine. I can be his empress. Together, we can prepare for the Melians' retribution. Maybe he'll listen to me and try to communicate with the Hunduns so we won't be fighting on two fronts. All I have to do is trust him.

My head goes woozy. Tingling pain reignites in my burn wounds. I guess the numbing effect of the healing substance wears off after a while. I grasp the tops of my thighs and double over in my seat. My eyes squeeze shut.

"Empress?" Qin Zheng's voice drifts nearer. His fingertips land on my shoulder. "What's wrong?"

My eyes flash open. I detach my sword from my hip and plunge it into his heart.

CHAPTER FIFTY-FIVE

THE DRAGON AND THE PHOENIX

He has the audacity to look surprised. Confused, even. As if he genuinely convinced himself I felt enough for him that he was safe with me.

By the next second, his battle reflexes catch up. A transformative fury sweeps over him. In an instant, he seizes control of the combined spirit metal on us, preventing me from driving my sword deeper.

"*Why?*" he chokes out.

"You know why!" I tug at my sword, yet I can't break his mental hold. I'm locked in place by my own armor.

Hand digging into my shoulder guard, he winces in concentration. I feel the spirit metal of my blade liquefying in his chest and swirling around his failing heart. Beat by beat, with conscious pulses of the metal, he keeps his blood pumping.

I go cold all over.

This can't be happening.

He can't survive even *this*.

"For . . . him?" Qin Zheng's eyes peel open before immediately fluttering near closed again. Sweat beads across his paling skin. Beyond him, Yizhi floats with Helan above their seats, his jaw hanging open.

"For *me!*" I cry. "Don't you get it? You are to me what the gods were to you. I can't breathe freely as long as you live!"

Qin Zheng's focus lapses. He forgets his next heartbeat.

Through my connection to the hull, I feel for the Stinger Dame and free it from the spirit metal attachments in its dock. Then I split my armor apart and shed it like a husk, kicking out of it. I can't wear that thing any longer if I want to get away. So long as I have a single stretch of it on me, Qin Zheng could control it with just a thread of contact.

In nothing but my conduction suit, I push away from him and grab Helan. "Get us out of here before he kills us all!"

Helan looks utterly stupefied by this turn of events but taps the heels of their shoes together twice. The boosting power activates in their soles. With me and Yizhi, one in each arm, they haul us to the nearest spiral hatch in the cockpit. A hoarse, incoherent shout drags out from Qin Zheng. Over my shoulder, I see him doubling over in the air, armor wings wavering, before the hatch seals us into a corridor.

He can't keep his heart beating by willpower alone forever. He *can't*.

Helan lets go of Yizhi to hit a red button on a side panel. The hatch makes a hissing noise as it presumably locks against Qin Zheng.

I latch onto Yizhi's elbow so he doesn't fall behind when Helan's shoes blast us onward through the corridor.

"Don't assume this is forgiveness!" I yell at him.

"*The baby's not yours!*" Yizhi says in a jumbled rush.

I nearly lose my hold on him. "What?"

"Probably not, anyway! I did my best to sabotage the procedure. If it worked, the baby's biological mother should be Auntie Wei herself instead of you." He breathes through his teeth, then releases a tremendous sigh of relief. "Fuck, this is the hardest secret I've ever kept!"

My mind spins in the vortex of hatches we're passing through. "But you said . . . 'probably'?"

"I can't guarantee the sabotage worked. I'm not a specialist." He scrubs his free hand down his face. His voice wobbles. "I'm sorry. I had to betray you in some way to get him to trust me."

I don't know how to react to this. I don't know if this makes what he did okay when he still let doctors do procedures on me without my knowledge.

"Are you bullshitting me again?" I say, colder than I mean to be.

"No," Yizhi says, a wet shine in his eyes.

"I . . ." My heart twists at the sincerity in his expression. Yet he can fake it so perfectly when he lies. "I don't know if I can believe you."

His throat bobs. "That's okay. I understand."

I pry my focus away from him. Now is not the time to get into this. I don't even know if we'll survive the next ten minutes.

We take a different route through the corridors than the one we smashed and tore our way through to get in. We lock each hatch after us. The thudding sounds of Qin Zheng slashing at them with his sword travel muffled through the walls. I pray that his lack of functioning heart will slow him down enough for us to escape the Hive Queen.

In the cargo hold we find the Stinger Dame free-floating. I mentally thank my foresight for uncoupling it when I had the chance. Once we make our way into its cockpit and plug into its pilot seats, I use the spirit metal connection to help Helan remove the clamp around their mouth. They cough, rubbing the weeping red outline on their pale skin. They aim a pained look at Yizhi, but they activate the ship without delay.

We ram our way out of the Hive Queen through the thinly patched hole we blasted to get in.

With my spirit sense reestablished via my pilot seat, I feel for Qin Zheng's location. He has reversed direction, heading back toward the Hive Queen's cockpit. Once he gets there, he'll be able to control the Stinger Dame if he makes even the slightest contact with us.

"Go, go, go!" I lean into my steering handles, pulling as much distance from him as possible.

As I scan the star-strewn void of space, considering our next move, I sense a faint trace of Shimin's signature again—from the trade station's dispersing wreckage.

Many thoughts streak through my head at once.

"Give me full direction control!" I slap my steering handles. "We need to get to the shards of the Vermilion Bird! If I put on Shimin's spinal brace, I might be able to pull them together again!"

Yizhi makes a choked noise. I'm not sure if he's horrified or awed at the idea, but neither he nor Helan objects. I orient the Stinger Dame with both its steering system and my mind. A muscle jumps under my eye from the exertion. Human bodies weren't built to do this much in one day.

I don't open my eyes more than I have to while we zoom toward the expanding cloud of destruction. The clear cells holding the Hundun husks swivel like dice among the explosion of matter. Chunks of debris enlarge in our view, going from small as toys to larger than buildings when we fly closer. Whole sections of the habitat rings spin in the form of metal and glass ruins, scattering dirt, vegetation, and globules of water in scrawling trails. Colliding pieces shatter each other into smaller fragments. Many plunge in blazing arcs toward our planet like meteors, streaking smoke above the oceans and landmasses as they disintegrate.

Some of the evacuation ships pass us, giving us a wide berth. Judging by their silver gleams, their hulls are regular metal, more similar to Helan's civilian ship than anything dangerous. I don't bother shooting at them. It takes all my concentration to navigate through the debris field. Random objects bombard our ship with unexpected force, jostling us this way and that. I think of nothing but reaching Shimin's signature. It's so close . . .

"There!" I pinpoint it. "The one with more scattered fragments than others!"

Helan shouts a command at the dashboard. A tether shoots out from the front of the Stinger Dame and attaches to the cell. The tether retracts, pulling the cell toward us. I grimace as the silhouette of Shimin's body becomes visible, tiny compared to the Vermilion Bird fragments. Unconsciously, I reach out.

A blast of qì hits our ship from the side. I feel it like a psychic scorch. Our screams warp as we go spiraling. Warning noises blare from the ship's systems.

Around and around, we spin out of control, the planet and the universe blurring in the cockpit's display. Our ship and the cell holding the Vermilion Bird swing each other down, down, down, as counterweights. We plunge through clouds and increasingly brighter surroundings. Helan shrieks out desperate commands, but red flashes persist across the dashboard. The ship gets so hot in my senses that I thrash and yell like I've been set ablaze. Then my connection needles retract on their own from my spine, breaking my awareness of the hull. It makes things only marginally better. Heat rises even in the cockpit. Its view display flickers around us. The scent of smoke reaches my nostrils. Our tether to the Vermilion Bird snaps.

"Shimin!" I scream as the sudden release flings the cell away, molten-red and orange against blue skies. Its glass walls burn up, fleeing like radiant sand in the wind. The last thing I see is its blaze flaring like wings before our view display sizzles out completely.

"The ship's too damaged!" Helan cries in the sweltering dark, translation trailing their words. "Brace yourselves! Stinger Dame, eject for emergency atmospheric reentry! Eject! Eject!"

"Got it," the system chirps in Hanyu.

Our seats slide together. The cockpit walls cram inward. Wide bands clamp around our upper arms.

"Projected impact surface will be open ocean," the system continues over the cacophony of noises. "Atmosphere breathable without filtration. Temperature within human tolerance. Gravity one point one times galactic standard. Please follow basic aquatic evacuation procedures. Good luck, and so long."

With a loud hiss, the cockpit pops free from the ship.

There's no other explanation for the sensation. We suddenly tumble faster, and sound roars outside the cockpit. Bile churns in my stomach, yet I can't defy the pressure on my body to lift my hand and clamp my mouth. Every breath is an effort, as if I'm stuck between two walls.

I black out. I don't know for how long.

I'm shocked alert again when a hefty force tugs the cockpit upward. A parachute deployed? We fall differently afterwards, swaying drastically from side to side instead of spinning like mad. Several more jolts rock us, rattling panels in the cockpit, before we slow into a steady descent. One we might actually survive.

My relief doesn't last more than a few seconds. I failed to kill Qin Zheng. I lost the Vermilion Bird. Even if I live, what do I do?

Before I reach an answer, we hit what must be the ocean. It pushes back at us, buoying the cockpit up and down. With a groan, Helan unbuckles from their seat and manually opens a hatch. Spurts of seawater spill in, accompanied by the overwhelming smell of salt.

We help each other out of the cockpit. The moment we splash into the ocean, the bands placed around our arms inflate, keeping us afloat. Gasping for breaths of natural air, I survey our surroundings. It's so surreal to see colors stretch on for infinity back in an open world.

Too open.

All around us are nothing but waves upon waves upon waves. No land. A large parachute pools beside the bobbling cockpit. The sun sits low on the horizon, beginning to set.

"Where are we?" I ask, voice raspy. I can't tell if we dropped into an ocean that borders Huaxia. For all I know, we could be on the other side of the planet.

Yizhi, Helan, and I gawk at each other. None of us have anything more to say. Helan's gaze darts around our world, their breaths coming faster. Yizhi reaches for them. Helan flinches, kicking away in the undulating water. After the concentrated amount of betrayal they witnessed within a few minutes, I don't blame them.

The incongruous sight of their pink-and-blue hair spears me into my new reality. I really did just go to the stars and back. Burning debris continues to streak across the sky. A meteor shower. I saw a few with Big Sister in our village, but none so stunning. None I personally caused.

I'm watching in a daze when one meteor curves in its path and heads right for us.

Every muscle in my face goes stiff.

"Go!" I push Yizhi and Helan, arms splashing. "Go, go, go!"

We swim as fast as we can, but our efforts are pathetic. The thing grows larger as it approaches us, shiny and golden in the setting sun.

The Hive Queen.

A thunderous rumbling sound comes ahead of it, vibrating through the air. Pulsing winds churn the waves higher and shove us without mercy. Several times, the water closes above my head. The flotation devices on my arms keep me from sinking deeper, but at this point, drowning might be the better fate. I spit out mouthfuls of seawater, my nostrils stinging.

When the Hive Queen gets close, so large it blocks out the sun, the waves intensify. The pressure ahead of the ship punches a wide dent in the water beneath. The Hive Queen rights itself and makes a smooth descent onto the roiling waves a short distance in front of us. Ice crystallizes across the ocean surface, freezing it mid-motion and trapping our heads and arms above our bodies.

As I cry out from the cold that stabs through my bones like needles, the ship's roar quiets to a persistent hum. I can hear whimpering, from either Yizhi or Helan, but I can't see them. I'm frozen in the middle of a sloping wave.

The platform of ice bobbles in deceptive peace. My teeth chatter, and darkness pulls at my mind. I wish I could sink into it and be free of this agony, yet my body refuses to give out.

Metallic noises emerge from the top of the Hive Queen's at least twelve-story height. My last hopes are extinguished when a fully armored figure slides down its curve on a fluid piece of its surface.

At least he doesn't land gracefully. He tumbles over when he reaches the ice, grasping his chest. It takes him quite the effort to get up. A line of spirit metal connects him to the ship. I don't know how he managed to fly it down so precisely, but it makes me feel a little better about failing to kill him. There was no beating him. His existence is a force of nature. If a god of war really exists somewhere, he has its blessing. I did my best.

Step by struggling step, he staggers toward me. The cold numbs even my dread. I simply stare at him when he stops in front of me, the frozen wave holding me at his chest level.

He stares back, breathing laboriously. He looks as half dead as he biologically should be, all the color gone from his face. How long will he outlast me?

"Let Yizhi and Helan go," I say through my chattering teeth. "If we all die, there'll be no one to warn Huaxia about the retaliation."

"That is not for you to worry about," he rasps out, wincing as though the mere act of speaking is too much. "A ship full of our tributes surrendered to me."

"Oh."

So that's how he got down. He had help.

The relief of our girls making it out is a good enough feeling to take with me to the beyond.

"Kill me then," I say, refusing him the satisfaction of seeing me afraid. "You were going to do it the moment we got back to Huaxia, anyway."

"No." He shakes his head slowly, gazing at me with a weariness deeper than physical. He clutches his chest tighter. "No, empress. I loved you."

A surge of unwelcome emotions shatters the perfectly fine peace I was ready to die with.

"No, you didn't!" I scream. "You didn't love me! You loved the fantasy version of me in your head, who resists you enough to be exciting but will always bend to your will in the end, and will forgive you no matter how you hurt or control me!"

Hot tears spill from my eyes, running over the frozen water on my cheeks. Great. Leave it to him to ruin my last moments.

I choke down air to catch my breath. "Now your fantasy ends."

The rage I expected from the beginning reanimates over him. The ice bobbles in greater swells and dips. I see it: the change in his eyes, the moment I become dead to him. I don't look away. May I haunt him for however much longer he keeps himself alive.

His hand goes to his sword.

Cracks split across the ice on a rising tide. He stumbles backward. The water doesn't stop swelling. A red glow brightens through the breaking ice.

Something shatters out from beneath us.

I fall loose from the ice and slip down a hot surface. Grappling for purchase among pouring water, I feel the texture of Fire-type spirit metal. A bird cry pieces the air.

I grasp an edge with my stiff hands. A wing edge. It spans out to my side, Fire-red qì seeping beneath its metal feathers. The heat stings like static against my numb flesh. Steam rises everywhere. When the wing tilts higher, I shimmy down its edge until I'm on its body.

The Vermilion Bird's body.

It's about ten times smaller, but undoubtedly the same shape as the Vermilion Bird's Standard Form. My mind stutters, trying to process what's happening.

How . . . ?

The memory of the clear cell burning up as it plunged through the skies flashes in my mind.

The heat of the reentry. It melted the pieces back together.

"Shimin?" I ask, not believing what's happening.

There's no response, but when I grab hold of two feathers, the Bird swoops down again, skimming its other wing through the ocean. Yizhi and Helan appear when the water spills off, looking just as befuddled as me. Helan slips down the wing. Yizhi catches them by the waist. I stretch to seize Yizhi's hand and pull him more securely onto the Bird's back.

Our eyes meet.

Before either of us can muster a reaction, more large things bobble out of the ocean. Bright bolts of red and green fire at the Hive Queen.

Hunduns.

What in the skies is going on?

The chaos of the battle recedes as the Bird flaps its wings, flying up and away. I think I see Qin Zheng dodging the blasts while reeling himself back into the Hive Queen. Rage and relief bloom in me in unison. Which makes no sense. I press my throbbing head into the crook of my arm.

I don't know if I'm dreaming, because this can't be real. I don't know what exactly just happened and what it means. The only thing I'm sure of is how good the heat beneath me feels. I rest my cheek against the warm metal feathers. Slowly, my body stops shivering. The darkness takes me.

CHAPTER FIFTY-SIX

TENGRI KHAGAN

I awaken amid the swaying motions of flight. Wind caresses my face and streams over my matted hair. The Vermilion Bird's wings flap every few seconds, still soaring over the ocean, though night has fallen.

The slightest attempt at lifting my head sends a sparking pain across my brows. I lay my cheek down again.

Beside me, Yizhi is also on his stomach, resting his chin on one hand and gazing ahead at the moonlit waves. He does a double take on me. Our hands remain entwined.

I jerk mine away. No hurt strikes his eyes, only resignation.

I turn my attention to the Bird's backlit feathers. I brush my hand across them. "Shimin?"

"I've gotten no response so far," Yizhi says.

My hand curls into a fist. My first instinct is to refuse to engage in conversation with him. A few seconds of silence later, my pettiness fades. We're alone out on the ocean with no idea where we are. We need to work together to find our way back to Huaxia.

"Then what is this?" I mumble, pressing my ear to the Bird's back. There's a faint hum inside. I don't know what that means or how long it will last. I should've kept a spinal brace from the Stinger Dame's pilot seats. Then I'd be able to use my spirit sense.

"I don't know," Yizhi says, more quietly. "But he must be in here somehow."

I recall the ambush by the Black Tortoise, the moments when Shimin piloted the Vermilion Bird alone to hold it back from getting to me and Yizhi. That wasn't supposed to be humanly possible. Did his ... spirit ... transfer into the Vermilion Bird?

"Would Helan know more?" Gingerly, I crane my head to see over Yizhi. "What are they doing?"

"Sleeping." Yizhi glances aside at Helan. "Our gravity is higher than the trade station's. It's going to be tough on them. I'm not used to it anymore either, but at least my muscles and bones were developed for it to begin with."

Stars twinkle above. For the first time in untold centuries, no gods orbit among them. Chunks of destruction are still blazing across the sky. Can the whole planet see them? Everyone must be wondering what's going on. I hope no one's unlucky enough to get hit.

"Do you think those station people who evacuated will come down here, too?" I question.

"I assume so. They've got nowhere else to go. Those evacuation ships aren't built for interstellar travel. Technically, the reason they take a few of us up there every year is so they're not so isolated from us that our diseases would kill them if they had to come down here in an emergency. Though, in their terminology, we're 'migrants,' not 'tributes.'"

There's a silence where I should've asked more about how they treated him and those girls. All of this is already too much to process. I don't think I'm ready for details.

A chill skitters up my spine when I imagine each meteor above as a ship full of Melians, who have no problem being worshipped as gods, landing in the fields of regular folk who have no spirit armor to defend themselves. I imagine Qin Zheng—if he gets back to Huaxia alive—taking his rage at me out on Wan'er, Taiping, and others of the Phoenix Alliance. Tremors travel up from my fingers.

"Yizhi, what have we done?" I say, my voice faraway to my own ears. I grip the metal feathers beneath me, feeling on the verge of falling off. "I shouldn't have stabbed him, should I? Did I kill Huaxia's best chance of surviving the retaliation?"

Yizhi puts his hand near mine, close but not touching, as if we're back under Qin Zheng's rules.

"When I saw you again, I almost didn't recognize you," he says, softly. "It was like the light in your eyes was gone. It didn't come back until you drove that sword into his chest."

Tears surging, I bury my face between my arms. "Do you know the mess I had to clean up after you left? The people I had to convince him not to kill? Your own little brothers and sisters, Yizhi."

"I'm sorry," he says, barely audible.

I wish he would hold me, but I can't give in to that kind of dangerous weakness again. Craving someone I can't trust has no good ending. When our roots sink into each other, there's no way of coming apart without ripping a thousand bleeding holes in us both.

Something hard digs into my sternum, making me realize I'm still wearing the phoenix half-pendant. I grasp its gold chain, about to pull it out of my salt-encrusted conduction suit, but think better of it. I'm not giving up my claim to being the Empress of Huaxia.

I try to sort out some sense in my mind. For at least another month, Qin Zheng can't announce what I did or execute anyone in my name. Not if he wants his child to be legitimate. Wan'er and Taiping do invaluable work; he can't kill them without proper reason. If we get back to Huaxia as soon as possible, we can warn them. Also, the Iron Widows and Phoenix Ladies should still be loyal to me. I'll tell everyone about the truth of our world and help them prepare for what's coming while they have all the facts, which they should've had all along. I will not be complicit in the lies about the Hunduns, nor their slaughter, any longer.

Yizhi and I speak no more for the rest of the night. I slip unconscious again, qi-exhausted beyond belief.

At daybreak, he calls my name. My eyes blink open to the sight of land on the horizon. No Great Wall beyond the beach and forests. It's not part of Huaxia, but it's a start.

After the Vermilion Bird touches down on the beach, it lowers its wings. I slide to the sand on one side while Yizhi helps Helan, who can't even stand up, down the other. They both stick close to the ground once they're there, panting. It's the first time *I've* been the steadiest person in a group.

The Bird's head droops. Its eyes dim.

"No!" I stumble in front of it. That can't be it, can it?

I press against its chest to listen for its inner hum. Right as my hand touches the feathered surface, red light splits out. Warm, molten fingers emerge to lace with mine. A winged humanoid outline rises before me, shaping itself out of the Bird's chest. It looks like someone wearing the Vermilion Bird's spirit armor, except every bit of them is metallic, and a feathered, beaked mask like that of its Heroic Form sculpts out on its face.

I can do nothing but stumble back with my mouth hanging open when the figure steps down to the ground. Light fades behind it once its vast wings shake free. To the side, Yizhi and Helan watch with matching awe.

How is this possible?

After an eternity in the limbo between hope and answers, I summon the courage to utter the question:

"Shimin . . . is that you?"

The figure puts its hand to its forehead. The glow of its angular eyes brightens and wanes several times through its bird mask. Then, in a low voice, it speaks.

". . . *Mei-Niang?*"

EPILOGUE

When Qin Zheng startles awake, for a moment he believes he's back in the lab, hooked up to devices meant to measure and study him. He nearly rips the tubing out of his chest before remembering he now needs it to stay alive. It connects to a machine beside his bed, pumping his blood through a spinning component that resupplies it with oxygen before streaming it back into his body. He no longer has a heartbeat. Until they can find him a compatible transplant, this is how he has to live.

It's more tolerable, at least, than hanging on to the edge of existence with nothing but a conscious effort to sustain every beat of his heart, as he had to do during his entire return journey to Huaxia. He tasked two of the tribute girls with jolting him awake if they felt no pulse for more than five seconds.

He ought to reward them lavishly. According to them, after witnessing the Heavenly Court's destruction, they allied with tributes from other regions and overpowered the false gods on their evacuation ship. They then sent the Hive Queen a transmission in Hanyu, surrendering to him, because the Huaxia tributes trusted him as their ruler. He hardly had the mental capacity to observe the foreign tributes closely once they docked aboard, but they were a curious sight, with hair and skin colors in a wider range than he had ever seen.

Landing the Hive Queen in Chang'an with them, along with their heavenly prisoners, caused quite the commotion.

"The gods are not gods but subjugators as human as ourselves," he told the nearest cameras in the crowd that amassed on that mountaintop. "The Heavenly Court is no more. I destroyed it. More information to come. Now leave my presence and bring me a heart surgeon."

He remembers little of the rush to the operating table, only squeaking wheels and blinding lights. Huaxia must be ablaze with speculation. He has to gather his wits soon to give his people answers.

By habit, he reaches for the other side of the bed for comfort. Then he curses himself.

How dare she?

She is a prideful, arrogant creature, he knows. So is he. They had not begun on the best terms, but did they not reach an understanding over the nearly full year they had known each other? Together, they overthrew gods.

And yet. *And yet.*

The dragon half-pendant he's still wearing slips to his shoulder. He grasps it, about to tear it off his neck and throw it against the wall, but thinks better of it. He will not accept defeat so easily. He remembers how she would push him away when conscious but curl up to him when deep asleep. How accomplished he felt when she unconsciously clung to him as he left for morning assemblies, forcing him to pry her arms off himself to not be late. Knowing her true feelings, he remains baffled by her dedication to self-deception. All because she can't accept the idea of submitting to a man? If she refuses to see reason, he shall do it for her. He has been far too lenient with her, too tolerant of her insolence. He should never have linked into a dream realm with her night after night, knowing the dependency it would create. Sentiment weakened him. For the first time in his life, he understands the logic behind binding the feet of a woman. This nonsense is intolerable.

He is not entirely sure how she slipped away when the Hunduns overwhelmed him. He thought he saw a flying Chrysalis, yet why would that have been in the ocean? The situation was much too chaotic, and he was under much too dire a strain to retain many details. It is a mystery he will have to find her again to solve.

He feels for her spirit signature. She is not the only one who has trained to sense one particular signature over a tremendous distance. Every time she headed to the war front, he honed it. If he knows her as he knows himself, she will not cower beyond the bounds of Huaxia. She will find her way back, and when she does, he will sense her.

He calls for a staffer to summon Secretary Shangguan and Minister Gao. Her precious lady friends. So long as he holds their lives in his hands, she is bound to return to him. She'll come home, even if he has to break her legs and drag her.

After all, his son cannot grow up without a mother.

To be continued . . .

ACKNOWLEDGEMENTS

This book took inspiration from both Empress Regnant Wu's reign of terror to consolidate her rule and the First Emperor of China's draconian legalist policies. I would obviously not call either of these historical figures "revolutionaries," given that they were born into social ranks much higher than those of their reimagined counterparts in this series, but relative to their eras, they both induced a dramatic overhaul of the systems of power in their world. Empress Regnant Wu became the empress through shattering the influence of the aristocratic class and lifting up commoner scholars. The First Emperor abolished feudalism and enforced centralized governance across China after conquering all seven Warring States. Although the tyrannical lengths he went to in order to achieve his vision caused his dynasty to fall shortly after his death, it is no coincidence that the dynasty following his was founded by a commoner instead of the centuries-old aristocratic clans that ruled the Warring States. Empress Regnant Wu, on the other hand, pulled back the terror she had imposed with spies and secret police once it was clear that her position was no longer threatened.

In this sci-fi world with material circumstances closer to our modern era, it felt natural to me to make the characters challenge capitalism as a system of power instead. But I want to stress that no revolution would ever, ever look like this in real life, and neither can the events in this book be responsibly compared to any historical revolutions. What I've imagined is more of a military coup, in any case. Two-hundred-year-old legends don't come back to life, and eighteen-year-old girls can't descend from the sky in a giant mecha dragon. In our reality, the only way to enact change on a mass scale has been and will always be to get out and get organized. It is our bonds that will liberate us. Unionize, talk to your community, join organizations, protest, and don't be fooled into resenting women, people of color, queer people, immigrants, or other groups of people that seem to be cared more about nowadays but don't actually hold the bulk of power in society. Do what you need to do to survive under capitalism—this book itself had to be published by a large corporation for you to read it—but always keep in mind that a better world is possible through direct action and solidarity. Because it is not human nature to accept subjugation.

My most heartfelt thanks to Rebecca Schaeffer, Sara Wolf, Akana Phenix, and Sofia Robleda, for narrowly saving this book from going out as a disaster. To Molly X Chang, who's single-handedly responsible for certain scenes getting increasingly intense. You are a terrible influence ♥.

To my publisher, for waiting so long and bearing with me as I slowly lost my mind while drafting this. To Emily Varga and Sarah Mughal, for helping me through that whole ordeal.

To my former agent, for everything we achieved together in the five years we had. I'm not sure if you're allowed to read this, considering what happened, but know that I will always keep you in my heart for picking me up when no one thought I would amount to anything.

To Ashley Mackenzie, for turning my shoddy sketch of the Yellow Dragon armor and my request to make Qin Zheng look "more like a douchebag" into this incredible cover.

To the team at Picturestart, for believing in *Iron Widow*'s potential and working tirelessly to get it adapted for screen. To Dual Wield Studio, for making such incredible *Iron Widow* merch (find the link on my website if you haven't seen it 😌!).

To Kiran V, Zoë Wren Boyd, and Franklyn S. Newton, for help with Qin Zheng's occasional Cockney accent. (Yes, I assigned him a natural Cockney accent because people were confused about what they were supposed to imagine when I just wrote "working-class dialect." Feel free to imagine the rest of his dialogue in snobbish British received pronunciation.)

To Qiu Jin, Alexandra Kollontai, Rosa Luxemburg, Angela Davis, Thomas Sankara, Kristen Ghodsee, Paul Cockshott, and Allin Cottrell, whose speeches and writings were a huge source of inspiration for this book.

To old friends and new friends, for keeping me grounded as my life turned more and more unbelievable. Sorry that I can't even *attempt* to list you all. I'm already in trouble for how long this book is.

Finally, to every reader, reviewer, bookseller, librarian, and others in the book community, whose enthusiasm for *Iron Widow* propelled it into becoming an unexpected hit. Even in the most grandiose of my fantasies while I was a teenage aspiring writer, I didn't dare imagine the level of achievement this book has reached. You changed my life, and I owe everything I have to you.

XIRAN JAY ZHAO is the #1 *New York Times*-bestselling author of the Iron Widow series and *Zachary Ying and the Dragon Emperor*. Their books have been a finalist or winner of many awards, including the Nebula, British Science Fiction Association, Locus, and Astounding awards. A first-gen immigrant from small-town China to Vancouver, Canada, they were raised by the Internet and made the inexplicable decision to leave their biochem degree in the dust to write books and make educational content instead. You can find them @xiranjayzhao on Twitter for memes, on Instagram and TikTok for chaotic skits, and on YouTube for long videos about Chinese history and culture.

www.xiranjayzhao.com